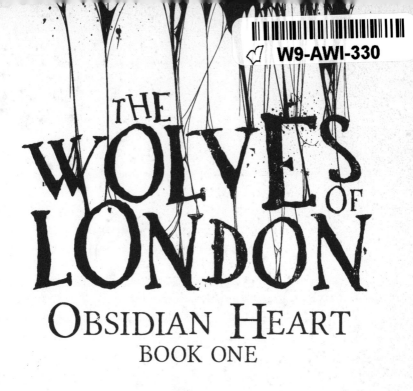

THE WOLVES OF LONDON

OBSIDIAN HEART
BOOK ONE

COMING SOON FROM MARK MORRIS
AND TITAN BOOKS

OBSIDIAN HEART
Book Two: The Society of Blood
Book Three: The Wraiths of War

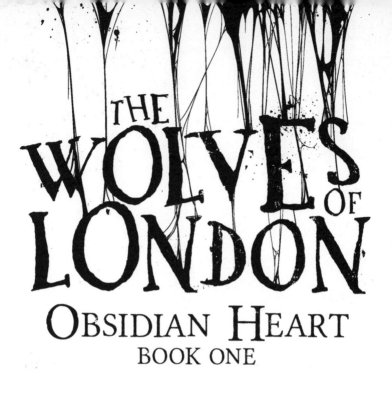

THE WOLVES OF LONDON

OBSIDIAN HEART
BOOK ONE

MARK MORRIS

TITAN BOOKS

Obsidian Heart Book One: The Wolves of London
Print edition ISBN: 9781781168660
E-book edition ISBN: 9781781168691

Published by Titan Books
A division of Titan Publishing Group Ltd
144 Southwark Street, London SE1 0UP

First edition: October 2014
1 3 5 7 9 10 8 6 4 2

Visit our website:
www.titanbooks.com

A CIP catalogue record for this title is available from the British Library.

Printed and bound in the United States.

To Stephen and Patricia Volk, with love.
"Monster? But we're British, you know!"

ONE

FRIDAY, 26 JULY 1996

I was nineteen years old and scared to death. So scared that I had to clench my teeth to stop them from chattering. Which was ironic, because it was the height of summer, 32° in the shade. The inside of the car was rank with the smell of sweat, testosterone and baked leather.

I was aware of Chris sitting beside me, his black-gloved hands gripping the steering wheel as if it was a safety bar on a roller coaster. His face, what I could see of it, was a lumpy, dark blur in its stocking mask, like a sculpture of a human head worn smooth by the wind and rain. Neither of us had said anything for the past five minutes. I didn't know about Chris, but I was worried that if I spoke the waver in my voice would give away how terrified I was. I stared out through the windscreen at the terrace of derelict houses opposite, and tried to pretend I was calm, in control. But really I was thinking: *Why the fuck am I doing this?*

I knew why, though. I was doing it for Candice. That's what I told myself anyway, though in hindsight I have to admit that that wasn't strictly true. The thing is, with what I earned driving a furniture delivery van six days a week (plus overtime), I *could* have managed to pay Michelle for Candice's welfare, *and* pay my rent on my grotty bedsit in Dagenham, *and* just about scrape by on a weekly diet of baked beans, mashed spuds and cheap mince. I *could* have. People do, don't they? But I was nineteen, and I wanted a bit of a life. Nothing special, nothing extravagant. Just a few extra quid to go out on a weekend, buy some decent clothes, maybe get a car.

So when it boiled down to it, I suppose you *could* say that I was about to hold up a security van with my mates just so that I wouldn't have to stay in every night, eating Pot Noodles and staring at my little black-and-white telly. I know that sounds pathetic, but what you've got to understand is that crime wasn't such a big deal where I was brought up. To most of the kids I knew, and many of the adults too, it was a way of life, of getting by. Though when I say 'crime', I don't necessarily mean the sort of crime that we were about to commit. I didn't live my early life surrounded by murderers and rapists and armed robbers – though I knew of a few people who fell into one or other of those categories. No, I'm talking about petty crime: shoplifting, nicking cars, selling drugs, robbing houses. More serious crimes were still a bigger deal – but at the same time they weren't *that* huge a leap. The prospect of being drawn in, as I had been, wasn't as shocking or unthinkable as it would have seemed to the law-abiding majority.

I'm not sure whether that's an explanation or an excuse for my actions. I'm not sure whether I'm trying to make you understand or gain your sympathy. I'll leave my words for you to judge as you see fit. Because the thing is, everyone's unique, and everyone interprets what they see and hear based on their own experiences. I'm a different person now to the one I was on that hot summer's day in 1996. And what I've learned over the years is that we're each of us a stew of physical and psychological ingredients, shaped by genetics, environment, upbringing, peer pressure and human interaction. So what's acceptable, or at least understandable, to one person is going to be unacceptable or inconceivable to another. *C'est la vie*. When it comes down to it, there's no black and white. Only grey.

So there I was, sitting in the passenger seat of a ripped-off Ford Mondeo next to my best mate Chris Langtree. From where we were parked, in the shadowy forecourt of one of a row of abandoned warehouses, we had a view of the long, quiet road almost up to the mouldering brick wall at its far end. At that far end, although we couldn't see them from our position, Ray Duffy and Cosmic Dennis were sitting in a brown Vauxhall Vectra, also ripped off. The Vectra was tucked into the pot-holed entrance of a long-disused textile factory, so snug against the high wall which enclosed the factory grounds that Cosmic Dennis wouldn't have been able to open his door more than an inch even if he'd wanted to. This meant that the car would be unseen by any vehicle turning on to the street at its far end. I couldn't help imagining the Vectra as a funnel-web spider, poised in the darkness of its lair, ready to leap out on unsuspecting prey.

The heist had been Ray's idea. By the time Chris got me involved everything was sorted, all the details worked out with military precision. I didn't know what I was getting into at first. Chris rang me at work one day – I couldn't even afford a home phone – and said that he had a proposition for me. I went round to his flat that night, expecting... I don't know... something mildly dodgy, I suppose. I'd known Chris since primary school and we were like brothers. We didn't live in each other's pockets, we didn't always see eye to eye, but we trusted each other implicitly. Chris worked in a shop selling electrical equipment for DJs and bands – record decks, sound systems, that sort of thing – but he made most of his money from fencing (the kind that involves stolen goods, not poking people with swords) and from selling dope to muso potheads on the side. In the past he'd slipped me a few quid to store ripped-off gear in my bedsit or to look after his stash while the cops were sniffing around. I'd once had a pair of speakers taking up most of the floor space in my bedroom with 'ZZ Top' stencilled on the side.

This time it was different, though.

The second I stepped through the door of his grotty Housing Association flat I heard voices. Chris handed me a tin of McEwan's, which wasn't anywhere near cold enough, and cast me an odd glance, half sly and half apologetic, which immediately made me uneasy.

'Come through,' he said, turning away from me. 'We're in here.'

I followed him down the narrow corridor, breathing in the musty scent from the damp-mottled walls, and into a square room which doubled as his bedroom and main living space. The floor was carpeted with a sludge-brown nylon weave and the walls were lined with haphazard stacks of electrical equipment. The low central table was cluttered with crumpled beer cans, empty coffee mugs and joint-rolling paraphernalia. To my left, slumped on the sagging sofa-bed beneath the big window which looked out on to the street, Dennis Jasper snorted in apparent mirth, snagging my attention. He was a rangy, raddled man with a long, bony, deeply lined face and stiff, mousey hair that stuck out at all angles. He wore a ratty old waistcoat over an off-white T-shirt, drainpipe jeans which made his legs look as spindly as broom handles, and tan leather cowboy boots. He was sucking on a spliff pinched between the thumb and forefinger of his right hand, his mouth wrinkling inwards like a contracting anus. He took a good lungful of smoke, the end of the spliff crackling and glowing orange as it burned down, then offered it to me.

I shook my head, not because I was averse to weed, but because I couldn't face the thought of putting my lips where his fingers had been. Dennis Jasper – known as Cosmic Dennis because of the bullshit he spouted whenever he was high (which was most of the time) – was one of life's grubby men. His teeth were brown, his over-long fingernails were permanently clogged with black gunge, and his moist-looking, dirt-ingrained skin exuded a faint odour of old toilets.

He gave another cackle, as though my refusal was the punchline to a private joke, and said something incomprehensible about the 'angel of death'. Still holding the unopened can of beer in my hand, I looked away from him, turning my attention to the other man in the room. He was already leaning forward, an old dining chair creaking beneath his solid, meaty bulk, as he offered his hand across the cluttered table. The chunky bracelet encircling his wrist and the thick silver rings on each of his fingers gave the impression that his body had been strengthened with metal joints, like a cyborg from a sci-fi movie.

'Alex,' he said, his voice a husky croak, 'good to see you, mate.' He had the amiable but vaguely threatening presence of a man who was so hard that he didn't feel a need to prove it.

I took the hand and shook it. 'How you doing, Ray?'

'Doing good, mate. How about you?'

'Can't complain.'

He nodded, his sleepy eyes assessing me, his gaze unwavering. After a moment he said, 'Sit down, mate, have a drink.'

I couldn't help feeling I was about to be interrogated, that as soon as I sat he would drop his nice-guy persona and start to pump me with questions. I racked my brains, wondering what he thought I'd done, what he'd been told I might know, but I couldn't think of anything. I wanted to ask what was wrong, whether someone had been bad-mouthing me, but I thought that might sound like an admission of guilt, so I stayed silent.

I glanced at Chris, who was standing behind me with his arms folded, looking pensive. He nodded at me – encouragingly, I hoped. I sat.

'Aren't you gonna open your beer?' Ray said, nodding at the can in my hand.

'Sure,' I said. I popped the ring-pull, took a swig of the fizzy, metallic-tasting stuff, and forced it down.

He nodded in approval, his close-cropped hair gleaming with styling wax. When he moved, his black puffa jacket made a dry, slithering sound like a snake. Over by the window Cosmic Dennis watched the sweet-smelling smoke coiling above his head and chuckled for no discernible reason.

'Chris says you can be trusted, says you can keep secrets. That true?'

Ray's voice was a rasp in the otherwise silent room. I shrugged, trying not to feel intimidated. 'I think so.'

'Think so? Don't you know?'

I sensed rather than saw Chris tense behind my right shoulder.

'No,' I said, 'I can definitely.'

'Can what?'

'Be trusted.'

'You sure?'

'Yes.'

He stared at me a moment, then nodded. 'Okay.'

I waited. Ray reached across, lifted a can from the table and tilted it towards his mouth, before replacing it carefully on the ring of moisture it had formed on the scarred wood. After a moment he said, 'I hear you've got money problems, Alex. That you'd jump at the chance to earn a few extra quid.'

'Doing what?' I asked.

'Does it matter?'

'It might.' I swallowed. 'I don't want to hurt anybody.'

Ray flashed his teeth in a sudden grin, as though the idea was ludicrous. 'Nobody's gonna get hurt.'

Over on the sofa-bed, Cosmic Dennis muttered, 'We're not in the crying game, Mr Churchill,' and dissolved into breathy laughter.

Ray ignored him. 'So you interested?'

'I might be,' I said carefully, 'but I'd need to know what you want me to do.'

Ray narrowed his eyes and tilted his head to one side, as though contemplating how much to tell me. He'd been in the year above me at school, but I knew him more by reputation than anything; we'd never been on much more than nodding terms.

'You wouldn't need to do anything except back us up,' he said eventually. 'There's this geezer, Amir Mahoon, Paki businessman. He owns half a dozen supermarkets round Leyton, Wanstead, Hackney.'

I nodded. 'I've seen them.'

'Right. Well, every Friday afternoon Mahoon's brother collects the takings in his van and drives to the NatWest in Walthamstow to pay it in. He follows the same route every week, and part of it takes him along March Road near the cemetery. One side is houses, the other's warehouses and factories – but it's all derelict, due to be knocked down. There's only one way in, one way out. Do you see where all this is leading?'

I nodded. 'How much will he be carrying?'

'I'm reliably informed it'll be somewhere in the region of a hundred grand. Interested?'

I blinked. All I could see at that moment was pound signs in front of my eyes. I felt my throat closing up, my stomach clenching, my limbs tingling. I suddenly got the impression that I was sitting on the edge of an abyss, and that if I leaned forward I'd fall, and keep falling, down into endless blackness. I tried desperately to keep all of this hidden, to not allow any of it to show on the surface. Although warm, fizzy beer was the last thing I wanted in my stomach at that moment, I forced myself to raise my arm slowly, to tilt the can towards my mouth. The liquid lubricated my throat enough for me to ask, 'Split four ways?'

Ray rocked backwards in his seat as though I'd punched him. His response, though derisory, at least had a bark of laughter in it.

'Fuck off! You honestly think I'd set all this up and give you equal fucking shares? Do you take me for a muppet?'

I felt my face growing hot and knew my cheeks were blazing red. 'Course not,' I mumbled. 'Sorry, Ray, I wasn't thinking.'

'Too fucking right you weren't.' He stared at me so intently I thought I'd blown it, but after a moment he shook his head, like a teacher resigned to dealing with dim pupils. 'I get fifty per cent,' he muttered. 'You three share the other fifty. Take it or leave it.'

I made a quick calculation. A third of fifty grand was still about seventeen – which for me was well over a year's wages. 'I'll take it,' I said.

'Yeah, me too,' said Chris quickly behind me. Over by the window Cosmic Dennis seemed oblivious to the conversation. He had a grin on his face and his eyes were darting about the room. I wondered what hallucinatory wonders were cavorting in his frazzled brain.

Chris spent the next hour talking us through what the job would entail, and over the following few weeks we met on at least a dozen more occasions to discuss the finer points. By the end of that period even Cosmic Dennis knew exactly what was expected of him. It did occur to me to wonder why Dennis was on board, but that would have been questioning Ray's judgement, so I kept my mouth shut. In the end I was glad I did, because when I mentioned my misgivings to Chris one night over a pint he looked at me like I'd just walked unwittingly across a minefield.

'You know Dennis is Ray's uncle, don't you?'

I goggled at him. It had never occurred to me that they might be related. 'Seriously?'

'Yeah. Dennis married Ray's mum's sister. Sometime in the late seventies this was. Got her pregnant, I think.'

I thought back on all the meetings we'd had over the past few weeks, of how Ray had seemed to push Dennis around, to control him in the same way a dog owner would control an unruly puppy. I wondered what the true nature of the relationship was between them. Was Ray babysitting his uncle? Did he feel he could trust and rely on him because he was family? Or was he maybe trying to help out his mum's sister financially by bringing Dennis on board? Whatever the reason, it struck me as a weird family dynamic. And it made me uneasy too. It made me feel that Dennis might prove to be Ray's blind spot.

Chris, though, shook his head. 'Ray knows what he's doing,' he said confidently. 'Everything'll be fine.'

I hoped so. I was still hoping so when Amir Mahoon's brother's grey van turned the corner on to March Road and began to rattle along the pitted tarmac towards us.

I described it as a security van earlier, but it wasn't really. It was little more than a ramshackle Transit with bald tyres and a bad paint job. In many ways it was crying out to be robbed – Ray had said on more than one occasion that the Mahoons were taking the piss, and that by robbing them we'd be teaching them a long-overdue lesson. He even made it sound as though we'd be doing them a favour, saving them from a much bigger fall along the way.

That's not how I felt, though, as Chris tensed in the driver's seat beside me. Not for the first time I felt as though I was getting in way over my head. Compared to the average nineteen-year-old, I was a pretty hard lad from a rough estate, who had taken more than a few knocks in life. Even so, as Chris said, 'Here we go,' and slammed the car into first, it suddenly struck me for the first time how fucking *real* this was, how *serious*.

At the same time I knew there was no backing out now, that I had no option but to follow it through. I couldn't do it half-heartedly either. I'd spent weeks thinking that Dennis might prove to be the weak link, so there was no fucking way I was going to allow it to be me. I gripped the edges of my seat as Chris accelerated and the car shot forward out of the warehouse entrance, veering in front of the van. Through the gauze of the stocking mask, I caught the barest glimpse of a shocked brown face – a boy's face – in the passenger seat, all wide dark eyes and a gaping oval of a mouth. As the driver tried to take evasive action, Chris twisted the wheel of the Mondeo and turned us sharply to the left, directly into the path of the already swerving van. I saw a wall of grey metal hurtling towards the passenger window, and then – BANG! – the door next to me buckled inwards and the window shattered, a thousand tiny cubes of safety glass showering into my lap and across my legs.

My entire body jolted with the impact, sending hard, jagged shock-waves shooting through my limbs, back, ribcage and head. For an instant I was aware of my body as an inter-connected unit, if only because it felt as though my flesh, bones, heart and brain had suddenly become dislodged from one another. The feeling lasted for no more than a split second and then everything dropped back into place. Next thing, the two vehicles were scraping against one another as they careened sideways, but only until the van hit the high kerb side on and crunched to an abrupt halt.

The Mondeo lurched, skidded in a half-circle so that we were facing the van almost nose to nose, and stopped with a screech of brakes and the sharp tang of scorched rubber. Before I'd even recovered my wits, Chris had snatched up one of the two baseball bats lying in the well between the front seats and was shoving open the driver's door. I grabbed the other bat and tried to push open the door on the passenger side. But it was jammed solid in the frame, too twisted and buckled from the impact of the crash. I kicked at it a couple of times, then gave up and scrambled over the front seats to exit via the driver's door, almost falling on to the road in my eagerness to show willing. By the time I'd jumped to my feet and joined Chris, he was already holding his baseball bat out in front of him and screaming, 'Get out of the fucking van!'

Adrenaline was pumping through me. I felt wild, exhilarated, abandoned. I ran up and smashed my bat down on the van's bonnet, putting a big dent in it. Through the windscreen I saw Mahoon's brother, a chubby man with a thick black beard, a white skullcap on his head. He looked terrified, and the skinny kid next to him – who couldn't have been more than ten or eleven – was crying in fear, mouth wide and drooling as he blubbed.

Out of the corner of my eye I saw Ray and Cosmic Dennis getting out of the Vectra, which had come screaming up behind the van and was now jammed tight up to its rear bumper. Like me and Chris, Dennis was wielding a baseball bat, but Ray had a sawn-off shotgun. He strode unhurriedly to the driver's side of the van, and pointed the shotgun at Mahoon's brother's bearded face through the window.

'Open the fucking door,' he said, his voice business-like, brooking no argument. When Mahoon's brother hesitated, he barked, 'Now! Unless you want to lose your fucking head!'

Mahoon's brother became a mass of jittery movement as he complied with Ray's request. As soon as he had pushed the door open, Ray reached in, grabbed his thick beard and wrenched him out. Although I still felt high on adrenaline, I winced as Mahoon's brother hit the tarmac hard and sprawled in front of us, his baggy white trousers tearing at the knee. The skin beneath tore too, blood mingling with dirt on the white cotton.

Mahoon pushed himself up with one arm. The other he raised as if shielding his face from the sun. 'Please,' he begged, 'please... please...'

Ray stood over him, staring down, and even through the stocking mask I could see the contempt on his face. A chill went through me. For a second I believed that Ray was about to end Mahoon's brother's life – and maybe even that of the boy still cowering in the van, goggling at us with big dark eyes. Then Ray jerked his head up and looked at Dennis.

'Open her up,' he said.

Dennis cackled and loped like a big black stick-insect towards the side of the van. Curling his long fingers around the handle of the side door, he tugged, and the door slid open on gritty, squealing runners. Inside was a heap of dirty nylon sacks with draw-string tops. Dennis hopped up into the van and tugged one open. He reached inside and plucked out a thick white envelope which he waved above his head.

'Christmas presents for all the little children!' he cried gleefully.

We spent the next minute or so loading up the boot of the Vectra with the sacks from the van. Some of them were full of coins, which it took two of us to carry, and which caused the Vectra to creak in protest as we dumped them in. Before leaving, Ray made Mahoon's brother and the boy – who was so terrified he had to be wrenched from the interior of the van by the scruff of his neck – lie spreadeagled on the road, face down. Both were shaking violently and the man never stopped begging for mercy, even when Ray told him to shut the fuck up. I'd never seen anyone in genuine fear of his life before, and despite the adrenaline still buzzing through me, it made me feel dirty and ashamed for my part in putting the two of them through such an ordeal.

Ray locked the van doors and threw the keys into the overgrown garden of a derelict house across the road. Then the four of us piled into the Vectra – the Mondeo was a write-off, and would have attracted too much attention even if we *had* been able to start her up – and fucked off. As we drove away, I peeled the now-sweaty stocking mask from my face and looked out of the back window. The last thing I saw before we turned the corner was Mahoon's brother slowly raising his head to watch us go, his bearded face betraying shock and wonder at the fact that he was still alive.

TWO

SUNDAY, 30 SEPTEMBER 2012

'You all right, Dad?'

Her voice was soft, but it still startled me. She saw the cigarette jerk in my fingers as I lifted it to my mouth and expressed her amusement the same way she'd done since she was two or three years old, by crinkling her nose in such a way that it tugged the corners of her lips into a smile and squeezed her eyes into slits. Even at eighteen it was an adorable expression, and gave me an unexpected pang of nostalgia, an almost melancholy sense of time slipping away.

'Sorry,' she said, putting a hand lightly on my arm. 'Didn't mean to make you jump.'

'I was miles away,' I told her.

'What were you thinking about?'

I shrugged. 'Nothing much. The past. Everything that's happened. How much you've grown.' I turned on my heel to face her, then leaned forward and kissed her on the cheek. 'I mean, look at you, Candice. You're a beautiful young woman.'

She rolled her eyes. 'Dad,' she said, drawing out the word like she used to as a kid when I was mucking about, embarrassing her. I put my arm around her shoulders and we stood for a moment, side by side against the wall of the pub, watching the tourists and post-performance theatre-goers streaming to and from the bustling attractions of Covent Garden. The Rusty Bucket, whose upstairs function room Candice had hired for her eighteenth, was a sturdy old London boozer on Russell Street, whose wooden fittings had apparently been constructed from old ship's timbers. Its status as a grade II listed building meant that it had retained its etched mirrors and embossed ceilings, though that hadn't stopped the current owner from turning it into a trendy bar-cum-gastro-pub.

After a few moments Candice sighed and snuggled against me. 'Thanks for coming,' she said.

A good foot taller than my daughter, I leaned forward and kissed the top of her blonde head. 'Christ, you don't have to thank me. I wouldn't have missed this for the world.'

'Yeah, I know, but...'

'But what?'

'Well, it can't have been easy for you, can it, what with Glenn's family here and everything?'

I grunted a laugh. 'Into the lion's den, you mean?'

'Well... yeah, I suppose so, sort of.'

I gave her shoulder a squeeze, suddenly aware of how slight, almost frail, she was. 'That's all water under the bridge now,' I said. 'It was a long time ago.'

'Doesn't mean you haven't still got the scars to show for it, though.'

I laughed again. 'They're old scars. Old scars, old me. I'm not the cocky little yob I once was.'

She muttered something that I didn't quite catch and I asked her to repeat it. After a moment she sighed and said, 'I'm not sure Glenn's changed that much.'

I frowned. 'What do you mean? He doesn't knock your mother about?'

'No, nothing like that. It's just... well, his attitude.' She paused. 'He's like a big kid. Always going on about "students" and "getting a proper job instead of sponging off the government".' She rolled her eyes. 'He does my head in. I reckon he'd be happier if I was working in fucking McDonalds. Sorry.'

Listening to her, I felt my stomach knot with long-standing contempt for the man who had married Michelle, Candice's mother. But I also felt a surge of satisfaction that my daughter was confiding in me, viewing me as an ally against someone who I suppose had been more of a father to her over the years than I had.

Michelle and I had never actually *been* together as such. Candice had been conceived on Christmas Eve 1993, when I was sixteen. Back then Michelle had been a hard-edged punkette, her hair as red and spiky as her attitude, and on the night in question I had staggered out of The King's Head, where I'd been drinking since mid-afternoon and was feeling the worse for wear after God knew how many pints of Special Brew, to witness a blazing row between Michelle and her long-term boyfriend, a steroid-popping skinhead called Glenn Dass. Once the fireworks were over and Glenn had stalked off after calling Michelle a 'piss-ugly cunt', I stumbled across and stupidly asked if she was okay.

Swiping away black lines of mascara that were trickling down her tearful face, she snapped, 'What does it fucking look like?'

'Sorry,' I said, flinching as if I'd been stung. Sober, I might have walked away, but because I was pissed (and horny) I hovered a moment, peering at her through beer-blurred eyes.

'Is there anything else?' She spat out the words like bullets, her face scrunching aggressively.

'Weren't you in my year at school?'

'So? What do you want – a fucking medal?'

'No, I just...' I shrugged and looked down at my feet, waiting for inspiration to seep into my drunken brain. Finally I asked, 'What you doing now?'

'Apart from freezing my tits off in a pub car park, you mean?'

I squinted at her, half-grinned. For a boy of sixteen, a girl mentioning her own tits, regardless of the context, was a big turn-on. 'You don't have to stay out here,' I said. 'We could go inside.'

'Oh yeah, and do what?'

My grin widened. 'I could buy you a drink.'

Her panda eyes, bloodshot from crying, narrowed to slits. 'It'll take more than that, you know. I'm not a fucking scrubber.'

'I never said you were. Forget it if you're not bothered.'

She stared at me sullenly for a moment, then gave an abrupt nod. 'Go on then.'

I remember little about the rest of the evening, though I do know that an hour or so later Michelle and I were shagging in a cubicle in the women's toilets. My abiding memory of that encounter was the wet floor, the stink of puke which clogged up one of the sinks, and having to constantly change position in the tiny cubicle because cold, sharp edges kept jabbing me in the buttocks, legs and back. Ultimately our desperate rutting became more a war of attrition than an expression of mutual desire, both of us wanting it to be over but determined to see it through to the bitter end. When it *was* over we went our separate ways, disheartened and battle-weary, neither of us expressing any inclination to see each other again.

Just over a week later, on New Year's Day 1994, Glenn Dass and a couple of his mates jumped me outside the local chippy. I rolled into a ball as they kicked me repeatedly in the spine and stamped on my ribs and head, before rolling me, barely conscious, off the road and down a steep railway embankment choked with weeds and nettles. It was a bitterly cold night and I might well have died if an old geezer hadn't walked past with a Jack Russell half an hour later. The dog sniffed me out and started barking, and the old boy phoned an ambulance. I was admitted to hospital with three broken ribs, a cracked vertebra, a fractured wrist and various head injuries. The worst part of the experience was not the beating itself, but waking up in a hospital bed a few hours later. Everything had swollen and stiffened up, and despite the heavy-duty painkillers I'd been prescribed, each tiny movement sent an eye-watering jolt of agony through me. Just blinking and breathing were bad enough, but when I tried to chew or swallow it felt as if rusty gears were grinding into life inside my body, each one connected to a cluster of exposed nerve endings. And as for moving my bowels... well, let's just say it was probably the closest to the torment of childbirth that a man is ever likely to get.

There was never any possibility of Michelle and I getting married, not even when she burst into The King's Head two months later – just after my seventeenth birthday – screaming the odds and telling me that I was 'gonna fucking pay' for getting her up the duff. I was in no mood for a row; the cuts and bruises were only just starting to fade, and I was still moving gingerly. But for the next month or so I refused to accept that the child was mine – until my appointment finally came through for a DNA test, which confirmed what I felt (at the time) was the awful truth.

Glenn was back on the scene by then, and to his credit he stuck by Michelle, despite the fact that she was carrying another man's child. I think partly because he'd proved his physical dominance over me, and partly because I hadn't grassed him up, which in his eyes was like me admitting that I'd been out of order and deserved the beating, it helped him come to terms with the fact that I'd violated his 'property'. It even enabled him to put aside any resentment he might have felt towards Candice and, despite his limitations, become a pretty decent stepdad for her.

In the almost two decades since that New Year's Day encounter, he and I had never seen eye to eye, though I suppose we'd tolerated each other well enough when we'd been thrown together in family situations. Even so, the fact that he'd once bested me, regardless that he'd caught me by surprise and had been backed up by his mates, was clearly still a big thing for him. It was almost instinctive the way he adopted a cocky, swaggering manner whenever we met, the way a slightly contemptuous arrogance would creep into his voice. Many times I'd felt the urge to tell him to grow the fuck up and move on, but I'd always managed to bite my tongue, and so keep the peace.

As for me and Michelle... well, I can't pretend that it hadn't been tricky between us over the years. We were like repelling magnets, always rubbing each other up the wrong way. The main problem was that we had different outlooks on life, which had led to a hell of a lot of resentment, at least on her part. Whereas Michelle had obstinately dug herself into a rut and refused to change her circumstances, even though (according to Candice) she was bitter and unhappy, I had pig-headedly rejected what it seemed at one time was the path laid out for me, and had done my best to turn negatives into positives – most obviously by viewing the misery of prison life as a watershed, an opportunity to motivate myself into crawling out of the sewer, shaking off the shit and moving on to better things.

I don't mean that to sound smug. I'm not saying it to make you think that I consider myself superior to Michelle. It's just the way things were, just an illustration of our different personalities. Maybe you have to fall a long way in life before it hits you what a fuck-up you're making of it, and maybe Michelle had simply never had a jolt big enough to persuade her to change her situation. I don't know. All I knew was that we were polar opposites, and that it had led at times to arguments over how we each thought Candice should be raised. My worry had been that Michelle and Glenn were holding her back, stifling her natural intelligence, whereas I knew Michelle had been obsessed with the idea that whenever Candice had been with me she'd been exposed to some kind of weird, academic, cultural life that might turn her into a snob, or make her want something that Michelle didn't understand and couldn't provide.

Despite all that, though, I think both of us were agreed that Candice had turned out all right – more than all right. She was bright, sensible, funny, tolerant, all the things that ought to make any parent proud. In spite of Glenn's sneery attitude towards students, she had just started the second year of her A levels and wanted to do Hospitality and Event Management at Loughborough University. Everything was going brilliantly for her.

Or so I thought.

After her outburst about Glenn, I gave her another squeeze and asked, 'What are you sorry for?'

'Swearing,' she said.

'You don't have to worry about that,' I said with a grin. 'I was swearing like a trooper before I could walk. I think my first word was "bollocks".'

An elderly woman with coiffured hair and expensive-looking jewellery turned to give me a disapproving glance as she tottered past, and both Candice and I burst out laughing. Her laughter died quickly, though, which prompted me to give her another reassuring squeeze.

'Ignore what Glenn says,' I told her, 'and I'm not just saying that because of the history between us. You do what you've set your heart on, and don't let anyone sway you. I know your mum's proud of you, and so am I.'

'Thanks, Dad,' she said, and sighed.

'But?' I asked.

'But what?'

'But that's not the only thing that's bothering you, is it? There's something else.'

This time the sigh was big enough to make her shoulders slump as if the air was leaking out of her. 'Is it that obvious?'

'Well, maybe not to the untutored eye,' I said, 'but I'm a psychologist, remember. I'm trained to notice these things. I can always spot those little signs of discontent – the downturned mouth; the constant sighing; the tears running down the cheeks; the scribbling of the suicide note; the noose around the neck...'

'All right, Sigmund Freud,' she said, poking me in the ribs as a smile crept back on to her face, 'you can shut up now.'

I took a long drag on my cigarette, giving her space to breathe, to think. Sure enough, after a few seconds, she said, 'Can I talk to you about something?'

I spread my hands. 'Talk away.'

'Not here,' she said, looking around. I couldn't see who she thought might be listening – the rest of the smokers standing out in the cold with us were strangers – but her expression was furtive all the same. 'Let's go inside, get a drink and find a quiet corner in the downstairs bar.'

'Lead the way,' I said, taking a last drag on my cigarette before dropping the stub, stamping on it and following her back inside.

There was a little round table next to a group of fat, beardy blokes in T-shirts who were laughing a lot. Candice squeezed herself through to the built-in padded leather bench that ran the length of the wall while I queued at the bar for drinks. By the time I got back she was texting on her phone, a troubled expression on her face, her fingers tapping the tiny keyboard so swiftly they were almost a blur. The tink of our wine glasses on the wooden tabletop and the glassy scrape as I pushed hers towards her caused her face to bob up and produce a tired smile.

'Cheers,' I said, sitting down and raising my glass towards her, 'and happy birthday again.'

'Cheers,' she responded, the Sauvignon Blanc catching the light in little darting shimmers as she lifted her glass and touched it to mine. As I took a gulp of my plummy Merlot she barely wet her top lip before putting her drink back down. She pressed her hands together, aligning her fingertips, and hunched her shoulders as if she was drawing herself in. Her eyes flickered downwards and her lips tightened, as though she'd spotted something unsavoury in the bottom of her glass.

'Think a bit harder,' I said. 'My mind-reading powers aren't what they were.'

This time my comment didn't provoke even the twitch of a smile. 'Sorry,' she said. 'This isn't easy.'

'Why? Because it's embarrassing? Because it's complicated? Because you think I'll be angry?'

She made a face, snatched at her glass and took a hefty swig. The beardy blokes on the next table burst out laughing, drawing her gaze for a moment. Then she said, 'You know I've got this boyfriend, Dean?'

'The one you're hiding from us?'

'I'm not hiding him.'

My comment was meant as a joke, but her reply was enough of a snap to make me raise my hands. 'Sorry if I touched a nerve. You mean the one who couldn't come to your party because he had to work a shift at Nando's?'

'Yeah... but that's not the reason.'

'Not what reason?'

'The reason why he couldn't come.'

I looked at her and frowned, but she purposely averted her gaze. 'So what *is* the reason?'

It wasn't only the expression on her face that told me she was in trouble; it was her body language too. She held herself stiffly, the tautly clenched muscles in her neck and exposed arms making me think of a rabbit or deer poised to flee at the slightest sign of danger. I felt a flutter of nerves in my stomach; it was a feeling I hadn't had for a long time, but it was instantly familiar nonetheless. It seemed to take an age before she said, 'He's scared.'

Even now I hoped I was reading the situation wrongly, that my sudden apprehension was misplaced. 'Scared of meeting us all?' I asked, but she shook her head.

'Scared of being out in public. Scared of being seen by... certain people.'

'What people?' Unconsciously my voice hardened. 'What's he been up to, Candice?'

My daughter flinched as though I'd raised a hand to her. 'Don't get angry with *me*, Dad. None of this is my fault.'

I controlled myself, took a swig of wine. 'I'm not angry with you, sweetheart. I'm just worried about you. It's obvious that whatever this boyfriend of yours has done, it's had a knock-on effect. So why don't you tell me what you're involved in?'

'*I'm* not involved,' she said. 'But that doesn't mean they won't take it out on me.'

'Who?' I asked, and this time the nerves didn't just flutter in my stomach, they cramped.

The beardy guys on the next table burst out laughing again, and I glared at them. One had a Dalek on his T-shirt, which was stretched across his fat belly. He caught my eye, and instantly the mirth dropped out of his face and he glanced quickly away. I might be a psychology lecturer these days, but I apparently still have the kind of face that makes people uneasy.

Instead of answering my question, Candice said, 'Did I tell you that Dean was an art student?'

'You have now.'

'Right, well... one night about, I dunno... eighteen months ago, he went to this party in Shoreditch with some friends of his, and met this guy, Mitch, who told Dean that he was a businessman. Mitch talked posh, and had a really expensive suit, and a girlfriend who looked like a model, and Dean was pretty much in awe of him, even though Mitch was only two years older than him. In fact, Dean said that Mitch made him feel like a kid – not in the way he treated him or anything, but just because he was so confident and... sorted, you know?'

I nodded and finished my wine. I could have done with another, but I didn't want to interrupt Candice's flow.

'Anyway, in spite of this, Mitch was really friendly towards Dean, and asked him what he did, and seemed really interested in Dean's art and everything. They talked for a bit and then Mitch told Dean he had some really great grass and he asked him if he wanted to go outside for a smoke.'

Candice stopped there and gave a little shrug. She reached out almost shyly and ran a forefinger through the frosting of condensation on the side of her glass.

'By the way, I don't want you to think Dean's a druggie or anything, Dad, cos he's not. He just smokes a bit of pot now and again when he can afford it.'

She glanced at me and I wafted a hand to show it was of no consequence. Where I grew up the use of recreational drugs was an everyday occurrence. Taking a couple of Es or some speed, or smoking a joint to chill out, was no different to having a few pints down the pub. That doesn't mean I would have condoned Candice popping pills every day, but despite the recent scare stories about marijuana causing long-term mental health problems, I didn't know anyone whose brain had become fucked up just from smoking the odd joint.

Encouraged by my response, she said, 'So Dean and Mitch went out on the balcony. And while they were there Mitch started asking Dean about his student loan, how he managed to live on a pittance, all that. At first Dean thought Mitch was taking the piss, but then Mitch said he knew a way that Dean could earn a bit of extra cash.'

'Let me guess,' I said. 'He wanted Dean to sell drugs for him?'

A look of shame crossed Candice's face. 'Only grass. There's no way Dean would have touched the hard stuff. And it's not like he was getting kids addicted or anything. He was only selling it to other students who would have got it somewhere else.'

'So what went wrong?'

Candice sighed. 'At first Dean was only getting a few ounces a time off Mitch. Every week or two Dean would meet some contact of Mitch's in a pub or a park or somewhere, and Dean would hand over the cash he'd made from selling the stuff, and would get ten per cent back for himself, and the contact would give Dean more weed to sell. Then the last time they met, two weeks ago, Mitch's contact told Dean that Mitch was pleased with the way things were going, and that this time he was going to arrange for Dean to have a few months worth of grass all in one go, so that he and Dean wouldn't have to meet up so often.'

'I'm guessing he told him it was less risky that way?'

Candice nodded.

I sighed. 'So how much did Mitch let him have?'

'Fifty ounces. It was too much for Dean to carry home, so one of Mitch's men drove it round to Dean's flat.'

I whistled. 'That's a hell of a lot of weed to take possession of. How much does an ounce go for these days? Hundred and fifty?'

If Candice was surprised by my knowledge she didn't show it. 'More like two hundred.'

'So that's ten grand's worth of weed your boyfriend had hidden in his flat.' I could see where this was going. 'Didn't he suspect anything?'

Candice shook her head. 'Why would he? He'd known Mitch for over a year, and Mitch had always been straight with him. And Dean had built up a client base of about fifty people, which worked out at an ounce per person. Dean said an ounce would last the average user about ten to twelve weeks.' She shrugged. 'The maths seemed to add up.'

'But?' I said.

'But the next day, when Dean was out, his flat was broken into and the entire stash was stolen.'

I sighed. 'Did the burglars take anything else?'

'No,' said Candice in a low voice.

'Sounds like they knew exactly what they were looking for, doesn't it?' I muttered.

Candice was silent for a moment, then she said, 'Dean reckons the guys who did it were enemies of Mitch's, that they were from a rival gang.'

'Maybe they were,' I said, 'but I'll bet that when Dean told Mitch what had happened, he didn't get quite the response he expected.'

Candice grimaced. 'Dean rang Mitch straight away. He thought Mitch would be angry about the burglary, but sympathetic to Dean. But Dean said Mitch was really cold. He told Dean that it wasn't his problem.'

'And that he still wanted his money?'

Candice's face flickered with distress, and she swallowed as if trying to hold back tears. When she next spoke her voice was low, strained. 'Dean was set up, wasn't he, Dad?'

I shrugged, but tried to sound sympathetic. 'Looks like it, sweetheart.'

'But why? Why would Mitch do that? Dean was making money for him.'

'Yeah, but only dribs and drabs. People like Mitch are greedy, Candice – and totally ruthless.'

'But why pick on Dean? He can't afford to pay Mitch back.'

'Because he's weak. Because he's vulnerable. And because if enough pressure is put on him and he gets scared enough, he'll *find* that money somehow.'

Candice looked stricken, like she didn't know which way to turn. Gently I asked, 'Is that why you've told me all this?'

She looked surprised. 'What do you mean?'

'Because you want to know if I can lend you the money? Clear your boyfriend's debts?'

Shame and disappointment chased one another briefly across Candice's face, but they were quickly replaced by hope. 'Can you?' she asked. 'We'd pay you back, Dad, honest.'

'How much does Dean owe altogether? Ten grand?'

'Plus interest. Fifteen in all.'

I tried not to flinch. 'And when does he have to pay it by?'

'Mitch gave him two weeks, but that was nine days ago. He's got till this Friday.'

'Fuck me,' I murmured, looking down into my empty glass.

'*Can* you help us, Dad?' There was no pretence in Candice's voice now. Her words were a desperate plea.

I sighed. 'I wish I could, sweetheart, but I'm not that plush. I do all right, I make enough to get by, but I haven't got a lot of savings. I've got maybe... six, seven grand in my account. You're welcome to that if you want it.'

'Could you maybe borrow the rest from the bank?' Candice suggested. 'I hate to ask, but... we're desperate, Dad.'

I felt a flare of anger – not at Candice, but at Dean, for dragging my daughter into his mess. 'And tell them what? I can't just borrow nine grand from the bank without offering an explanation.'

'Can't you make something up? Tell them Kate needs an operation or something?'

I scowled. 'I'm not dragging Kate into this. And I'm not lying for the sake of your boyfriend, Candice – not with my record.'

She put a trembling hand up to her face. Now she really *did* look as though she was about to burst into tears. 'Sorry, Dad,' she said, her voice so low in the crowded room I could barely hear her. 'It was unfair of me to ask.'

I glanced quickly around the pub, but no one seemed to be paying us any attention. I still had a burning knot of anger in my belly, but I kept my voice calm.

'What about Dean's parents? Can't he ask *them* for a loan?'

She gave a brief, jerky shake of the head. 'His dad's dead. And his mum's not that rich. And she's ill a lot of the time, in and out of hospital. He says something like this would really upset her.'

She'd be a lot more upset if her beloved son was found in a skip with his throat cut, I thought.

'Hasn't Dean got stuff he can sell?' I suggested. 'A car? A computer? An iPhone? At the risk of sounding like an old codger, don't you kids have all sorts of fancy gadgets these days?'

'It's not enough, Dad,' Candice's voice was dwindling. 'Mitch wants all the money in one go. We'd never be able to raise enough.'

'I'm sure he'd be open to negotiation. Half now, half in a few weeks' time. People like Mitch might be evil bastards, but at the end of the day they're more interested in getting what they think is owed to them than in meting out punishment. Physical violence is messy and hard to hide. It often leads to the police getting involved, even if the victim is too scared to go to them himself.'

Candice listened to me intently, but as soon as I'd finished she shook her head. 'That might be what it was like in your day, Dad, but people like Mitch aren't bothered about the police. One of Mitch's guys told Dean that if he didn't come up with the money in time, his loved ones would suffer. He knew Dean's mum's address, and he said something like "Wouldn't it be a shame if your pretty girlfriend suddenly lost her looks?"'

Candice's crumbling resolve gave way, and all at once tears were running down her face.

'I'm scared, Dad,' she blurted through her sobs. 'I'm scared of what's going to happen.'

My guts were twisting now, partly with fear and anxiety, but mostly with a boiling rage. How *dare* this dumb, fucking boyfriend of my daughter's get himself into a situation where she might be harmed! How *dare* some vicious, jumped-up low-life threaten and frighten my little girl!

The natural response of the average law-abiding citizen might have been to advise Candice to go to the police and tell them everything. Far more preferable for her boyfriend to get a rap on the knuckles, they might say, than for her to end up badly hurt or worse. But I knew better than to suggest such a thing. I knew that although the police would take Candice seriously – maybe even seriously enough to find Mitch and bring him in for questioning – their hands would effectively be tied. They wouldn't be able to detain him for long without evidence, and people like Mitch usually had all the bases covered. Besides which, Mitch had no doubt already informed Dean that if he *did* go to the police, and if Mitch *was* arrested, then plans already laid would immediately spring into action – plans which would most likely involve certain of Mitch's friends paying visits to both Dean's mother and girlfriend.

Reaching across the table, I took Candice's small, limp hands in mine and gave them a squeeze. With more confidence and conviction than I was feeling, I said, 'Nothing's going to happen, Candice. Nothing at all. I promise you that.'

She looked at me through swimming eyes, and the desperate hope in her face almost broke my heart. 'What are you going to do?' she whimpered.

I thought about the past I'd vowed never to go back to, the telephone number I'd once been given that I'd vowed never to use.

'I know some people,' I said. 'People who've been around a lot longer than this Mitch bloke, and who've got a lot more influence.' I felt my stomach clench again, but I kept my gaze as steady as my voice. 'I'll give them a call. They'll soon sort this out for us, sweetheart. Don't you worry.'

THREE

KATE

The bomb dropped from above, a direct hit that crushed my ribs and expelled the air from my stomach in one painful gasp.

'*Dadeeee!*' the bomb cried, slithering off my belly and snuggling with a wriggle of limbs into the warm gap between my left arm and now-aching torso.

Before responding I drew in an experimental lungful of air and slowly breathed it out again. I was surprised and relieved to discover that everything seemed to be working normally. With sleep-gummed eyes I squinted at the squirming creature in the crook of my arm, its fan of tousled, chestnut-brown hair shaking and bouncing as it burrowed into a more comfortable position.

'Morning, trouble,' I murmured.

The tumble of chestnut locks suddenly jerked upright to reveal a sleep-creased little face. 'I'm not trouble!' a voice piped up indignantly. '*You're* trouble!'

'I don't dive-bomb people when they're asleep,' I pointed out.

The face pushed itself into mine. 'It's time to get up,' it argued. 'Time to get ready for *school*.' Then the face recoiled, its nose crinkling. 'Poo, Daddy, you *smell*.'

Reaching across to my bedside table, I grabbed my phone, which I was using as an alarm clock. After talking to Candice the night before, I'd come home and – armed with a three-quarters-full bottle of Jack Daniels and a packet of Marlboro Lights – had sat out for God knows how long on the narrow balcony of the third-floor flat that I shared with

31

Kate, my youngest daughter. Barely feeling the cold, I'd demolished the whisky and smoked most of the pack while staring unseeingly over the spiky, uneven Chiswick skyline, my conversation with Candice (and more to the point the promise I'd made her) circling in my head like some mad, clockwork toy. Finally, my guts acidic with alcohol and anxiety, and my throat raw and aching with tobacco, I'd staggered to my little bedroom next to the bathroom and collapsed into a restless, semi-drunken half-sleep, which I'd known even as I crawled under the duvet would leave me feeling more exhausted than rested.

Sure enough, as my senses slowly returned, I became aware of just how groggily hungover I was. Kate was right; I *did* stink. Even I could tell that my breath smelled like a fire-bombed distillery. I needed several pints of water, a bucket of painkillers, a hot shower and about a gallon of coffee before I'd begin to feel even remotely human again. I could have done with another twenty minutes to groan myself out of bed too, but there was no chance of that with Kate around. My five-year-old daughter was like a mad, clockwork toy herself, full of frantic energy, especially first thing in the morning when she'd just had her batteries recharged with ten or twelve hours of the kind of blissful sleep that only kids can enjoy. In a minute she'd be bouncing up and down, demanding her breakfast, after which I'd have to coax her to wash her face, and get dressed, and brush her teeth and hair, whilst at the same time trying to get my own thoughts in order for the day ahead.

Every week-day morning started like this. It was stressful, frustrating and madcap, but even with that day's added misery of a dozen pneumatic drills hammering in my skull, I wouldn't have changed it for the world. Kate was a handful, but what she took out of me in terms of energy, time and patience, she gave back a million times over in love, joy and laughter. I don't want to sound like a soppy, gushing idiot, but the bottom line is that she gave my life meaning in all sorts of ways – any parent worth their salt will know exactly what I mean. There's nothing as fierce as the love you feel for your child, and the fact that I was effectively the only parent that Kate had, that I was her sole guardian and protector, intensified those feelings still further.

Checking my phone, I saw it was 6.53 a.m., only seven minutes before my alarm was due to go off. Although I had no idea what time it was when I'd crashed, I doubted I'd had more than four or five hours' fitful sleep.

'Why don't you go and watch *Toy Story* for ten minutes,' I suggested, 'and then I'll come and make breakfast?'

Kate's big blue eyes widened in almost comical astonishment and glee. 'I'm not allowed to watch DVDs in the morning,' she said, as if it were some divine edict. 'You said it makes me late.'

'I know I did,' I said, 'but this is a special treat. If you go now, you can watch it for ten minutes, but then you have to switch it off and get ready for school. Deal?'

'Deal!' she yelled, loud enough to make my teeth ache. She leaped off the bed and scampered towards the door, a whirling dervish in yellow Little Miss Sunshine pyjamas. At the threshold she skidded to a halt and looked back at me as a sudden idea occurred to her. 'Can I watch *Toy Story 2* instead of *Toy Story?*'

Her round face was so earnest that I had to clear my throat to stop myself from laughing. 'Course you can.'

'Yay!' she bellowed, and shot out of the room like a bullet from a gun.

I flopped on to my back and stared up at the ceiling. There was a brown stain there shaped roughly like the British Isles, probably from some long-ago flood in the bathroom of the top-floor flat. The stain had been painted over, but it had seeped through in speckles and patches, as if the joists and floorboards above were still saturated with damp. Ever since Kate and I had moved in four years ago, the attic had been occupied by a little Jewish woman in her seventies called Mrs Hersh, whose husband was dead and whose four children were scattered all over the globe. Although she looked frail as a bundle of dry sticks, Mrs Hersh was a tough old thing – always out visiting friends, or getting her hair done, or lugging her shopping back from the supermarket on the high road, her feet clomping up and down the wooden staircase. I was dreading a time when the stairs might become too much for her and she'd be forced to move out. I had visions of some new, heftier tenant climbing into a brimming bath, only to come crashing through the ceiling as the spongy floor gave way.

I wasn't thinking about that this morning, though. Just as it had the night before, my mind returned to the promise I'd made to Candice. I felt like someone who'd lost a vital set of keys, but couldn't shake the urge to keep going over and over the same ground in case they'd missed something. I'd been trying to think of an alternative to getting in touch with the person I'd told my daughter would be able to sort out her mess, but even though my mind was working overtime, I knew that nothing else I might come up with would be anywhere near as effective. Just because I'd once – when I was young and stupid – been nicked for armed robbery, which had resulted in a nine-year jail sentence (of which I'd served six years and two months), that didn't make me a tough guy, or an anti-hero. And neither did it mean I had a string of underworld connections I could call on when I needed a favour.

I did have *one* connection, though. Just one. But it was a fucking good one.

The day before being released from prison I'd been given a phone number, and told to call it if I ever got into trouble or needed a favour. I'd thanked the man who'd given it to me and put the number away in a safe place. But even back then I'd vowed never to use it, never to look back over my shoulder like Lot's wife, never to open Pandora's box.

I'd never thrown the number away, though. Call it superstition, call it hedging my bets, but I'd not only kept the number, I'd made sure I knew exactly where it was at all times. Now, because of that, I felt torn right down the middle. Half of me wished I *had* thrown the number away, that it wasn't there to tempt me, whilst the other half saw it as my salvation – or at least Candice's salvation.

'It's not for me,' I said out loud. 'I wouldn't be doing it for me.'

I suppose I hoped that that might make it all right, but it didn't, not really. Whether I was doing it for me or not, it didn't change the fact that I was contemplating opening the door and letting the darkness back in. Because the thing is, nobody gets something for nothing in the world I was considering venturing back in to. If I rang that number, then it might mean Candice would be safe, but I would clock up a debt; it would make me beholden.

'Da-deeeee!' The call came from the living room beyond the flat's short hallway, and despite the way I was feeling I felt a smile sneak on to my face.

'What?'

'It's been ten minutes. Do I have to switch the DVD off now?'

My smile widened. Despite often behaving like a small but lively bull in a very cluttered china shop, my youngest daughter was a stickler for rules and regulations. I considered giving her two more minutes, but then decided that the rule thing was something to be encouraged, not let slide.

'Yep,' I said, swinging my legs out of bed and bracing myself to sit upright. 'I'm coming to make breakfast.'

The next hour was the usual chaos of knocked-over beakers of milk and lost trainers and misplaced spectacles. Kate had been born in difficult circumstances, having to be cut from her mother's womb because she was in a breech position with the cord wrapped around her neck. She was deprived of oxygen for longer than the doctors were happy with, and for a while it had been touch and go as to whether she might suffer permanent brain damage. In the event the effects, thank God, had been relatively mild – a few initial developmental and learning difficulties, which she was now more than making up for, and some minor optic-nerve damage, which meant that she currently wore cute, pink-framed spectacles to stop her from squinting when she was watching TV or trying to make out the words on the whiteboard at school.

Needless to say, she was always losing the specs – when she wasn't sitting on them and breaking them, that is. If I had a quid for every time I'd asked her where she was when she last took them off, I'd be a millionaire by now.

On this occasion, the specs, smeared with jammy thumbprints, were found under the sprawled-open pages of her *Toy Story* colouring book, which she'd been engrossed in while I was grabbing a quick shower. By 8.10 we were ready to go – or at least, thanks to me, *she* was. She stood impatiently by the door, watching as I laced up my boots, wearing her now-clean specs and her green-and-red duffel coat, a *Dora the Explorer* school bag slung over one shoulder. Despite taking two supposedly fast-acting Ibuprofen and downing three cups of sludge-thick coffee my head was still pounding. I was flushed and sweating too after my shower, though I told myself I was only imagining that the sweat oozing out of me and forming damp patches on my shirt smelled like pure JD.

'Come *on*, Daddy,' Kate said, rolling her eyes, as if *I* was the one responsible for the string of mishaps which had made us late, 'or Paula will go without me.'

'No she won't,' I said. 'She'll knock on the door first to find out where you are.'

'She might forget.'

'She won't.'

'She might have already knocked on the door and we didn't hear her.'

'I think that's unlikely, don't you? This flat is so small that if you trump in bed I can hear it in the kitchen.'

While Kate giggled I finished tying my laces and straightened up.

'Right then,' I said. 'Let's go.'

She turned and pulled down the door handle while I twisted the Chubb lock above it that she couldn't reach.

'Even if I do a quiet one?' she said as the door swung inwards.

'What?'

'Trump in bed.'

I grinned. 'Even if you do a silent one. An SBD.'

'What's an SBD?'

'Silent but deadly.'

'What does that mean?'

'It means a trump which you can't hear, but which smells really, really bad.'

Kate guffawed at this. The sound, echoing up and down the stairwell, was both delightful and alarming. She was still guffawing as she marched across the short hallway and rapped on the door of flat 4.

'Well, somebody's tickled by something,' Paula Sherwood said, pulling the door open.

'It's Daddy,' said Kate, her blue eyes widening behind her spectacles. 'He's been talking about *trumps*.'

Paula's long-lashed eyes flickered to regard me with amusement as Kate pushed her way into the flat, shouting for the Sherwoods' son, Hamish. Paula was a strong-jawed brunette with startlingly pale grey eyes and a scattering of girlish freckles across her nose and cheeks. I admit I fancied her, and sometimes I even flirted with her, but never seriously. I got the impression that she and her husband Adam were rock-solid, besides which he was a nice bloke, and there was no way I wanted to make waves in either my life or theirs.

I'd struck lucky with the Sherwoods. Because Hamish was the same age as Kate, Paula was only too happy to take the children to school every day, *and* pick them up, *and* look after Kate until I got home. She even babysat for me when I had to work late or on the rare occasions

– like last night – when I went out. To be honest, they were a lifeline, and what I'd do if they moved away I had no idea; I didn't want to think about it.

I shrugged now and gave what I hoped was a wry grin. 'What can I say? We'd covered politics and the economy. I was running out of subjects.'

Paula chuckled, and then asked, 'Are you all right, Alex?'

I felt suddenly self-conscious about the sweat patches on my shirt. 'Bit hot and bothered, that's all. You know what it's like, rushing around first thing in the morning.'

'But last night,' she said, 'when you got home? You seemed a bit... preoccupied.'

I shrugged again, trying not to look uncomfortable. 'Just family stuff. Nothing major. Thanks a lot for last night, by the way. Don't know what I'd do without you.'

That sounded a bit more intimate than I'd meant it to, but Paula had the good grace not to react. Instead she said breezily, 'No problem. Besides, you'd do the same for us – you *have* done the same for us.'

It was true. I'd had Hamish round for sleepovers with Kate when the Sherwoods were out – but it hadn't happened often. I owed them a lot more than they owed me.

Grimacing, I said, 'Listen, I don't want to take advantage, but is there any chance you might be able to have Kate for a bit longer tonight? There's something I may have to do after work.'

She wafted a hand. 'Sure. In fact, it's easier having Kate here than not, because she keeps Hamish amused. If it was up to him, she'd live with us all the time.'

As I thanked her there was a shriek from the depths of the flat. Paula raised her eyebrows. 'I'd better get the little horrors off to school before they wreck the place. Have a good day, Alex.'

'Yeah, you too.'

I went back into my flat and closed the door. I'd have to be heading off to work myself soon, but I had the first period free, so there wasn't a rush. I stood for a moment in the little hallway with the four doors leading off from it and took a deep breath, allowing my thoughts to settle. Then I walked slowly through to the kitchen to make myself yet another coffee, clearing away the breakfast things as I waited for the kettle to boil.

I knew what I was doing. It's called displacement activity. It's where you find a bunch of unimportant tasks to occupy your time in order to put off what you really *should* be doing. Once I'd cleared the kitchen, I carried my coffee through to the living room, apprehension gnawing at me. Tucked into the corner between the French windows and the kitchen door was my desk, on top of which sat my Apple Mac, the telephone, and a haphazard pile of textbooks, documents, lecture notes and student essays which needed marking.

I eyed the third drawer down on the left. That was my 'miscellaneous' drawer, which contained all the bits and pieces I had no real use for, but was reluctant to throw away. I stood in the middle of the room, hovering for a moment, and took a swig from my mug. Then I said, 'For fuck's sake,' and banged the mug down on the wooden blanket box in front of the settee, next to Kate's *Toy Story* colouring book. Marching across to the desk, I yanked the 'miscellaneous' drawer open, half-hoping the envelope might have mysteriously vanished in the weeks or months since I'd last seen it. But there it was, small and white and dog-eared, poking out from beneath this year's Father's Day card that Kate had made for me. I'd put the number in an envelope because I'd been reluctant to transfer it to my address book, or to the contacts file on my computer, thinking that doing so would have been like officially accepting it into my life, making it permanent somehow.

Lifting the envelope from the drawer, I stared at the name on the front and sighed. Then I opened the envelope and took out the folded sheet of paper, which was low-grade, flimsy, torn from a standard-issue prison notebook. Unfolding the sheet with one hand, I lifted the telephone with the other and thumbed the connection button. As soon as the receiver started to hum I dialled the number scrawled on the sheet.

When the phone rang at the other end my mouth went instantly dry and my head and heart started to thump in unison.

He won't be there, I told myself almost hopefully. *He gave me this number years ago. He's bound to have moved. He might even be back inside.*

After three rings the phone was picked up. 'Hello?'

The voice was wary, clipped, unwelcoming.

'Benny?' I said.

'Who's this?'

I licked my lips. They were so dry it was like pushing a stone between two sheets of sandpaper. 'I don't know if you remember me, Benny, but... it's Alex. Alex Locke.'

FOUR

THE HAIR OF THE DOG

I start each academic year by telling my new students about my less-than-illustrious past. I do this not to impress them, or frighten them, but simply because university campuses are hotbeds of gossip and hearsay, and if *I* didn't say anything then chances were that sooner or later they would stumble upon some far more distorted version of the truth.

Although kids of that age – or young adults, as our esteemed principal insists on calling them – like to pretend they're too cool to be impressed by anything or anyone that's older than they are, the initial response I never fail to get from each influx of students is wary respect bordering on awe. Many of my colleagues think I should milk this for all it's worth, but I'm not comfortable with the 'hard man' image – and not only because it's misplaced. The thing about violence is that it's so antithetical to the majority of so-called civilised society that in the eyes of those who've rarely been exposed to it, it attains an oddly glamorous, almost mythical status.

But real violence isn't glamorous at all. It's savage and ugly and squalid. People are often destroyed by it, both physically and emotionally. It leaves nothing but fear and misery in its wake; it fucks up lives, permanently, irrevocably.

This is something I take great pains to drum home when I'm telling my story. Career criminals might *seem* cool with their designer suits and their entourage of hangers-on, but they're really not the sort of people you want to be around. The majority of them are psychological

41

wastelands; sociopaths. Yes, they can appear loyal, friendly, even charming, but in truth they often only mimic human behaviour in order to get what they want. And woe betide anyone who becomes a nuisance to them, or outlives their usefulness, or just happens to be in their way at the wrong moment. I've heard of people being stamped and kicked to death for a minor slight or ill-conceived joke; I've heard of crooks shooting or stabbing other crooks – sometimes even their best friends, blokes they've known for years – simply because of a disagreement over a restaurant bill or a misplaced comment about the other guy's wife.

Benny Magee was such a man. If you met him with no prior knowledge of who he was you'd think he was amiable, open-minded, softly spoken. And yet he'd been involved in some terrible things, and had spent as much of his adult life in prison as out of it. There'd been a lot of respect for him in Pentonville; people treated him with deference, even though he wasn't the sort of bloke to throw his weight about and assert his authority. The first time I met him I was sitting cross-legged on the bunk in my cell, trying to concentrate on the psychology textbook in my lap. I had one finger stuck in my ear and my lips were moving in an attempt to block out the racket going on around me and get the words on the page to stick in my head.

That's one thing about prisons that they never focus on in movies and TV dramas. They never mention the noise. Morning, noon and night there's an unceasing barrage of people shouting to each other, yelling abuse, crying, screaming for attention, banging the hell out of the walls and doors of their cells. It never stops. It goes on and on. The first time I was exposed to it I was terrified, I thought there was something kicking off, but after a while I realised that this was what it was like all the time, and that if I didn't want it to crush me it was something I would have to get used to.

I only became aware that someone had stepped through the open door of my cell when a shadow fell across the page of the book. Immediately my head snapped up, my heart thumping. I knew there were plenty of screws around, but I knew too that sometimes they could be purposely distracted, or even persuaded to turn a blind eye.

When I saw Benny standing over me, my stomach clenched and the muscles in my shoulders went rigid. Until now I hadn't crossed his path, though I'd seen him around and knew of him by reputation. The stories that other inmates had told me about him were toe-curling. It was said that he'd once nailed an informant to a wooden floor before removing his fingers and toes with bolt cutters; that he'd dealt with a business rival by hammering a tent peg through his eye and into his brain; that he'd punished an ex-girlfriend's lover by tying him up, fastening electrodes to his testicles, throwing him into a bath of cold water, and then electrocuting him until he passed out, slipped beneath the water and drowned.

What made these stories even more horrifying – and oddly more feasible – was the fact that Benny wasn't much to look at. By that I mean he was unassuming – slight, with fine, sandy hair and a narrow, forgettable face. I'd have put him in his late thirties, which meant that he was about twice my age. Perhaps the one concession to his criminality was the fact that he had a small scar bisecting the left side of his upper lip. However, he could just as easily have got that from falling off his bike when he was a kid.

I felt an urge to scramble to my feet and stand to attention, but I thought that might be construed as squaring up to him, so I stayed where I was, cowering and submissive.

Benny wasn't alone. Standing behind him was a big man, running to fat but still formidable, with a black moustache and hands like the clawed scoops on a digger.

Bending at the waist, Benny leaned towards me until our foreheads were almost touching. He smelled fresh and faintly scented, of shower gel and deodorant, perhaps some kind of hair product. When he parted his lips to speak, my balls shrivelled and crawled into my belly, like a pair of snails retreating into their shells. I expected some blood-curdling threat to tickle my ears. But then I noticed that Benny's pale blue eyes were not trained on me, but trying to make out the title of my book.

'What you reading?' he asked.

Not quite trusting myself to speak, I held up the book.

'*Psychology of Behaviour*,' he said, and pulled a mildly impressed face. Straightening up, he turned to the man standing behind him. 'See this, Michael? Here's a boy who's using his time wisely. There ought to be more of his sort in here, don't you think?'

The moustached man grunted in what I took to be assent. I couldn't, though, work out whether Benny was taking the piss. Part of me was still convinced I was about to be punished for daring to try to rise above my station.

Turning back to me, Benny asked, 'What's your name, son?'

'Alex,' I said, but the word came out as little more than a dry, crackly wheeze. I cleared my throat and tried again. 'Alex Locke.'

Benny nodded sagely, as if I'd posited a workable solution to a difficult problem. 'How long have you been in this shithole, Alex?'

'Nearly a month,' I said.

'And what are you going to do when you get out?'

Still wary, I said, 'I'm not sure.'

'Just reading that for the hell of it, are you?' Benny said, nodding at the book.

'Oh... no. I'm doing some A levels. Psychology, maths and English. If I pass them I might do a degree.'

'A laudable ambition.' Benny looked at me. His eyes made me think of glaciers reflecting the pure, piercing blue of an Arctic sky. I tried not to shiver. 'Do you know what laudable means, Alex?'

I did, or thought I did, but his eyes were freezing my brain, rendering me incapable of thought.

'Good?' I said lamely.

'More or less. It means commendable. Worthy of admiration.' He paused for a split second, and then asked mildly, 'Do you know who I am?'

My mouth was suddenly so dry I couldn't swallow. I nodded and managed to tear my lips apart to whisper, 'Yes.'

Benny smiled. 'Then you'll know it's too late for me. I've gone too far down the road to damnation to turn back now.' He placed a hand on my shoulder and gave it a little squeeze. I imagined that hand wielding a hammer, banging nails into a rival's flesh, or a tent peg into an opponent's eye.

'But not you,' he said. 'There's still time for you to mend your ways. Do me a favour, Alex. Don't fuck it up.'

'I won't,' I whispered.

'I hope not. I'll be watching out for you. While you're in here I'll be your guardian angel. Anything you want, just ask. Okay?'

'Okay,' I said.

'Good lad.' He turned abruptly and nodded at Michael, who preceded him out of the door. At the threshold Benny turned back. 'Oh, and Alex?'

'Yeah?'

'Don't be afraid.'

I was never sure whether he meant of him, of anyone else in the prison, or of life in general, and I never asked. All I know is that from that day onwards I was under Benny's protection. I'm not saying that prison life was a breeze because of that – by its very nature it was a depressing, repetitive, soul-crushing experience – but after Benny's visit I got the very real sense that my fellow inmates had changed their attitudes towards me.

The first month I'd been there I'd felt like a gazelle around which a pack of lions was constantly prowling. However, apart from a few threatening comments – which were ten a penny in prison and rarely the prelude to anything more serious; violence, when it came, tended to be swift, brutal and unexpected – I'd managed to avoid any kind of confrontation. I'd felt, though, as if I was being assessed, mulled over, considered for future action. As a result, I was constantly on edge and had tried to keep myself to myself as much as possible, which was one of the reasons why I'd buried myself in study. Maybe my fears were all in my head, but I didn't think so. And even if they were, Benny's intervention helped a lot, because after he'd spoken to me I felt much easier in my mind. The belligerent stares I'd been getting (or imagined I'd been getting) before, and the muttered conversations I'd noticed among various cliques of prisoners whenever I'd walked past seemed all at once to melt away. People might not have been friendlier towards me, but they were definitely less hostile. I didn't make many friends in prison, but that suited me fine, because it meant I could get on with my studies without fear of interruption or distraction.

It might sound like a cliché, but prison was the making of me. In fact, you could go even further back than that, and say that if Chris hadn't suggested to Ray that he bring me in on the job he was planning, I might well have ended up pissing my life away on some shitty estate. But because I was in on the job I got caught. And because I got caught I ended up in prison. And because I was in prison, and had time on my hands, I started reading books. And it was through that that I started my studies, and got a degree, and ended up teaching psychology...

Cause and effect. A long chain of linked circumstances. Everyone's lives are like that, I suppose, full of 'what if's and 'if only's. Some people think it's fate or destiny, some think it's just a random series of events. Whatever your beliefs, the fact is we're all given a choice of multiple paths to follow, and the ones we choose to take are what determines who we are, what we become.

That might not be very profound, but it's true all the same. Looking back, I sometimes wonder what might have happened if I'd not made certain decisions at certain times. Knowing what I know now, all I see is the equivalent of a jumper unravelling, at first stitch by stitch and then more and more rapidly, or perhaps more accurately a wave engulfing all before it, which starts with the ripples caused by a single dropped pebble into an otherwise calm lake.

But I'm jumping ahead of myself, and it's important not to do that. I have to tell this story as I lived it, as it happened to me, and resist the urge to interject based on where I am now, and on what I know.

So. Benny Magee. The phone call. The next fork in the road. The next decision on whether to turn right or left.

It went like this:

'Hello?'

'Benny?'

'Who's this?'

'I don't know if you remember me, Benny, but... it's Alex. Alex Locke.'

'Alex Locke.' He repeated my name with no inflection, and therefore no apparent recognition, whatsoever. I was about to start the tortuous job of reminding him of our association, whilst again wondering if, by ringing him, I'd done the wrong thing, when he spoke again, a note of incredulity creeping into his voice.

'Fuck me. Alex Locke. The kid from Pentonville. What was it again? Psychology of Behaviour?'

'That's right,' I said, not sure whether to feel flattered or alarmed that he'd remembered.

'So tell me this, Alex,' he said mildly. '*Did* you fuck it up?'

Even though I was tense, I couldn't help but smile. 'I don't think so.'

'Glad to hear it. So where's life taken you?'

I hesitated, feeling like one of the little pigs reluctant to open the door in case the big bad wolf should enter. I felt like this even though I knew that eventually, if he was going to provide me with the help I needed, I'd have to tell Benny more than I was comfortable with. 'I'm a psychology lecturer.'

'Good for you.'

'So what are *you* up to these days?'

I blurted out the question to stem the ones he was asking me, but as soon as the words left my mouth I clenched my teeth and screwed up my face as if I'd bitten down on a sour lemon. What a dickhead! What was I thinking of, asking him that?

Luckily, though, Benny gave a dry chuckle.

'Perhaps I'd better not answer that, on account of the fact that I might incriminate myself.'

He laughed harder, and I laughed along with him, just two old lags sharing a joke.

'So,' he said, 'what do you want from me, Alex? Because touched as I am to hear your voice, I take it you're not ringing to reminisce about the old days?'

'Not really,' I said. 'Sorry. I need your advice.'

'About what?'

I hesitated. 'My daughter's in a bit of bother through no fault of her own, and I'm... well, I'm out of my depth, to be honest. I'm not quite sure how to handle things. I was hoping you might be able to help.'

I realised how flimsy that sounded. But I couldn't tell Benny what I really wanted – which was for him to scare the shit out of the thug who was threatening Candice. I had to let Benny come up with that suggestion himself. But how to manoeuvre him into that position? Benny wasn't stupid; in fact, he was sharper than the weapons he had reputedly used to silence his enemies. I was beginning to wish I'd thought this through a bit more – or better yet, come up with a different plan. For all Benny's pleasant manner, I couldn't help but feel that I had let the big bad wolf in after all, and was now holding on to its tail in the hope that it wouldn't unsheathe its claws and turn on me.

'You must be desperate,' he said, 'to call me.'

'I'm desperate to help my daughter,' I replied carefully.

'Is that so?'

I imagined his narrow face, shrewd and calculating, the coldness emanating from his ice-blue eyes, and I had to fight the urge to slam the receiver down.

A couple of seconds' silence stretched between us, and then I said, 'Look, Benny, maybe this wasn't such a good idea. You don't want to be burdened with my stupid little problems. I mean, why would you? You're a busy man.'

I clammed up, aware that I was starting to let my tongue run away with me. How old would Benny be now? Fifty? Maybe he'd retired; maybe he'd mellowed with age.

'Have you forgotten what I told you?' he said.

He had this knack of wrong-footing you, of making you feel as if he knew more than he was letting on. It was unsettling, and annoying too, because you *knew* he was being manipulative, and yet that didn't stop you wanting to please him, to keep up with his way of thinking and not let him down. I suppose some of that was based on fear – you were scared of him becoming angry, because you knew what he was capable of – but not all. Benny might be outwardly unassuming, but he was also oddly charismatic. He had what is commonly termed a magnetic personality.

'What do you mean?' I said, cursing myself for sounding dumb.

'In Pentonville. I said I'd look out for you, Alex. And I will. I'm a man who keeps his promises.'

Loath as I was to contradict him, I found myself saying, 'We're not in Pentonville now.'

'Matter of opinion. Life's just a bigger prison with better scenery.'

I didn't know what to say to that. Before I could think of anything, Benny added, 'Besides, when you sign up with me, Alex, you sign up for ever. It's a life sentence, son.'

He laughed suddenly, a gravelly bark.

'I'm joking. But seriously, Alex, I think we should meet up, talk about this. I can tell from your voice that you're at your wits' end – besides which, it would be a tonic to see your ugly mug again.'

Suddenly I wanted to backtrack, think of an excuse *not* to meet him, but I knew he'd see right through me if I hesitated. So instead I heard myself saying, 'That'd be great. Thanks, Benny. I really appreciate it.'

We arranged to meet in a pub called The Hair of the Dog just off Barking Road, near the West Ham football ground at 5.30 that afternoon. The campus where I taught was in East London, just north of the river, so it wasn't much more than a short northwards hop for me. I drifted distractedly through my day's teaching like someone with a doctor's appointment he wasn't looking forward to, and was out of the building and hurrying towards the local DLR station at Beckton Park as soon as my last lecture of the day was over. I could have hung around a bit, taken more time to answer the questions of the half-dozen or so students who always lingered after lectures as if they didn't have a million and one more interesting things to do, or even retreated to my tutorial room to catch up on a bit of marking. But I was restless, anxious to arrive at the rendezvous and stake out my territory before Benny arrived.

The Hair of the Dog was a corner pub on a busy road, its frontage decorated with hanging baskets as big as baby's cribs. The expanse of wall beneath the windows was faced up with shiny ceramic tiles, which looked as though the building was protected by a chitinous, cockroach-brown exoskeleton. The old-fashioned, swinging pub sign depicted a wolfish, grinning dog wearing a bowler hat and holding a tankard of frothing ale in its strangely human-like paw. The pub was the cornerstone of a row of businesses which included a noodle bar, a dry cleaner's and a hypnotherapy centre.

Stepping inside the pub, I was immediately assailed by that old-school and wholly comforting odour of stale cigar smoke (ingrained in the walls and still redolent), ancient cologne and the hopsy, earthy fumes of beer and whisky. The décor was old-school too – battered red leather and chipped mahogany tables. The central bar was shaped like a squared-off tug boat, which had clearly been designed in order to serve all four corners of the vast room which it bisected. The carpet was the colour of raw beef and the ceiling was still stained an acrid yellow-brown from the days when the place had been a smoker's paradise.

At this time of day there were only a couple of dozen people occupying the myriad tables, which made the place look empty. I crossed to the bar, aware of the click of pool balls from an adjoining room and the burbles and bleeps, like robotic indigestion, from the unattended fruit machine. As a young man I'd spent many a drunken night in pubs like this, but now I felt incongruous, a middle-class pretender trying to fit in with the workers. Stupid, I know. This was

London, after all. The great melting pot. My eyes scanned the bottles arranged on the shelf behind a young guy in a green polo shirt who was waiting patiently to serve me. I pondered a moment, then ordered a large glass of Chilean Merlot.

I've always loved that moment just before you start drinking when the barman sets your first full glass down in front of you. Today, though, my stomach was so jittery with nerves that even the gentle chink of the glass on the bar and the cherry red shimmer of light on the deep velvety surface of the wine failed to calm me. As soon as I'd paid him I all but snatched at the glass and gulped down my first mouthful. It was smooth, but it burned a little when it reached the bile in my stomach. I took another gulp, then another, and within a minute the glass was half-empty. I stopped myself from taking a fourth gulp and placed my hands on the bar. It wouldn't do to be half-cut when Benny appeared. I needed to keep a clear head.

I was over half an hour early. I took my drink to a nearby table and passed the time wishing he'd arrive, in order to get this thing over with. I wished I'd bought a newspaper too, so that I could appear to be sitting casually, leafing through it, when he walked in. I did consider popping out and getting one, but then I got a mental image of me leaving the pub just as he was coming in, and him maybe thinking I was chickening out – so I stayed put.

The door opened a few times over the next half-hour, first to admit a gaggle of students – none of them mine, thank God – then a trio of brassy blondes, dolled up for a night out, one of whom gave me the eye, and then a couple of blokes who looked like they'd been working on a building site. Eventually, feeling like Johnny No-Mates, I took out my mobile and busied myself with it. I'd had a message from Candice asking if I'd had any further thoughts about our conversation last night, so I texted her back to say I was working on it. Then I logged on to the internet and looked at the news and sport headlines without taking anything in. I finished my wine, and at first decided not to get another until Benny turned up, then thought it'd look a bit pathetic if I was sitting there with nothing in front of me when he arrived. So I got up from my seat and went over to the bar, purposely ignoring the blonde who'd eyed me earlier and who I could see out of the corner of my eye was doing so again.

I ordered another Merlot, and was rooting in my pocket for change when I sensed a presence behind me. Thinking it was the blonde, I turned, and suddenly there he was.

'Hello, Alex,' he said.

He'd aged well. He had a few lines around his eyes and mouth, and his sandy hair, now cropped short, had turned grey at the temples, but otherwise he was tanned, slim and fit-looking. He was wearing a grey suit and a pale blue shirt with no tie – classy, but not too flash. Seeing him gave me a renewed and vertiginous realisation that I'd reached into the past and pulled it into the present despite my good intentions, and that there was now no turning back. I covered my apprehension by smiling and holding out my hand.

'Benny. It's good to see you. Thanks for coming.'

His grip was firm and dry. I was surprised to find he was shorter than I'd remembered, certainly a good three or four inches shorter than my own six-two. In prison he had always seemed to dominate any room he was in, and I supposed in the intervening years I'd mistakenly linked the force of his personality with a physical presence more intimidating than he actually possessed.

'Good to see you too, Alex. What are you drinking?'

'My shout,' I said. 'It's because of me that you're here, after all.'

His expression didn't change, nor his stance. Yet suddenly I became aware that his pale blue eyes were fixed on me, and it was as if a chill had crept in from somewhere. I felt the muscles tighten in my cheeks.

Pleasantly he said, 'Take it from me, I never go anywhere unless I want to.'

'Course not,' I said, trying to keep my own voice light. 'Which is why I'm so grateful you agreed to see me.'

His ice-chip eyes regarded me a split second longer, and then flickered away to assess the array of bottles behind the bar. 'I'll have a Scotch and soda,' he said. 'No ice.'

Rather than making small talk at the bar he turned and padded across to a table near the window. He moved confidently, almost daintily, like a dancer. He sat and turned his face to the last of the day's meagre daylight dribbling in through the distorted glass, his hands folded in his lap. He didn't move until I had placed our glasses on the table and sat down, and then he turned to me.

'Suppose you're good at reading people, picking up signals?' he said without preamble. 'Non-verbal communication and all that?'

I shrugged, wondering whether I was being tested, hoping he wouldn't ask me to psychoanalyse him. 'Well, I know the theory. But practical application's a different matter. What you become aware of more than anything, the further you read into the subject, is how many hang-ups you've got.'

Benny chuckled. 'In case you haven't noticed, that blonde over there's got the hots for you.' He indicated where he meant with the slightest twitch of his head.

I resisted the impulse to look over. 'I'd have to have been blind not to have noticed that.'

We laughed together, and I felt my tension slowly easing. Then Benny said, 'You've been regretting ringing me all day, haven't you, Alex? You've been wondering whether you made a mistake by picking up the phone this morning?'

I'd half-raised my glass to my mouth, but now I froze and looked at him. 'What makes you say that?'

He took a sip from his own glass, as if encouraging me to do the same. 'Relax, son. I'm not gonna bite your head off. It's just that I'm a bit of a psychologist myself. Purely amateur, of course. You have to be to survive as long as I have in my world. You have to know how people tick. You have to understand their motives and needs.'

'In order to manipulate them?' I asked, feeling suddenly bold.

He shrugged. 'Sometimes. Sometimes just so that you know who you can trust and who's likely to stab you in the back.'

I sipped my wine, trying not to rush it. 'So you know how I tick, then?'

'I know what a tough decision it must have been for you to ring me, and how you've been feeling since.'

'Oh?'

He smiled. 'No disrespect, but it's not exactly rocket science. Soon as you did what you did to land in Pentonville you knew it was a mistake. You decided then and there to put it behind you, to better yourself, and I admire you for that. Most of the kids inside, they're ignorant and lazy and they don't know any better. They think being a criminal makes them tough and independent, and that going straight, abiding by the law, means they're soft, that they can't hack it.

'But they're wrong. Because it takes a lot more guts to do what you did. For young kids the pressure inside to be meaner and badder than everyone else is immense. If the government don't want inmates to re-offend then they shouldn't put them together in the first place. Criminality feeds off criminality. Stands to reason.'

'So where *should* you put them?' I said. 'You can't build individual prisons for people. There aren't the resources to remove offenders from the environments that make them what they are.'

Benny gave me a crooked smile. 'Now that's the sixty-four thousand dollar question, isn't it?'

'And what about you?' I ventured. 'Aren't you putting yourself down by saying what you're saying?'

'I am what I am,' Benny said. 'I am what society made me. I'm not saying I'm proud of it, and I'm not saying I'm ashamed of it. It's just the way it is.'

'You seem to have done okay for yourself, though.'

'Well, that's because I was brought up right. I listened to my elders and respected what they told me. I kept my eyes and ears open and was encouraged to think for myself. I didn't rush into things and I didn't run before I could walk. It's all about planning. Using a bit of this.' He tapped the side of his head.

'But this isn't about me,' he continued. 'It's about you. When I gave you my number and told you to call if you needed anything, I thought the odds were I'd never hear from you again. And to be honest, I hoped I never *would* hear from you again. If I did, I knew it'd mean that you were in trouble, or that you'd somehow slipped off the straight and narrow. I knew you'd keep my number, though, and not throw it away. Even back then you were a smart boy, and a careful one, and I knew you'd keep it as something to fall back on, just in case.'

'And when I called you today,' I said, 'what did you think?'

'Like I said, I knew you must be desperate. I'm part of your old life, the one you were determined never to go back to, so I'm guessing that since putting the phone down this morning you've been regretting calling me, dreading this meeting, wondering what it'll lead to. You're trying to act like you're pleased to see me, but you're not really. You're scared.'

It was disconcerting, having my layers stripped away so unceremoniously.

'You're very astute,' I said, 'and I have to admit that's a pretty accurate assessment.' I paused, then asked, '*Should* I be scared?'

Benny shrugged. 'Probably. Not of me, though.'

'Of what then?'

'Of whatever it is that made you pick up that phone, and of what you might have to do to put it right.'

I sighed and took a gulp of wine. 'Like I said, my daughter's in trouble.' Briefly I told him what Candice had told me last night.

After I'd finished Benny was silent for a moment. He sat there, staring at me. I tipped my head back, tilting my glass towards my lips to avoid meeting his eyes.

Then, almost callously, he said, 'So what do you expect me to do about it?'

I shrugged, trying not to appear intimidated. 'Like I said on the phone, I'd value your advice.'

'No,' he said.

I blinked, taken aback. 'Sorry?'

'I mean no, that's not it. That's not what you want me to do.'

For a moment I wasn't sure how to respond, and then tentatively I said, 'Isn't it?'

He looked almost disappointed. 'At least have the courtesy to be honest with me, Alex. What you really want is for me to deal with this scrote, don't you? You want me to make your problem go away?'

I licked my lips, which had suddenly gone dry. 'Well... I suppose I *was* hoping you'd suggest that,' I mumbled.

'So what's in it for me?'

'I... I don't know. I suppose I thought...'

'That I'd do you a favour? Old times and all that?'

I shrugged again. I felt two inches tall. And despite what Benny had said, I *was* scared of him.

'I suppose so. Look, I'm sorry, Benny. Maybe this *was* a mistake. Maybe I should never have bothered you.'

Silence fell between us again. Then Benny sighed and stood up. I thought he was going to walk away without another word, and wretched though I felt, I was grateful that I was about to be let off so lightly.

Then he said, 'Let's have another drink,' and walked across to the bar. I sat there in a daze until he came back.

'Now,' he said, putting the drinks on the table, 'let's talk about this thing. And no fucking about this time. Agreed?'

'Agreed,' I said.

'Right then. First off, I'm not your fucking pit bull. You don't just let me off the chain and order me to kill. Understand?'

I swallowed. 'Yes,' I said. 'Sorry.'

'All right. Now, second thing, I sympathise about your daughter, and it's clear that this cunt needs taking down a peg or two, but this is your fight, not mine, so if you want him sorted out you're going to have to do it yourself.'

I grimaced, thought of the conversation I'd had with Candice last night. I'd been the tough guy then, enraged and vowing I'd take control of the situation. Now I felt nineteen again, floundering and out of my depth.

'I hear what you're saying,' I said, 'but... I'm not sure I can do that. It's... well, it's not really my forte.'

I winced at how feeble that sounded, but Benny took it in his stride – maybe he'd even been expecting it.

Spreading his hands, he said, 'So your only alternative, it seems to me, is to pay this fucker off.'

'Yeah, but how? The bank won't lend me the money, and there's no one I can borrow it from.'

Instead of answering, Benny reached into the inside pocket of his jacket and produced a black leather wallet with a gold clasp. As he opened it, I thought for one horrifying moment that he was going to lend me the money; I even had an image of him handing over the thousands I needed in cash, right there in the pub. If there was one thing I definitely *didn't* want, it was to be in debt to Benny Magee. However what Benny took from his wallet was a midnight-blue business card, which he placed on the table in front of me.

I picked it up. Embossed in silver across the middle of the card was the word 'Incognito'. In the bottom left-hand corner, in smaller letters, was an address in Soho.

'What's this?' I asked.

'Gentlemen's club run by a friend of mine.'

I looked at him, waiting for him to elaborate. He took a sip of his Scotch and said, 'My friend is looking for someone smart and reliable for a one-off job. Very easy work, very good money. If you're interested, I can make a call on your behalf right now.'

Despite the wine my mouth was dry. I had the sudden feeling that I was stepping into quicksand.

'Am I allowed to ask what kind of work it is?'

'If I told you, I'd have to kill you,' Benny said, his face deadpan. He held the expression for a little longer than was comfortable, then suddenly grinned. 'Seriously, Alex, it's nothing too heavy. It's the easiest twenty-five grand you'll ever make. You'll be able to pay off your daughter's debts and have enough left over for a nice holiday.'

'Twenty-five grand,' I repeated slowly.

'I know what you're thinking,' he said. 'You're wondering if I'm setting you up to be the fall guy in some dodgy deal.'

'I don't—' I said, but Benny held up a hand, stemming my protestations.

'I don't blame you. That's how *I'd* feel. Look, why don't you just go and talk to my friend, find out what the job entails? No strings attached, and if you decide it isn't for you, you can walk away.'

'Just like that?'

'Why not? Makes no odds to me. I'm not going to lose out, so I won't hold it against you.'

'But won't it put me in a compromising position, knowing things I shouldn't?'

Benny chuckled. 'This isn't James Bond, Alex.'

'I don't know,' I said.

Benny shrugged. 'Up to you. Look, I'll go for a piss, give you a couple of minutes to think about it.'

He stood up and walked away from the table. There was a part of me that wanted to stand up too and run out of the door before he came back. On the other hand I knew that if I did I'd be forever wondering what kind of opportunity I'd turned down. I couldn't imagine the job would be legal, not for that sort of money, but on the other hand Benny was right. It would easily pay off Candice's debts and leave me with a nice little nest egg. But could I risk everything I'd built up, my life with Kate, my career? Then again, what was my career worth compared to

Candice's safety? And it wasn't as if I couldn't turn the job down if I decided it was too risky, or if I was asked to do something I wasn't comfortable with. I wasn't a kid any more. I couldn't be intimidated into doing something I didn't want to do.

'All right,' I said to Benny when he came back. 'Tell your friend I'll go in for a chat. But please make it clear that that doesn't mean I'll take the job.'

If Benny had gone off somewhere else to make the call I might have been suspicious, but he did it right in front of me. He produced an iPhone from his pocket and tapped in a number.

'Monroe?' he said. 'It's Benny. Listen, I might have someone for that job you want doing.' He listened a moment, then looked at me. 'Can you get over there right away?'

My instinct was to say no, that I needed time to think, time to arrange childcare for Kate, but even as these responses popped into my mind I knew they were nothing but excuses, and that if I didn't act immediately I'd talk myself out of grabbing for the branch that Benny had held out for me. I licked my lips, then gave a brief nod.

'He'll be there in an hour or so,' Benny said. 'His name's Alex. But listen, Monroe, he's just coming for a chat, okay? No obligation... What? Yeah, I'll tell him... Right, I'll speak to you soon. Bye.'

Benny cut the connection and put the phone back in his pocket. 'It's all fixed up,' he said. 'Knock on the door and when someone answers, ask for Monroe.' He drained his glass and nodded at mine. 'You'd better drink up and get going.'

I gulped at the remainder of the wine in my glass, trying not to feel flustered. This was all happening with indecent haste, and no matter how much I told myself I could walk away from it at any time, I couldn't help feeling like an insect in the already closing jaws of a carnivorous plant. I stood up, bumping my knees on the table, and held out my hand.

'It was good to see you again, Benny,' I said. 'And thanks.'

He shook my hand and looked me in the eye, his gaze as pale and fathomless as ever.

'The pleasure was all mine,' he said drily.

FIVE

INCOGNITO

From the business card that Benny had given me, I expected Incognito to be one of those exclusive little places located within a Victorian town house. I expected white pillars, stone steps, perhaps a polished brass plaque beside a glossy black door. What struck me when I arrived, though, was that the snazzy card in my hand was nothing but the equivalent of a silver-plated fish hook. No doubt management strategy was based on the hope that once potential customers had gone to the trouble of finding the chipped grey entry door tucked down a side alley off one of Soho's less populated thoroughfares, few would turn away without at least satisfying their curiosity.

Maybe they were right, but I hesitated a long time before knocking. It wasn't simply the appearance of the club – which was stuck between a grotty dry cleaner's and a driving school called 'L' To Pay, with the dirtiest windows I'd ever seen – that put me off, but the inkling I'd had since punching in Benny's number that morning that I was venturing into dark and dangerous territory.

More than anything, what being in prison had taught me was how precious and wonderful it is to have your freedom. That might sound trite, but it's not until the things that you take for granted are denied you that you realise how much you relish them. Simple things like spending time with your kids, walking to the corner shop for a paper, a quiet pint in the pub on a Sunday lunchtime, watching a late-night film on the telly – was I prepared to put all of that at risk? I knew this job that Benny had lined up would be dodgy, but sitting on the tube the question I'd been asking myself was: *how* dodgy? Maybe this Monroe bloke would want me to be a getaway driver, or courier, or drug mule? Maybe he'd want me to provide an alibi for one of his mates in a court case, or add a note of respectability to a scam he was running? What would I be prepared to do to get Candice out of trouble? How far would I go? If you had asked me yesterday I might have glibly said I'd do anything to help my kids. But if it really came down to it, would I break the law? Would I be prepared to risk everything I'd striven to achieve – my position, my reputation, most crucially my life with Kate – to protect my eldest daughter?

Well, yes, I probably would, if that turned out to be the *only* way. But what would it take to convince me that that was the case? In all honesty I couldn't believe that a chat with this friend of Benny's would be enough at this early stage to knock me off the straight and narrow, certainly not when there were other potential avenues to explore, other possible solutions (even though I couldn't see what they might be yet) to ponder.

Which rather begged the question: why was I here at all?

Up close I realised that Incognito's dented, chipped door was only grey because it was plated with steel. And it wasn't *just* dented; it looked as though a mob had gone at it with pickaxes, hammers and baseball bats. I gave a deep sigh, raised my hand, and after hesitating for a few seconds longer, finally knocked. It was dark and cold by this time, and the alleyway smelled of garbage. An oily streak that must have been a cat slipped through the shadows beside an overturned bin. Rusty light bleeding in from the street lamps beyond the alley's entrance glinted on broken glass outside an abandoned barber's shop whose windows were patched with sagging sheets of brown paper.

There was a grind and a clank that reminded me of my old cell door opening at slopping-out time, and then a black line appeared between door and frame.

'Help you?' The voice was female but smoke-roughened. It came from a face that was hardly more than a pale glimmer cratered with shadows.

'I'm here to see Monroe,' I said.

'We're not open till eight.'

'I'm not a punter. I've got an appointment. I'm a friend of Benny Magee's.'

The face hovered a moment, the eyes black pits. 'Hang on.' Then the door slammed in my face.

I waited so long I thought I'd been rejected on sight. I was contemplating thumbing the 'Menu' button on my mobile to call Benny and tell him it was a no go when the door opened again.

'Come in,' said the same voice as before, the woman who had spoken shuffling backwards as she hauled the door open.

I stepped into a widening wedge of light. As soon as I was inside, the door banged shut behind me. The woman peering at me suspiciously was around fifty. She was fat and red-cheeked, her black hair scraped into a tight bun. Her heavy eye make-up and dark lipstick made her face look like it had been painted on a balloon by a little kid. Her evening gown was a glittery black tent, and rings and bracelets clinked and jangled on her pudgy hands and wrists.

'Follow me,' she said, and swept off down the corridor, massive buttocks swaying under her black dress. The effect should have been comical, but she gave off the vibe of someone you really didn't want to mess with. I followed her along a corridor covered floor to ceiling in red leather panels, like a padded cell or a kinky sex dungeon. At the end of the corridor was another door, this one black. The woman opened it and bustled through, making no attempt to hold it for me. I caught it as it began to swing shut and followed her out on to a balconied walkway.

We were overlooking a high-ceilinged room with a bar running the full length of the left-hand wall. A square stage in the middle of the room was surrounded on three sides by rows of empty seats. From up here the stage looked to be made of semi-transparent Perspex, and was lit from below, so that it glowed like ice. Three poles extended from the ceiling, as if pinning the stage into place. A red-haired girl in a leotard was entwined around one of the poles, going through what were presumably some of her moves for later with a bored look on her face. Apart from the glowing stage, the lighting in the room was subdued – which no doubt hid a multitude of sins.

Without a word the woman led me down a set of steps to the floor below. At the bottom she half-turned and pointed at the bar.

'Wait there. Order yourself a drink if you like. On the house.'

'Thanks.'

She clumped away, heading for the shadows on the opposite side of the stage.

Behind the bar a handsome man with blond highlights was polishing glasses.

'What's your poison?' he asked.

I looked at the rows of optics behind him. They were illuminated by orange down-lighters, which made the bottled spirits glow like elixirs. I was tempted, but decided not to add fuel to the red-wine headache now starting to throb behind my eyes. 'Just some still water, thanks,' I said.

He looked at me like I'd leaped on to his bar and taken a dump on its polished surface.

'Ice and lemon?'

I bared my teeth in a grin. 'Please.'

While he poured water from a bright blue bottle, I climbed on to a bar stool shaped like a giant golf tee and watched the girl on the stage. She was skinny, long-limbed, with a pale, doll-like face. I was hoping to catch her eye and exchange a smile, not because I fancied her, but because I felt the need for some friendly human interaction. But she was in her own world, plugged into her iPod, eyes half-closed. After a while her sinuous movements began to have a mesmeric effect.

'You like her? Her name's Lotus.'

The voice came from behind me. It was soft and huskily warm, but its unexpectedness made me jump. As I turned, glass in hand, water slopped on to the floor. The woman who had spoken raised her eyebrows in amusement.

'Sorry. Didn't mean to startle you.'

I could tell by her face she was being playful rather than mean. 'You sure about that?' I asked with a smile.

She laughed, showing straight white teeth.

'Well... maybe a bit. It's just you looked so absorbed.'

I couldn't think of a response that wouldn't make me sound like I was trying to deny being a dirty old man. In the end I asked, 'Is Lotus her real name?'

'Yes and no,' the woman said. 'Her name's Zuzanka. But Zuzanka means Lotus in Latvian.'

I didn't know whether she was pulling my leg. 'Is that so? And what's *your* name?'

'Clover,' she replied, offering me a hand so stiff she looked like she was about to karate chop wood.

I shook the hand. It was cool and dainty, but her grip was surprisingly strong.

'I'm guessing you work here too?' I said.

'You could say that.'

I glanced towards Lotus, who was still coiling around her pole. 'You don't regard it as work?'

She gave that same amused smile, dimples appearing in her cheeks. She was around twenty-seven, twenty-eight, with a large, upturned mouth and widely spaced eyes either side of a snub nose. Her hair was thick and glossy and might have been dyed a deep maroon colour – it was hard to tell in the dim light. She was strikingly beautiful, though not in a conventional way.

Leaning closer she murmured, 'Before you dig yourself a hole you can't climb out of, perhaps I ought to come clean. I'm Clover Monroe. I own this place. I'm the person you've come to see.'

I felt surprised and a bit irritated, but tried to cover it by lifting my head and barking a laugh.

'Admit it,' she said. 'You were expecting a man.'

The look on her face, half-teasing, half-apologetic, made my anger evaporate. Raising my hands, I admitted, 'Guilty as charged.'

'Shall we start again?'

'I think we'd better.'

'Hi, I'm Clover Monroe. I'm the owner and manager of this establishment.'

Once again she offered her hand, but this time in an ironic way. I shook it with exaggerated formality. 'Alex Locke,' I replied. 'Lovely place you've got here.'

'It's a dump,' she said. 'But it's mine and it's a living.'

'So you're a friend of Benny's?'

She smiled. 'You sound surprised.'

'Well I am, a bit.'

'Because I'm not some suited thug with the demeanour of a great white shark?'

I laughed, but I was wary. I wondered how much of our conversation might get reported back to Benny.

'You said that, not me.'

She grinned as if she was pleased with my answer, and nodded at my glass. 'Let's talk in my office. Sure you don't want anything stronger?'

'Cup of tea would go down a treat.'

She gave that hearty laugh of hers again. 'I like your style, Mr Locke.' She turned and called to the barman, 'Robin, ask Mary to bring us some tea, would you?'

'Sure thing,' Robin said.

'Shall we?' Clover gestured towards a door marked 'Private', which was set into the back wall behind the staircase.

I nodded and we walked across. Clover unlocked the door and led the way into a corridor narrower and shabbier than the one upstairs. 'So how do you know Benny?' I asked as we walked.

'Family ties,' she said, in a way that suggested she was unwilling to elaborate.

We reached a wooden door, which, with its brass doorknob and eye-level panel of opaque, bevelled glass, looked like something out of a Charles Dickens novel. I half-expected to step into a gas-lit office with wood-panelled walls, but the room beyond the door was more mundane. A grey filing cabinet was tucked into an alcove next to a desk on which stood a computer, a printer, a mug of pens and a pile of paperwork. Clover turned on the light and I glanced around, looking for personal stuff – anything that might give me an insight into her background and personality. But there were no family pictures, no framed certificates, no trophies or knick-knacks. In fact, apart from a cork board pinned with flyers for takeaways and cab firms, everything in here was work-related. Either Clover was unsentimental or she protected her privacy carefully.

'Pull up a pew,' she said, nodding towards one of two wooden chairs against the wall. As I grabbed a chair, she moved around the desk and sat down. When we were settled she laced the fingers of her hands together and leaned forward, exposing a bit of cleavage. I tried to keep my eyes on hers as she said, 'How much did Benny tell you?'

'Not a lot. He told me you had a job you wanted doing, and that you were looking for someone reliable.'

'Did he say anything about the nature of the job?'

'No, but knowing Benny...'

She arched an eyebrow. 'Knowing Benny?'

I forced myself to take my time, consider my words. 'Look, I don't want to offend anyone...'

'...but given Benny's history you assume that what I need doing is illegal?'

'Well... yeah. It did occur to me that it might be a bit dodgy.'

Before she could reply there was a knock on the door.

'Come in,' she called.

The smoke-roughened answer was a growl of irritation. 'I would, but my hands are full.'

Clover gave me a gleeful look, as if this was some practical joke we were colluding in. 'Alex, would you mind?'

'Sure.' I crossed the room and pulled the door open. The woman who'd let me in entered with a tea tray, looking flustered and grumpy.

'As if I haven't got enough to do,' she muttered. 'We open in forty minutes, you know.'

'Yes, but Mary, you're so magnificent I just *know* you'll have everything running like clockwork by then,' Clover said.

It sounded like she was taking the piss, but I'm sure I saw Mary flush with pleasure as she dumped the tray on the desk. All the same she said, 'Don't think you can wind *me* round your little finger with your bloody sweet talk, *madam*.'

'I wouldn't dare,' Clover said, trying not to smile.

When Mary had gone Clover's half-smile turned into a grin. 'What a darling. I love her to bits.'

'Does *she* pole-dance too?'

Clover treated me to another of her full-throated laughs. 'Only on special occasions. Biscuit?'

I took a chocolate digestive from the plate, and waited as she poured the tea. 'So about this job...?'

Clover took a sip of tea, the steam wreathing her face, then settled back in her chair. 'There's a story involved.'

'I'm all ears.'

'Just over a year ago, I was bequeathed some money, which I used to set myself up in business here. But before that I was working as a girl

Friday for a... well, I suppose you'd call him an eccentric millionaire. His name was - is - Barnaby McCallum, and he's... *ancient*. In his nineties at least. He's a virtual recluse. He lives in a big Victorian house in Kensington, and he does nothing all day but sit in a wheelchair and stare out of the window. He's still got his marbles, but he hardly says anything, hardly moves. He employs a housekeeper who cleans and cooks for him, an odd-job man who maintains the property as best he can, and a girl Friday, who deals with all his correspondence - finances, ongoing business concerns, the charities he patronises, that kind of thing.

'Despite his age and lack of mobility, McCallum still has his fingers in a lot of pies - at least nominally. Apparently in his younger days he had an almost supernatural ability to identify fledgling companies which would later go on to become mega-bucks corporations. He made a stack of money buying shares in around thirty of these companies. But the weird thing is he didn't show this aptitude for business until well into middle age. Before that he... well, to be honest, he's got a bit of a dubious past.'

'Dubious how?'

She wrinkled her nose. 'Maybe "dubious" is the wrong word. Maybe "secretive" is more accurate. Like I say, he's at least in his nineties, which means he must have been born around the end of the First World War. But there's no documentation for his early life - and I should know; I had access to pretty much all his existing records, apart from his will, when I was there. The earliest document that refers to him... well, it isn't really a document at all. It's a poster.'

'A poster?'

'It's on the wall of his... I suppose you'd call it the drawing room. It's a framed poster from the late forties - 1948, I think. It's for a performance at the Hippodrome Theatre by the world-famous magician, The Great Barnaby. I asked Mr McCallum about it once, and he confirmed that it was him. He wouldn't tell me any more though. He's a nice enough old man, but he clams up whenever you try to probe into his personal life. Ask him a question he doesn't like and he feigns deafness - just stares right through you. So, having failed to get it from the horse's mouth, I tried to find out more from other sources, but I didn't get very far. He's got no family - none I could find anyway – and even googling "The Great Barnaby" drew a virtual blank. There's a one-line Wikipedia entry, which says that he was one of the world's leading magicians for ten years or so after the war, but that he faded into obscurity and his true identity remains a mystery. Plus there are a few mentions of him on other magic sites, but nothing that gives any clues to his past.'

'Maybe he's foreign,' I said. 'Could be he was originally from Germany, or from one of Germany's wartime allies. You'd understand him wanting to keep *that* quiet.'

'Yeah, I thought that too,' Clover said. 'But... I dunno. I could understand him wanting to keep it quiet at the time. But now?' She shrugged.

Trying to steer her back to the point, I said, 'This is all very interesting, but you still haven't told me what the job is.'

Clover gave me a calculating look. 'McCallum has... an artefact in his possession. It's a human heart about the size of a goose egg, carved out of obsidian. He keeps it in a glass case in his drawing room, the same room where the poster is. I was recently approached by a consortium of Japanese businessmen, who claim that McCallum acquired the artefact illegally from their country years ago, and that they've been trying to track it down ever since, in order to restore it to its rightful owner.'

I could see where this was leading. 'Don't tell me – and this *consortium* approached you because they found out you'd worked for McCallum and thought you might be able to get the artefact back for them? Or at least give them information which would help *them* get it back?'

She nodded. 'Apparently a representative of the consortium had already approached McCallum directly and made him an offer for the artefact.'

'Which he'd refused?'

She gave a secretive smile, as if she'd won a bet with herself. 'Benny said you were perceptive.'

I shrugged off the compliment. 'Well, let's see just how perceptive I can be. I'm guessing either this consortium thought you had the influence to lean on McCallum and persuade him to come round to their way of thinking, for which they'd pay you a commission, or that you had information about – what? – the house's security system? Something that would make the artefact easier to nick.'

'Right on the second count,' she said. 'The consortium's representative told me they had offered McCallum a quarter of a million for the artefact, but that he'd told them where to go. They then tried threatening him with legal action, but he just laughed at them. So what they wanted from me were details of the artefact's location within the house, and the security measures in place to protect it.'

'But you strung them along, didn't you?'

She looked surprised. 'How did you know?'

'That's why you got Benny in on this. You wanted him to find someone who could nick the artefact for you, so that *you* could sell it to the consortium and make a load more money than you would if you were just acting as advisor.'

That laugh again. 'Bloody hell, you're good. In fact, you might almost be *too* good. It certainly looks like Benny has found me the right man.'

'Hang on,' I said. 'I haven't said I'll do the job.'

'You will, though, won't you?' she said confidently.

I thought about Candice. I thought about the twenty-five thousand pounds that Benny had mentioned. I would never forgive myself if Candice got hurt, but I wasn't desperate just yet. There had to be other – less illegal – ways of raising the money. Had to be.

Hoping I wouldn't live to regret it, I shook my head. 'No. Sorry, Clover, but I think you need to find someone else.'

She looked momentarily stunned, then understanding crossed her face. 'Oh, I get it. You want more money. Well, I'm sure that can be—'

'It's not about the money,' I said. 'It's about whether I'd be able to face myself in the mirror the next morning.'

She stared at me in bewilderment. 'Are you serious?'

'I'm afraid so. Look, I know you must think I'm soft in the head, but I can't take the risk – and I don't want to.' I shrugged. 'I know you and Benny must have had a conversation about me while I was on my way here.'

Again she looked surprised, almost guilty, in fact. 'How would you know that?'

'You said that Benny had told you I was perceptive – and he certainly never told you that when he called you. I heard everything he said.'

'Touché,' she said wryly.

I smiled. 'So did Benny tell you what I was inside for?'

'Armed robbery, wasn't it?'

'That's right. But it's not as impressive as it sounds. I was young and stupid and under too much pressure. I did it because... well basically, because I was more or less living on the bread line despite working all the hours God sends, and I needed the money. And it was well worked out. It seemed like... if not exactly the perfect crime, then a pretty safe bet.'

'So what happened?' Clover asked. 'How did you get caught?'

'There was a weak link, a bloke called Dennis Jasper. He was a crackhead who thought he was an anarchist. After the heist we divided up what we'd nicked, and the guy who'd organised it, an old school friend of ours called Ray Duffy, told us to keep a low profile and not to splash the cash. Dennis managed to keep quiet for about two days, and then he got hammered down the local pub and started shooting his mouth off about how he'd fucked the system.

'Next thing I knew, I was woken at five in the morning by a crash that made me think an oil tanker had ploughed into the side of the house. Then the police flooded into my bedroom, dragged me out of bed and punched me in the guts so hard I pissed myself. Before I knew what was happening, I was thrown into a Black Maria and driven to the local nick.'

Clover was half-smiling, like she didn't know whether to look sympathetic or amused.

'And that's pretty much it. I got sentenced to nine years and served six years and two months of that.'

'And what happened to Dennis Jasper?'

'I've no idea. I never saw him again. I heard on the grapevine that he'd got a shorter sentence than the rest of us for dropping us in it. Some say he buggered off up north when he got out, but others reckon he's buried in a farmer's field somewhere.'

'And meanwhile you went straight?' Clover said.

'Yes. I became an upstanding member of society. I still am.'

Clover's expression had changed, but I couldn't quite read it. It might have been pity or admiration or something else entirely. I shrugged. 'Sorry to disappoint you.'

She shook her head. 'It's not that. I respect your integrity. No, it's... Would it change your mind if I were to tell you that McCallum is alone in the house at night, that he sleeps soundly, that his security system – despite what I told my associates – is non-existent, and that I can provide you with a key for the French windows that lead directly into the drawing room? I know it's easy for me to sit here and say this, Alex, but the opportunity I'm offering you will be marginally less difficult than taking candy from a baby. In fact, it'll be the easiest twenty-five grand you'll ever make in your life.'

I regarded her for a moment. 'Can I ask you a question?'

'Ask away.'

'If this job's so easy, why do you even need a middle man? Why not do it yourself?'

She smiled but looked away, her cheeks flushing red. 'You really want to know?'

'Yeah, course.'

'It's because, despite my association with Benny, I'm not a natural criminal. And frankly I'd be shit-scared. Bloody terrified, in fact. Creeping through that garden at night, letting myself into that pitch-black house... just the thought of it gives me palpitations.'

'You don't *look* the nervous type.'

'I'm not – when I'm in my comfort zone. But out there...' she shuddered. 'No thanks.'

I was silent for a moment. I couldn't decide whether to believe her or not. 'So you're prepared to give up twenty-five grand just to save yourself from being spooked for half an hour?'

'Definitely. Because I don't see it as giving up twenty-five grand. I see it as *earning* two hundred and twenty-five by doing sod all. All *I'd* have to do is sit tight here drinking tea and eating biscuits while you do all the leg-work.'

'Plus it would give you an alibi if anything went wrong,' I said.

'Nothing *will* go wrong, but... yes, there is that.' She tilted her head, her smile widening. 'I can see you're tempted.'

'Good try,' I said, 'but I'm afraid the answer's still no. It's not that I don't appreciate the opportunity, and it's not like I couldn't do with the money, but like I said earlier, it's a crime. You're asking me to enter someone's premises illegally, to steal their property—'

'Property which they obtained illegally in the first place,' she reminded me.

'That's as may be. But two wrongs don't make a right.' I spread my hands. 'Sorry, but... there you go.'

Clover sat back, looking disappointed. 'Pity,' she said. 'I really thought you and I had the makings of a good partnership.'

I wasn't sure what she meant by that. Was she trying to flatter me? Even flirt with me? Trying to make light of it, I said, 'Well, if you've got any jobs which *don't* involve breaking the law...'

'I'll be sure to let you know,' she promised.

She held my gaze for a long moment. I stood up and stuck out my hand.

'Well, great to meet you,' I said, feeling suddenly awkward. 'No hard feelings?'

'No hard feelings,' she confirmed, and shook my hand with what seemed to be genuine warmth. She held on to it for a bit longer than she needed to and I looked at her quizzically.

'Maybe our paths will cross again,' she said.

I couldn't think how they might, but I tried to sound encouraging. 'Who knows?' I said. 'Maybe they will.'

SIX

REFLECTION

By the time I got home I was shattered. I'd been on tenterhooks all day, and the emotional toll that that had taken combined with the wine I'd drunk in The Hair of the Dog had pretty much wiped me out. I staggered into the darkened flat, slapping lights on as I went, and straight into the kitchen. With tiredness gnawing at me, I pinballed from cupboard to drawer to fridge, dragging out crockery and cutlery, coffee, milk, bread, ham, margarine and mustard. Moving like an automaton I made myself a coffee and a sandwich and then stumbled back into the front room, leaving the kitchen debris behind me. I put my mug down on top of Kate's *Toy Story* colouring book on the toy chest which doubled as a coffee table and then sank on to the settee with a rusty groan to match the creaking of the springs.

It was only as I tipped my head back and closed my eyes that I became aware of the silence. Not that it was ever completely silent in London, of course, but compared to the clamour I'd been surrounded by all day it seemed, temporarily at least, as hushed as I had ever known it. Then, little by little, sounds filtered through – the humming of the fridge, the rumbling whoosh of distant traffic, the faint but constant white noise of the city. Hadn't I read somewhere that the infinitesimal background hiss we hear in even the quietest of environments is the ceaseless, ever-expanding echo of the big bang rolling on into infinity? Was that a scientific theory or just an old wives' tale? With my eyes closed I lifted my sandwich to my mouth and took a bite. Chewing the bread and meat slowly into a pulp and gulping it down was a bigger effort than I'd been expecting.

Next thing I knew I was jerking awake, shocked and disorientated, as if from a nightmare. Salmon-pink light streaked with purple bruises was seeping in through the French windows. I gaped blearily at the still-full mug on the colouring book, the coffee now scummy and cold. I clearly hadn't moved because the plate containing my ham sandwich, the bread now a little curled and dry at the edges, was still on my lap. I shifted and groaned. My back was aching like a bastard and my hands were numb with cold.

What time was it?

I pushed the plate aside and stretched out my legs so I could extricate my phone from my jeans pocket. Even after trying to massage some life into my hands, my fingers were like dead meat, and I was reminded of those three-pronged claws in amusement arcades which you have to manipulate with levers to pluck a prize from a glass booth. At last, however, I managed to prise out my phone and gaped at the display screen. It was 6.25 a.m. I'd slept for over seven hours.

In thirty-five minutes it would be time to get Kate up and ready for school. Great. But at least, unlike yesterday, I had half an hour's grace before the whirlwind hit. Last night, once I'd realised I was going to be back too late to put my daughter to bed, I'd rung Paula and arranged for Kate to stay the night over there.

Moving like an old man I pushed myself to my feet and shuffled through to the bathroom. I didn't have a hangover this morning – or not much of one at any rate – but my sleeping position and the chill that had seeped into my limbs during the night made me feel almost as wretched. I cranked up the temperature in the shower and luxuriated in the sensation of hot water battering my skin, unknotting my clenched and aching muscles. As I soaped my body and washed my hair, I thought about my meeting with Benny, and Clover's offer, and wondered whether I'd made the right decision, and how the hell I was going to help Candice.

She'd be wanting answers and I didn't have any. Not yet anyway. Having closed the door of opportunity that had been opened for me made it doubly imperative that I come up with a solution to Candice's problem. Maybe the thing to do was to bring Michelle and Glenn in on this, get everything out in the open, work as a family to clear up the mess. Candice would hate it, of course, but perhaps if we all pooled together we'd raise enough to pay off this Mitch guy. There'd be repercussions, bitterness, accusations – I could see Glenn using the incident to insist that Candice get a job to pay off her debt, for a start – but we could deal with all that once the bigger threat was out of the way.

Or maybe we *should* just tell the police and have done with it. Despite the threats that Mitch had made, it wasn't *really* in his interests to inflict physical damage on his accusers, was it? Not over what to him must be a paltry sum; and not when it would mean the finger of suspicion being firmly pointed in his direction.

By the time I stepped out of the shower my flesh was tingling and I felt... if not exactly raring to go, then at least reasonably human again. From where I was standing, towelling myself dry, I could see my reflection staring back at me from the mirror screwed to the wall above the sink. It looked pissed off, accusatory, its short, dark hair sticking up in damp spikes. Its face was thin, maybe a bit *too* thin, the cheekbones high, the skin pulled tight around the jaw line. Its nose was long, bony – I think the polite term is *aquiline* – and its eyes, though I say so myself, were a fairly startling blue (before she went loopy Kate's mum, Lyn, used to describe them as 'Paul Newman blue').

Though a fair number of women seem to have taken a liking to my face over the years, I've always thought it a bit shifty. I know I've got a tendency to frown a lot, narrow my eyes and not smile much, because people have remarked on it.

'Don't look so mean,' Lyn used to say when we were out together.

'I'm not,' I'd reply.

'Yes you are. You always scowl at everybody. You look at people like you want to rip their heads off.'

Her words always surprised me, and for a while I'd make an effort to smile more. But eventually my face would slip back into its default expression of 'moody git'. I must admit, it's got me into a few of those 'What you looking at?' situations over the years. On the other hand it was a boon in my younger days. If you looked anything but mean on the estate where I grew up the jackals would quickly close in.

I got dressed and made myself coffee and toast, then carried it through to the front room. I watched the news while I waited for the hammering on the door that would herald Kate's pyjama-clad, tousle-haired arrival.

By 7.10 she still hadn't turned up, though, and I wondered whether she'd insisted on breakfast with Hamish before heading home to get washed and dressed. I had a quick smoke out on the balcony, then brushed my teeth and crossed the landing to knock on the Sherwoods' door. I half-expected to hear the shrieking of excited children from within, the rapid thump of elephant-like feet, Paula's voice raised in encouragement bordering on exasperation.

But all was oddly silent, and no one responded to my knock. I put my ear to the door and knocked again, louder.

'Hello?' I called. 'Anyone there? It's me, Alex.'

The silence was eerie. I felt discomfited by it – not exactly worried yet, but baffled all the same.

I took out my phone, dialled the Sherwoods' number. After a moment I heard a strange double-ring, the phone in the flat and the same one in my earpiece. The phone rang five times and then Paula's voice broke in, its tinnier echo, coming from my phone, telling me to leave a message. Instead of doing so I cut the connection and dialled Paula's mobile number. This time, when her voicemail cut in, I *did* leave a message, trying to keep my tone light, as if that alone would make everything okay.

'Hi Paula, it's Alex here. Just wondered where you were. It's twenty past seven. I've just popped round to get Kate, but there's no answer.' I hesitated, toying with the idea of speculating aloud where she might be, but then I said, 'Call me when you get this message, just to let me know everything's okay. I'm sure it is. Bye.'

I put my phone away and hovered for a moment on the landing. I felt out of sorts, wondering what to do next. I couldn't go to work not knowing where Kate was. As I wandered back into my flat I was already formulating theories and explanations.

Maybe one of the Sherwoods' parents had been taken ill and they had been called away unexpectedly. But if that was the case would they have taken the children with them? Wouldn't one of them have gone and one of them stayed at home? Well, maybe it was Adam who had been taken ill then? Or Paula? Or maybe Adam was working away from home – he did that sometimes – and Paula had had no choice but to rouse the kids and take them with her? But in that circumstance, wouldn't she have called me and left a message? It was the silence that was odd. Paula was usually so efficient, so reliable. Although if she'd had a shock – if one of her parents had had a heart attack, say, or if they'd been involved in an accident – then it would be perfectly understandable if she'd simply forgotten because her mind was elsewhere.

I called her mobile again and got the same response. They couldn't all have just overslept, could they? No, Kate was an early riser – unless, of course, she and Hamish had been up till all hours, bouncing off the walls, and had succeeded in exhausting everyone so much that they had all slept through their alarms, the phone calls, the banging on the door...

No, that was stupid and unbelievable. But I clung to it for a few minutes, if only to delay my thoughts from taking a darker turn. However, as I marched back across the landing and thumped on the door with renewed vigour, I knew that lurking in the back of my mind were lurid news stories of fathers who had suddenly gone mad and killed their wives and children before taking their own lives, of faulty gas fires poisoning entire households, of families being discovered slaughtered in their beds...

I conjured a picture of Paula in a nightshirt, face slack with sleep, tugging the door open and murmuring, 'Alex? Wassamatter?' I willed this image to become a reality, but again there was no reply to my knocking. I went back to my flat and paced for a moment. It was now 7.30 a.m. Was it too premature to call the police? Probably. Almost certainly. But something was wrong. I knew it. I could sense it.

Perhaps I should smash the door down? It might lead to embarrassment later, even to disgruntled accusations of over-reaction, but I could deal with that. If I knew that Kate was okay I could deal with anything. I thought about the shitty week I was having. First Candice, now Kate. What had I done to deserve this? Suddenly realising that I didn't *need* to kick the door down, I darted back into my flat and into the kitchen. In the drawer beneath the wall-mounted water heater was all the flat-related paperwork: instruction books for the various appliances; gas, electricity and water supply info; a laminated list of rules and regulations; emergency numbers... ah.

Whipping out my mobile phone I thumbed in my landlord's number, immediately storing it for future use. On the third ring a heavily accented voice barked, 'Hello.' The owner sounded resentful, as if I had caught him in the middle of something important.

'Mr Grzybowski? This is Alex Locke from 22 Fountain Road in Chiswick. I live in flat 3. I need you to come over right away.' Haltingly I told him why, my words tumbling over one another in my urgency to explain.

Mr Grzybowski was nonplussed. 'This is a long way to come for such a paltry matter,' he said. 'Your friends must have simply gone out.'

'Where would they go at 7.30 in the morning?' I replied, trying not to sound sarcastic.

After some to-ing and fro-ing he agreed to come over, though not before I had threatened to kick in the door of flat 4 if he didn't turn up. Breaking the connection I wondered about kicking in the door anyway, but instead I diverted my energy into running upstairs and knocking on the door of flat 5 where old Mrs Hersh lived.

She hadn't seen the Sherwoods either, or heard them go out. 'But I'm sure there's nothing to worry about,' she reassured me, and invited me in for tea. I refused as politely as I could and pounded all the way downstairs, almost slipping and falling in my haste. I knocked on the doors of the two ground-floor flats, whose occupants I barely knew, to ask whether they had seen or heard anything.

They hadn't, and so at 7.45 a.m. I found myself upstairs again, perched stiffly on the edge of my settee, teeth clenched and hands clasped tightly between my knees, like a first-time parachutist waiting for the call to jump. I'd exhausted my immediate options, and yet I couldn't shake the feeling that I should be doing *something*. I called Paula's mobile again, and when the answer phone cut in I left a second message. I heard the waver in my voice as I did so: 'Hi Paula. Alex again. Can you let me know where you are? I'm getting worried now.'

It was about fifty minutes later when I heard slow, heavy footsteps ascending the stairs. I ran out of my flat (I'd left the door propped open) to greet the new arrival. I guessed it would be Grzybowski, but that still didn't prevent my heart from giving a little surge of hope that it might be Paula returning after having dropped the kids off at school. Again a little mind-movie ran inside my head. Paula would be flustered, full of apologies and explanations: 'We went out to get croissants for breakfast, but got snarled up in traffic and had to go straight to school.' Or: 'I had to run Adam to the station to get an early train, so I took the kids with me. I did think of knocking on your door, but I didn't want to disturb you.'

But, as I had expected, it was the rotund, panting figure of my landlord who rounded the bend in the staircase and stumped up the last half-flight towards me. He was dark-skinned and grey-haired and raised jaundiced, bloodhound eyes to regard me balefully.

'I do not appreciate threats, Mr Locke,' he growled as he approached. 'If you damage my property you find somewhere else to live. It is a simple rule.'

Edgy as I felt, I was in no mood to waste time arguing the toss with him. Instead I fixed my face into what I hoped was an expression of apology and said, 'I'm sorry, Mr Grzybowski, but I really am worried. My daughter stayed over with my neighbours last night, and there's no reason why they shouldn't be there at this time in the morning. It doesn't make sense.'

Grzybowski grunted as though unconvinced, but made no further comment. Clumping to the Sherwoods' door he pulled a set of keys from the pocket of his shapeless, olive-green jacket and picked through them laboriously with his thick fingers. I hovered at his shoulder, fighting an urge to tell him to hurry the fuck up. He smelled of stale cooking oil and aftershave made more pungent by an under-hint of day-old sweat.

Finally he found the right key and fitted it into the lock. I all but tumbled in behind him as he pushed the door open. Like my flat the entrance hall was gloomy until you put the light on. When he clicked the switch I gasped.

The hallway was empty. Not just of people, but of everything. Where were the pictures on the walls, the slim bookcase on the right, the little bamboo side table on which the phone usually rested atop a stack of local directories? I pushed past Grzybowski, who grunted in protest, and ran from room to room, checking out the rest of the flat.

Empty. Stripped bare. Furniture, books, clothes, ornaments, everything... gone. It was as if a removals van had come in the night and taken away every single thing the Sherwoods owned.

My heart dropped into my stomach. I started to shake. I swung round to confront Grzybowski, who stepped back, alarmed, at what must have been a wild-eyed look on my face.

'Where are they?' I demanded, though it was clear that the empty flat was as much a surprise to him as it had been to me.

'Gone,' was all Grzybowski said, raising a hand as if that made everything clear.

My fear for Kate made me suddenly angry, furious. 'But *where* have they gone? Because wherever it is, they've taken my daughter with them!'

SEVEN

UNKNOWN NUMBER

The interview with DI Jensen and DS Earnshaw lasted about twenty minutes. It was DS Earnshaw who did most of the talking. He was a bulky, solid Mancunian with dark-framed spectacles and hair that looked like it had been slept on then forgotten about. He had a slow, deliberate way of speaking, and I got the feeling Jensen – a tall, balding man with a knobbly face – let Earnshaw ask the questions in order to lull most of the villains he dealt with into a false sense of security. Yet although Earnshaw might have seemed a plodder, behind his droning voice and sleepy eyes I sensed a thorough, methodical brain motoring away. He had certainly done his homework on me.

I don't mean that the interview was a grilling, or that Jensen and Earnshaw gave the impression that they thought I had engineered my daughter's disappearance, but they did know of my past form and of Lyn's history of mental health problems and her current long-term incarceration in Darby Hall Psychiatric Hospital. When they asked whether any of my fellow inmates in Pentonville might have had reason to harbour a long-standing grudge against me I thought fleetingly of Benny – was it a coincidence that this had happened just as he had come back into my life, especially as I had turned down the job he had set up for me? – but I said nothing. Not because I was scared of how furious he would be if I should happen to drop his name into the pot only to then discover he was innocent, but simply because I couldn't see what he would gain out of arranging to have Kate abducted. He was ruthless when he needed to be, but he wasn't the sort of man who did things purely out of spite. So, although it was an instinctive decision, I decided I would prefer to keep Benny as a potential ally by withholding his name rather than earn his wrath by sending the police sniffing round his door.

After the interview was over, Jensen and Earnshaw crossed the landing to look over the Sherwoods' now-empty flat. All they found was Paula's voice on the answer phone and half a dozen messages which they told me were unusual only in that the incoming calls all seemed to be of a business or practical nature – nothing personal at all. They ordered Grzybowski, who had been hovering on the landing like a spare part, to lock the door and to open it for no one but the forensics team, who would be arriving within the hour to go over the flat with a fine-tooth comb. Jensen asked me if I would like a family liaison officer appointed to the case, who would remain with me for as long as I required his or her services and 'provide me with a link to the ongoing investigation'. When I said no, he nodded as though in approval at my fortitude, and told me how sorry he was that this had happened and that they would let me know the minute they had any news. Then they shook my hand, thanked me for my co-operation and assured me they would leave no stone unturned in their hunt for the Sherwoods.

It wasn't until after they had gone that the anxiety, which I'd been bottling up for the past half-hour or so, hit me like a virus. Suddenly I was shaking and the strength went out of my legs. I just about made it back into the main room, where I dropped on to the settee as if the tendons behind my knees had been cut. Staring blankly in front of me I suddenly registered what I was looking at, and swallowed to clear a lump in my throat. It was Kate's beloved *Toy Story* colouring book, surrounded by a scattering of coloured pencils. I'd bought this for her after the two of us had seen *Toy Story 3* in 3-D earlier that year. Kate had loved the film, but she had huddled up to me during the scary bits. It was heart-breaking to recall how cute she had looked with the 3-D specs perched on the end of her nose over her pink-framed glasses. After the film we'd had dinner in Pizza Express and she'd bounced up and down in her chair with excitement at what she'd seen, chattering away as she relived her favourite scenes.

It was only as I was leaning forward and stretching out a hand towards the colouring book that I realised what I was doing and checked myself. The way I was feeling I knew that opening the book and looking inside would be unbearably painful. Even so, I might still have opened the book if my mobile hadn't just then started to ring. I yanked it from my pocket to see who was calling, but my screen informed me it was an 'Unknown Number'.

'Hello?'

'Alex,' said a female voice. 'It's Clover Monroe.'

I guessed Benny must have given her my number and assumed she was calling to ask whether I'd reconsidered her job offer. Irritated I said, 'Sorry, but this isn't a good time right now.'

'I know,' she said. 'That's why I'm ringing.'

My thoughts were too scrambled to make sense of her words. 'Sorry?' I said. 'What?'

Her voice was urgent, willing me to understand. 'I need you to come and see me right away,' she said. 'It's about what's happened to Kate.'

EIGHT

MUTUAL ACQUAINTANCE

I felt like ripping the world apart. Getting angry, and staying there, was the only way I could handle the gut-wrenching terror and helplessness threatening to overwhelm me. I'd been in some tricky situations before, situations where I thought I might die, but the mortal fear I'd felt then was like a pinprick compared to how I was feeling now. Not knowing where my beautiful little girl was, or why she'd been taken, was like harbouring a bubbling volcano that was about to erupt. Although I knew it was futile, I had an almost irresistible urge to be *out there*, running through the streets, looking for Kate.

The best I could do right now, though, was head across London to see Clover. She was the only lead I had. The journey was maybe ten stops on the tube, changing from the District line to the Piccadilly at Hammersmith, but it felt like an eternity. All the way there I was gripped by a kind of madness. I hated my fellow commuters for calmly getting on with their lives like there was nothing wrong in the world. When a French tourist on the platform at Hyde Park Corner prolonged my agony by throwing himself at the closing doors and forcing them open again, and then laughing merrily with his girlfriend as the two of them entered the carriage, I could quite happily have rammed something sharp and pointy into his eye.

Clover had been unwilling – or unable – to tell me much over the phone.

'What do *you* know about what's happened to Kate?' I said, struggling to keep my voice under control. 'What's going on, Clover?'

'Let's not talk now,' she replied. 'It'll be better face to face.'

'Why will it? I haven't got time for this shit. Where the fuck's my daughter?'

'I don't know. Genuinely. Just come and see me, Alex.'

'If you're fucking me about...' My voice choked off. Suddenly it felt as though there was cotton wool jamming my throat.

'I'm not fucking you about,' she said.

My brain was buzzing, whirring. I couldn't think straight. I knew that if I was going to be any help to Kate I needed to stay calm, keep my head clear, but that was easier said than done.

Swallowing the obstruction in my throat, I said, 'What if I tell the cops about this phone call? Send *them* round to see you instead?'

'That would be a mistake,' Clover said. 'I'm not your enemy, Alex.'

'How do I know that?'

'You'll just have to trust me.' Her voice was persuasive, even sympathetic. 'I'll explain it all when you get here.'

I didn't like it, but it seemed I had no choice. 'It'll take me a while to reach you.'

'Just be as quick as you can.'

Thinking she was about to ring off, I said desperately, 'Please, Clover. Just tell me if Kate's safe.'

She hesitated. 'As far as I know.'

'As far as you know? What does that mean?'

'See you soon, Alex.'

The phone went dead.

For the latter part of the journey I sat hunched over, staring down at my hands, which were clenched between my knees. I didn't look up, didn't move. I felt like I was conserving my energy for some ordeal. I went through everything that had happened, trying to find some new insight, some clue in the conversations I'd had with Paula, with Benny, with Clover. I tried to work out whether I was doing the right thing by going back to Incognito. I'd been there last night, so if Benny or Clover meant to do me harm they had already had ample opportunity - yet even so I couldn't shake the suspicion that I was the equivalent of some unsuspecting woodland creature wandering blithely into a hunter's trap. Then again, if I was the real target, kidnapping Kate seemed like an odd move. Wouldn't it have been easier to have put a bullet through my head and dump my body in the Thames in a weighted sack? After all, a missing kid is big news. National news. It's emotional, it tugs on people's heart strings. But a single guy? If *he* goes missing, or does a bunk, nobody much cares outside his immediate family.

The other factor that disturbed me about Kate's disappearance was that it seemed to have been no spur-of-the-moment thing. Assuming that the Sherwoods had been her kidnappers, didn't it follow that they had moved into the building with the sole purpose of abducting her? They had been living across the landing from us now for... how long? The best part of a year? I couldn't remember exactly, but they had certainly taken the time and effort to gain my trust over many months. It now appeared that they had bided their time, waited for the optimum moment... and then simply vanished with my daughter.

And all this stuff with Candice and her drug-dealing boyfriend, and with Benny and Clover – had that been part of the plan too? Was Mitch's threatening of Candice merely the first of a chain of pre-planned events leading to this moment? Or had the Sherwoods – whether acting alone or as part of some group or organisation – simply taken advantage of the situation, seizing their moment while my back was turned and my attention diverted elsewhere?

Round and round it went in my head, and each time I came up with different questions, different possibilities, different permutations. But no matter how hard I tried, I just couldn't seem to get the pieces to fit.

Maybe it *would* be better simply to hand everything over to the cops. They were the experts, after all. They had the manpower, the know-how, the authority. Then again, they would just play things by the book. They weren't emotionally involved like I was. They wouldn't be prepared to bend the rules, to negotiate.

I was still trying to work it all out when I arrived at Incognito. In the daylight the neighbourhood looked more of a shithole than ever. The alleyway was filthy and stank of overflowing bins. I wondered if any of the other businesses flanking the club or facing it across the street were still operational. This whole place had the feel of a corpse that was long dead and rotting. I raised a fist and banged on the metal door.

As I stood waiting I got the feeling that someone was standing behind me. I felt a chill across my back, a prickling in my shoulders and neck. It was as if someone had stepped up close enough to blot out what little warmth and light was seeping from the grim sky after that morning's rain. I spun round, ready to defend myself – but there was no one there. I saw a flash of movement in the grimy glass of the building opposite, but it was just the reflection of my own body, raising its fists.

Next thing, the door to Incognito was grinding open and Mary was peering out at me. I glared back at her without saying anything. I wasn't prepared to take any of her bad-tempered bullshit today.

She let me in and led me through the labyrinth of corridors to Clover's office with hardly a word. Clover rose from behind her desk, hands clasped in front of her. She looked sympathetic, eyes sad and mouth downturned, as if she understood exactly what I was going through. I wondered how much of that was show, and whether she was deliberately keeping the desk between us as a shield. Mary hovered in the background, waiting for instructions.

'Would you like some tea, Alex?' Clover asked.

'No,' I said.

Clover glanced at the older woman. 'Thanks, Mary. If anything crops up can you deal with it? I don't want to be disturbed.'

Whatever Mary's response was, I didn't see it. I kept my eyes on Clover. A couple of seconds later I heard the door close behind me.

As soon as Mary had gone, Clover said, 'I'm so sorry about what's happened, Alex. You must be worried sick.'

'Just tell me what you know,' I said. After my inner turmoil on the tube, I was pleased to hear the calmness in my voice, even if my throat did feel a little tight.

She nodded. 'Of course.' Glancing down at the computer screen in front of her, she put her hand over the mouse, moved it an inch or so and left-clicked. 'A couple of hours ago I got this.'

She stood to one side, indicating that I should join her behind the desk. I walked round and looked down at the email she had opened. I made myself concentrate on it, read it slowly.

From:	**A Friend**
Date:	2 October 2012 8:55
To:	Clover Monroe
Subject:	Alex Locke

Dear Ms Monroe,

You don't know us, but we have a mutual acquaintance, Alex Locke. I would like you to contact Mr Locke immediately and inform him that we are currently in possession of his youngest daughter, Kate, and that in order to maintain her well-being and facilitate her release he must follow our instructions to the letter.

We know that you contacted him yesterday with regard to obtaining a particular artefact. What we require Mr Locke to do is to obtain the artefact, as per your offer, and deliver it to our mutual clients, representatives of the Ishikawa Corporation, who will be awaiting his arrival in Suite 5 of the Royal Gloucester Hotel on Frith Street at precisely 2 a.m. tomorrow morning (Wednesday, 3 October).

At present Kate is being well looked after. She believes she is in the care of a friend of her father's, and that her father has been called away unexpectedly on business. As a treat she has been allowed to choose her favourite food for lunch (Hawaiian pizza and Super Noodles, with Ben & Jerry's Phish Food ice cream to follow) and is now watching her favourite movie Toy Story 3 on DVD.

If you and Mr Locke accede to our request, Kate will be returned unharmed tomorrow morning. If, however, our requirements are not met, then we will kill the child. Please be assured that this is not an idle threat.

The situation, therefore, is clear. Mr Locke will obtain the artefact and deliver it to our clients at the previously specified time and location. It is a simple task, and one which we are certain he will perform admirably. Naturally, neither yourself nor Mr Locke will inform anyone else of the task, or allow them to become involved in its execution. Any suggestion of police involvement – or indeed of the involvement of friends, colleagues or family members who you may feel tempted to contact – will result in Kate's immediate death.

Any attempt to track this email to its source will similarly result in Kate's death. Please be assured that your actions are being monitored at all times, and that any attempt to deviate from the course set out for you will be met with the direst of consequences. To remove temptation, we feel compelled to inform you that this temporary email account was created in an internet café, and that all traces of its creator have been excised from online records.

Finally, please don't think that once the task has been completed to our satisfaction and Mr Locke's daughter has been returned to him, either of you will be free to entertain notions of justice and/or retribution. It would serve you well to remember that you, Ms Monroe, together with Mr Locke and his daughters, will remain for ever vulnerable.

That was it. No goodbye, no 'Yours Sincerely', no name. At some point during the reading my hand had crept up to cover my mouth, as if to stifle a scream. Now I became aware that the hand was trembling, and also that I felt cold, sick, trapped. I leaned against the wall, worried that if I didn't support myself my legs might give way.

Clover was looking at me, a frown of concern or apology on her face. Although my mind was frozen with shock, I tried to read the email again, searching for clues hidden within the text. The message had been sent at 8.55, but what did that tell me? I had no idea what time the Sherwoods had left their flat and started their journey to wherever they had taken my daughter, which meant that Kate could be literally anywhere in the world by now. Having said that, if the bit about the pizza, Super Noodles and Ben & Jerry's ice cream was to be believed – and the fact that they *were* Kate's favourite foods led me to think that the sender was telling the truth – then presumably she had to be somewhere where those products were readily available. Not that that narrowed things down a great deal.

Toy Story 3. Mention of the film sent a pang through my chest. It was unsurprising that Kate had asked to see it, but combined with what the sender had said about my actions being monitored at all times, it gave me the creepy sensation not only of being watched, but also of my thoughts being accessed. However, even as I recalled how I had reached out for the colouring book in the flat earlier, whilst remembering mine and Kate's visit to the cinema, I was telling myself that I mustn't think that way, I mustn't allow myself to get paranoid. I had no idea who had sent the email, or who – if anyone – he was working for, but I mustn't start to imagine him as some invulnerable supervillain.

So where did that leave me? And what should my next move be? I didn't realise Clover was talking until she shouted my name so loudly that it was clear she'd already repeated it several times.

Startled, I looked at her. 'What?'

'Are you all right?' she asked, reaching out tentatively and placing a hand on my arm.

I laughed without humour. 'What do *you* think?'

She rolled her eyes as if the question was too big to answer. 'What I think is that we're probably out of our depth.'

I scrutinised her face, looking for signs of deception. 'You *really* have no idea what this is about?'

She shook her head. 'Not a clue.'

'Because what strikes me is that this would be a sure-fire way of getting me to do the job you want me to do.'

Her eyes widened, as if that hadn't occurred to her. 'I swear, Alex, this is nothing to do with me. I would never stoop so low...'

'But how can I be sure? I don't even know you.'

She shook her head. 'I don't know. You can't, I suppose.'

'And this *is* your job. Your idea.'

'Then someone must have hijacked it.'

'Who?'

'I don't know.'

'But who else knows about this? Who else knows about *me*?'

Either she was a bloody good actress or she was genuinely shocked as the penny dropped. 'Only Benny.'

'So it must be him.' I took my phone out of my pocket, started to dial.

She reached out as if to snatch the phone off me. 'What are you doing?'

'I'm calling him. What do you think?'

'But what if it *isn't* him?'

'It is. It's got to be.'

'But what if it *isn't*, Alex? Remember what the email said about not telling anyone else. Are you prepared to take that risk?'

I paused, turned off the phone. Thinking hard, I said, 'If it *was* Benny, he would say that, though, wouldn't he, to keep us off his back? It's got to be Benny. And if it's not Benny, then it's you.'

'It's not me,' Clover said. 'And I can't believe it's Benny either. But if it *is* Benny, and he's got Kate, then won't he kill her if you call him? I mean, you'd still be going against his instructions, wouldn't you?' She paused. 'It must be someone else.'

'Must it? Who?'

'Well... Benny could have told someone. Or the Japanese – the Ishikawa Corporation – could have been keeping tabs on us.'

'That doesn't make sense,' I said. 'Kate's abduction was no spur-of-the-moment thing. It looks to have been carefully planned. The people who took her were her regular babysitters, friends and neighbours of mine; they've been living next door for about a year. They have a little boy called Hamish. But this morning their flat was empty, cleaned out.'

Clover looked baffled, but I could see that she was trying to figure it out. 'Well... maybe it was just *made* to look as though they'd taken her, to throw you off the scent.'

'Maybe, but...' I thought about it, but I still couldn't seem to make the pieces fit. There were too many possibilities, too many variables. And too many suspects – including Clover herself. What really baffled me was why *I* was so important to the plans of whoever was behind this – because that was what it looked like. Someone had gone to great lengths to manoeuvre me into a corner. But why? Why did *I* have to be the one to steal the artefact? Why couldn't they get some other guy, someone who was happy to do the job, someone with less baggage? Frustration boiled up inside me and I thumped the desk. 'Fuck!' I blurted. 'Whoever's behind this has got us over a fucking barrel, hasn't he?'

'Looks that way.'

'Fuck! Fuck! Fuck!'

Clover waited until I'd simmered down, and then she asked, 'So what are you going to do?'

I pulled a face. 'I don't think I've got much choice.'

She shrugged, but her expression seemed to confirm it. Nodding at the computer screen she asked, 'All that stuff about our movements being monitored... isn't that just bullshit? Scare tactics.'

'Maybe, but...'

'But what?'

I grimaced. 'Monitoring equipment is very sophisticated nowadays. I guess if they've got the resources they can follow us pretty much wherever we go – as well as keep tabs on our texts and calls and emails.'

Clover glanced quickly around as if searching for hidden cameras, a look of paranoia on her face. 'I hate the thought that someone could be watching us at this very moment. Do you think they're listening to this conversation?'

'Who knows? It's probably a bluff. But in a way I hope they *are* listening.'

'Do you? Why?'

'Because then I can tell them' – I tilted up my head and raised my voice, addressing the room – 'that I agree to their terms. That I'll do their fucking job for them.'

Clover pulled a sympathetic face. 'I'm sorry you got involved in this, Alex. I can't help feeling it's my fault.'

'Maybe it is and maybe it isn't.'

'What will you do until tonight? Go home?'

I thought about it. With Kate missing the spotlight would be on me. What if the police decided to monitor my comings and goings? What if the press got their teeth into it and set up camp outside my building? I couldn't afford to be under scrutiny, not if it might jeopardise Kate's welfare.

'It's probably best to lie low,' I said, 'keep out of the public eye. Can I stay here until it's time?'

'Sure,' said Clover, making a sweeping gesture with her hand. 'I'll get Mary to send in some sandwiches.'

Twenty minutes later the two of us were sitting at Clover's desk, eating ham and cheese toasties and drinking coffee. Clover picked at her toastie, breaking tiny pieces off the corner and nibbling at them. When my phone rang I snatched it from my pocket and answered it without considering the consequences.

'Hello?'

It was my head of department wanting to know where I was. He told me that there was a lecture hall filling with students and no sign of the lecturer.

'Sorry, Mike,' I said. With everything that had happened I'd completely forgotten to inform the college of my whereabouts. 'My daughter's gone missing. I'm afraid my head's all over the place at the moment.'

'Oh my God,' he said. 'When? How?'

I told him that I'd let him know when I had more details, that I wasn't sure when I'd be back in, and that I had to get off the line in case the police were trying to call. I spent the rest of the day drinking coffee, smoking Marlboro Lights, reading the email over and over, and fielding calls from Candice and – yes – the police. DI Jensen wanted to know where I was (I told him I was staying with a friend because I couldn't face being in the flat with all Kate's stuff around me) and informed me that the search of the Sherwoods' flat had yielded nothing. He also told me that background checks had revealed that Adam, Paula and Hamish Sherwood had never really existed, their carefully constructed false identities stretching back no more than eighteen months. He said that Adam's and Paula's likenesses, lifted from falsified online records, had been widely distributed among the nation's law-enforcement agencies, but that as yet they remained unidentified.

'Don't worry, though, Mr Locke,' he said glibly. 'We'll find them. It's only a matter of time.'

I wanted to scream at him for telling me not to worry, but instead I thanked him and cut him off.

Despite my years in prison, during which I had been forced to turn patience into a fine art, as the day wore on I found myself becoming increasingly stir crazy. By early evening I was pacing Clover's office like a tiger, all but climbing the walls.

The hours passed slowly.

NINE

McCALLUM

Kensington High Street, with its swanky shops and posh restaurants, is surrounded by parks and gardens. There's Holland Park (I've taken Kate to the adventure playground there a few times because it's not far from Chiswick), Hyde Park and Kensington Gardens. The rest of the space is taken up by streets and squares lined with big and generally well-kept houses. In one of these lived Barnaby McCallum, the man I'd come to rob.

I left Incognito around eleven and arrived at High Street Kensington station not long after half-past. I was wearing the black zip-up jacket and jeans I'd left home in that morning, plus a dark blue baseball cap that Clover had lent me. The idea of the cap was that I'd be harder to identify if nosey neighbours happened to spot me on McCallum's street. It made sense, but I couldn't help feeling I was more noticeable and suspicious-looking with the cap on. As far as I was concerned, I looked like what I was about to become: a burglar.

I didn't feel too nervous about the job itself; I was just eager to get it over and done with. My main focus was on Kate's well-being, and any anxiety I had stemmed from the fact that I couldn't afford any slip-ups for her benefit. I tried not to distract myself with thoughts about whether email man would fulfil his side of the bargain; all I could do was fulfil mine and hope that he would be true to his word. As I travelled across London I wondered whether my movements were being monitored, as email man had claimed. In a way I hoped they were. At least then he and his associates would know that I was doing all I could to follow their instructions, and that if I was stopped or prevented for whatever reason it wouldn't be my fault.

Clover had given me a key to the French windows that led into McCallum's drawing room, reiterating several times that I wouldn't have any problems. She said that McCallum's street was tree-lined and dark, the houses set back from the road and not too close together. She told me that McCallum had chosen the house specifically for its seclusion, and that whenever she'd been there at night the street had been graveyard quiet.

Although I was eager to get the job done I was anxious not to rush it. I was determined to keep a clear head and take my time. I had over two hours before I had to deliver the artefact to email man's contacts at the hotel, so I had plenty of leeway. For that reason I stopped and ordered a takeaway latte at the still-open coffee booth in the station concourse. As I waited for my coffee I tried to stay relaxed, to keep looking straight ahead, even though my instinct was to check out the people who were still streaming back and forth even at this late hour. I paid for my coffee and strolled down the road, drinking it. I had a tatty old A–Z (something else which Clover had given me) tucked into the inside pocket of my jacket, but I'd had time during the hours spent mooching around in Incognito that afternoon to commit the route to memory, so I doubted I'd need it.

I didn't. Crossing the high street, I took a right up Campden Hill Road, and ten minutes later, after another couple of turns, I was standing at the end of Bellwater Drive. By now the only sound I could hear was my own footsteps. I turned up the drive without hesitation, dropping my empty coffee cup over a garden wall as I did so.

Clover had been right. The street *was* dark. There were street lamps, but the orange glow they gave out seemed to get tangled in the black branches of the trees surrounding them and never reached the ground. I walked up the street slowly, but knowing that there was nothing more suspicious than someone deliberately trying to be unobtrusive I didn't make any particular attempt to keep to the shadows or stay out of sight. Nearly all the houses I passed had soft light glowing behind at least one or two mostly curtained windows, but I didn't see a soul, either out on the street or as a silhouetted head staring out of a window.

McCallum lived near the end of the street, at number 56. Not all the houses had visible numbers, but enough of them did for me to tell when I was getting close. I passed number 50, then another house, then one with 54 interwoven into its wrought-iron gate. Then there was a high hedge which looked black and shaggy in the darkness, and all at once I came to an opening in the hedge, and there, through a metal gate a couple of feet taller than I was, was McCallum's house.

What can I say about it? I don't know much about architecture, but like the rest of the houses I'd passed it was big and old and impressive. It was mostly white, with stone steps leading up to a front door tucked away underneath a porch supported by pillars. There were tall windows and lots of fancy bits of carved stonework and a rounded tower to the right with a roof that tapered to a point. From my point of view, I was pleased to see that the building was set back from the road beyond an expansive front lawn, that it was separated from its neighbours on both sides by a high wooden fence edged with trees and shrubs, and that it was completely dark, not a single light burning in any of its windows.

As well as the cap, the A–Z and the keys, Clover had also given me a pair of black leather gloves. I pulled them on and gave the gate a little push. I expected to have to climb over, and was already hoping I'd be able to do it without impaling myself on the spikes on top, but the gate shifted inwards a couple of inches before stopping with a metallic clatter. A quick look showed me that all I had to do was reach through a gap in the ironwork and lift a latch to get in. This I did, pushing the gate open, which creaked, but not too loudly. I shut the gate and stepped to one side, so that I couldn't be seen from the road. Then I took a minute or so to let my eyes roam across the house and garden, checking out the terrain.

The layout was pretty much as Clover had described. From what I could see, she was right about the lack of security too. There was nothing to indicate a system had been installed since she'd last been there. The building itself, and the grounds, looked reasonably well maintained, though there were enough ragged edges to show that McCallum was no perfectionist. That also fitted with what Clover had said about the old man employing a skeleton staff to keep things ticking over. Pushing myself away from the hedge, I started to walk up the path towards the house, but it was crunchy with loose stones and gravel, so after a few metres I side-stepped on to the lawn.

The grass, spongy from the day's rain, absorbed my footsteps completely. Not that I expected anyone to hear me. According to Clover the old man was in bed by eleven every night and once his head touched the pillow he was pretty much dead to the world. I knew the French windows that led into the drawing room were round the back, so I made my way there, scanning the ground ahead so that I knew exactly where I was putting my feet. Once the shadow of the house had fallen over me, it was almost pitch-black, only a few shreds and speckles of light leaking in from the street and the sky above to give any definition to my surroundings. I slowed down, worried about tripping over or into something and injuring myself. There would be nothing worse than messing up due to my own clumsiness and stupidity.

I reached the French windows without mishap and felt for the lock. As soon as I had it I slotted in the key and turned it with a rusty creak. I pushed the metal handle down and the door opened easily. A couple of seconds later I was inside.

The room I was standing in smelled of dry old carpets and furniture polish. I couldn't see much. There seemed to be lots of empty floor space, some items of furniture – possibly armchairs – over to my right, flanking what I guessed was probably a fireplace and mantelpiece, and something long and flat-topped – a bureau or a sideboard – against the wall to my left. Directly opposite the French windows the wall looked extra-dark and oddly uneven, which puzzled me for a second before I realised it was a floor-to-ceiling bookcase. Somewhere in the building I could hear a clock ticking, and there were the usual tiny creaks you get in any old house as the structure settles and shifts. But apart from that, nothing. Right at that moment it was hard to believe I was in the middle of one of the busiest cities in the world.

Leaving the French windows ajar, I made my way across to what I guessed was the sideboard on my left. Clover had told me that this was where the old man kept the obsidian heart, on a little velvet stand beneath a glass dome. As I approached it, it suddenly occurred to me to wonder what I'd do if the old man had moved the heart. It was possible, especially considering that people had been offering him pots of money for it. What if he'd put it in a safe, or even a safety deposit box in the bank? Would email man blame me if I couldn't fulfil the task through no fault of my own? More to the point, would he carry out his threat to harm Kate?

My anxiety lasted all of three seconds. I was within a couple of steps of the sideboard when I made out the gleam and vague shape of a glass dome. I stepped closer, trying to identify what was beneath it. All I could see was a fuzzy black blob, which could have been anything. I reached out with both hands and carefully lifted the dome aside. Despite what Clover had said I half-expected an alarm to go off, but nothing happened.

Although it was still too dark to see clearly, I could now tell that the object was roundish and gleaming dully. I reached out and picked it up, lifting it from the plinth it had been resting on. It was heavy for its size and sat snugly in my palm like a slightly misshapen egg. It had to be what I'd come for, but I tugged the glove off my left hand with my teeth so that I could touch it with my fingertips to make sure. I was thinking that if the old man was worried someone might try to steal the heart, he could have put a decoy here. I felt like a blind man reading Braille as I ran my fingers over the object's smooth, cool surface. I tried to picture what a human heart looked like, with its valves and veins and bulges. From what I could tell this was a pretty accurate representation.

Satisfied that I'd got what I came for, I put the glove back on, and was about to zip the heart into my jacket pocket when I heard the creak of a floorboard behind me. I spun round, and a shape rushed at me out of the darkness. Immediately I realised someone must have been sitting in one of the armchairs by the fire, hidden in the shadows, the whole time I'd been here. I could just make out a thin, stooped figure waving something above its head – a walking stick or a cane. As I turned to confront it, the figure let out a shrill, ragged screech. Then it brought the cane sweeping down towards me.

I jumped to the side and the cane smashed down on the sideboard – right on to the glass dome, shattering it to pieces. From the way he moved I could tell my attacker was a frail old man, so guessed it must be McCallum. As glass flew everywhere, McCallum gave a grunt and the cane flew out of his hand. I heard it go slithering and clattering away even as I was turning towards the open French windows. Next thing I knew the old man had thrown himself at me and was clinging on like a giant spider. He wrapped his thin limbs around me, digging his bony fingers into my arm and back. I tried to shake him off, but he clung on tenaciously, hoisting himself up and curling his legs around mine.

'*Give it back!*' he screeched into my ear. '*Give it back!*'

His chin was digging into my shoulder blade. I struggled with him, trying even harder to push him off. But he just tightened his grip, like that bloody face-hugger thing in *Alien*.

'Please... get off...' I gasped.

'*Give it back!*' he screeched again.

I didn't want to hurt him, but I had to get him off me. I could smell his stinking breath, like sour milk and rotting fish. Despite his strength, his body felt wrong, twisted and sinewy, the skin too thin, the bones too sharp. The easiest thing would have been to give him back his property and leg it out of there, but I couldn't do that, not with Kate's life at stake.

Still holding the heart in my hand, I brought my arm round, intending to give him a little bash on the head with it, just enough to make him loosen his grip. But something happened. As the heart made contact with his skull, there was a sort of *zing* noise, and then a horrible gristly crunch. Next thing I knew something hot and wet was splattering the side of my face and McCallum's suddenly limp body was falling away from me, tumbling to the floor.

For a few seconds I stood, panting and shaking, not knowing what the fuck had happened.

'Mr McCallum?' I said. 'Mr McCallum?'

He didn't answer, didn't move. He just lay there, a black heap on the carpet.

I hesitated for a couple of seconds. The easiest thing would have been to run off and leave him to it, but I had to see what had happened, had to check whether he was okay. So I walked to the far corner of the room to where I could just make out what looked like a doorway to the left of the fireplace and felt around on the wall until I found a light switch.

After the darkness the light was so bright that for a moment I couldn't see anything. I screwed my eyes up tight, trying to squint through the glare. I imagined neighbours swarming to the house, attracted to the light like moths. I wondered how visible I was through the French windows. More to the point, I wondered how visible the old man was, lying motionless on the carpet.

Probably sooner than it seemed, the glare faded enough for me to open my eyes. I blinked a couple of times, then looked down at the old man.

My guts lurched. The first thing I saw was the halo of blood fanning out around his head. I stepped closer and saw his open eyes, already glazing over. Above his eyes was a neat round hole, which was where the blood was coming from. It looked like the sort of hole an apple corer would make in a piece of fruit.

How the fuck had that happened? I'd only tapped him.

I looked down at the obsidian heart in my gloved hand.

To my amazement a black, vicious-looking spike, about the length and thickness of my index finger, was sticking up out of the middle of it. I stared at it stupidly. That hadn't been there when I'd run my fingertips over its surface. My first thought was that it must have sprung up out of a hidden compartment, like a flick-knife blade, but I couldn't see anywhere it might have come from. Besides, it looked too long to fit inside the object in my hand. What was happening here?

I nearly cried out and dropped the heart when the spike suddenly retracted. It was like... how can I describe it? Like when you touch the eye stalk of a snail and it draws it back into its body. One second the spike was there, the next it had been... *absorbed*. I thought I was going mad. My brain was trying to tell me I was holding something alive, but my eyes were telling me that it was nothing but a human heart carved out of hard, black, shiny stone.

If it hadn't been for Kate, I would have thrown the heart across the room and run like hell. It was only the thought of what would happen to her if I fucked this up that enabled me to keep my head together. I took another look at McCallum's body, and saw for the first time just *how* withered and twisted he was. He looked like an ancient, dried-out vampire who had finally succumbed to a stake through the heart or a blast of sunlight. I walked back across the room and turned out the light before dropping the heart into my jacket pocket and zipping it up. I felt nervous carrying the heart, as if it was a vicious animal that was currently asleep, but which might wake up at any moment. As soon as my eyes had readjusted to the darkness and I could make out the layout of the room, I walked across to the French windows, giving McCallum's body a wide berth, and let myself out into the garden, locking up behind me. All I wanted to do was run, get to the hotel as quickly as possible and offload the thing in my pocket. Little did I know at that moment what I had set in motion, and what fate had in store for me.

TEN

ABATTOIR

I'm not the sort of person normally given to panic. Then again, I'm not the sort of person normally given to stabbing old men through the cranium and killing them stone dead. It wasn't until I had retraced my steps across the garden and reached the gate that the full impact of what had happened hit me. For the second time that day I started to shake and the strength went out of my legs. I staggered over to the hedge, squatted down and threw up.

For a minute or so afterwards I kept going hot and cold, shivering like I'd come down with a fever. For Kate's sake I knew I had to get myself together. I pulled off one of the gloves and brought my hand up to wipe the sweat from my forehead, and that was when I felt the stickiness on my face and neck and remembered how I'd been spattered by McCallum's blood as the spike had gone into his brain.

It was the shock of this, more than anything else, which brought me back to my senses. What would have happened if I had gone out on to the high street with blood all over me? There might have been some parts of London where no one would have batted an eyelid, but Kensington was not one of them. I had to think this through, cover my tracks – both for Kate's sake and my own.

Pulling a handkerchief from my pocket, I used it to wipe off as much of the blood as possible. I could have done with checking myself in a mirror, but there was no way I was going back into McCallum's house to search for one. I wondered how much forensic evidence I'd left at the scene – footprints, hairs – but knew it was pointless worrying about things I could do nothing about. I was certain I had left no fingerprints, which was something at least.

Unsure whether you could get DNA from someone's puke, I kicked soil over mine just in case, burying all traces. The last thing I did before opening the gate and stepping out on to the pavement was take off the baseball cap Clover had lent me and stuff it into my pocket along with my bloodied handkerchief. I might be more recognisable without the cap, but I was more suspicious-looking (and therefore more memorable) wearing it. Plus there might have been some of the old man's blood on it, which someone might remember later if they saw a news report about his murder.

Hoping I wouldn't walk smack into someone exercising their dog or on their way back from the pub, I took a deep breath, then pulled open the gate. I stepped smartly on to the pavement, tugged the gate shut behind me and began to walk away from the scene of the crime. Every nerve in my body screamed at me to run, but I kept to a steady pace. It took a real effort to keep looking ahead instead of glancing around, but somehow I managed it.

Fortunately the street was empty, though that didn't mean there might not have been someone looking out of a nearby window. Again, though, there was nothing much I could do about it. I would just have to face that problem if and when it arose. By then, at least, I hoped to have fulfilled my part of the bargain and done enough to secure Kate's release. At that moment nothing else mattered.

I walked as far as Campden Hill Road, where I spotted an empty bus shelter. Stepping into it, I sat on one of the plastic flip-up seats. Even though I hadn't been running I was sweating and panting with tension. I put my head back against the Perspex wall and tried to will myself to calm down, but my heart was going like crazy. Eventually I took the A–Z out of my pocket, gripping it tightly in both hands in an effort to stop them from shaking. Instead of walking back down towards the high street, where even at this hour there would be people around, I decided to skirt around the edge of Holland Park and head north to Notting Hill.

I kept away from the high-population areas around Holland Park and Notting Hill Gate tubes, and called a cab from a street off Ladbroke Grove. When it arrived I ducked into the back and told the driver to take me to Dean Street, which ran parallel to Frith Street. The driver was middle-aged, Asian, jowly and unshaven. He glanced at me once disinterestedly in his mirror, then nodded.

Luckily he wasn't the chatty type, and apart from constant pick-up requests over the tinny radio from a woman with an Essex accent the journey passed in silence. By the time we arrived in Dean Street it was after 1 a.m., and I was feeling a bit more together. I paid my fare, giving the driver a decent tip, but not one so big that he'd remember it, and looked around, wondering how to kill the next fifty minutes.

Incognito was only a few minutes' walk away, but I couldn't face the thought of explaining to Clover what had happened. In any case, I was reluctant to deviate from the plan; the last thing I wanted was to do anything that would give email man a reason to get twitchy. I walked up Dean Street and spotted an all-night café across the road beneath an overhang of darkened offices. It looked like a dive, but that was fine. The grottier the clientele, the less I'd stand out.

The first thing I did when I stepped through the door was to duck into the toilets. I hoped there would be a mirror on the wall, and there was – part of one at least, in the form of a jagged triangle clinging to a single screw. I checked myself out, and noticed a couple of smears of now mostly-dried blood just under my jaw line, which I'd missed. After cleaning myself up with a wet paper hand towel and flushing away the evidence, I went back out into the café and ordered tea and toast.

The tea was pantile-red and the toast soggy and hard to stomach, but I stolidly worked my way through it. I sat at a corner table furthest from the door, my back to a transparent display case, where cheese and ham pasties, slices of limp pizza and greasy-looking doughnuts offered themselves to the hungry and desperate. Over the heads of the few other customers – a pair of bleary-looking students and a brown-toothed old woman in a filthy headscarf – I watched the comings and goings in the street outside. Already what had happened an hour before was starting to seem unreal, like a vivid nightmare that it had taken me a while to shake myself out of.

Ironically, however, it was then – just as I was feeling a little calmer, and the incident was turning dream-like in my head – that the brutal reality of what I'd done suddenly side-swiped me. I realised, as if for the first time, that I was now a murderer, and that nothing I could do would ever change that. Whether I had meant it or not, I had ended the life of a man who had been on this planet for eighty or ninety years, a man who had been well into his fifties when I was born. And what made it even worse was that this man – Barnaby McCallum – had, from all accounts, lived a life of colour and variety and excitement; he had taken risks and grasped opportunities and worked hard for his achievements. Surely, I thought, such a man deserved to die peacefully in bed surrounded by his family and friends? And yet, thanks to me, his flame had been abruptly and brutally snuffed out, and he was now lying all alone on a cold, hard floor in a pool of his congealing blood.

The thought made my gorge rise and I lowered my head, breathing hard in an effort to stop my tea and toast from making a re-appearance. I couldn't believe how, in the space of a couple of days, my life had turned to shit. Maybe email man *would* let Kate go, and maybe I *hadn't* left enough evidence at the scene for the cops to catch me, but at that moment it felt like the walls were closing in. Eventually my stomach settled and I slowly raised my head – only to see a police car slowing to a stop at the kerb outside.

My heart lurched, and I almost dived under the table, before realising that the car wasn't stopping, but was simply slowing down as a result of the natural ebb and flow of the London traffic. Logically I knew that even if I *had* left evidence at the murder scene, there was no way the police would get to me this quickly.

Not unless I had been set up.

Thinking about that, I suddenly wondered why the old man had been sitting in the dark. It was almost as if he'd been *expecting* me to break in. Had he had a tip-off that I was coming? Or had he just been paranoid since being offered a quarter of a million for the heart? In which case, why hadn't he moved it to a more secure place?

As before, my mind was full of questions. Had McCallum known what the heart was capable of? And what about the people who wanted to get their hands on it? Did *they* know? Then again, what *was* it capable of – apart, obviously, from what I had seen it do? Was it a weapon or...

I couldn't think what else the heart might be *apart* from a weapon, and to be honest I didn't want to ponder it too much. The thing gave me the creeps, and the sooner I was able to hand it over and get it out of my life, the better.

The clock on the wall said 1.41. I watched the minute hand creeping round until it got to 1.50 and then I stood up. Walking to Frith Street, I half-expected to be intercepted or apprehended, but less than five minutes later I was standing outside the Royal Gloucester Hotel.

Despite its name it wasn't that grand. But neither was it a dump. In fact, it was pretty nondescript, which I suppose made it ideal for an illegal transaction. I entered through a set of revolving doors and found myself in a lobby with a spinach-green carpet. The reception desk to my left was dark, gleaming wood and the wallpaper was a lighter shade of brown imprinted with an over-fussy pattern of tangled leaves. A couple of sprawling, over-large pot plants completed the impression that I had walked into a building that wanted to be a forest. I spotted a set of lifts over to my right and strode towards them with the confidence of a paying guest.

No one tried to stop me or ask what I was doing, but it wasn't until the lift was ascending that I breathed a sigh of relief. None of the lift buttons had said 'Suite' next to them, so I just pressed the button for the top floor and hoped for the best.

My hunch turned out to be right. I stepped out of the lift on to a landing with three widely spaced doors. Above the door closest to me was a wooden sign with the words 'Suite 4' carved into the wood and highlighted in gold paint. Half a dozen steps brought me to 'Suite 5'. I checked my watch. 1.57 a.m. Perfect timing. I raised a hand and knocked gently.

It was so silent that you could almost hear the air hum. When I leaned forward to put my ear to the door, the rustle of my jacket seemed to reverberate from the beige walls.

I couldn't hear anything from inside the room. I waited a few more seconds, then knocked again. My tongue rasped across lips which were dry with nerves. I shifted from one foot to the other – and then, for the first time since stepping out of the lift, I heard a sound.

It didn't come from behind the door of Suite 5, though. It came from above me. I looked up at the ceiling, not that I expected to see anything. The sound was like claws scrabbling on a rough surface. I imagined an owl landing on a roof a few metres above my head. Maybe even rats running about in the air conditioning ducts.

The sound continued for a few seconds and then stopped. I looked at my watch. 1.59. Raising my fist, I knocked louder. Glancing up and down the corridor, I leaned forward again, my face so close to the door that I could have kissed it, and in a low, urgent voice, said, 'Hello?'

Still no answer. 'Fuck,' I said, though so quietly that the only audible sound was the wet 'ck' in my throat. I knocked again, louder.

'Hello?' I repeated. 'Anyone there?'

2.01. My anxiety was turning to paranoia. What if I'd got it wrong – the time, the place? What if I'd not read the email properly?

But I had. I *knew* I had. Not only had I read it properly, I'd read it at least twenty times. The details were seared into my brain. There was no way I'd made a mistake.

Email man had told me and Clover not to ring anyone – that if we did, he'd know – but surely that didn't apply to us ringing each other? I took my phone out of my pocket. A quick call, just to double-check the details. Before thumbing the buttons, however, I tried the handle of the door.

It opened.

I was so surprised I jerked back, almost yanking the door shut again. I managed to stop myself, and for a few seconds just stood there, my hand wrapped around the handle, the door open half an inch. I couldn't see much. A line of light, a sliver of something brownish that might have been a desk or a table.

'Hello,' I said into the gap. 'I think you're expecting me. I've got something for you.'

Silence. I sighed and pushed the door open. Hesitated for a second, then stepped forward into a typical hotel sitting room, nice but anonymous. Desk to the left, three-piece suite, low table, TV, rust-coloured curtains billowing in the wind.

It was empty, but there were signs of recent occupation. A folded Japanese newspaper on the brown leather settee, a china cup containing half an inch of what looked like weak, milkless tea on the low table.

'Hello?' I called again, but I'd now pretty much accepted the fact that there was no one here. I wandered over to the window, which was open as far as it would go, and looked out. From here London was a mass of lights, some moving, some not, with dense patches of blackness in between. I debated what to do. Wait here till the people I was supposed to meet came back? Leave the heart where it would be easily seen and vacate the premises? Call Clover to find out whether there'd been a change of plan?

I decided on the last option, but first I wanted to check out the other rooms. There were doors on opposite walls, to my left and right. The one on my right was closest, so I tried that first. I opened the door on to a bedroom containing a king-sized double bed, which looked not to have been slept in, or even sat on. In fact, there was no sign that anyone had been in here at all – no luggage, no clothes, no glass or book on the bedside table.

I went back into the sitting room. The door on the opposite wall was just beyond the desk. I crossed to it, guessing that it must be the bathroom. I was reaching for the handle when I heard the scrabbling sound again. It seemed to come from directly above my head, and I got the odd feeling that whatever was up on the roof was tracking my movements. Again I looked up, but there was nothing to see except a white ceiling. I glanced across to the open window, where the curtain was still billowing like a listless ghost. Suddenly I felt the urge to be as quiet as I could. Gritting my teeth, I pushed the handle of the door down slowly and eased it open. The first thing I saw was white walls streaked and spattered with red. A single word jumped into my head: *abattoir*.

The shock made my fingers spring apart, jerk away from the handle. Letting go didn't stop the door from swinging all the way open, though. Inch by inch the room was revealed. I stood, stunned and gaping, my mind like an expanding balloon that was being filled not with air but terrible images. I wanted to recoil, but instead felt myself taking a step forward, as if tugged by invisible wire. The door gave a final creak and came to a halt.

The light was on in the bathroom, and its barely audible hum was like a tiny, almost subliminal scream. A scream that went on and on, as if reacting to what it illuminated.

There were two men in the bathroom. Both were dead. They were not *just* dead though – they had been taken apart, piece by piece. Their blood was pooled on the floor, spattered up the walls and across the mirror, and was even dripping from the ceiling.

Their heads were in the sink, cheek to cheek like lovers, glazed-eyed and open-mouthed. Their torsos and severed limbs were stacked in the bath like firewood – except for one hand, which was resting on the lowered toilet seat, dead fingers still curled around the butt and trigger of a chunky black handgun.

The instant effect of seeing so much carnage was like a stinging, open-handed slap across the face. It was a flash of sensation, so awful and vivid and unexpected that I felt almost blinded by it. It was only little by little that I noticed specific details associated with the two men and how they had died. Even then, shocked as I was, it struck me that some of the details were very odd indeed.

The first detail – the obvious and most mundane one – was that the men were Japanese. Their faces were slack, blood-flecked, horribly distorted by death, but there was no mistaking their nationality. The second detail was that they had been smartly dressed in suits and ties and crisp white shirts. They looked like businessmen. But businessmen with guns. Which is where it began to get odd.

The gun in the severed hand resting on the lowered lid of the toilet seat had not been fired. If it had been, there would have been evidence – a bullet hole in the wall or door or ceiling, or, if the bullet had embedded itself in the killer, a trail of blood leading from the bathroom, across the floor of the sitting room and presumably out into the corridor. But there were none of these things – which seemed to indicate that although one of the dead men had had his gun in his hand, he and his companion had been attacked so swiftly and savagely that he hadn't even had time to pull the trigger.

Maybe I was being paranoid, but I couldn't help thinking, as I stared down at the hand, that the killer wanted me – or whoever else might have found the bodies – to know this. That was why the hand had been placed so carefully where it was – as evidence of the killer's incredible speed and agility.

He's showing off. I was still so shocked that I wasn't sure whether I actually whispered these words or merely thought them. I wasn't *so* shocked, though, that I didn't notice another detail. And again, like the unfired gun, this was one that seemed so impossible that, despite the evidence, it couldn't be true.

Admittedly I haven't seen many dismembered corpses in my time, but it still looked pretty obvious to me that the men hadn't been taken apart in the normal way. There were no clean cuts that I could see, no evidence of the kinds of marks made by axes or swords or chainsaws. No, these men seemed to have been *ripped* apart, their skin stretched and torn, their exposed bones shattered and twisted. I thought of roast chicken, the gristly sound of sinews snapping as the legs were wrenched off the bird.

Oddly it was this thought, rather than what I was looking at, which nearly made me throw up for the second time that night. I managed to keep my gorge down through sheer willpower, telling myself what a bad idea it would be to puke at two separate murder scenes on the same evening. Leaning forward, so as not to get blood on my boots, I grabbed the door handle and pulled the bathroom door shut. As it clicked I heard a flapping sound behind me and almost jumped out of my skin, but it was only the curtain blowing in a particularly strong breeze.

With the door shut, my mind went into a sort of automatic self-preservation mode. I'd already used my handkerchief to clean blood off my face, so now I untied my right boot, pulled off my sock and used it to wipe all the door handles I'd touched. I wished I'd had the foresight to put my gloves back on before entering the room, but it had never occurred to me that I would have to worry yet again about leaving physical evidence behind. When I'd done all I could to cover my tracks, I left quickly, using the stairs this time instead of the lift. The fact that I didn't meet anyone on the way down or crossing the lobby was a stroke of luck, I suppose, though after the day I'd had it felt like the very least that the universe owed me. I stepped out into the street and started walking up the road, and it was only when I'd taken a couple of dozen steps that I wondered where the hell I was going.

ELEVEN

FLESH AND METAL

It was when I turned right, cutting down Bateman Street, that I realised my subconscious had made the decision for me. I was heading towards Incognito. Of course I was. It was five minutes' walk from the hotel, and I needed somewhere close and familiar where I could get my head together.

My head was very much *not* together as I trudged the quarter of a mile or so from Frith Street to the little alleyway off Poland Street in which Incognito lived up to its name. The chaos in my head reminded me of something a work colleague, Stephen Carrier, had once told me. Stephen was a lecturer in modern literature and a committed bibliophile. He *loved* books, *adored* books, couldn't get enough of them. He pored over catalogues and publishing websites with the gleeful enthusiasm of a child. At weekends he travelled the length and breadth of the country to spend hours browsing in second-hand bookshops or visiting book fairs. He had a phrase to describe the moment when he entered a room full of books for the first time: 'book blindness'. Confronted by an overabundance of sensory input, he told me that for several seconds, sometimes even a minute or two, his brain could simply close down, unable to cope with the barrage of information it was attempting to assimilate.

Walking through the streets of London in the early hours of Wednesday morning, I understood for the first time exactly what he meant. My thoughts were like a mass of trapped flies, buzzing, never settling, impossible to catch. I couldn't focus on my surroundings;

cars and buildings and people were nothing but smears of light and shadow. How I reached Incognito I'll never know. Automatic pilot, I suppose. A combination of instinct, desperation and self-preservation.

It was only when I came to the alleyway that the fog in my head started to clear. The gap between the buildings on either side was so black it was like an absence in the world. If it hadn't been for the ascending seepage of light from the surrounding streets, it would have been impossible to tell the difference between the tops of the buildings and the muddy strip of sky which separated them. Beyond the blackness the only light that made any impression came from a caged bulb above Incognito's entrance. The bulb illuminated the club's name and highlighted the dents and scratches in the metal door, but that was about it.

At least it gave me an oasis to head for. I started forward, crossing an area so dark that there could have been a whole gang of muggers standing in my path and I wouldn't have seen them. My foot knocked against something, which bounced away with a clunky tinkle. Only a bottle, but the sudden noise made my body spasm with tension.

As if reacting to the sound, something moved in the blackness. It was more an impression than a certainty, but it made me stop and stare, screwing up my eyes as if that could make me see better. It hadn't been a quick, darting movement, like a cat would make, but a kind of slow, bunched-up *oozing*, like a slug or a snail – and hadn't it been briefly accompanied by a sly, metallic tapping noise too?

Stupid, I thought. Just my eyes trying to create shapes out of nothing. Even so, I trod a bit more carefully as I crossed the last few metres of darkness, scanning the ground ahead as best I could.

It was only when I thought about raising my right hand to knock on Incognito's door that I realised it was resting on the bulge of the heart in my jacket pocket. It must have strayed there when I'd entered the alleyway, but even though the movement had been an unconscious one I still found it unsettling. It reminded me of a villain reaching for a gun – which in turn made me think of the severed hand of one of the murder victims back at the hotel, still curled around the butt of a pistol which had been no use at all.

I tried to tell myself I had no reason to be worried about the same thing happening to me. I had no quarrel with anyone. I was merely following orders; I was nothing but a pawn in a game I didn't understand. However the darkness had a way of pulling such reassurances out of shape, of turning logic on its head. But it wasn't just the fear of violence which bothered me; it was also the prospect of deliberately using the heart as a weapon that made me sick to my stomach. I had no idea what the thing was, or what it was capable of, but I knew that people had died because of it. I moved my hand away from my jacket, clenching my fist as if that would make me forget the shape and weight and feel of the heart in my palm. And then, scowling, I bashed on the metal door.

As the echo of my knocking faded I sensed movement above my head. I looked up, and caught a glimpse of something leaping the six or so metres from the top of the building on the opposite side of the alleyway to the one beside which I was standing. The thing moved so swiftly that it was there and gone in a flash, leaving me with nothing but an impression of something as ragged and flappy as a crow, and as spindly-legged as a spider, but far larger than both. For a few seconds after it had disappeared I stared up at the black clouds drifting through the murky sky like blood clots. My mouth was dry and a rash of goosebumps crawled up and down my arms and back.

I was so unnerved that when the door of Incognito opened I almost leaped out of my skin. I pushed straight past Mary and slammed the door behind me, ignoring her indignant cry of, 'Do you mind?'

'Where's Clover?' I asked, clenching my fists to stop my hands from shaking.

Mary pursed her lips, her face hardening, and then she must have seen something in my eyes. 'She's in the bar,' she muttered, 'having a well-deserved—'

'Is that door unlocked?' I interrupted, pointing at the black door at the end of the corridor.

Mary nodded, and I all but ran along the corridor and shoved the door open. Immediately the heat of the club enfolded me in a sweaty hug and the bass beat of the music thumped in my teeth and chest. On the stage a small, muscly girl in a red bra and thong was pole-dancing, her back arching and her blonde hair flying as she coiled and contorted like a snake. At a glance I'd say there were forty or fifty people in the room, all but half a dozen of whom were men. I could see Clover at the bar, dressed in a little black number which showed off her slender legs. She was sitting on one of the plastic stools, her hand curled around a tumbler containing something red. As I watched she leaned forward and took a sip through a black straw. Next to her was a fat man in a light blue suit whose conversation seemed to be a series of punchlines followed by roars of laughter. Clover was smiling and nodding, but even from the walkway I could tell she was listening to the man more out of duty than because she wanted to.

I hurried down the steps, marched across to the bar and took her arm. She turned with a scowl, and then smiled as if she was genuinely relieved I'd made it back in one piece.

'Alex,' she said. 'Is it done?'

'Not exactly,' I muttered.

The relief on her face changed to concern. 'Why? What happened?'

I glanced at the fat man. 'Can we go somewhere else?'

'Sure.' She turned back to her customer and dabbled her fingers across the top of his forearm. 'Excuse us, Clive, would you? Duty calls.'

The fat man looked daggers at me. 'Will you be long?'

'I may be. Have a drink on the house.' She beckoned to Robin the barman and pointed at Clive's glass.

Two minutes later we were in Clover's office and she was checking her emails at my request. She shook her head apologetically.

'Nothing. So tell me what happened.'

I told her. About the old man. About what I'd found at the hotel. She paled and her lovely features tautened with fear, her breath starting to come in panicky gasps.

'Oh shit,' she said. 'Oh shit.'

'Is there anything you're not telling me?' I asked.

She looked startled. 'What do you mean?'

'I mean is there anything you're not telling me? Anything you forgot to mention?'

If the hurt look on her face was an act, she was a bloody good actress. 'Is that really what you think?'

'I don't know *what* to think, Clover. This is all so... fucked up.'

'What you said about the heart...' She hesitated. 'There's no way you might have been mistaken?'

116

'About what?'

'About the way the blade... retracted?'

'It was *absorbed*,' I said. 'That's the only word I can think of to describe it.'

'Maybe it folded up. Maybe the... opening it comes out of is so tight it looks seamless when it closes again.'

I shook my head irritably. 'You weren't there. You didn't see it.'

'Can I see it now?'

I felt weirdly reluctant. Possessive even. 'I thought you'd *already* seen it?'

'I have, but only under glass. I never really paid much attention to it when I worked there.'

I hesitated for a couple of seconds longer without really knowing why – it wasn't because I was afraid the heart might suddenly become a weapon again; at least, I don't think so – and then I unzipped my jacket pocket. I reached in gingerly, as if afraid I might get bitten, and lifted out the heart, cupping it delicately in my hand, as if it was a living creature. When I placed it on the desk between us, Clover craned forward to examine it, her face wary.

'Be careful,' I said.

'I *am* being careful.'

For a few seconds neither of us spoke, both of us staring at the heart.

'Can I touch it?' Clover asked finally.

I shrugged and she tentatively caressed the thing, her fingertips moving over the veins and bumps and protuberances. After a minute she got bolder and picked the heart up. I felt a stab of anxiety.

'Watch it.'

'Don't worry. I'm not going to put it close to my face.'

She rolled it slowly from hand to hand, scrutinising it from all angles. 'It looks like it's carved from a solid lump of obsidian.'

I nodded and asked, 'What are we going to do?'

She sighed and put the heart back on the desk. 'Wait for further instructions, I suppose.'

'And then what? I'm a murderer now. A hunted man.'

Clover frowned. 'I don't know. For now our options are limited. We don't know who our contact is. And we don't know who killed the men at the hotel, or why.'

'I'm guessing whoever killed them wanted that,' I said, nodding at the heart.

'Which is our only trump card at the moment. The fact that *we've* got what everyone else seems to want.'

I snorted. 'That's hardly comforting. I feel like the bloke holding the meat while hungry lions close in on all sides. I wish I could just get rid of the thing and let whoever wants it fight it out between themselves.'

'But where would that leave Kate?' Clover said. 'If the heart falls into the wrong hands...'

'Do you think I haven't thought about that?'

She looked away. 'Sorry.'

I felt bad for having a go at her. Unless she was playing a devious game, none of this was her fault.

'Me too,' I said. 'And you're right. We need to sit tight and wait for email man to get back in touch. Once he finds out about the Japanese guys he's bound to, isn't he?'

Clover looked at me strangely.

'What?'

'I don't really want to say it, but...'

'But what?'

'What if he thinks you killed them?'

For a minute I was stumped. My head was so messed up that that hadn't occurred to me. At last I said, 'He won't.'

'How do you know?'

'Because why would I? What could I possibly gain from it? Besides, those guys had been torn apart. They didn't even get a chance to fire their guns. I'm not Superman, Clover.'

'You think whoever killed them is?'

I hesitated. I had already told her that the men had been ripped apart, that I'd found a hand still clutching a gun on the toilet seat, but I don't think she had fully considered the implications. 'I think *what*ever killed them... well, I don't think it was human.'

She gave a nervous half-laugh. 'What do you mean? That it was some kind of animal?'

I shrugged. 'If it was, it would've had to have been something like a gorilla. But a bloody fast one. One that moved like lightning.'

She frowned, and almost tetchily said, 'Come off it, Alex. Isn't it more likely that the men were killed – shot maybe – and then chopped up? Maybe the hand was planted there as some kind of sick joke.'

I was sorely tempted by her theory, but I couldn't shake the image of how the dead men's flesh and bone had been twisted and torn.

'You didn't see them,' I said. 'Besides, I haven't told you everything.'

'Oh?'

'I've a feeling I might have been followed back here by whatever killed those men.'

Her eyes widened. 'What do you mean?'

I told her about the thing I'd seen outside, that had jumped across the alleyway from one roof to another.

'But that's impossible!' she said. 'The gap's about... eight metres.'

I shrugged.

'You must have seen a bird or something. Or a plane in the sky.'

I was about to reply when, faintly, we heard a crash from upstairs.

Our eyes met. I wondered if she was thinking the same thing as me: *Here it comes.*

The crash was followed by screams, shouts, a tinkle of breaking glass so faint it was like the sound of distant wind-chimes. Instinctively I snatched up the heart and zipped it back into my pocket.

'Is there a back way out of here?' I asked.

Clover circled the desk and ran to the door.

'Clover!' I snapped.

She yanked the door open. 'I have to see what's happening.'

'I don't think that's a good idea—'

But she was already out the door and heading down the corridor. I hesitated a second, wondering whether to find my own way out of there, but even as the thought crossed my mind I knew there was no way I could abandon her. 'Fuck,' I said and gave chase.

I caught up with her unlocking the door into the club. From beyond came the sound of mayhem – people shouting and screaming, things breaking and falling over. I grabbed her hand as she reached for the door handle.

'Clover, wait.'

She tried to twist out of my grip. 'Let me go.'

'Listen to it out there,' I said.

She swung to face me, her eyes wide. 'Alex, it's *my* club. *My* responsibility.'

I clenched my teeth in exasperation. 'All right,' I muttered. 'I won't stop you. But we need to be careful. Clover, look at me.'

There was anger on her face, but she did as I asked.

'The likelihood is that whatever's on the other side of this door killed the two guys at the hotel. That means that even though this is your club, you can't just walk out there and start shouting the odds. So let's not be reckless, okay? Let's take this nice and slowly. Do you understand?'

She still looked angry and scared, but she gave a quick, sharp nod. 'Yes.'

'Okay,' I said. 'So let me go first. You stick close behind me.'

'What are you?' she asked. 'My indestructible human shield?'

'Hardly.'

As carefully as I could I opened the door. Just a crack at first, and then I pulled it wider. The first thing I saw was a man lying on his face a few metres to my left. He was motionless, but in the dim light it was hard to tell what had been done to him. I heard Clover gasp and knew she had seen him too.

'Take it easy,' I whispered.

I eased my way through the gap, Clover sticking close, like a shadow. Although the music was still thumping away, in the last minute all the other sounds we'd heard – the crashes and thuds and screams – had ceased.

Further to my left I could see that many of the optics behind the bar had been smashed, various coloured liquids dripping from the jagged remains of the upturned bottles. There was no sign of Robin the barman, or anyone else for that matter – no one upright and moving, at any rate. From where we were standing in the doorway, partly sheltered by the stairs to our right, I could see three other bodies. One belonged to the fat man in the light blue suit who had been talking to Clover earlier. He was spreadeagled on the floor like a cartoon drunk, his head propped against the bottom of the bar. There was a dark, lumpy smear on the glassy surface above his head, and for a few seconds I was puzzled by the fact that he appeared to be wearing shades which had partly melted and dribbled down his face, before realising that his eyes had been gouged out and the empty sockets were leaking tears of blood.

I looked away from the fat man and focused on the other two bodies, both men, sprawled in awkward positions as if they'd been felled while running. At first I wondered whether they had been shot and then I saw that what I'd taken to be a bunch of dark clothing on and beside the belly of one of the men were his innards. He'd been gutted.

I was about to suggest to Clover that we go back through the door and lock it behind us when she gave a squeal of shock. I looked to my right and saw a squat figure appear round the bottom of the staircase and come blundering towards us. I tensed, ready to defend myself, and then realised it was Mary. At first I couldn't see what was wrong with her, apart from the fact that her eyes were bulging and her mouth was open in a silent scream. I noticed she had something around her neck, something that appeared to be part thick grey muffler and part... what? In the dimness I could make out what looked like the cannibalised innards of an old clock: cogs and spools and little brass levers all working against one another.

What the hell could it be? A collar of some kind? A torture device? Whatever it was, it was wound tightly around her neck and those parts that weren't mechanical seemed to be made of some strange, glistening material. I stepped forward with the notion of aiding Mary in some way, and that was when the collar came alive. It whirred and *slithered*, and a portion of it reared up behind Mary's head.

Clover screamed.

The thing had the face of a grey-skinned baby. But one that had been nightmarishly modified, stretched over some kind of circular brass frame and held in place with metal pins as long as my own fingers. It had black, gleaming orbs instead of eyes and its plump grey lips were peeled back to reveal not gums and a tongue, but a whirring, clicking mass of minuscule clockwork components. The body of the thing was eel-like, but as thick as my arm and several times longer. As it tightened its coils around Mary's throat, she dropped to her knees. Her hands came up and scrabbled weakly at the creature's glistening grey flesh. Her face was purple now, the whites of her eyes filling with dark spots as the blood vessels burst. Her mouth was all tongue, which stuck out between her lips, so bloated with blood it looked almost black.

Although the thought of getting close to the thing disgusted and terrified me, I couldn't just stand there and watch Mary die. I stepped forward, but as soon as I reached out the creature's 'neck' flexed and its head shot forward like a striking snake. I snatched my hand back, horrified as a double row of jagged metallic teeth concertinaed out on an extendable jaw made of fused bone and metal, and clacked together on empty air that a split second earlier had been occupied by my fingers.

'Fuck!' I shouted. 'I need a weapon!'

Clover was pressed against me, fingers digging into my arm tightly enough to leave bruises. Her voice was a thin shriek. 'Use the heart!'

'How?'

'I don't know! Just try it!'

I dug into my jacket pocket and pulled out the heart. Despite what had happened earlier the idea of using it as a weapon seemed ludicrous. I held it up, pointing it at the creature. But as I waited for something to happen, I heard a horrible crack, and the life went out of Mary's swollen face, her eyes rolling back in her head. Clover screamed, 'No!' as Mary's body spasmed and went limp. The heart continued to sit there in my palm like a lump of useless black stone as the eel-creature slackened its grip on poor Mary's throat and her body hit the floor like a spud-filled sack.

Uncoiling itself from her neck, the eel-creature reared up like a cobra, its grotesque baby-face weaving from side to side. I backed up, almost treading on Clover's toes, ushering her towards the partly open door from which we had emerged. As we retreated, Clover's breaths rapid with the distress of what she had seen, something moved over by the stage. Keeping the eel-thing in my peripheral vision, I glanced in that direction.

Clover whimpered as something unfolded from the stage. Bathed in spotlights, which blazed from above and below, it gave the impression it was rising from an effulgent sea. Squinting, I initially thought that it was some kind of vast bird. And then, as it extended to its full height and stepped forward to stand at the front of the stage, like a diver perched on the edge of a diving board, I realised it was a man.

It was not a normal man, though. He was impossibly tall and thin, a ragged overcoat hanging from his bony shoulders like the wings of a gigantic bat. His head was long and white and narrow and completely bald, and he was wearing rimless round spectacles – either that or his eyes were nothing but pale, reflective discs.

At first I thought his mouth was tiny and thin-lipped, but then he smiled, and the smile split his face like a widening vertical wound. It stretched and stretched, and grew redder and redder, and as it did so he slowly raised his arms, like a conductor poised to begin a concert performance.

Immediately the arms began to grow, to elongate, to stretch towards us. I heard a clicking and a whirring as they did so, and then I saw the tips of his long, pale fingers peel back like the opening petals of a flower. I watched with horror and astonishment as syringes, each one tipped with a hypodermic needle, emerged from the holes of the fingers of his left hand, a succession of scalpels and drills from the fingers of his right. The syringes were transparent, and filled with a cloudy fluid. I even saw a bead of liquid at the tip of one of the needles catch the light and glitter like a tiny jewel.

Then Clover was screaming my name and wrenching my arm, pointing upwards. I looked up and was appalled to see that I had been so distracted by the man on the stage that I had failed to register his army of freaks, which were now slithering and buzzing and clacking towards us. It was a nightmare conglomeration of flesh and machinery, the heads and limbs and viscera of children and animals intermingled with components that appeared to have been gleaned from Victorian engines and time-pieces and weaponry.

There was something that looked like a large mechanical beetle, albeit with the dangling limbs of a small child, chugging through the air towards us, leaking a trail of oily vapour; there was a stubby, brass-coloured cannon-like device that swooped and darted through the air, propelled by the white, outstretched wings of an owl; there was a clicking, spider-like contraption with the face of a mewling cat that scuttled sideways along the wall, defying gravity; there was a limbless girl in a glass bell jar who rolled and lurched towards us on a complex lash-up of pipes and pulleys and caterpillar tracks.

So fascinating and hideous was this advancing parade of horrors that I might have stood, gaping, and allowed them to overwhelm us if Clover had not grabbed me by the collar and wrenched me backwards. A split second later a dozen or so metallic needles buried themselves in the wall beside my head. Startled, I realised that all of the advancing creatures were armed in some way. Even now weaponry of one sort or another – nozzles and tubes and whirling blades – was shunting into place, powering up, swivelling in our direction.

Stumbling and almost falling over one another, Clover and I threw ourselves back through the door and slammed it behind us. Clover locked it while I shoved the heart back in my pocket.

'Where now?' I yelled, my heart racing with adrenaline, my limbs tingling with shock, my thoughts jagged with sheer disbelief at what I had seen.

She led me back along the corridor, past her office and into a room on the left. It was nothing but a poky storeroom, stacked with boxes across which was laid a thick swag of faded blue curtain. Against the far wall leaned a set of stepladders, an old ironing board and half a dozen fold-up chairs. I looked around for a hidden door but couldn't see one. I even looked up at the ceiling, searching for a skylight.

'What—' I started to say, but Clover, bent almost double, barged me aside. Off-balance, I stumbled, throwing up my hands to stop myself crashing into the wall. I twisted angrily, to see that Clover was dragging aside a rug I'd been standing on. Underneath was a trapdoor with an iron ring set into a circular groove so that it was flush with the floor. She dug her fingers under the ring and heaved and the trapdoor started to open. I rushed forward to help, shoving the trapdoor all the way up until the folding hinge that supported it had snapped into place.

Cold air wafted up from the opening, accompanied by a dank smell like mouldering stone and old farts. I saw a square shaft inset with rusty but solid-looking rungs. After a few metres the shaft was swallowed by darkness.

Kneeling, I peered into the shaft and saw white splinters of light reflecting on black moving water far below. I could hear it too – a rushing sound so faint it was like a gentle breeze through dry grass.

'What is this?' I asked.

'Escape tunnel.'

I blinked at her. 'Handy.'

'In the late seventies this place was owned by a friend of Benny's. George Lancaster?'

She said the name as though I might have heard of him. I shrugged.

'He had a lot of enemies, so he had this installed for when he needed a quick getaway.'

She had already taken hold of the top rung and was lowering herself into the shaft.

'Where does it go?' I asked.

The shadows were swallowing her now, closing over her head like black water. Her voice echoed off the stone walls. 'Does it matter?'

TWELVE

ADRENALINE CRASH

George Lancaster's escape tunnel came out round the back of a Chinese restaurant in the tangle of roads leading off from Leicester Square tube station. It took us ten minutes, maybe less, to get there. As soon as we had reached the bottom of the ladder beneath Incognito – having pulled the rug back across the trapdoor and closed it behind us in an attempt to cover our tracks as best we could – Clover grabbed a torch from a stone shelf, peeled off the plastic bag it was wrapped in and turned it on.

I was not sure what I'd been expecting to see. My sole knowledge of London sewer tunnels came from old Sherlock Holmes movies and the like. I suppose I thought they might have been modernised since the 1890s, but I was wrong. Clearly those Victorians knew what they were doing.

Stretching ahead of us was what looked like a huge brick pipe with a flat floor. There were smaller pipes, thick grey plastic ones, about the width of my thigh, attached to brackets running along the left-hand wall. I half-expected to have to wade through a river of human waste, but there was only a modest flow of rusty-looking water running along the central drain. Even the smell wasn't so bad, dank and farty but bearable.

Clover led the way, hurrying along despite the high heels she was still wearing, as if she knew exactly where she was going, the torchlight leaping eerily across the greasy walls. My mind still felt like a bag of broken glass, tinkling and sharp-edged with shock. Mostly it was occupied in trying to come to terms with, and make sense of, the incredible things I had seen tonight. Were those creatures *real?* If so, where had they come from? What did they want? But struggling to fight free of the bomb-blast debris in my mind came random, and more practical, thoughts and observations.

I wondered whether Clover had had need to use this particular exit before; I wondered briefly whether we should call the police in case those... *creatures* swarmed out of the club and began to cause havoc in the London streets (and almost immediately I rejected the notion, thinking, entirely selfishly, of email man's orders, of Kate's safety). I wondered too whether the creatures were *associated* with email man – whether, in fact, the figure on the stage with the extendable arms and the too-wide smile was email man himself. My mind shied away from that possibility like a frightened horse. The thought of Kate in the clutches of those *things*...

Eventually we came to another rusty-looking ladder and climbed up it. At the top was a square manhole cover, and it took the two of us, clinging awkwardly to opposite sides of the ladder, to push it up and over to one side. I had visions of climbing out and getting instantly mown down by a truck, but as I say we emerged to find ourselves in a dark alley round the back of a Chinese restaurant. Ironically, having just walked quarter of a mile through a sewer tunnel, it was the stale smell of steamed fish and vegetables drifting out of an air vent at the back of the building that made me double over with a sudden attack of stomach cramps.

'You okay?' Clover asked.

I nodded and straightened up. 'Just got to me for a second. I'll be fine.'

She switched off the torch and looked around. Her face was white and I could see she was trembling.

'Back there,' I said. 'Those things. What were they?'

She shook her head. Suddenly her face crumpled and she was sobbing.

'Hey,' I said softly. 'Hey.' I stepped forward and held her in my arms.

Although I was comforting her I felt like a fraud. I felt like sobbing myself. She clung to me until the tears had run their course, and then she broke away, sniffing and wiping at her eyes, bringing herself under control.

When she spoke her voice sounded almost normal. 'Where to now?'

'Back to my place?' I suggested. 'Cup of tea? Work out what to do next?'

We both knew it was a risk, but our options were limited and we needed somewhere to get over what we'd been through. We trooped out into the street, which was still not deserted even though it was getting on for three in the morning. There were a few late-night revellers around, and one or two places that were just about open, but looked as if they'd be closing soon. We passed through the Chinatown arch on Gerrard Street and headed up to Shaftesbury Avenue looking for a cab. Finding one, I told the driver my address and then the two of us sank back into our seats. For the rest of the journey we sat in stunned and mutual silence, each affected by the night's events and lost in our own thoughts.

It was only when we turned the corner into my road that I stirred from my slumped position, leaning forward to scan the vehicles parked nose to tail along the length of each kerb. If I had spotted a police car, or even a vehicle with people sitting in it, I would have told the driver to keep going, but all seemed quiet.

After instructing the driver where to stop, I roused Clover, who appeared to have slipped into a light doze. I paid the fare, then we hurried across the forecourt to the door of my building, my eyes darting right and left as my hand rooted in my pockets for keys. It was a relief to get inside and to hear the reassuring clunk of the lock behind us. As we trudged up the stairs it struck me how weary and hollow I felt – the result, I guessed, of adrenaline crash after the traumatic events of the evening. From the way Clover was moving – like someone leaving hospital after an operation – I guessed she felt the same way.

We reached my landing and came to a halt. For a couple of seconds we simply stared at my door hanging off its hinges, a big dent edged with splintered wood visible beneath the handle. It looked as though the lock had been shattered with one almighty kick or perhaps with a whack from a sledgehammer.

Clover and I exchanged glances. She was so exhausted that she looked drawn and disappointed rather than scared. I understood the expression, because I felt exactly the same way. I took a deep breath, gathering what little resources I had left, and said, 'Wait here.' I tiptoed across to the broken door and slowly pushed it open, reaching around the frame to switch on the light.

There was nothing to see or hear. Just the small hallway, doors leading off. The doors to the bathroom and both mine and Kate's bedrooms were open, the rooms beyond small enough for me to tell at a glance that they were unoccupied. The only closed door was that which led into the main room and the adjoining kitchen. Had I closed it earlier as I had left the flat? I couldn't remember. Bracing myself, I sprang forward and shoved the door hard with both hands.

If there had been someone crouched on the other side the door would have knocked them flying. But it didn't happen. Instead the door just swung back, showing me a dark but apparently empty room.

I glanced at Clover, standing in the corridor, looking anxious. 'All clear, I think.'

I was aware of her edging cautiously over the threshold and into the flat as I stepped into the main room. Backlit by the light from the hallway I knew that I made an obvious target, and so reached immediately for the square of plastic to my left. I slapped the switch down, squinting a little at the sudden glare, though my vision didn't take much adjusting. I felt Clover at my back, trying to see around me.

'Oh my God,' she breathed.

It was only when the light came on that I saw that the room had been trashed. The sofa and chairs had been shredded and turned over; books – including Kate's *Toy Story* colouring book – had been torn apart and strewn about like dead birds; CDs had been dashed to the floor, their plastic casings crunched underfoot; the TV was lying on its back with a saucepan embedded in its glass screen.

Clover's exhalation had not been a response to the devastation, though. Spectacular though it was, her eyes – and mine – had been drawn almost immediately to the opposite wall. Spray-painted in big red letters on the pale wallpaper were five words:

BEWARE THE WOLVES OF LONDON

THIRTEEN

THE EYE OF THE STORM

Clover was asleep, breathing deep and long, her dark hair spread over the hotel pillow, and her face, now peaceful and relaxed after the traumas of the day, looking younger than her twenty-odd years. Her closed eyelids were a pale lilac colour and reminded me of butterfly wings in the dim light. One limp hand was resting against her cheek, as if she'd fallen asleep while sucking her thumb.

Looking at her, I felt a protective ache in my belly, an urge to keep her from harm. It was nothing to do with sexual attraction. It was as if my feelings for Kate, with nowhere to go, had latched on to Clover instead.

Although I was exhausted, my head was too busy for sleep. As well as feeling a duty to watch over Clover, I had so much to think about I barely knew where to start.

After seeing the words daubed on the wall of my flat we had decided it was too risky to stay there. So we hit the streets again, sticking to the shadows and looking all around us as we hurried away from the building in case the Wolves of London, whoever they were, were still hanging around. We came to a panting, jittery halt outside the closed, dark entrance to Chiswick Park tube station and called a cab from there. I suggested trying Clover's place, but it turned out she lived in a flat above the club, so that was a no go. We therefore got the cab to take us back into the West End, where Clover and I both withdrew £500 each from a cash machine. Then we found a quiet little hotel near Bloomsbury Square and took a double room for the night – just somewhere to sleep and, if possible, recharge our batteries. We were so shattered we literally couldn't think beyond that. A proper, coherent plan would have to wait until the morning.

As soon as we locked the door of the room behind us, Clover staggered over to the bed and collapsed. Within seconds she was asleep, her body shutting down like it was deploying some kind of defence mechanism. I pulled off her shoes – God knows how she'd managed in those high heels all night – and threw the spare blanket from the walk-in wardrobe over her. Then I turned off all the lights apart from the little reading lamp above the desk, made myself a cup of tea and settled down in the armchair.

I thought about taking a shower – I felt grubby and kept getting sharp, sweaty wafts of what was probably the by-product of concentrated adrenaline whenever I shifted position – but thinking about it was as far as I got. Not only did it seem like too much effort, I also didn't like the thought of leaving Clover in the room on her own, or indeed of making myself vulnerable by standing naked behind a plastic curtain with water running into my eyes. So I did nothing but sit there, drinking tea and trying to make sense of what was going on. It struck me I was turning into a kind of Jonah, insomuch as many of the people with whom I'd been associated these past few days – my daughters, Clover, Barnaby McCallum, the two Japanese 'businessmen' – had suffered in one way or another. I wondered for the thousandth time what was happening and what my role in it all was. And I wondered too whether there was still further yet to fall, and how I would cope if there was.

Sitting in the semi-darkness, Clover's soft, slow breathing filling the room, I had the feeling that I was currently in the eye of the storm, huddled in a protective bubble, while all about swirled chaos and death and destruction. It wasn't a comforting feeling. I knew that Clover and I couldn't stay here for ever, and that sooner or later we would have to emerge and face the storm head on.

At my request, Clover had checked her emails on her phone a few times since we'd fled the club, but there had been no further contact from email man. I'd checked my phone too, of course, and continued to do so, obsessively, every ten minutes or so, but zilch. Without realising I was doing it, I began, as I sat there thinking, to trace the outline of the obsidian heart in my breast pocket with my fingers and then to caress it through the material. As soon as it struck me what I was doing I felt uncomfortable, disturbed by my actions. I had the odd sense that the heart was almost like my own heart, or more specifically like a heart that was giving me trouble – burning in my chest, weighing heavily. There was no doubt that it was at the centre of everything that had happened. It was both a curse, in that it had caused so much trouble, and a blessing, because when it came to the question of keeping Kate alive it was my only bargaining tool.

But what exactly was it? Where had it come from? Was it *only* a weapon or something else? Thinking of the tall man and his menagerie of half-organic, half-clockwork creatures, I even found myself wondering whether the heart was of this world or whether it was from... where? Outer space? Some secret world within our own where things existed that had managed to keep themselves hidden for hundreds, maybe thousands of years?

Though outwardly I was calm, inwardly my thoughts were still raging, my mind crippled with anxiety for Kate, and struggling to come to terms with what it had seen tonight, trying to fit square pegs into round holes. I took the heart out of my pocket and began to pass it from hand to hand, playing with it the same way someone might play with a set of worry beads. My fingers moved restlessly over the knobbly, veined surface as if feeling for a hidden catch, a secret opening, a way in. Funnily enough, it never occurred to me that the thing might be dangerous, that what had happened to McCallum might happen to me too. Maybe I was so beset with worry and confusion that I simply didn't care, though I don't think that was it. It was more a sense, almost a conviction, not only that I was the heart's protector, but that it somehow *knew* that I was.

I leaned to one side so that the yellow light from the lamp beside me shone on the heart's gleaming surface. I went over every millimetre of it with my fingers and eyes, looking for cracks or... I don't know; just wanting it to give up its secrets, in the hope that I might better understand what was going on. At one point I even held the heart up in front of my face, like a jeweller examining a diamond. But nothing happened. Just as in Incognito, the heart stubbornly refused to become anything other than what it appeared to be, an egg-sized human organ carved out of black stone.

At last I sighed and sat back, the seat creaking beneath me. On the bed, Clover gave a little moan and half-turned over, then settled again. For once London was silent. I could hear nothing outside the room but the faint background hum of the universe. I looked at the heart for a couple of seconds longer, then curled my fingers around it and squeezed.

'Come on,' I muttered. 'Come on.'

I closed my eyes, then opened them again. The room was the same as before. The heart was still a rock-like lump in my hand, unmoving, unyielding.

'Fuck you then,' I whispered, and slipped the thing back into my pocket. Needing a piss, I leaned forward to push the dead weight of my weary body out of the seat. I looked across at the half-open door of the bathroom, at the wedge of darkness between door and frame.

The darkness moved.

My own heart leaped like it had been jump-started and my hands gripped the arms of the chair. My brain told me I should be on my feet, leaping into action, but I couldn't move. I watched as the bathroom door opened slowly and soundlessly, not all the way, just enough to reveal the silhouette of a figure. The figure was slight, and beneath its black bulb of a head it seemed to glimmer like a ghost. Then it stepped out of the shadows and light fell across it, and I gasped in recognition.

It was Lyn, the mother of Kate. But Lyn was in a psychiatric hospital on the south coast; had been there for five years. Her presence here now was astonishing, not only because she was here at all, but also because this wasn't the raddled, reduced Lyn I now visited on an irregular basis, but the beautiful, gentle, radiant Lyn I had first known and loved years before. And what pushed the visitation from astonishing into the realm of the impossible was the fact that this was also *pregnant* Lyn, five or six months gone, before all the trouble had started. I stared in amazement at the bulging belly beneath the knee-length nightshirt she wore.

I remembered that nightshirt. I might even have bought it for her. It was white with a repeated cherry design on it, and it had short sleeves edged in lace trim. I noticed that Lyn was even wearing the bangles and rings she wasn't allowed to wear any more, and her fingernails and toenails (her feet were bare) were painted a bright candyfloss pink. She was smiling at me, that old mischievous smile that exposed her dimples, her eyes wide and blue beneath her ash-blonde fringe.

I opened my mouth, but no words came out. It wasn't until she shimmered that I realised I was crying.

She looked at me for several seconds, and on her face was compassion, love even. Then she spoke, and her voice was not the cracked mutter or the barbed-wire screech I was now used to. It was soft and warm and sexy, like it used to be.

'Take care, Alex,' she said. 'The wolves are coming.'

Then, her hands cupping her pregnant belly, she stepped back into the bathroom and was swallowed by the shadows.

'No!' I croaked, and that was when I felt my body jerk and my eyes tear open, and I realised, with a mixture of despair and relief, that I had been dreaming. The dream had been so vivid, though, that I stood up, the heart rolling off my lap and on to the floor with a thump. I rushed across to the bathroom, wrenched open the door and turned on the light. I was half-thinking that if I was quick enough I might still catch Lyn before she went back to wherever she had come from. But the bathroom was empty, and the harsh light reflecting off the white tiles was like fingernails scraping down the blackboard of my brain.

I don't know whether it was this, or the dream, or simply a delayed reaction to everything that had happened that night, but suddenly, for about the fifth time in as many hours, I got a fierce attack of stomach cramps. This time I knew I wouldn't be able to will it away, and so I threw myself down on the floor in front of the toilet and stuck my head in the bowl. A second later I hurled up everything I had eaten and drunk since killing the old man, which wasn't much – tea, toast, a couple of shortbread biscuits that had been on the tea tray in the hotel room. It took several good heaves to get my stomach empty and then I was retching up foul-tasting bile which burned my throat.

Eventually my guts stopped cramping and I slumped away from the vomit-spattered toilet and on to my back. The light on the ceiling looked impossibly high and impossibly bright, like an icy sun glaring down on a cold, white desert.

My last coherent thought was that I had to go back into the other room, protect Clover and safeguard the heart.

Then the light above me seemed to flare like an exploding sun, and I remembered nothing more.

FOURTEEN

THE DARK MAN

When I offered to buy her a drink, she laughed tipsily and said, 'I'll have something cheap and tarty.'

'Like what?' I asked.

'Oh, I don't know. Something with sambuca in it.'

I knew she was teasing me. Testing me, even. Matching her grin with my own, I said, 'I hope that's not what *you* are?'

'What?'

'Cheap and tarty.'

She looked at me again – *properly* looked at me this time – and despite the fact that she was a little drunk, I saw intelligence, shrewdness and humour in her eyes. 'Do you *really*?' she asked.

'Yes I do.'

And that was how it started. At the end of the evening Lyn wrote her phone number in bruise-red lipstick on the inside of my forearm and made me promise to call her.

2003, that was. June. I was twenty-six years old and two months out of prison. I had a master's degree in psychology and had enrolled in teacher training college. I'd been told that because of my criminal record it was 'unlikely' I would ever be allowed to work with impressionable minors, but that – depending on how 'enlightened' my potential employers were – there was a possibility I might eventually find work in further or adult education. I knew it was going to be tough, but I was optimistic and determined. And on the night I met Lyn, in a packed pub called The Punch and Judy in Covent Garden, I was still reeling with joy at the sheer novelty of being able to do my own thing for the first time in over six years – of being able to go where I wanted to go, to eat what I wanted to eat, of simply being able to stand under a vast open sky, and to walk for miles and miles.

Those first few years with Lyn were the happiest of my life. We were ridiculously loved up, soppy for each other; she was my soulmate, or so I believed. Her dad, Terry, owned an accommodation agency and fixed us up with a nice little flat in Shepherd's Bush, just round the corner from the Empire. He was a good bloke, Lyn's dad. Originally from Plymouth, he talked with a West Country drawl that made him sound like a bumpkin, even though he was anything but.

When Lyn told me she was pregnant in November 2006 I thought my life was complete. By this time I had gained my level 4 further education teaching certificate, and was teaching night classes four evenings a week and loving it.

I can't remember exactly when Lyn started cutting herself, but it must have been around May or June of 2007. She started on the backs of her wrists, and then moved on to her upper arms and thighs. Round about the same time, or maybe just before that, came the nightmares and the sleepwalking. Lyn could never remember the full details, but she became convinced that someone was watching her, someone who wanted to harm her baby. She talked about 'the dark man', or sometimes 'the man from the shadows', but whenever I asked her to elaborate she became confused and upset. Doctors put it down to depression, hormonal imbalance, and the first few times I took her to A&E after she had slashed her arms, they simply patched her up, gave her some anti-depressants and sent her back home.

Hoping that the doctors were right and that her increasing instability was nothing but a temporary aberration, I watched her like a hawk, but it was impossible to keep tabs on her 24/7. I had my teaching job to do in the evenings, plus I admit to becoming complacent at times. Interspersed with the bouts of self-mutilation and paranoia would be periods where Lyn would become more or less her old self – loving, rational, *normal*. When this happened I would breathe a sigh of relief and hope that this time the doctors had got her medication right and that the worst was over.

It all came to a head one Sunday morning maybe six or seven weeks before Kate was due. Leaving Lyn dozing in a warm bath, steam curling from her scarred, pink, shiny-wet body, I popped down to the corner shop for bread, milk and a paper. Apart from a couple of bad dreams, she had been relatively stable for the past week or ten days, and I thought she'd be fine for ten minutes. Despite the tightly stretched dome of her belly, I remember looking at her lying in the bath and thinking how vulnerable she looked, how childlike. She had tied up her blonde hair loosely, and trailing strands of it were clinging to her neck. Bobbing above the water, her nipples had become so dark during her pregnancy that they resembled twin islands in a milky sea.

I kissed her forehead and asked her if she would be all right. She grunted and half-nodded, as if she was mostly asleep and dreaming.

When I got back ten minutes later the flat was silent. Although it's almost certainly hindsight, I recall thinking it was an odd sort of silence, the silence of a child who has broken his mum's favourite vase and is waiting in fear for the repercussions.

'Lyn?' I called, taking off my jacket and hanging it up. It was then I noticed the small, wet footprints. They led from the bathroom, across the wooden floor of the landing to our bedroom, and back again, crossing over at several points.

I called her name a second time, my heartbeat accelerating. Then, telling myself I was over-reacting, I put the milk, bread and paper on the floor by the front door and ran up the hall to the bathroom.

At first, when I shoved the door open, all I could see was blood. The vividness of it was like a slap in the face. There had been blood before, of course, every time Lyn had cut herself. But there was more of it this time – a whole bath full of it – and against the shiny white tiles of the little room it made more of an impact.

After the first shock my mind went into overdrive, taking in the details. I saw the twisted wire coat hanger on the floor, surrounded by spatters and spots of dark-red arterial blood; the wet footprints across the lino, into some of which more blood had seeped like a marbling of pale red veins; and I saw Lyn herself, lolling in a bath of water-diluted blood the colour of ripe tomatoes, her skin deathly grey, her mouth hanging wide and her eyes rolling beneath half-closed lids.

'Jesus Christ, Lyn!' I shouted. 'What have you done?'

I scanned what I could see of her body above the red water, but there was no sign of any scratches or cuts. She had obviously used the coat hanger on herself, but I didn't know how and where. Reluctant to drag her out of the bath in case it opened up any concealed wounds, I put my hand into the bloody water between her feet and yanked out the plug. As the water swirled away, exposing the rest of her body, I pulled out my mobile and rang for an ambulance.

It wasn't until after I had rung off, and the water had almost drained away, that I could see what she had done to herself. Between her legs, beneath her swollen belly, was a torn mess of flesh, leaking a thick red ribbon of blood. I like to think I've got a pretty strong constitution, but at the sight of her mutilated genitals I had to grab the sink to stop myself passing out. I knelt there, breathing hard, as waves of sickness rushed up through my body and black spots swam in front of my eyes.

What kept me upright and focused was the knowledge that I had to look after Lyn. I could see that she was already shuddering as her body went into shock. I hauled myself to my feet, staggered to the bedroom and grabbed the duvet off the bed. Heading back across the landing, I almost slipped on the wet floor, but just managed to stay on my feet. I stepped carefully around the pools of water and blood by the bath and draped the duvet over Lyn's body, tucking it in around her neck to keep her warm. Leaning over the bath, I put my arms round her as best I could and kissed her clammy, wet forehead. I held her till the ambulance came, telling her over and over that she was going to be fine, that everything would be all right.

I didn't believe it, though. I knew she had stepped over the line this time. Up to now the opinion of the doctors had been that she was hormonal, seeking attention, and that once the right meds kicked in and the baby was born, everything would go back to how it was. But what Lyn had done to herself wasn't attention-seeking, it was the action of someone who was severely disturbed. Not only that, but she hadn't just harmed herself this time; she had been trying to harm the baby too.

At least that was what I thought at first. My immediate assumption was that she blamed the baby for the way she'd become, or maybe she felt resentful, trapped by her pregnancy. I was scared to death and sick with worry as I climbed into the ambulance, but there was also a part of me that was angry. We had been happy, things had been going well, so why had Lyn screwed it up? Didn't she *want* to be with me? Didn't she *want* us to be a family?

I sat numbly in the ambulance while the paramedic, a Welsh guy called Luke with the build of a rugby player, did his stuff. He was setting up a drip in her arm when Lyn started to mutter my name, her head jerking from side to side.

Luke spoke softly to Lyn, then turned to me and beckoned me forward. 'I think she wants to talk to you, mate.'

I moved across to a chair beside the wheeled stretcher and sat down. Lyn was still pale, though she didn't look as deathly as she had twenty minutes earlier. Her eyes were unfocused beneath her drooping eyelids, as if she was drifting into sleep again. Her lips were moving, though no sound was coming out, and her face looked drawn and waxy.

'Hi,' I said softly, not knowing whether she could see or hear me.

She raised a hand and clutched at the air, as if my voice was a fluttering moth.

I reached out and took the hand, partly to comfort her and partly because her gesture was so pitiful it distressed me. Earlier I'd thought how childlike she seemed. Now she resembled a feeble old woman.

'It's all right, I'm here,' I said.

The contents of the ambulance rattled as the vehicle took a corner. Although the siren was silent, we were moving at speed.

Lyn blinked sleepily and again I wondered if she was aware of me. Her lips were still moving, but the engine was too noisy to make out what she was saying, so I lowered my head, tilting my ear towards her mouth.

Her breath smelled bad, as if the violence she'd inflicted on herself had turned her sour inside. She was whispering something. I leaned in closer. So close that her breath stirred the hairs lining my earlobe, tickling like insects' feet.

'She needs to come out,' she said, gasping between each word.

'Who does?' I asked.

Instead of answering, she grimaced, and her free hand, the one I wasn't holding, hovered in the air for a few seconds before settling on her belly.

'She needs to come out,' she whispered again. 'Otherwise the dark man will get her.'

I wasn't sure how to respond at first, and then I said gently, 'She's not ready yet, Lyn. She still has a few weeks to go.'

Lyn's face creased up and her head thrashed from side to side. 'She's ready... she needs to come out... help her... don't let him get her...' Her voice trailed off, as if her own agitation was exhausting her.

I covered her little hand between both of mine and squeezed gently, trying to give her some of my strength. I knew it was pointless to argue, that it would only upset her more, and so I fell back to what I had been saying in the flat – I told her that she and the baby would be fine, and that everything would be all right.

As soon as we arrived at A&E she was whisked away to be examined and stitched up. I hung around in the waiting room, gravitating between the snack machine and the tatty magazines on the low table surrounded by plastic chairs. I didn't read the magazines. I just turned the pages to give my hands something to do. I ate a Kit Kat and drank several cups of sludgy, bitter coffee. After an age a doctor came to speak to me, a stocky man with flared nostrils and wiry black hair that made me think of the Action Man I had had as a kid. He introduced himself as Dr Sangster and shook my hand.

'How is she?' I asked.

'Oh, physically she's fine,' Dr Sangster said almost airily, 'and so is your baby. The damage your wife did to herself was nasty but superficial. However, there's going to be some swelling and soreness in that area for a while – but it shouldn't affect the birth.'

I nodded, relieved that she and the baby were okay. I didn't bother mentioning that Lyn and I weren't married.

'What we *are* concerned about, however,' he continued, 'is her mental health.'

'Me too,' I said. 'It started about three months ago. The doctors we've spoken to so far seem to think it's hormonal, and that she'll get better once the baby arrives.'

He looked at me thoughtfully. 'I'm sure it's been a great strain, and I think it's time we took some of that strain away from you. With your permission, Mr Locke, I'd like your wife to remain in hospital, at least until your baby is born.'

For a while now Lyn had been like a ticking bomb, and so the relief I felt at being given the opportunity to hand that bomb over was far greater than my distress at the prospect of her spending the next five or six weeks in hospital.

Dr Sangster placed a reassuring hand on my shoulder. 'I appreciate that this is probably not how you envisaged these weeks leading up to the birth of your child, Mr Locke, but believe me, I really do think it's the best option for all three of you. The safety of all parties is paramount in this case, and your wife's psychological condition is giving us genuine cause for concern. Without constant monitoring there's a real danger that she could inflict serious harm on both your baby and herself.'

He told me not to worry, and that Lyn would be well taken care of, and that I could visit her whenever I liked. Finally, he patted my shoulder and said that he was sure Lyn and I would look back on this period as nothing more than a minor bump on the long road of life.

He was wrong. Lyn never recovered. Over the next few weeks, leading up to Kate's birth, she became increasingly obsessed not only that 'the dark man' would steal her baby from her, but that he somehow had the ability to spirit Kate away from inside her womb. Lyn thought the only way her unborn child would avoid this fate would be if Kate was out in the open, where she could be seen and protected. There was no arguing Lyn out of this point of view, no reasoning with her. In the end she had to be permanently restrained to stop her from clawing at herself, and often she had to be sedated too, because she would work herself up into a state of screeching panic.

Lyn was beautiful when I met her, but she went downhill fast after Kate was born. She never did come home. She stayed in hospital for a long time, and eventually she was transferred to a private institution. She receives the best treatment possible, but it has never made the slightest difference. The day that 'the dark man' came into her life was the day I lost her.

FIFTEEN

SCORCHED EARTH

'Alex! Alex!'

The voice sounded distant at first, and then suddenly seemed to rush at me, like a crow swooping from the darkness. I shouted out and jerked awake.

My body was so stiff and cold it hurt to move and my eyes were filled with stinging light. I felt hands on me and fought against them. 'Hey, calm down.'

Bits of memory started to filter through, and then it all crunched in and I remembered where I was and what had happened. Putting up a hand to shield my eyes, I squinted into the face looming over me.

'You okay?'

I saw Clover nod. 'Yes.'

'What time is it?'

'I don't know. Morning.'

I sat up, groaning. I felt like an old man. Then again, I *had* been asleep on a hard bathroom floor for God knew how long. I rubbed a hand across my forehead. My mouth tasted like something had died in it. With Clover's help I climbed to my feet, turned on the cold tap and swilled my stale, sickly mouth out with water. Then I remembered something else, and felt a stab of panic.

'The heart!'

'Don't worry, it's safe.'

Clover held on to my arm as I staggered into the bedroom and dropped into the armchair with a grunt. The heart was on the dressing table, directly under the reading lamp which I'd turned on last night and which was still shining light down upon it. It looked like a black egg in an incubator, which was being kept warm until it was ready to hatch.

Sitting on the edge of the bed, Clover asked what had happened. I hesitated a moment, then told her. Her eyes widened as I recounted how Lyn had stepped out of the darkened bathroom, as if I was describing something that had actually taken place. Although I had wanted it to be real last night, I frowned when she asked me what I thought it meant.

'It didn't mean anything,' I said. 'It was a dream.'

She looked at me like she expected more.

'What?' I said irritably.

'Are you *sure* it was a dream?'

'Of course I'm sure.' I frowned. 'It was finding the men in the hotel bathroom last night, seeing all that blood on the white tiles. It must have reminded me of something that happened a few years ago.'

She was looking at me, encouraging me to go on.

'Lyn used to self-harm. One day she was in the bath and she cut herself really badly.' I looked away from her. 'I don't want to talk about it.'

She leaned back as though to give me space. 'From the way you describe it, I still think it might have been more than a dream.'

'How could it have been?'

She pursed her lips. Even with no make-up on and hardly any sleep she looked fresh and bright-eyed. 'You said you were examining the heart, trying to get it to do something?'

'So?'

'So what if it *did* do something? What if it brought Lyn here?'

I scowled. 'For what?'

'To warn us.'

'To tell us that the wolves are coming? Not exactly helpful, is it? Not exactly specific.'

'Maybe it wanted to tell us not to get complacent, to remind us that wherever we are we're not safe.'

I felt anger rising in me and tried to swallow it down. 'Sorry, Clover, but I don't buy it. It's just... crazy. Lyn's in a psychiatric hospital called Darby Hall just outside Brighton. She's a shadow of the person I once knew. The Lyn I saw last night – *dreamed* about last night – was how

146

she used to be when I first met her. She was lovely back then...' I felt my voice faltering and cleared my throat.

'What happened?' Clover asked softly.

'Long story.'

'Don't give much away, do you?'

I shrugged. 'It's not relevant, that's all. Maybe I'll tell you some day. When we've got all this sorted out.'

She was silent for a moment. Then she said, 'Okay, so maybe it wasn't *actually* Lyn. But it could have been some kind of... projection.'

I groaned. 'It was a dream, Clover. Don't go making it out to be anything more.'

'Just hear me out a minute.' There was a sharpness to her voice, which I found oddly heartening. Last night she had seemed so done in that I was worried she might go to pieces. 'What I'm saying is that maybe you *did* activate the heart in some way, and it latched on to your memories and showed you an image you'd find... I don't know... familiar. Comforting, even.'

'Latched on to my memories? You're talking about that lump of rock like it's a living thing. Something that thinks.'

Clover looked uncomfortable. 'Well, we don't know *what* it is, do we? We don't know what it's capable of. It's more than a lump of rock, though, that's for sure.'

I held up my hands. 'Okay, granted. But let's not confuse ourselves more than we are already by coming up with mad theories. Let's just keep things simple for now, take it one step at a time.'

'Agreed,' she said. 'But can I say one more thing?'

I sighed. 'Do I have a choice?'

'Not really.'

'Go on then.'

'Well, it's just that last night, after you used the heart to...' She cupped her hand and swung her arm round.

'Kill McCallum?'

She grimaced. 'Yeah. After you'd done it, didn't you say you threw up? In the garden?'

'So?'

'And then after the vision or the dream about Lyn, you threw up again... and then passed out.'

I jerked my shoulders grumpily. 'So what's your point? I'd say it was a fairly natural reaction after—'

'No, no, you don't get it. What I mean is, what if the heart made you sick? What if using it is bad for you?'

'Like smoking?'

'I suppose. But with more immediate effects. What if...' She paused and I could see she was thinking the theory through. 'What if every time you use it, it takes something out of you? A bit of your life-force? Your soul?'

I couldn't believe we were having this conversation. In the ordinary scheme of things it would have been ridiculous. All the same, I found myself putting a protective hand lightly on the centre of my chest, as if trying to hold something in. 'Nice thought.'

She leaned back on the bed, resting on her elbows. 'It's just a theory. I don't know any more than you do.'

Her words seemed to hang in the air. Despite everything we'd been through together, I still wasn't a hundred per cent sure that I could trust her, or if she knew more than she was letting on. At the same time I felt instinctively that I could – but how far could I trust my own feelings? I rubbed my hands vigorously over my face to try to wake myself up, and got a whiff of sweaty armpits.

'I need a shower,' I said.

'Well, I didn't like to say anything, but...'

This time her tone was playful. She grinned at me and I grinned back. It struck me how amazing it was that we could still dredge up even a fraction of a sense of humour after what had happened. It was a good thing, I suppose, though as the grin stretched my mouth I was aware of a voice inside my head, reminding me that Kate was missing, that I was a murderer, that Clover and I were in deadly peril.

'Have you checked your emails this morning?' I asked, pulling my own phone out of my pocket.

Clover nodded. 'Yes. Sorry. There's nothing.'

There was nothing in my inbox either, or on my voicemail. Nothing from email man, that is. And my battery was worryingly low.

'Why don't I order some breakfast while you take a shower?' Clover said. 'Then when we've eaten and cleaned ourselves up, we'll go out and buy some new clothes? Something cheap, practical and anonymous.'

I nodded. 'Sounds like a plan. We need phone chargers too. Have a look in the London Guide. See if there's a Fugitives From Justice R Us near here.'

The shower was one of those power jobs that blasts water at you so hard it feels like it's scouring your skin. It was just what I needed. I turned it up as hot as I could stand and worked up a lather with the shampoo and soap, giving my hair and body a good scrubbing. I felt a need to strip last night's dirt away. Not just the physical dirt, but the dirt of what I'd done and what I'd seen. I felt like I could have stood under those pounding jets for hours, but after five minutes I started to get anxious about leaving Clover on her own. I switched off the shower, grabbed a fluffy white towel and started to dry myself. I was just wishing we had some toothpaste, and made a mental note to add it to our list of purchases, when Clover shouted, 'Alex!'

There was urgency in her voice, but I couldn't tell whether she was excited or scared. I had an image of her answering a knock on the door, to find that instead of the room-service guy it was the tall man from last night, his arms stretching out towards her.

'What?' I shouted, frantically wrapping the towel around my waist.

'Come and see. Quick or you'll miss it.'

Still damp, water trickling down my face, I pulled open the bathroom door and stepped through a cloud of steam into the bedroom. The TV was on, and Clover, perched on the edge of the bed, was leaning forward, eyes fixed on the screen. Following her gaze I saw wobbly footage of a building on fire, lines of white text on a red banner scrolling underneath. A newsreader's clipped voice was providing information in bite-sized chunks. I was trying to make sense of what I was seeing when Clover said, 'It's Incognito.'

'Shit,' I said, and looked at her as the news report ended. 'What did they say?'

Clover looked stunned. 'They said police think the fire started in the main bar and took hold quickly. They said it was near closing time, so the club wasn't full, but that they think there are at least a dozen casualties.'

'Did they mention you?' I asked.

She shook her head.

'Scorched-earth policy,' I said.

She blinked at me. 'What?'

'It's a military strategy used against Napoleon's army when they advanced across Russia in the 1800s. The retreating population burned all the land so there was nothing for Napoleon's men to use – no food, no shelter, nothing.' I shrugged. 'What's being done to us reminds me of that. All our resources are being cut from under us.'

'Except the difference is that we're not the advancing army. We're the ones on the run.'

'True. And at least we've still got money and shelter for now.'

There was a knock on the door. 'Room service.'

'And food,' Clover said, pushing herself up from the bed.

'Tell him to leave it outside,' I said quietly. 'Just in case.'

Clover nodded and repeated my request.

'No problem, madam.'

Clover put her ear to the door and after fifteen seconds or so she said, 'I think he's gone.'

'Give me a minute,' I said and went back into the bathroom.

With no other alternative, I put yesterday's clothes back on. After my shower they smelled even staler than before, but that couldn't be helped. When I was dressed and had laced up my boots I went back into the bedroom, walked across to the door and listened. Hearing nothing, I opened the door a crack, looked up and down the empty corridor, and picked up the tray that had been left there.

'Is it going to be like this all the time now?' Clover asked as I pushed the door shut with my foot.

'Like what?'

'Us skulking about, scared of our own shadows?'

'We just need to be careful,' I said, knowing it wasn't much of an answer. I put the tray on the dressing table, then picked up the heart and pocketed it. As I did so my mobile rang, and I jumped. For a moment I thought the sound had come from the heart.

I took out my mobile and looked at the display screen:

Candice calling.

Glancing at Clover I cautiously pressed 'Accept'.

'Hey, sweetheart.'

'Hi, Dad. I just wanted to say thank you *so* much!'

For a moment I was silent, wrong-footed by the joy and relief in my eldest daughter's voice.

'What for?'

She laughed. 'The money, you idiot. How did you manage to get hold of it – or shouldn't I ask?'

The money. Immediately I realised what must have happened. Someone had paid off Candice's boyfriend's debts. But who? And why?

Winging it, I said, 'So it arrived, did it?'

'Dean rang me ten minutes ago to say that Mitch had been paid in full, and that we were in the clear.' She gave a heartfelt sigh. 'I can't tell you what a relief it is. You're a total star, Dad. We'll pay you back, I promise.'

'No hurry,' I said, my mind working furiously.

She paused slightly. When she next spoke her voice was sombre. 'Are *you* okay? Any news about Kate?'

'Not yet. I'll let you know the instant I hear anything.'

'Do you want me to come over?'

'No, thanks, sweetheart. In fact, I'm staying with a friend.'

'Okay, well... call me if you need anything. Even if you just want to talk. I hope everything works out, Dad. And thanks again. I love you.'

I felt myself welling up, and realised that my emotions were closer to the surface than I'd thought. I cleared my throat. 'I love you too. See you soon.'

I cut the connection and looked at the phone in my hand for a moment.

'You okay?' Clover asked.

I cleared my throat again and put the phone in my pocket. 'Someone's paid off my eldest daughter's debt,' I said. 'Fifteen grand.'

She blinked. 'Who?'

'No idea. Benny?'

'Why would Benny do that?'

'I don't know. Maybe it wasn't him.'

We stood there in silence, as if each was waiting for the other to offer an explanation, and then Clover gestured at the tray on the dressing table.

'Come on,' she said. 'Food's getting cold. Tuck in.'

I wasn't sure I had much of an appetite, but as soon as I started eating I realised how hungry I was. Clover had ordered the full works: orange juice, coffee, cereal, bacon and eggs with all the trimmings, toast and marmalade. After throwing up last night, my belly was growling and I went at it ravenously, relishing every mouthful. As I ate, I thought about that scorched-earth policy and how important it was to get sustenance when we could. What if our enemies, whoever they were, were powerful enough to freeze our bank accounts and credit cards so that we couldn't get access to money? Within a few days we'd be reduced to living on the streets with nothing to eat, where we would be easy prey for our pursuers. If that happened I decided we would be better off going to the police and telling them everything. Despite what email man had said, Kate would have a better chance of survival if I was alive and in a position to influence the search for her.

For now, though, I thought it was more to Kate's advantage if I stayed out of the clutches of the law. Of course, I could have been playing this completely the wrong way. I was under no illusions that I was out of my depth, and was operating purely on instinct, reacting to circumstances as they happened. I was still clinging to the hope that email man would get in touch, proposing a magical solution which would leave all parties satisfied and me somehow in the clear.

We had almost finished breakfast when the room was filled with a noise like rippling wind-chimes. I jerked out of my seat, sloshing coffee over my hand, before realising it was Clover's metallic-pink iPhone. She snatched it from the bedside table and looked at it.

'Speak of the devil,' she said, turning the phone around to show me the display screen.

Surrounded by little dancing musical notes, I read the words:

Benny calling...

'Should I answer it?' she asked.

I hesitated, then nodded.

Fixing her eyes on me, Clover put the phone to her ear. 'Benny, hi.'

I heard the scratchy murmur of Benny's voice, but couldn't make out what he was saying. After a few seconds Clover said, 'Yeah, yeah, I'm fine, don't worry.'

I guessed that Benny was asking Clover about the fire because after a few seconds she said guardedly, 'I'm not sure how it started. The police are looking into it.'

When Benny next spoke, Clover raised her eyebrows at me, silently asking me what she should say, how much she should tell him. I held out my hand for the phone and she gave it to me without debate. Benny was still talking, but I cut in on him.

'Benny, it's Alex. Alex Locke.'

There was a moment's silence and then, apparently unruffled, Benny said, 'Alex, what's going on?'

I looked at Clover and said, 'Benny, have you ever heard of the Wolves of London?'

His silence pretty much answered my question. When he next spoke his voice was warier than I'd ever heard it. 'Why do you ask?'

'Because whoever they are, I think they're after me and Clover.'

Another silence, even longer this time. So long, in fact, that eventually I said, 'Benny, are you still there?'

This time he answered immediately. 'I think you both need to come and see me. Tell me where you are and I'll send someone to pick you up.'

SIXTEEN

BAD DEEDS

Two hours later we were sitting in the conservatory attached to the back of Benny's house, drinking coffee so strong it was like a slap to the senses. The caffeine, combined with my lack of sleep, made my limbs tingle and my thoughts quick and feverish. I looked out over Benny's back garden, which was the size of a football stadium and dominated by a lawn like a billiards table. Although it was October, the grass was such a bright emerald green in the autumn sunshine that to my gritty eyes it seemed to vibrate with life. The flower borders must have been a riot of colour in the spring, but at this time of year they were full of little bushes and twiggy things that looked brown and dead. The garden was surrounded on all sides by a double enclosure of tall trees, which were shedding their leaves, and a high wooden fence.

Benny's wife, Lesley, a pretty, soft-spoken woman, perhaps ten years Benny's junior, was out on the lawn, playing with a little yappy dog, throwing a red ball for it over and over.

Whoever it was that said crime doesn't pay clearly didn't know what they were talking about. I knew Benny had been born and raised in Hoxton, but he had obviously done well enough out of his chosen profession to rise above his humble beginnings and leave the horrible council estates of East London far behind. His house, which was maybe not *quite* palatial enough to be called a mansion, was in a genteel, leafy suburb just south of Guildford. It was only a forty-minute train journey to Waterloo, but it seemed a million miles away from the noise and dirt of London.

Within half an hour of speaking to Benny, a dove-grey X-type Jag with tinted windows and a dark-suited chauffeur who looked capable of snapping an average-sized man in two had cruised into the private car park abutting the hotel. I had told Benny that we needed to buy clothes, toiletries and phone chargers, that we didn't have anything with us except what we were standing up in, but Benny had said that he would sort that out for us, that under no circumstances were we to venture on to the streets.

'Are we really in that much trouble?' I asked.

Benny's response had been characteristically non-committal. 'It's best not to take any chances.'

Despite his calmness, his swift response to my mentioning the Wolves of London served only to turn my paranoia up another notch. Every second that Clover and I spent in the open – even leaving the hotel and hurrying across the car park to where the Jag was waiting for us – I half-expected some sort of attack. Where that attack would come from, or what form it would take, I had no idea. In the past twenty-four hours the world had become an unpredictable place, one in which it seemed that literally anything was possible.

I didn't start to relax until we had worked our way out of the snarl of traffic in central London and were accelerating south on the A3. Even then, when Benny's Jag was sliding smoothly through the southbound traffic, eating up the miles, I couldn't shake off the notion I would never feel truly safe again. I glanced at Clover, who was staring anxiously out of the window on the opposite side of the car, and guessed that she felt the same. Sensing that I was looking at her, she turned and a nervous smile flickered on her face.

'You all right?' I asked.

'Yeah,' she said, then surprised me by reaching across the gap between us and gripping my hand tight. For the rest of the journey we sat holding hands like a couple of daft teenagers.

Benny's house, The Redwoods, was at the end of a private road lined with impressive, widely spaced dwellings, all of which had been individually designed and built. It could hardly be seen from the road because of a high brick wall and a tightly packed screen of tall trees beyond it. We only knew we had arrived when the chauffeur stopped in front of a pair of black iron gates, opened the glove compartment and extracted a silver remote no bigger than a credit card. Opening the window, he pointed the remote at the gates and pressed a button. When the gates swung soundlessly open, he replaced the remote in the glove compartment and guided the car up the drive.

The house was on our left, attached to a double garage, whose closed doors were directly in front of us. I expected the doors to open like the gates had done, but the chauffeur halted in front of them and cut the engine. As he stepped out of the car to open Clover's door for her, I got out on my side. I was standing up straight, stretching my back, when Benny appeared at the door of the house, beneath a porch with a red-tiled floor, over which jutted a wooden canopy, painted blue and decorated with hanging baskets.

Wearing a pair of silver-framed bifocals and a blue polo shirt untucked over designer jeans, Benny looked like a businessman relaxing at home on a Sunday morning.

Mildly he said, 'Hello, Alex. You look as though you've been crapped out of a cow's arsehole.'

'Thanks,' I said. 'I'll take that as a compliment, because I feel even worse.'

To my surprise Clover ran past me and straight into Benny's arms. He hugged her like a father greeting a long-lost daughter and then led us inside.

The house was light and spacious, the cream walls and carpet contrasting with the dark wood of a Victorian grandfather clock ticking sonorously to our left and an antique writing desk which faced it across the hallway. The paintings on the walls were bold, hot slashes of autumnal colour – reds and oranges, yellows and browns – and there was a piece of modern sculpture on a plinth by the stairs that looked both shell-like and vaguely sexual, its sensuous curves and crevices like an invitation to probe and caress.

Moving nimbly for a man of his age, Benny led us upstairs to a landing from which the corridor branched right and left. The right-hand corridor was slightly elevated, accessed via a trio of steps set at right angles to the main staircase. Benny skipped up the steps and strode along the corridor, jabbing a finger at the first door on the left. 'Alex, you're in here. Monroe, yours is the fourth door on the right, next to the bathroom.'

He waved away our thanks and told us that Lesley had been down to 'the village' to buy us what we needed, all of which we would find in our rooms. Then he said he would stick some coffee on and see us downstairs in fifteen minutes. His words brooked no argument – not that I was tempted to offer one. Wary as I was of his motives, my over-riding emotion was gratitude that he was willing to help us. It's possible that, left to our own devices, Clover and I might eventually have rallied and formulated a plan, but without Benny's intervention we would, for a time, have been like boxers on the ropes, reeling from a barrage of blows and able to do little more than react to what was being thrown at us.

The room he had pointed out to me had an oatmeal-coloured carpet and a double bed with a blue and orange duvet. In place of the right-hand wall was a long fitted wardrobe unit with mirrored doors, whereas the upper two-thirds of the wall opposite the foot of the bed was an expanse of leaded windows overlooking the back garden and the fields beyond. On the bed, still in their bags and with the labels attached, were two pairs of jeans – one blue, one black – a couple of long-sleeved tops, a grey, zip-up hoodie, a three-pack of boxer shorts and a six-pack of new socks. It was nothing fancy, but it was decent, practical gear with no designer logos or flashes of colour to distinguish it. Making a mental note to find out how much Lesley had spent and pay either her or Benny back later, I changed out of my smelly clothes into a light grey top, the blue jeans and the hoodie.

After transferring the heart from my black jacket into the hoodie's side pocket, and setting my phone to charge using the new charger, I picked up a small plastic bag of toiletries bearing a Boots logo, which had been sitting next to the clothes, and wandered up the landing until I found a bathroom. I ripped my new toothbrush out of its wrapper and cleaned my teeth, and then squirted some body spray under my armpits. Feeling not exactly refreshed, but at least less like a refugee, I went downstairs.

Ten minutes later, at Benny's request, Clover – who had changed into a black sweatshirt and jeans – and I were recounting our experiences. I started by describing how, the previous morning, I had gradually come to realise that my daughter had been abducted, and then Clover took over, telling Benny about the anonymous email she had received. Still half-suspecting that Benny had either sent the email himself or was otherwise involved in Kate's disappearance, I studied him closely as Clover handed over her phone so that he could read the message. However, if Benny *was* involved, the expression on his face gave nothing away. He handed the phone back, then listened to the rest of our story silently, his mouth set in a grim line, his pale eyes fixed unblinkingly on whichever of us was talking.

It was when I came to the part about how McCallum had died that things became a little awkward. As I described how the black figure had come screeching at me from across the room, Clover butted in, flashing me a look which I interpreted immediately. Benny was a tough, straightforward man, with a set view of the world and it wasn't, therefore, difficult to picture him not only dismissing our wild tales, but accusing us of wasting his time and taking advantage of his hospitality. We had enough enemies as it was, and if Benny wasn't one already, then he wouldn't be a good name to add to the list. For that reason, when Clover said, 'Alex didn't mean to hit the old man as hard as he did – did you, Alex?' I shook my head, trying to look ashamed.

'No,' I said. 'I swear, Benny, I only tapped him, but he went down like a ton of bricks.'

Benny nodded gravely. 'He was old. His skull must have been as thin as an egg shell. Don't blame yourself.'

We glossed over the attack on the Incognito, told Benny we'd heard screams and crashes and had guessed that the place was under attack and that the attackers had come for the heart. We said that when we had peeked round the door we'd seen people lying dead and a man standing on the stage with some kind of weapon in his hand.

'We felt bad, but there was nothing we could do,' Clover said. 'So we shut and locked the door, then got out of there as fast as we could.'

'You did the right thing,' Benny assured her. 'Playing the hero's all very noble, but at the end of the day you wouldn't have been any less dead.'

Apart from my dream about Lyn, which I didn't mention, the rest of the story was straightforward enough. When I had finished telling it, Clover asked, 'So who are they, Benny, these Wolves of London?'

Benny sighed and took a sip of coffee, his eyes swivelling to regard his wife playing happily with the dog outside. I was on tenterhooks as I watched him. I could have murdered a cig, but I had had neither the time nor the opportunity to light up since my disastrous encounter with McCallum.

At last Benny said, 'They're a superstition, an underworld rumour, a story told by villains. They're supposed to be... how shall I put this? A dark force. Unstoppable. Something to strike fear into the hearts of fearless men.'

I exchanged a look with Clover. 'A dark force? You mean they're... supernatural? Is that what you're telling us?'

Benny gave a soft snort of laughter. 'What I'm telling you is that they're a *story*. I'm not for one minute suggesting the story is true.'

'So you don't believe in them?' I said.

'I believe that whoever is invoking their name means serious business.'

'But where do these stories come from?' Clover asked. 'They must have *some* basis in fact.'

Benny shrugged. 'Maybe. But what *you've* got to worry about is that a lot of bad deeds have been committed in their name.'

'Bad deeds?' I said.

'More than bad.' Benny's voice was quiet, lacking in drama. 'Unspeakable. Deeds that can turn the stomachs of even the hardest men.'

Clover's lips had tightened. 'Like what?'

'Things it's probably best not to hear about.'

Clover abruptly slapped the arm of her chair. 'Come on, Benny. You can't not tell us. If these Wolves of London – or whoever is using the name – are after us, we need to know what they're capable of.'

A leaf the colour of fire swirled from a nearby tree and bumped against the window. More leaves were already darkening the conservatory roof, pressing against the glass like tiny yellow and brown hands.

Benny sighed. 'Murders,' he said. 'But not *just* murders. Torture. Mutilation. Things you wouldn't believe. Things which no one was ever arrested for. Which the suspects all had cast-iron alibis for.'

'So these Wolves are what?' I asked. 'A vigilante force? Mercenaries?'

Benny shrugged. 'Maybe. But the things they do...'

'Go on,' I muttered.

Once again he glanced out of the window at his wife, and for the first time, as the sun caught his face and shone in his pale eyes, I got the sense – whether real or imagined – that whatever terrible things he had done in the past, it was now all over, that he had lost the taste for it. He might still be head of the pride, but I suspected (or perhaps simply hoped) that the loyalty and respect he commanded these days was based on former glories, not present deeds.

'There was one bloke I knew,' he said quietly. 'Back in the late eighties, early nineties. He had a couple of kids, a boy and a girl. The boy was six or seven, the girl a couple of years younger. One night, while they were asleep, someone came in through their bedroom window, anaesthetised them and cut out their eyes. From what I heard it was a neat job, like a surgical operation. Whoever did it even cauterised the wounds so they wouldn't bleed to death.'

His voice betrayed no emotion, but I felt a chill of dread and revulsion run through me. Clover was gaping at Benny in shock.

'Is that true?'

He nodded. 'Oh yeah.'

'But why would someone do something like that? It's... *horrible!*'

'It was a warning,' Benny said, 'or maybe a punishment for something the father had done. Lots of people got hurt because of it. But the bloke never did find out who it was.'

'So how do you know it was to do with the Wolves of London?' I asked.

'That was the rumour. That the Wolves of London had done it. That was what everyone said.'

'So is it just the case that they get blamed for every unsolved underworld crime? Villain against villain? Is that what you're saying?'

Benny frowned. His voice was clipped. 'No. Because it isn't as simple as that. It's the *type* of crime. What's done and where it's done. Some of the things the Wolves have done, or are *supposed* to have done, are... how shall I put this? Hard to believe. Impossible even.'

'In what way?' asked Clover.

Benny looked thoughtful, perhaps sifting through which stories to relate, or even deciding how much he should reveal of the world in which he operated. Finally he said, 'There was this one bloke, Ray or Roy something. He wasn't much – a drug dealer, driver, odd-job man, fence, small time stuff, you know? Anyway, he cut in on someone's business, and the next thing anyone knew, he'd disappeared. He was found three days later in a field in Kent.'

Benny paused, his cold gaze sweeping across us. Then he went on, his voice quieter, heavier.

'His body was smashed to pieces. Literally. Scattered across the ground. The story was that he looked as if he'd been dropped from a plane.'

'Maybe he had,' I said.

'The police investigation could find no evidence that a plane had flown over that area. That doesn't mean that there hadn't been one, just that they could find no evidence of it. But a contact of mine on the force told me the body had weird marks all over it.'

'What kind of marks?' asked Clover.

'He said they were like claw-marks. Like some big fucking bird had flown away with him, and then dropped him.'

'And what do you think?' I asked carefully.

A ghost of a smile crossed Benny's face. 'I haven't a clue. But there are other stories too, of people being torn to pieces in their homes. Not chopped up, but literally *torn* to pieces.'

My guts turned over. I hadn't given Benny the details of what I had found in the hotel bathroom, had said only that the men had been dead and that they hadn't died easily. I glanced at Clover, wondering whether I should tell Benny the full story, but she gave the tiniest shake of her head.

If Benny noticed he didn't let on. He drained the last of his coffee. 'Look, I don't want to scare you half to death with horror stories. The chances are, whoever wants that heart of yours is just trying to put the shits up you.'

At the mention of the heart, my hand crept to the lump in my hoodie pocket. When Candice was little she had had a pet rat called George, which used to fall asleep on her belly while she was reading or watching TV. As I touched the heart I was reminded of George. I even kidded myself that the stone felt warm beneath my palm.

'I don't suppose you've heard anything, Benny?' Clover asked. 'Why people are after the heart, I mean?'

Benny shook his head. 'Not a thing. But I'll put a few feelers out, make some discreet enquiries.'

'Thanks,' Clover said. 'It would be good to know exactly what we're up against.'

Benny gave a curt nod and turned his attention to me. 'Mind if I have a look?'

As ever, his scrutiny made me feel as though he'd caught me out in some way. 'What?'

'At the heart. I'd like to see what all the fuss is about.'

He held out his hand, like a school bully demanding money. Oddly reluctant to comply with his request, I licked my lips. I glanced at Clover, and she raised her eyebrows, as if to say, *What are you waiting for?* So I forced a smile and handed it over.

Benny examined the heart closely, turning it in his hand, feeling its weight, his surprisingly slim and dextrous fingers probing at it. I felt like the curator of a museum nervously watching a visitor handling a precious artefact. Weirdly, despite what it had done to McCallum, it wasn't Benny's welfare I was worried about, but the heart itself. I knew how tough it was, and yet I had to fight an urge to tell him to be careful.

'Nice piece of work,' he said, but he didn't appear overly impressed. When he offered the heart back to me I had to make a conscious effort not to snatch it out of his hand.

Outside on the lawn, Lesley or the dog had finally grown tired of the game. Lesley turned and trooped off to our right, towards the back door that led directly into the kitchen, the dog leaping at her heels. She glanced up once, her face flushed with cold, and waved at us. I saw Benny's icy countenance melt into a sudden and surprisingly tender smile. Opposite him, Clover drew up her legs, tucking her feet beneath her, and slumped back in her chair with a heart-felt sigh.

'It's so peaceful here,' she said, looking out at the back garden. 'I could just curl up and go to sleep.'

'Well, why don't you?' Benny said.

'Because we need to be... doing something. Looking for Alex's daughter.'

Benny leaned forward, elbows on knees. 'Oh yeah, and how would you go about that then? Where would you go?'

Clover hesitated. 'Well... I don't know. We'll think of something.'

'Is that right?' His voice was quiet and without inflection, and yet it was pitched in such a way that it exposed the flimsiness of our situation, the sheer folly of our intentions.

'What would you suggest, Benny?' I asked.

He gave a brief upward flick of the eyebrows, as if the answer was so obvious I hardly need to have asked. 'You'll stay here till this thing's sorted out.'

'We can't,' said Clover.

'You can and you will.'

'What if the Wolves of London come looking for us?' I said. 'We don't want to put you and Lesley in danger.'

Benny looked not at me, but at Clover. 'I promised your dad I'd look after you,' he said, 'and I never break my promises.'

I looked across at Clover too, realising there was still so much I didn't know about her. We'd barely had a chance to get to know each other in the normal way. 'Your dad?' I enquired.

She rolled her eyes. 'Long story.' And then she changed the subject quickly enough to make me determined to return to the topic at a more opportune time. 'Benny's right, Alex. Our best bet is to lie low here for now. There's nothing the two of us can do on our own. At least Benny can use his contacts to try to find out what's going on.'

The idea of sitting around while Kate was out there somewhere was excruciating, but I knew Clover was right. Reluctantly I said, 'Okay. But if you can find out anything that might lead us to Kate, Benny...'

Benny was already rising to his feet. 'I'll make some calls right now. Relax, Alex. Put your feet up. Make yourself at home.'

He stalked out of the room. We heard his footsteps cross the hallway and then the creak of the stairs as he ascended them.

Neither of us said anything until he was out of earshot and then I released a rattling sigh.

'Relax, he says.'

SEVENTEEN

MUSTARD GAS

Something woke me, though I had no idea what. All I knew was that one second I was in a sleep so black and dreamless it was like death, and the next I was lying on my back with my eyes wide open and my heart pounding so hard it was throbbing in my ears.

My limbs were tense too. No, not just tense – rigid. My fingers were claws digging into the mattress and I could feel the ache of stretched tendons in my shoulders and down the backs of my legs.

It was dark. Quiet. Not exactly silent – a wind had got up in the night and I could hear it rushing through the trees, causing branches and dry leaves to scrape together – but hushed enough to tell me it was the dead of night, and that if a sound *had* penetrated my subconscious enough to stab me awake it had subsided again now.

Perhaps I'd been woken by a sound that had already been and gone? The cry of an owl? The screech of a fox in the darkness? Maybe even the creak of a footstep on the landing from someone who'd got up to use the loo, or a door closing as they went back to bed?

Or maybe it hadn't been a sound at all. Maybe it had been a bad dream, instantly forgotten, or even the after-effects of a good dinner and several glasses of red wine. I couldn't deny that my belly was uncomfortably full and my mouth tacky with dehydration. I also needed a piss, but for the time being I lay where I was and listened to the world around me, acclimatising myself.

It had been a restless day. I had spent it feeling exactly the same as I had after Kate had disappeared – that I should be out there doing something, making things happen. But there was no denying that Clover and I were currently at a dead end. Until email man got back in touch with us, or Benny's contacts unearthed information that might lead me to my lost daughter, there was little we could do but wait.

To be honest, I still wasn't sure that I could trust Benny – or even Clover for that matter. I had been watching him carefully that day, looking for indications that he knew more than he was letting on, but if he did he hid it well. At dinner I had even asked him outright whether he had been the one who had paid off Candice's boyfriend's debts, but he had scoffed at the idea. But if it hadn't been Benny, then who? And more to the point, why? I didn't know anybody who had that much disposable income – or at least nobody who would pay out that kind of money with little chance of a return.

Of course, I was glad that Candice was out of imminent danger, but mulling over the possible identity of her mysterious benefactor still made me uncomfortable. In the last few days I had come into contact with a lot of dangerous people, and I was all too aware how rare it was to get something for nothing. Even if it wasn't immediately obvious, there was nearly always a price to pay.

I knew that lying in the dark worrying about it wasn't going to solve anything, though. The thoughts buzzing in my head were only serving to make me increasingly agitated. For that reason I decided that I needed to *do* something, even if it was only switching on the light and going downstairs for a smoke and a cup of tea. With a groan I turned slowly on to my left-hand side and stretched out a hand towards the lamp on the bedside table.

And froze.

Although the room had taken on a basic shape around me in the few minutes since I'd opened my eyes, it was still too dark to make out details. The chair in the corner on which I'd dumped my clothes was a squatting lump of blackness, and the curtains over the leaded windows on the opposite wall were a dim, ripply expanse of greyness, like corrugated iron. The lamp on the bedside cabinet was a thin spear of black with a spherical blob on top. But under the lamp was...

...what?

I knew what it was *supposed* to be. I knew what it had been when I had put it there a few hours before. It had been the heart. I had taken it out of the pocket of my hoodie and placed it on the bedside table under the lamp. Don't ask me why. I had had a lot of wine, followed by a couple of whiskies, and my thoughts hadn't been too clear. I guess I had just wanted it close to me, so that I could... I don't know... protect it?

But the thing was, it didn't look like the heart now. Whatever was sitting in its place looked two, maybe three times bigger.

And it was *moving*.

As I say, it was dark, and my head was pounding, and I was still a little disorientated, but even so, I could have sworn that the heart – if that was what it was – had swollen, expanded, and grown what looked like tentacles. The tentacles were rippling, curling upwards, slowly and sinuously, like the fronds of some undersea plant. And the main body of the heart seemed to be rising and falling, as if performing the function of a real heart, as if blood was pumping through it, in and out. Although there was no sound, for those few seconds I had the feeling that on the bedside table next to me was some creature the size of my head, something like an octopus or a fat black spider, or a mixture of the two.

Half-expecting the tentacles to respond and wrap tightly around my wrist, I jerked my hand towards the lamp and switched it on. The instant light flooded the room it was as if the real world had snapped back into place and everything was normal again. The heart, dwarfed by the lamp, was nothing more than a carved lump of shiny, black obsidian. I touched it, closed my hand over it, felt its coldness, its solidity. I picked it up and put it down again gently. It made a satisfying clunk, one hard surface against another.

I breathed out slowly, then sat up. With the light on, the room seemed smaller, less fluid. I had never been scared of the dark, and I wouldn't say I was exactly scared now. It was just that, with what had happened these past couple of days, the dark suddenly made the world seem less trustworthy, and not only because things could hide in it. It was as if the dark had properties of its own, as if it could stretch matter, expand boundaries, create doorways. I shook my head to rid myself of ideas that didn't seem quite my own, and threw back the duvet.

Checking my mobile I saw that it was 4.25 a.m. Shivering at the pre-dawn chill, I crossed to the chair and pulled on the clothes I'd peeled off earlier before collapsing into bed. I hesitated a moment, wondering whether I needed my socks and boots, and then put them on anyway. The events of the past few days had triggered the long-dormant sense of self-preservation I'd nurtured during my years in prison. To survive inside, even with the promise of Benny's protection, I had needed to be ever watchful, ever alert, ever prepared for fight or flight.

The bedroom door creaked when I opened it, and the floorboards under the landing carpet groaned beneath my feet. Tiny sounds, but they seemed as loud as gunshots in the sleeping house, even with the wind rattling outside. I left my bedroom door ajar, so that a glow of light spilled from it, but it only stretched halfway down the stairs before petering out. I crept across to the toilet for a piss, and then hesitated, wondering whether to flush and risk waking everyone up. In the end I left it, simply lowering the toilet seat as if that was some sort of compromise. At the top of the stairs I stood for a moment, peering down into the hallway below, even screwing up my eyes as if that could make me see better.

There were no street lights lining the private road outside, which meant that there wasn't even a faint glow leaking in through the half-moon of stained-glass panels in the front door. As a result the blackness looked thick as tar, and as if it stretched for ever. My only point of reference was the heavy ticking of the grandfather clock somewhere down to my right. It wasn't much, but it was better than nothing.

As I descended the stairs and the blackness rose to meet me, I felt my hand creeping to the hard bulge of the heart in the pocket of my hoodie. I'd snatched up the heart before leaving the bedroom; it had already become second nature to either carry it around with me or have it within reach. It wouldn't be over-stating it to say that I now thought of it as my lifeline to Kate, a sort of talisman. Deep down I might even have developed the idea that it was linked to Kate's own heart, and that as long as it was in my possession and under my protection, my daughter's would keep on beating.

I reached the bottom step and peered once again into the blackness, telling myself that it was only the lack of visual reference that made it seem to swirl like fog. Using the ticking of the clock as a guide, I turned left and walked straight ahead, knowing that the front door – or more specifically the old-fashioned brass light switch beside it – would be about five metres in front of me.

As I took small, shuffling steps I thought of a book that Kate had loved – that she *still* loved: Maurice Sendak's *Where the Wild Things Are*. In the story the bedroom of a boy called Max slowly transforms into a moonlit forest. Blinded by darkness, I imagined my own surroundings undergoing a similar transformation. I pictured myself stretching out a hand to feel tree bark and hanging vines, or even something worse. What if I touched hair? A face? A mouthful of long, jagged teeth?

I had taken a dozen, maybe fifteen steps when my outstretched hand *did* bump against something: a hard surface, which jarred my fingers. I paused a moment, and then felt my way across a chunky Yale lock and the ridges of a door frame. At last I located the light switch I'd been looking for and clicked it down. Turning from the door, I squinted into the light.

And was confronted by a small, childlike figure standing at the bottom of the stairs.

I jumped out of my skin – and then realised it was Clover. She looked sleepy, her maroon hair hanging in tousled curtains around her face, half-obscuring her features. In her long nightshirt, and with nothing on her feet, she looked like something out of a Japanese horror film. She gave a huge yawn and stood blinking at me as I clapped a hand to my chest.

'Don't do that!' I hissed. 'You nearly gave me a heart attack.'

'Sorry,' she said through the end of her yawn. She widened her eyes, trying to wake herself up. 'What are you doing?'

'My mouth was dry. I was about to make a cuppa. Do you want one?'

'I'll have a hot chocolate if there is any. What time is it?'

I flipped a thumb at the grandfather clock. 'Half-four. Sorry if I woke you up.'

'S'okay.' She pushed hair out of her face. 'I was having bad dreams. Or think I was. Can't remember.'

'Why didn't you say something to let me know you were there?'

'Didn't want to wake up Benny and Lesley.'

'Come on,' I said, 'let's go and stick the kettle on.'

I went ahead, and she padded slowly after me. She sat at the kitchen table while I busied myself looking through cupboards and drawers for mugs, spoons, teabags and hot chocolate. When I'd made the drinks we carried them through to the conservatory, where we could chat without fear of waking up our hosts. Despite her thin nightshirt and bare feet Clover didn't seem to feel the cold. She switched on a table lamp with a tasselled shade that gave off a cosy red glow, and sat in the wooden-framed armchair she'd occupied for most of that afternoon, tucking her feet underneath her and tugging her nightshirt down over her bare legs.

I wondered whether, in other circumstances, I might have found her attractive, whether there might have been a spark of romance between us. She was certainly a beautiful girl, and I was only seven or eight years older than she was, but my mind was too full of anxiety for Kate, and fear for myself, and a dislocating sense of confusion at what we'd seen and experienced over the past few days, to have time for anything else.

Sipping my drink, I wandered over to the glass-panelled wall of the conservatory and tried to make out what I could of the back garden. In the daylight the view across the lawn with the trees flanking it on all sides was restful, but right now I felt like a goldfish in a bowl, vulnerable and exposed. It was so black that all I could see was the reflection of my own red-hued face in the glass and the dim ghostly image of the room behind me. I knew Benny had motion sensor lights out there, attached to the back of the house, which blazed white if anything bigger than a hedgehog moved so much as a muscle, but that didn't help me shake off the fear that there might be unseen eyes in the darkness, staring back at us.

'You're like a caged lion,' Clover said behind me.

I glanced at her reflection in the glass. Her white skin and nightshirt glowed with soft red light.

'I'm just drinking my tea,' I said.

'All the same, you've got that look in your eyes. I keep expecting you to drop to all fours and start prowling in front of the window.'

I sighed. 'Sorry. I'm just feeling a bit stir crazy. My little girl is out there somewhere, in the clutches of God knows who, and I'm... sitting around having dinner and drinking wine.' I raised a hand. 'And before you say it, yes, I know we don't have much alternative, and I know that Benny has got people out there asking questions and gathering information. But even if we do get answers, what are we going to do? Formulate a plan? Go on the attack?'

'That depends on what the answers are,' she said.

I snorted, feeling helpless and frustrated, my stomach knotted up. I rested my hot, throbbing forehead against the window. The glass was so cold it seemed to exacerbate the pain rather than relieve it.

'Don't lose hope,' Clover said softly. 'We'll find her, Alex.'

'Will we?'

'Course we will.'

I turned to her. My stomach was churning. 'I'm going to level with you.'

She gave a mock grimace. 'That sounds ominous.'

I glanced towards the door of the conservatory, and instinctively lowered my voice. 'I know Benny's helped us, but I still don't know whether I trust him. And to be honest...' I hesitated. '...I'm not entirely sure whether I can trust you either.'

I looked into her eyes, wondering how she would react. I half-expected her to be upset or disappointed, but in fact she looked stoic, sympathetic even.

She was silent for a moment, and then with a sigh she said, 'I can understand that. After all, it was me and Benny who dragged you into this in the first place.'

I shook my head. 'No, I got myself into it. But there's no denying that you were there, conveniently placed, to nudge things along. And it was only when you and Benny got involved in my life that everything started to go haywire.'

She gave a little tilt of the head to acknowledge the fact. 'I can see how it looks that way to you. Believe me, I can. And it probably won't make any difference if I were to tell you that I'm one hundred per cent on your side. But I'm going to say it anyway, just for the record.' She gave an ironic smile. 'I'm one hundred per cent on your side, Alex.'

'Well, that's nice to know. But it doesn't stop you from keeping secrets from me.'

'Secrets?' she said innocently.

'Earlier today, when I asked how you knew Benny, how he knew your father, you changed the subject. So who *is* your father, Clover? Some big gangland boss?'

She smiled. 'Hardly. He was a vicar.'

'A vicar?'

'I grew up in a village in Kent. My dad was the vicar there. But when

I was five or six he was transferred to a new parish in London. Benny's mum used to come to his church, and my dad was at her bedside when she died. Because of that my dad and Benny struck up quite a friendship. Then, when I was sixteen, my mum died, and a couple of years later my dad did too. I'd just started a business degree when my dad had his heart attack, and Benny took me under his wing, helping me out with a solicitor to deal with everything, and sorting me out with a flat. After I finished my degree I worked for Barnaby McCallum for a while, and then when Benny's friend George Lancaster decided to sell Incognito, Benny helped me buy it. He thought it would be a nice little starter business for me.'

'And has it been?'

'I was doing all right – until all this stuff with McCallum and the heart. I wish I'd never got involved now.'

'Crime doesn't pay,' I remarked drily.

Clover wafted a hand to indicate her surroundings. 'Benny doesn't seem to have done too badly out of it.'

I was about to respond when suddenly she stiffened and her gaze shifted. 'Alex,' she said apprehensively, fear blooming on her face. I realised she was looking not at me, but at something beyond and above me. At something outside.

I felt the hairs stiffen on the back of my neck. 'What is it?'

'I don't know,' she said, her voice hollow. 'Look.'

I stepped away from the window, not liking the fact that I was pressed up against the glass, and turned to look. At first I saw nothing but darkness and wondered what had frightened Clover. Then I realised that the darkness wasn't darkness at all – it was something more solid. Something that was moving.

It was like oil or smoke in the shape of a thousand writhing snakes. But snakes that were so densely packed that they formed a constantly coiling mass. The mass was pressing itself against the outside of the conservatory, spreading across the glass panels and up on to the roof, as if looking for a way in. Although it didn't seem solid enough to move the dry leaves that had blown on to the roof, it seemed somehow to absorb them, or maybe draw them into itself, like a whale swimming through the sea with its mouth open, hoovering up plankton.

'What is it?' Clover asked, her voice quiet but strained.

'I don't know.' I sniffed. 'Can you smell something?'

'Like what?'

'Garlic or...' I'd been about to say 'mustard' when I suddenly remembered a documentary I'd seen about the aftercare (or lack of it) of the thousands of men who had been badly injured during the First World War. I recalled how one centenarian, who resembled a mummified corpse hunched in a wheelchair, had described a particular smell.

'Oh shit,' I breathed.

Clover's eyes flickered towards me. 'What is it?'

'That smell. I think it's mustard gas.'

'Mustard gas. What's that?'

'It's highly toxic. It causes chemical burns on the skin. In extreme cases it can lead to blindness and internal bleeding. We need to get out of here. Go upstairs and get dressed and wake Benny and Lesley.'

'What about you?'

'I'm good to go.' When she still didn't move I barked, 'Go on, Clover, *now!*'

She jumped to her feet as though given an electric shock. Keeping her eyes fixed on the black mass, which was still slithering over the conservatory, she darted out of the room. I pulled the collar of my hoodie up over my mouth and nose as I heard her running upstairs. I knew I ought to get out of there too, but I was reluctant to let whatever was crawling over the house out of my sight. Above me the glass ceiling creaked, as if the darkness had a weight to it. I backed hurriedly to the doorway, remembering something else I'd heard or read somewhere: that the safest place to stand during an earthquake was directly beneath a door frame.

The ceiling creaked again – and then with a sharp crack a line appeared down the centre of one of the glass panes. Although the pane held, it could only be a matter of time before the glass gave way under the pressure. And when that happened the thing, whatever it was, would bulge or ooze into the house, bringing with it more of that lethal mustard gas.

The blackness enveloping the conservatory was like a leather-gloved hand curling around a glass paperweight. I half-turned my head to yell up to Clover, but then something happened out in the darkness that dried the words in my throat.

Directly opposite me an insipid light suddenly appeared in the seething blackness, the darkness around it appearing to shrink back like the centre of a sheet of cellophane exposed to a naked flame. Within the light stood a figure. At first it appeared small and distant, and I had trouble making it out. But as it got closer, strolling casually towards the house, it became more distinct, until I could see that it was a young man, perhaps twenty years old, with a pale, thin face and dark hair that was slicked down and gleaming with oil.

Accompanying the man, growing louder as he approached the house, was a sound. Faint and distorted, like a far-off radio signal carried on the wind, it was nevertheless distressing enough to cause my stomach to tighten and my balls to shrivel up into my belly. I had never been involved in a war, and yet I identified the sound immediately as the clamour of a terrible battle. I could hear explosions and gunshots; cries of fear and mortal agony; grown men reduced to terrified children, screaming for mercy, or for their mothers, or simply begging desperately for their lives.

If I hadn't been holding the collar of my hoodie over my nose and mouth I might have clapped my hands to my ears. Instead I tried to block the awful sounds from my mind as best I could, and to focus instead on the man walking through the darkness towards me. He didn't look particularly threatening; in fact, he wore an expression that I can only describe as haunted. His eyes, set in hollows so deep that from a distance they looked like the pits of a skull, were intense – the eyes of a man who has seen too much at far too young an age. His complexion was sallow, his lips almost bloodless, and as he walked he puffed greedily on a roll-up no thicker than a lollipop stick, which he brought to his mouth every few seconds, his arm going up and down like a metronome.

Perhaps even odder than the man himself were his clothes. He looked as though he had stepped out of a World War One period drama. His double-breasted demob suit was a couple of sizes too big, his white shirt was wrinkled and grubby and the knot of his tie was askew. The only smart things about him were his black brogues, which had been polished until they gleamed. He cut rather a sad figure – and yet there was something intrinsically, chillingly *wrong* about him. It wasn't the darkness, or the smell of mustard gas, or even the sounds of battle that he carried with him. No, it was more that the misery, fear and desperation that clung to him seemed so powerful, so profound, that I got the impression it could suck the very life out of you.

I watched, my skin creeping, as he walked up to the glass. When he reached it, he simply stood there, looking in, smoking his little cigarette, his face expressionless. From upstairs, above the muted cacophony of battle, I could hear the thud of movement and raised voices, but it seemed like it was coming from another world, another time.

I knew it was a bad idea, a *terrible* idea, but I felt myself taking a couple of steps back into the room. Above me the glass ceiling creaked again, as if the darkness sensed my proximity. But I felt, for Kate's sake, that I had to take a closer look at this man, perhaps even make an effort to communicate with him.

'Who are you?' I asked, my voice as fragile as the glass above my head.

I was almost shocked when the man's eyes swivelled to regard me. He seemed so other-worldly that I'd assumed he would be unaware of my presence, or at least would consider me unworthy of his attention. Yet although his dark eyes met mine, the expression on his face didn't alter. He looked as though he had seen so much that nothing would surprise him, or scare him, or shock him, or make him happy, ever again.

Instead of answering my question, he slowly raised his right hand. It wasn't a gesture of greeting, and neither was he reaching out in supplication. His palm was facing inward, as though he was about to cover his face, or perhaps even peel it off like something from a horror movie. For a moment he simply stood in silence, the two of us staring at each other – and then his fingernails started turning black.

It happened slowly, beginning with the half-moon cuticles. First they went a smoky grey, then they darkened as the colour began to creep upwards. I watched, fascinated, as the blackness filled the fingernails completely, right to their tips. It was like watching five tiny containers filling with dark liquid.

As the darkness reached the tips of the man's fingernails it began to seep into the air, curling and twisting like treacly black smoke. The man's lips parted and more of the blackness crept out of his mouth. It drifted lazily in all directions, a few wispy tendrils rising to explore and partly smother his face.

Another pane of glass above my head cracked – which was enough to break the spell. My head jerked up, and I backpedalled rapidly to the door leading into the house – just as several panes burst in unison. As glittering shards of glass hit the floor with a jagged tinkle and exploded into splinters, I turned and ran back into the house, slamming the conservatory door behind me.

Running through the kitchen and along the corridor to the front of the house, I heard more glass breaking in my wake. I reached the hallway just as Clover, Benny and Lesley were coming downstairs. Benny looked grim, Lesley as frightened as the little dog that was shivering in her arms, and Clover, now dressed, looked hassled. I guessed she had had a hard time persuading them of the danger they were in. Benny glared at me as more glass shattered at the back of the house.

'What the fuck's going on?'

'We're under attack,' I said.

'Under attack?' He looked outraged. 'Who the fuck by?'

'It's more of a what than a who.'

His jaw tightened, his eyes narrowing into razor slits, and all at once I found it easy to believe the stories I'd heard about him.

'What are you talking about? Speak fucking English.'

I held up my hands as if to hold back his anger. 'There's something out there. A kind of...' I struggled to put it into words. '...a kind of living darkness.'

'A *what?*'

'It's true, Benny,' said Clover quickly. 'I've seen it. It's like an oil slick.'

'There's a man too,' I said, looking at Benny but aware of Clover's eyes widening in fear. I glanced at her. 'Not the one we saw at Incognito. Someone else.'

Benny stepped towards me, lithe as a dancer, dipping a hand into the pocket of the blue suit he was wearing. When the hand reappeared there was a gun in it, a pit bull of a weapon, compact and powerful.

'What are you doing?' I said. 'You can't go in there, Benny.'

He halted abruptly, stared at me, as if I was something new and strange. He was perfectly still, but it was a stillness brimming with menace.

'Who says I can't?' he asked quietly, almost reasonably.

'You don't know what you're up against,' I said.

A thin smile appeared on Benny's face. It was the coldest expression

I had ever seen. 'Neither does he, whoever he fucking is. Now get out of the way, Alex, or I'll put a fucking bullet through you.'

I could see he meant it. I raised my hands and stepped aside. Benny slipped past me, pushing open the door into the corridor that led to the conservatory. I looked at Clover. Should I go after him or wait here? Or should the three of us flee the house while we had the chance? For twenty seconds we stood in silence, bracing ourselves for shouts or screams or gunshots.

Finally I said, 'What do—' and then I spun round as I sensed movement behind me.

It was Benny. He was still holding the gun.

'The place is a wreck,' he said. 'But there's no one there.'

'What about the darkness?' I asked.

He gave me a long, silent look, then strode purposefully across the hall towards the front door.

'Be careful,' I said, but he ignored me. Without hesitation, he opened the front door and stepped outside. He stood in the porch, staring out into the darkness, gun held in front of him. The night framed his sinewy physique. It was deathly quiet and almost preternaturally still out there. The wind from earlier had died down.

'Where's—' Clover whispered, and then all hell broke loose. The darkness suddenly erupted towards us, black tendrils flying out of the night. Before Benny could react they swarmed over him and invaded the house. Like thousands of snakes released from a box, they spread in all directions, coiling around the door frame, slithering across the walls, stretching along the ceiling. They moved with incredible speed, obliterating the light as they came. They swept over us like a huge shadow blotting out the sun.

There was no substance to the darkness, so there was nothing to touch, nothing to grab hold of or fight. All the same I felt it engulfing me, crushing all that was good and hopeful and optimistic. I felt as if I was being torn from my body, as if my soul, my essence, had been swept away into a cold, endless void, a suffocating world of shadow. It wasn't like death, but like the *fear* of death, because at least with death would have come the bliss of oblivion.

I have no idea how long the experience lasted. Physically it may only have been seconds, but mentally it felt as if time was no longer relevant, as if a micro-second and a billion years were one and the same. I know that sounds hard to grasp, but that was how it was. Sometimes experiences go beyond words; sometimes words are too restrictive to convey the true depth and scope of what we think and feel.

For what seemed an age I was adrift in a limbo of fear, hopelessness and desperation. I thought I'd never get out, that I was trapped for ever, but what pulled me back into the real world was excruciating physical pain. It ripped through me like a hot blade; it was more agonising than anything I'd ever experienced. And yet there was a part of me that welcomed it, that latched on to it and clung to it for all it was worth, purely because it was physical, because it was mine, and because it reminded me that I was alive.

It was the pain which brought my body and soul back together. I snapped into awareness, as though waking from a trance, to find myself still on my feet and scrabbling at my chest. I thought for a second I was having a heart attack, and yet at the same time I felt as though the blazing white shell of agony which encased me was protecting me even as it was making me suffer – or rather, that it was protecting me *because* it was making me suffer. I felt my senses sizzling back into life as my hand clawed at my chest. And then it hit me where the pain was coming from, and my hand dipped into the pocket of my hoodie and closed around the heart.

Immediately I knew that it was this which had found me and yanked me out of the darkness. I knew it as surely as if a pulse of information had passed through the cold stone and into my brain. I took the heart out of my pocket, and suddenly it was as if some connection had been made, and the heart was part of me, or *I* was part of *it*. The pain faded, and as it did so I became aware that I was thinking differently, that all at once I knew what the heart was and how it worked. It didn't seem strange to be thinking this way, it didn't seem as though my mind was being manipulated or influenced; on the contrary, it seemed logical and natural. I held the heart in my palm and watched it change, and *as* it changed I got the impression that *I* was changing *it* as much as *it* was changing *itself*.

It wasn't merely the consistency of the stone which changed, becoming soft like putty; it was the nature of the thing itself. It transformed from a cold, hard inanimate object into something organic, alive. It spread out across my hand and extended into what I can only describe as some sort of tail or limb, which coiled around my wrist and slithered up my arm to the elbow. I felt tiny spines or suckers connecting with the pores in my skin, locking themselves into place. It should have been an alarming sensation, but it wasn't. Instead I felt complete, and also partly as though I was doing this to myself. It was as though my body and the heart were different components of the same machine, which needed to mesh together in order to work properly.

When the process was complete it was as though I was wearing a black, spiny, pulsating glove that extruded slowly waving sensor-like filaments, or tentacles. These filaments made me hyper-sensitive to my environment, made me able to taste the air, or more specifically to analyse the nature of the darkness which filled it. On some instinctive level I recognised that the darkness was something wild and primal, something dredged up from a fiercely burning core of anger and terror and human suffering. It was an emotional weapon made physical, unleashed with the purpose of invading and overwhelming the atoms and molecules of everything around it.

Not only did I perceive and understand this, but I could see a way to remedy it too. All at once the answer seemed simple and obvious, as if it was second nature to me, something I barely had to think about. It seemed as basic as parking my car in an empty space rather than in one that was already occupied, or of opening a door before going through it.

I flexed the muscles in my hand and wrist and suddenly the pulsating black substance which coated my arm was riven with dozens of thin fissures. From the fissures shone a piercing blue-white light, which sliced through the darkness, causing it to retreat, to shrivel back, in the same way that it had done earlier when the man in the demob suit had walked through it. As the darkness shrank away, objects and people began to appear, fading slowly into view like photographic images in a bath of chemicals. First Lesley was revealed, standing at the bottom of the stairs, still clutching the dog, and then Clover, a little way ahead of her. They were motionless, their faces taut, their eyes wide, as if frozen at the instant of some appalling memory or revelation. But as the blackness fell away from them they began to stir and blink, their faces relaxing, as if they were waking from a long and terrible nightmare.

Leaving them to recover, I walked forward, pushing the darkness ahead of me. It was breaking up, separating like curdled milk, folding in on itself as it retreated. It drained away through the door and back out into the night, revealing Benny in the porch, still clutching his gun, shaking his head and groaning like a boxer recovering from a knock-out punch.

As the last clots of darkness shrivelled and died in the light, Benny turned groggily and looked at me. His face went slack with astonishment and his eyes opened wide. It was strange and oddly disconcerting to see him with his guard down, his emotions so exposed.

'What the fuck?' he muttered, but I didn't try to explain. I couldn't. Its job done, I felt the fissures resealing themselves, the spine-like attachments disconnecting from my skin as the heart shrank back into my palm.

'We have to go,' I said, and then I turned as someone behind me made a shrill, inarticulate sound of distress.

It was Lesley. She was swaying on her feet as though about to faint. Her face was deathly pale, but there were feverish flares of red on the tips of her prominent cheekbones, and she was still holding the cringing little dog to her bosom like a talisman.

'What are you?' she hissed.

I shrugged. 'I'm not anything. Just a person.'

She glanced at my arm and her lips curled with fear and revulsion. 'Then what's that?'

The heart was little more than a gelid mass in my palm now, but even as I glanced at it, it retracted further, hardening into its familiar shape.

'I don't know,' I admitted. 'It's not mine.'

'You should get rid of it.'

I nodded, though I was surprised to find how much the suggestion alarmed me. 'You're probably right.'

She gave me a last look – part distaste, part fear – and then she buried her face in her dog's fur, whispering words of reassurance.

Clover moved across to me. 'You okay?'

Her face was hard to read. There was concern, confusion. A little bit of fear. Maybe even a hint of awe.

'I think so.'

Like Lesley, she glanced warily at the heart. 'What happened?'

'I'm not sure. Did you see?'

She gave a hesitant nod. 'Some of it. The heart changed, didn't it? Came alive.'

'It saved us,' I said. 'I... communicated with it.'

'It spoke to you?'

'Not as such, but... we worked together.' I shook my head. Already my understanding of the heart's nature and purpose, and my knowledge of how I had naturally and effortlessly achieved symbiosis with it, was slipping away. 'I can't explain it. We didn't exactly have a conversation, but... we shared an understanding. It's intelligent, I'm sure of that. Whatever it is.'

Clover shuddered, though whether at what I had said or at the memory of the darkness flooding into her I had no idea.

'So what happened to the dark?' she asked.

'It's been temporarily routed. I don't think I – we – destroyed it. I don't think it *can* be destroyed.'

'So it'll be back?'

'Maybe.'

'Then we *should* go.'

I nodded and she moved across the hallway towards Benny, who had been listening silently to our conversation, his eyes narrowed.

'What the fuck is going on?' he said.

'We need to get away,' Clover said. 'We're not safe here.'

'Not safe. This is my fucking house.'

'Yeah, and it'll be your tomb if we don't leave now!' Clover snapped, causing Benny to blink in surprise.

Before he could comment she half-raised a hand. 'Sorry, Benny, it's just... we've brought this on you. Alex and me. And we're really sorry. I know we all hoped that whoever's after us wouldn't find us here, but we were wrong. So the only way that you and Lesley will be safe is if we go, draw them off. You can still help us, but you'll have to do it from afar. We'll keep in touch.'

'I can't just let you walk out of here,' Benny said. I presumed that he meant he wanted to carry on protecting us, but the gun in his hand and the grim expression on his face seemed to give his words a more sinister meaning.

'We'll be fine,' Clover said.

'You think so, do you?'

She sighed. 'To be honest, I don't know. But it's clear we're not safe wherever we are, so perhaps it would be best if we kept on the move. You can take us into town, drop us at the station. We'll get a train back to London from there. And I think you and Lesley should book into a hotel and stay there until it gets light. Just to be on the safe side.'

Benny started to shake his head, but before he could say anything Lesley piped up, 'Clover's right, Benny. I think we should go. Now.'

I expected Benny to dig in his heels, but instead he sighed.

'Looks like I'm outvoted, doesn't it?' Before anyone could comment he turned away, indicating with a jerk of his gun that we should follow him out of the house.

As Clover and Lesley complied, I turned back towards the stairs.

'Where the fuck do you think you're going?' Benny snapped.

'I need my jacket and my phone. If the people who've got Kate try to get in touch—'

He nodded abruptly. 'Just hurry up about it.'

I ran upstairs and was down again within thirty seconds. As we followed Benny outside I asked Clover whether she had *her* phone, and to my relief she nodded.

The night was cold and the wind had picked up again. It rustled in the treetops as if something was alive and moving up there. The Jag was still parked in the driveway, where Benny's driver had left it earlier. I looked around nervously as we walked towards it, my hand still wrapped around the heart, which I'd now slipped back into the inside pocket of my jacket. As Benny pressed a button on his key fob, and the car unlocked with a chirrup and a flash of headlamps, I became aware of a fleeting pinpoint of orange light, like a dying firefly, at the edge of my vision. It had come from somewhere to my right, where the blackest shadows were clotted beneath the trees in the far corner of the front garden. I looked in that direction, and almost immediately saw the point of light flare again. I realised it was caused by the burn of tobacco as the pale-faced man in the demob suit sucked on his skinny roll-up. He was standing under the trees, watching us, the brief glow from his cigarette illuminating the bland expression on his face. Unlike before, when he had seemed to generate his own light-source, I couldn't see anything *except* his face this time. I got the odd impression that he simply wanted me to know that I hadn't beaten him, that he was still around. We stared at each other for a couple of seconds and then I got into the car with the others.

As soon as Benny backed out of the driveway and swung the car round, I felt a great lethargy sweep over me. It was more than just tiredness, more even than the normal crash that always follows a surge of adrenaline. This was bone-deep, as if a gigantic syringe had been plunged into my core and was sucking out all my energy. All at once I could neither speak, nor raise my limbs, nor even turn my head. I felt my heartbeat slowing, my senses shutting down. My surroundings blurred, became a monochrome smear of dark and light. It would have been alarming if I hadn't felt too exhausted to care. As my mind drifted, I suddenly remembered watching the tiny white dot in the centre of my gran's ancient black-and-white TV that the picture collapsed into when she switched it off. As the dot greyed out and faded into the darkness, so did I.

Whether it was Clover's raised voice that dragged me back into consciousness or the urge to throw up I have no idea. I knew only that if I didn't get out of the car quickly, or at least wind down the window, I would soon be pebble-dashing Benny's leather upholstery. Half-blind and as weak as a kitten, I clawed at the door handle on my left. I didn't know whether the car was moving or stationary, and my brain was too scrambled to care. More by luck than judgement, I pulled something and heard a clunk, and as the door yawned away from me I crawled towards the cold breeze that I felt pawing at my face until I sensed space and blackness, and then I leaned over as far as I could and puked.

As the stinking gruel geysered out of me, I recalled Clover's theory about the consequences of using the heart, and wondered whether she might have hit on something. My thoughts, however, were vague and incomplete; it was something I would have to consider at greater length when I was more alert. It took four or five big heaves, my body jerking like a fish on a beach, before I was done. Afterwards I didn't have the strength to do much more than lie there, panting and sweating, my face wet with the tears and snot that the violence of my convulsions had forced out of me, my throat burning with bile.

Eventually I became aware of a hand on my back, gently stroking me, and a soft voice speaking my name. It was the softness of the voice which made me realise that I couldn't hear the tiger-purr of the engine or feel the gentle thrum of movement.

Pushing myself up on wobbly arms, I looked blearily around. The first thing I saw was Clover, her face shocked and tense. I was about to tell her I was okay when over her shoulder I noticed that Benny had twisted around in the front seat and was pointing his gun at my face.

Before I could say anything he muttered, 'Get out of my fucking car.'

My first confused thought was that he was angry about me throwing up. I put up my hands and was about to tell him that I was pretty sure I'd got it all on the ground when Clover said, 'Please, Benny, be reasonable.'

It was dark, so I couldn't see Benny's face clearly, but from where I was sitting it looked to be all sharp angles and glittering eyes.

'Reasonable?' His voice was quiet, but there was no mistaking the steel in it, the thread of barely contained fury. 'You honestly expect me to be fucking reasonable after what happened?'

'It wasn't Alex's fault we were attacked,' Clover said.

Benny gestured at me with the gun. 'Isn't it? I don't even know what he fucking *is*.'

Clover spoke quickly, urgently. I still wasn't sure what was going on, but I couldn't help thinking she was talking for our lives. 'That's not fair, Benny, and you know it. He saved our skins back there. And it's my fault that he even got involved in this in the first place. If there's anyone to blame, it should be me.'

It was hard to tear my eyes from the circular black hole of the gun barrel less than a metre from my face, but as my brain got back up to speed, I started to get an idea of our surroundings. With the car door open, I could hear the rustle of wind in trees and bushes, the faint cries of nocturnal birds and animals. I didn't need to look around to tell that we were enclosed by darkness on all sides, that there was not even a hint of illumination from street lights or buildings.

'What's happening?' I asked cautiously. 'Where are we?'

'Shut your mouth!' snapped Benny, the gun jerking in his hand.

'For fuck's sake, Benny,' said Clover. 'He was only asking a question.'

I admired the way she managed to sound stern and placatory at the same time. Turning her head towards me, as if making a point, she said, 'We're in woodland. Somewhere near Wotton, I think. My understanding was that Benny would drive us to Guildford to catch a train to London, but instead he's brought us here.'

I licked my lips. Glanced from the staring black eye of the gun to Clover's face and back again. My mind was not only up to speed now, it was starting to race. I wondered whether Benny was so on edge that another word from me would be enough to make him pull the trigger. And if he *did* pull the trigger I wondered whether the heart would erupt into life in my pocket in time to save me.

Reaching into my pocket and squeezing the heart, I heard myself blurting, 'Why?'

Benny *didn't* pull the trigger. But for a long moment – during which I asked myself whether I had *really* just put the potential capabilities of the heart to the test – time seemed frozen. I stared into the barrel of the gun, the heart gripped in my hand – and then Clover inclined her head and said, 'Yes, Benny, *why* have you brought us here? Are you going to shoot us and bury us in the woods?'

Benny's face tautened, shadows flooding into the hollows of his cheeks. I held my breath; I knew he was capable of far worse than what Clover had suggested. Beside him, in the passenger seat, Lesley sat staring straight ahead, saying nothing, the dog in her lap.

Finally Benny muttered, 'Don't be soft. I just want *him* away from us. *Far* away. There's something not right about the cunt.'

'But we *were* going away, Benny,' Clover said. 'You were going to take us to the station and we were going to get a train back to London. That was the plan.'

Benny gave a brief shake of the head. 'Not good enough. Because if you're with him when he goes down, Monroe, you'll go down too, and I'm not having that. Which is why he's going to get out of my car now and walk away.' He jerked the gun at me dismissively. 'Off you go, Alex. Door's open.'

I considered saying no. I considered calling his bluff, and seeing whether he *would* shoot me, and more to the point whether the heart would save me if he did. But what was the point? I didn't want to risk Clover getting hurt, and I would only have been being defiant for the sake of it. And so I sighed and started to slide towards the open passenger door.

'How dare you,' Clover said in a low voice.

For a second I thought she was talking to me, but when I turned I realised she was looking at Benny. 'How dare you presume to make my decisions for me. I'm a big girl now, Benny, and I'll do what I fucking like, and if you don't like it then you'll just have to shoot me.'

She slid across the seat towards me, pushing me almost roughly ahead of her. 'Come on, Alex, we're going.'

I scooted along the soft shiny leather and had one foot out the door, trying to find a bit of ground that didn't have puke on it, when Benny said, 'Don't be stupid, Monroe.'

Clover turned back to face him, whipping her head around so quickly that her hair lashed my face. 'I don't call it being stupid. I call it being loyal.'

He grunted. 'Loyal? You hardly know the guy.'

Beside me, I felt Clover's body tense. For a second I thought she was going to smack Benny in the mouth, gun or no gun, and I half-raised a hand to stop her.

'You wouldn't understand,' she said. 'I was wrong about you, Benny. I thought you had more bottle than this.'

I clenched the heart again, willing her not to goad him, but a crooked smile appeared on Benny's face. 'It's not about bottle,' he said. 'It's about making the right decisions, knowing when to cut your losses.'

'Yeah? Well, I've made my decision and I'm sticking to it.'

She gave me another push. I unfolded myself from the car and straightened up and she did too.

'Goodbye, Benny,' Clover said, stretching out a hand to slam the car door.

Before she could, I put a hand on her arm. 'Maybe Benny's right. Maybe you *should* leave me here, cut your losses.'

Clover's eyes searched my face. 'Is that what you want?'

My hesitation was answer enough for her.

'Thought not.' She made to shut the door again, but then she paused and leaned into the car. 'Stay safe, you two. Thanks for everything. I really do mean that.'

Lesley gave a tight, nervous smile. Benny sighed. Looking at me, he said, 'You look after this one, Alex. Keep her safe. Because if anything happens to her, you won't only have the Wolves of fucking London coming after you.'

I looked back at him, saying nothing, and Clover shut the door.

There was a moment of silence, then the engine purred into life and the car drove away.

EIGHTEEN

DAWN CHORUS

'Why does he call you Monroe?'

It was the first time either of us had spoken for several minutes. After being abandoned by Benny we'd begun to walk back towards what Clover claimed was the A25. She'd told me that halfway to Guildford, Benny had taken an abrupt left down a minor single-track road surrounded by woodland. Ignoring Clover's demands to know what was going on, he had driven for two or three miles before pulling into a lay-by and cutting the engine. It was during the ensuing row that I had started to come round.

Clover turned her head to look at me now, half-amused, half-puzzled. 'Is that really all you can think of to say?'

'I'm curious, that's all. It's never Clover, always Monroe. It just seems odd.'

Clover shrugged and faced front again, staring into the darkness. 'That's Benny for you. He's a hard man, who thinks that showing affection is a weakness. He's protective towards me, and he hugs me like a daughter whenever he sees me – but he never uses my first name. When I was younger it was always "Miss Monroe"; now it's just "Monroe". It's his way of keeping his distance, holding me at arm's length.'

I snorted. Trees and bushes formed shifting black walls on either side of us, the rustle of leaves and the scrape of branches in the wind made ominous by the fact that we couldn't see them.

'Funny way of showing his protective side – by kicking you out to fend for yourself.'

'It was my decision. Benny's a proud man. He'd already decided to kick *you* out. There was no way he was going to lose face by going back on that.'

'Not even if it meant leaving you at the mercy of the Wolves of London?'

'Like I say, it was my decision. What could he do? Force me at gunpoint back into the car? Shoot me if I refused?'

'I see your point.' I hesitated, then said, 'Do you think he'd have shot *me* if I'd refused to get out of the car?'

Clover was silent for a few seconds. Far off in the darkness I heard the mournful cry of a bird.

'Who knows?' she said finally. 'Maybe. Benny's unpredictable. I've known him for years, but I wouldn't claim to *know* him, if you get what I mean? With people like Benny, it's all about self-preservation. They're loyal and protective up to a point, but they would never lay their life on the line for you. If Benny thought you were a threat he'd kill you as soon as look at you.'

I wondered, not for the first time, what had prompted him to take me under his wing in prison all those years ago. Had it been a whim? Had he thought I might be useful to him in some way? Or was it pointless trying to work out his motives because, as Clover had said, he was unpredictable?

'Back at the house, and then in the car, was the first time I've seen him flustered,' I said. 'I'd always thought he was... unruffable. Is that a word?'

Clover made a sound in her throat that was barely a laugh. 'It is now.' Again she paused. 'I might be wrong, but I think the darkness, and then seeing that... thing on your arm, rocked his world – and not in a good way. Although Benny's unpredictable, his world is very black and white; it has very set parameters. He can cope with threats from other people, but I think what happened tonight took him so far out of his comfort zone that it scared the shit out of him. It made him realise he wasn't in control, after all, that there were things he couldn't understand and deal with. So he decided to jettison what he saw as the cause.'

'Me,' I said, and she nodded.

We trudged on in silence for another minute or so, the uneven ground crackling wetly underfoot. It was just before 6 a.m., maybe an hour or so before dawn, yet although the sky was only a fraction lighter than the landscape around us, courtesy of a half-moon that transformed the low-hanging clouds into smears of silver, the dawn chorus was beginning its first hesitant twitterings and warblings. Surrounding us was the mulchy odour of wet vegetation and the occasional sharp tang of animal musk.

'So what about you?' I said eventually.

She looked at me. 'What do you mean?'

'Well, Benny was right, wasn't he? You could have cut your losses, put yourself out of danger by staying with him and Lesley. But you chose to come with me instead. Why was that?'

Her features tightened as her eyes narrowed. 'Is that a serious question?'

'You tell me.'

She halted abruptly. Her fists were clenched and I could tell she was angry. In a tight voice she said, 'Has the world really become so... so fucking cynical? So *poisonous*? Does nobody think that loyalty and integrity are good enough reasons any more?'

Aware that I was playing devil's advocate, I muttered, 'Like Benny said, you hardly know me.'

She closed her eyes briefly, as if fighting to control her temper. Then, in a scarily calm voice, she said, 'I feel guilty, if you must know. Regardless of whether I like you or not – which I do – I feel a *duty* to hang around. If it wasn't for me you wouldn't be in possession of the heart; you wouldn't have the "Wolves of London", or whoever they are, after you; your daughter might not have been kidnapped.'

I shook my head. 'We don't know if that's true. If you're not bullshitting me – which I have to admit I'm still not sure about – then you're just as much of a pawn in this game as I am.'

'Game?' she said.

I flapped a hand. 'I use the term loosely.'

'I've lost my business,' she said, 'my home. Friends of mine, people I know, and in Mary's case loved, have died...'

Her voice choked off. I stepped towards her instinctively, as if to offer comfort, but she waved me back.

'I know,' I said. 'Sorry. I'm just so...' I shook my head. 'This is just so fucked up.'

She drew a long, shuddering breath. Swiped at her teary eyes as if angry at herself for getting upset. Eventually, almost challengingly, she said, 'So what's the plan now?'

It was a question that had been preying on my mind. Shrugging, I said, 'We hitch a lift back to London, I suppose.'

'And then what?'

'I don't know,' I admitted.

She sighed, though I'm sure she can't have been expecting anything more constructive than that.

'At least I've still got the heart,' I said. 'Hopefully that will protect us.'

'Hopefully,' she said, and sighed deeply, then began to look around as if searching for something.

'Are you all right?' I asked.

'I really need to pee,' she said.

I laughed. After the tension of the last couple of minutes her words struck me as funnier than they ought to have done.

'I'll just go behind those bushes over there,' she said. 'Wait for me, won't you?'

'Course I will.'

I watched her move to the side of the track and then blend into the blackness of the trees and undergrowth. The crackle and snap of small branches as she pushed her way through the dark tangle gradually faded to silence.

'You all right?' I called.

Her voice was fainter than I expected it to be. 'Fine.'

'You sound quite far away.'

'I didn't want you to hear me peeing. It's embarrassing.'

'I'll cover my ears.'

In fact, I didn't need to cover my ears. Any sound that Clover might have been making was masked by the still-muted tuning up of the dawn chorus and the occasional rustle of wind in the bushes. I stood and relished these gentle sounds, tilting my head back and drawing the fresh morning air deep into my lungs. I doubted there would be many more moments like this in my immediate future, moments when I could just stand in contemplation, secure in the knowledge that I was alone and undetected. Then I thought of how I couldn't hear Clover even though she was only thirty or forty metres away, which made me realise how oblivious the two of us would be if there *was* actually someone close by, monitoring our movements. Would we hear them if they began to stalk us? Would the heart alert me to danger?

Once again I slipped my hand into my pocket and stroked the surface of the heart, tracing its contours with my fingertips. I was aware that my desire to keep touching it was almost fetishistic, and yet I was not sure how much of that was based on my anxiety about Kate and my belief that the heart was a bargaining tool for her safe return, and how much was due to the influence - whether insidious or benign - of the thing itself. An hour or so before, I had felt at one with the heart, in harmony with it; I had felt not only that we were working together towards a common cause, but that I was on the verge of grasping its secrets and mysteries, of being granted understanding of its true nature.

But had that really been the case? Or had the heart simply been using me as a puppet, buttering me up for its own purpose? Was it merely a parasite that needed a human host to function effectively?

I liked to think that the heart and I were protecting each other, but perhaps we weren't; perhaps the heart had its own agenda and would discard me when it decided I was no longer useful. In which case, until then, was I invincible with the heart in my possession? Was I like some kind of superhero, impervious to attack? And how far did the heart's influence extend? What kind of powers did it yield? Could it - as I had wondered in Benny's car - stop a bullet? What if I wasn't directly linked to it - if I was shot or stabbed whilst asleep, say? Would it come to my rescue then? And what of the people in physical proximity to me, like Clover - would it save them too? I squeezed the heart in my fist, and immediately the questions crowding my mind dissipated, as if the black stone was absorbing my anxiety and confusion.

As my mind cleared, I became aware that, standing in the darkness, I had slipped into what amounted to a waking trance. I blinked and looked around me. Far off on what I presumed to be the horizon I could see the thinnest sliver of pale blue light. How long had I phased out for? One minute? Five? Longer? Clover had still not reappeared, so it couldn't have been *that* long. Unless, of course, something had happened to her, or her claim that she needed to pee had merely been a pretext for... for what? Perhaps she had slipped away. Or called someone on her mobile. Again I wondered how much I could really trust her. Perhaps she had her own agenda, after all. Perhaps she was playing me for a fool. Turning to where she had slipped into the trees, I saw a glimmer of white in the blackness.

It wasn't until I had stepped forward, and had opened my mouth to speak her name, that it occurred to me that Clover had not been wearing white. Apprehension bristled through me, raising goosebumps on my arms, as the pale shapeless thing drew closer, flickering among the trees. I wanted to speak, to challenge it, but I was loath to draw attention to myself. The pale thing drifted closer still, pushing between the last of the trees, and was suddenly on the road ten metres from me.

In the darkness it was little more than a grey-white smear that seemed to hover above the ground. It was motionless for a moment, and then it began to waver towards me. I stepped back, drawing the heart from my pocket. I was about to shout out whatever warning my dry throat could dredge up when a soft voice said, 'Alex?'

I drew in a breath so violently it sounded like a cry of pain. I recognised that voice. I had last heard it in what I thought had been a dream not more than twenty-four hours previously.

'Lyn?' I whispered. 'Is that you?'

The apparition neither replied nor came closer. It had halted six or seven metres away, a pearly smudge in the darkness. I wanted to walk up to it, but I was scared. Scared of getting too close; scared that if I *did* get too close it would disappear. I stood for a moment in an agony of indecision – and then I had an idea. Still clutching the heart in one hand, I slipped my other into my jeans pocket, took out my phone and switched it on.

This time the sound that came out of me was like a sob, though I was barely aware that I'd made it. Revealed in the icy glow of the mobile screen was Lyn as I had seen her in the hotel room, barefoot and pregnant and beautiful, dressed in the white nightshirt with the cherry design, which billowed gently around her body in the cool breeze. She was smiling and her hair shone like gold in the light.

'Are you real?' I asked.

Instead of replying to my question, she raised her arms as though to draw me into an embrace. 'Come to me, Alex,' she said.

I took a step towards her, but she shook her head, as though I had misunderstood. 'No. Come to *me*. I need you. Only you can bring me back.'

'Where are you?' I asked.

She smiled sweetly. 'Long ago and far away.'

I felt my throat thickening with emotion, the heat of tears at the back of my eyes. 'I miss you, Lyn,' I whispered.

The screen of my phone went dark.

After the glow of illumination, the blackness seemed so complete that I could no longer see even the glimmer of Lyn's nightshirt. I jabbed at the screen to light it up again and pointed it at where she had been standing.

She was gone.

I moaned, despair washing through me. But even as I slumped, like a man coming to a halt after pushing himself to his limits, I was surprised at how bereft I felt. It was as though I was suddenly standing outside myself, analysing my emotions from afar and finding them curious and alien. Then the moment passed and I stared at the spot where Lyn had stood, feeling tired and strung out. Although the real Lyn wasn't dead, I still felt as though I had found a way to make contact with her spirit – albeit haphazardly and so fleetingly that it was agonising. Just before my mobile screen went black again, I noticed that although the ground where she had stood was muddy, she had left no footprints.

Come to me, she had said, which could mean only one thing.

I heard a rustle in the darkness and turned my phone on again. Clover was struggling through the last of the undergrowth, pushing brambles and small branches aside. She staggered on to the dirt road with a gasp of effort and squinted at what to her must have been a small rectangle of blue-white light.

'Alex?' she said. 'That *is* you, isn't it?'

I turned the light on to my own face, plunging my surroundings into darkness. ''Fraid so.'

I sensed rather than saw her moving towards me. 'Are you all right? You look a bit... strained.'

'I've seen Lyn again,' I said. 'She was standing right there. She looked as real as you are.'

Clover hunched her shoulders and half-turned with a shiver, as if she expected my ex-wife to be standing beside her. 'Where did she come from?'

I gestured towards the trees, which I now realised were beginning to gain a little definition as the sky grew lighter. 'Out of the woods, right where you did.'

'Creepy,' she said, but I shook my head.

'No, it was... sad. I have to go and see her.'

'She's not real, Alex. She's an apparition, or a vision, or a trick.'

'No,' I said. 'She's real and she's lost. She needs me.'

Clover half-raised a hand, as if to stop me in my tracks. 'Hang on. This is the actual Lyn we're talking about, right?'

I nodded. Though I had no idea where it would lead, all at once I had a plan, a purpose. 'I have to see her, Clover. I don't care whether it's a good idea or not, but I have to go to Brighton.'

NINETEEN

MADHOUSE

'Oh my God,' Clover said.

It was two hours since Lyn had appeared. Clover and I were sitting hunched at a corner table of the Copthorne motorway services branch of Costa, trying to appear as unobtrusive as possible as we devoured breakfast paninis and drank seriously big mugs of hot, strong, milky coffee. Although it was only twelve hours since Lesley had cooked us a belt-bursting dinner of lamb casserole, mashed potatoes and honey-roast parsnips, and less than four hours since Clover and I had been in Benny's conservatory chatting over a pre-dawn cuppa, I felt as though I hadn't eaten for days. Of course, puking my guts out next to Benny's car and walking several miles in the autumnal chill of an early morning probably had a great deal to do with that. Finishing my panini in double-quick time I contemplated whether to order another or simply stock up on peanuts and chocolate bars from WH Smith and snack en route.

Finally reaching the A25 after a good hour's trudge, the two of us had managed to thumb a lift from a guy called Greg, whose ginger whiskers and stocky build put me in mind of Yosemite Sam. Greg was a draughtsman, who was originally from Sunderland, but who currently lived in Guildford and commuted to his job in East Grinstead each morning. Clover and I were so tired that we could both have done with a snooze, but Greg liked to talk, and as it was often an unspoken rule that a hitchhiker was obliged to pay for his journey in kind, I sat in the passenger seat and engaged him in conversation while Clover snatched forty winks in the back.

'I love the classics, me,' Greg said, nodding at the footwell between us, in which, among the chewing gum, sweet wrappers, pens and random bits of paper, was a CD case for Charles Dickens's *Barnaby Rudge*. 'I never read 'em when I was a kid cos I was too busy playing football and causing bother, but I'm catching up now. Once I've done with Dickens I'll be on to Thomas Hardy. *Tess of the D'Urbervilles* and all that.'

As he dropped us at the service station with a cheery wave I found myself envying Greg. He seemed to have it sorted – a good job, a nice car, a wife and kids who he mentioned with affection, and a determination to expand his horizons. His life seemed so neat and simple and organised, whereas mine was an unruly mess.

'It's in, then?' I said to Clover in response to her exclamation.

She was hunched over the open newspaper she had bought, which covered three-quarters of the table. She looked up, wide-eyed, pushing her glossy, maroon-coloured hair away from her face.

'Page three,' she replied, the newspaper making a fluttering crackle as she flipped it around.

The headline read: 15 DEAD IN LONDON NIGHTCLUB FIRE. There was no mention of murder, or of the club coming under attack. According to the report, the fifteen bodies discovered in the charred remains of the cellar bar were too badly burned to have yet been identified. The story stated that although there appeared to have been no survivors, the club was sparsely populated at the time because it was near to closing time. Fire officers were still investigating the cause of the blaze, though it was thought that the fire had started somewhere on the ground floor of the building, trapping the victims in the basement area below.

We read the story together, and when Clover gave a sharp intake of breath I knew she had reached the final paragraph, which stated that the nightclub's owner, Clover Monroe (27), was thought to be among the victims.

'Shit,' she murmured, looking across the table at me, an expression of shocked blankness on her face. 'Everyone thinks I'm dead. Which I guess makes me a kind of... non-person. That's weird.'

I hesitated to say what was on my mind, but then I said it anyway. 'On the plus side, if the police think you're dead it means they won't be looking for you, not until they've identified all the bodies.'

Clover narrowed her eyes. 'Do you think this is more of that scorched-earth policy you were talking about?'

'How do you mean?'

'Well, the fire must have been started to conceal evidence. But those freaks who started it – assuming it *was* them – know we're together and that we escaped. Could be they're isolating us, cutting us off from help.'

'Though if the worst came to the worst we *could* still go to the police.'

'And tell them what? Your daughter's gone missing, my club's burned down – we must both be under suspicion. If we told them that we were on the run from villains who had done both of those things we'd have to tell them why and that would only incriminate us. How long before the police link you to McCallum's murder? For all we know, these "Wolves" may have planted evidence at the scene.' She raised her hands and slapped them down on her thighs, a gesture of helplessness. 'No, if we go to the police they'd want to contain us and question us. We're on our own, Alex.'

I had never felt more trapped, more uncertain of where to turn. Even in prison I had had a plan, a sense of determination, hope for the future. I looked around, my gaze sweeping across the sparsely occupied tables, to the drift of people gravitating towards the toilets, or the other fast-food outlets, or into WH Smith to buy a morning paper or a bottle of water or a quick snack. There was a constant flow of bodies in and out of the main doors, commuters stopping off en route to the office, night-workers heading home after a long shift. To my eyes all of these people seemed purposeful, unburdened, in control of their lives. I wondered what we would do – what everyone would do – if the Wolves of London were suddenly to make an appearance in these most mundane of surroundings. I thought of the tall man with his syringe-fingers and his grotesque clockwork army, the man in the demob suit with his living darkness formed from the accumulated horrors of war. I couldn't imagine them here. They were creatures not only of the night, but of nightmare. How could they possibly exist in a world of McDonald's and piped music and vending machines?

As I was looking around, Clover was still browsing through the paper. Suddenly she froze. 'Look here,' she said.

The story was on page ten: BRUTAL MURDER OF RECLUSIVE MILLIONAIRE.

I swallowed, pressing my hands flat on the table to stop them from trembling as I read the story:

> Retired millionaire businessman Barnaby McCallum, who was thought to be in his early 90s, was found brutally murdered in his home yesterday. It is believed that he may have disturbed a burglar, who broke into his house on Bellwater Drive, Kensington, in the early hours of Wednesday morning. His body was discovered by his housekeeper, Cynthia Pritchard (59) who lives nearby. Police have revealed that Mr McCallum was killed by a single blow to the head. Detective Inspector Michael Rainey, who is leading the inquiry, described the murder as a 'vicious and cowardly attack on a defenceless old man.' It is unclear whether anything was taken in the attack, though police have confirmed they are pursuing several lines of enquiry. DI Rainey made a statement in which he said that the killer would almost certainly have had the victim's blood on his clothing, and he appealed for any information that might lead to an arrest. Mr McCallum is thought to have no surviving relatives.

'Vicious and cowardly,' I murmured. 'Is that what I am?'

I felt deeply ashamed. Not only of what I had done, but also that since the attack on Incognito I had been so wrapped up in my own problems that I had barely given McCallum a thought. But the story in front of me, full of the kind of newspaper speak that the majority of us skim over on a daily basis, suddenly brought it all crashing in again. This was real and unalterable. As extenuating as the circumstances may have been, and however unintentional my actions, the inarguable fact was that I was a murderer. And what I now knew about the heart – little though it was – made me wonder whether, in fact, I had *caused* the spike to appear and pierce his skull; whether, subconsciously, I had *wanted* to kill Barnaby McCallum.

Clover reached forward and slipped her hands over mine. 'Of course you're not,' she said. 'You mustn't think that.'

'But that's what it says here in black and white.'

She frowned. 'What do they know? They have no idea what happened. They just say these things as a matter of course.'

I stayed silent. I knew she was right, and yet I couldn't shake off the feeling that, whatever the circumstances, I deserved to be punished for what I had done.

As if guessing my thoughts, Clover said, 'It was an accident, Alex. You know that. You mustn't believe anything else.'

'Yeah, but—'

'But nothing. The old man attacked you. You were defending yourself. You didn't know that the heart was going to do what it did.'

'Didn't I?'

She gave me a curious look. 'Of course not. Why are you even doubting that fact?'

We left soon after, Clover dumping the newspaper into a bin on the way out. After checking our phones, which we had been doing on a regular basis, we trooped across to the lorry park in search of a lift.

We were in luck, chancing almost immediately upon a genial Glaswegian called Andy who was driving a consignment of frozen beef down to Brighton and was only too happy to let us tag along. The cabin of Andy's truck was spacious and warm and smelled, oddly and comfortingly, of something akin to Weetabix or freshly baked biscuits. It was only as we rumbled up the slip road to rejoin the M23 that I realised I had never been in a road-bound vehicle quite as large as this one before. In spite of everything, I felt an almost boyish thrill to be so high up, looking down on the cars and vans scurrying and darting around us.

Andy's accent was so thick I could understand only half of what he was saying, but that barely mattered as he did the majority of the talking, and seemed happy for Clover and I to punctuate his spiel with nods and laughs and grunts at the appropriate junctures. Most of his talk consisted of the downfall of Glasgow Rangers, the parlous state of Britain's roads and the exploits of his daughter, Maura, who was one of only a handful of girls doing chemical engineering at Birmingham University. The constant barrage of words – exacerbated by the blare of Radio 1 and the leviathan growl of the truck's engine – would have been tiresome if Andy hadn't been such a jovial companion. Even so, by the time he dropped us off close to Brighton Pier, our ears were ringing.

The soughing sea and bickering gulls were soothing by comparison. Even the rush-hour traffic on the road that ran parallel to the seafront seemed muted. It was a chilly, breezy morning, but dry and bright enough to encourage several early-morning strollers along the promenade to venture out without jackets. One of a quartet of lads, who looked as though they hadn't yet completed their previous night's drinking, was bare-chested, a West Ham United badge tattooed on his bulging left pec. As he and his friends approached, he leered at Clover and said something that the wind snatched away. I squeezed the heart in my pocket, but although the other lads cackled so much they had to lean against one another for support, the group barely broke stride as Clover turned her back on them, curling her hands around the railings edging the pebbly beach below and gazing over the churning grey water.

In comparison to what we had been through, the threat the lads carried seemed trivial. Nevertheless I watched them until they had swaggered away, and then I turned towards Clover, our shoulders almost touching as I gripped the topmost iron railing, which was shockingly cold.

'We came here once or twice when I was a kid,' I said. 'Me and my dad liked it, but my mum thought it was posh. The waiters in the restaurants made her uncomfortable because she imagined they were looking down on her. For that reason we mostly went to Southend or Selsey Bill. There was a Pontins at Selsey Bill, or maybe a Butlin's. One of the two.'

Clover's maroon hair was blowing in the wind. She raised a hand to hold it away from her face and turned her head to squint at me. 'How often do you visit Lyn?' she asked.

I kept my eyes on the sea. 'Not often. I find it too upsetting. And I'm not sure that Lyn gets much out of it. Sometimes she doesn't even recognise me.'

'Is it a private hospital she's in?'

'Yeah.'

'That must be expensive.'

I shrugged, feeling uncomfortable. 'Lyn's parents pay for most of it. I chip in when I can. I wish I could do more, but I've got Kate to look after...'

My voice tailed off as the simmering coal of anguish that had been present in my belly since Kate's abduction flared again. Although her disappearance was at the forefront of my mind every minute of the day, now and again there were particularly acute reminders not only of my loss, but of what the long-term implications of that might mean. I felt a trembling start in my arms and gripped the iron railing harder to try to neutralise it. I wished I hadn't left my last packet of cigarettes at Benny's, wished I'd bought some more at the service station when I'd had the chance. I was a casual smoker – I normally succumbed only when I was drinking – but at that moment I could have murdered a fag. I turned to Clover and forced a smile that made my face muscles ache.

'I'd better look for a taxi,' I said.

I began to stride along the promenade, towards the pier. Across the road a row of Regency-style hotels with bone-white facades reflected the cold sunshine like a vast, gleaming grin. Clover padded after me.

'Don't you mean we?' she said.

I slowed my pace. 'I'm not sure that would be a good idea. Lyn gets very unsettled around strangers, and if she saw us together I don't know how she'd react. I thought it'd be better if you waited in a café or something. I'll probably only be an hour or so.'

'Do you think that's safe?' she said doubtfully.

'Well, I guess that depends on how bad the coffee is.'

The joke was feeble, but she rewarded it with a brief, grunting laugh. 'Seriously, do you think it's wise for us to split up, even if it *is* only for a short time?'

'It's the heart they want,' I said, 'and I'm pretty sure it'll protect me if they come for it.' (I wasn't sure at all.) 'The hour you spend chilling out with a cappuccino will probably be the safest one you'll have spent in the past two days.'

'It's that "probably" that bothers me. How about if I come with you, but sit in reception while you see Lyn?' She gave me an innocent look. 'I promise I won't be any trouble.'

'All right then, if that's what you want. But if you break anything you won't get any supper.'

Darby Hall Psychiatric Hospital was a sprawling Victorian edifice in a leafy and residential area of Hove, four or five miles from the Brighton seafront. I called ahead to check that it was okay to visit at short notice, and then Clover and I hailed a taxi outside the Royal Albion Hotel opposite the pier. Hove put me uncomfortably in mind of the Kensington neighbourhood where Barnaby McCallum had lived and died, but if anything the houses here were larger and more opulent. Set well back in its own grounds, Darby Hall was the most grandiose of all, its series of banked lawns so immaculately manicured that they looked as smooth as snooker tables. The taxi driver dropped us at the main gates, which formed a forbidding arch of grey iron spikes held together with ornate cross-bands. I pressed the button on the intercom, gave my name and the gates hummed open. Once Clover and I were through, they closed with a gentle clang.

We crunched up the gravel drive, rhododendrons and laurel flanking us across a narrow stretch of lawn on our left, while the larger and more impressive lawns on our right climbed like a number of vast steps towards the house perched on a plateau above. By the time we arrived at the steps leading up to the building's wide front door we were both panting a little and, despite the autumn chill, I could feel a sheen of sweat on my forehead. In the summer the lawn would be dotted with residents – playing croquet or wandering about or simply sitting on the grass or in wheelchairs, enjoying the sunshine – but not today. It was evidently too cold or too early in the morning.

I pressed a buzzer marked 'Reception' and the same tinny female voice who had greeted me at the gate said, 'Come in, Mr Locke.'

There was a lower-pitched buzz and I pushed the door open.

Although the reception area was so spacious that a trapeze act could have performed in it, the abundance of cherry-coloured wood and the small front windows made the space feel cosy, if not claustrophobic. Our footsteps seemed to resound through the building as we approached the desk on our left, behind which sat a plump, smiling woman in her late fifties, whose flushed face could have been either a reflection from the wooden panelling or the result of high blood pressure.

'Good morning, Mr Locke,' she said. 'How nice to see you again. Would you take a seat?'

She indicated a pair of antique-looking chairs upholstered in some heraldic design, and picked up the telephone.

As she put a call through to the medical staff, I perched on the edge of the chair, my hands on my knees. Perhaps I had inherited something of my mum's inferiority complex, because I always felt uncomfortable here, and not only because I was unsettled at the prospect of seeing Lyn. It was the quiet gentility of the place that set me on edge, the fact that it seemed to go out of its way to disguise its true purpose. It was probably just me, but I couldn't help thinking that the patients were kept hidden because, despite the high level of care they received, they were considered a grubby and embarrassing secret.

The clack of descending footsteps accompanied by their echoes reached our ears several seconds before their owner. Looking up the wide shadowy staircase opposite the front door, I saw a ghostly flash of white, which resolved itself into a doctor's coat worn by a thin, freckled, ascetic-looking woman in her mid-thirties. This was Dr Bruce, who I had met several times, and who, though civil, possessed no sense of humour. As she descended I leaned forward to stand up, and was surprised to feel Clover's hand reaching out to give mine a reassuring squeeze.

I offered her a vague smile, then turned to greet Dr Bruce, who was now marching across the wooden floor towards me, extending her arm to offer her usual military-style handshake. Her hand was cold and bony as I enclosed it with my own.

'How are you, Mr Locke?' she asked.

'Fine,' I said. 'And you?'

'Busy,' she replied bluntly. 'I'm afraid you've caught us rather on the hop.'

'Sorry. I was in the area. Is Lyn not ready to see me?'

She paused before replying. 'As you know, Mr Locke, Lyn dislikes surprises. She has set schedules, set routines, and she becomes agitated whenever those routines are disrupted. Having said that, today appears to be one of her better days. Although the process has been somewhat rushed, I have been through the usual preparation procedures with her and she seems amenable to your visit. Of course, there is no guarantee that her composure will prevail.'

'Of course,' I murmured, glancing at Clover and wondering whether she was thinking what I was thinking: was Lyn calm because she had been *expecting* me?

Dr Bruce caught my glance and frowned. Giving Clover a fleeting, dismissive look, she said, 'I hope you're not thinking of springing a double surprise on Lyn, Mr Locke? Despite her current placidity I'm not sure how she would cope with that.'

I shook my head. 'Of course not. I wouldn't be so insensitive. My friend will wait here.'

Dr Bruce gave a short nod, and turned on her heel. 'Right. Well, if you'll follow me...'

I had been there often enough to know where Lyn's room was, but it was probably a house rule that visitors could only venture beyond the reception area if accompanied by a member of staff. Trying to avert my eyes from the doctor's skinny rump beneath her white coat as she clopped up the wooden stairs, I plodded in her wake like a recalcitrant schoolboy behind a stern headmistress. At the top of the first flight she led the way along a corridor with a thick green carpet and stopped at a wood-panelled door. She gave a perfunctory knock and stepped through the door so quickly it looked as though she was trying to catch the room's occupant unawares. Raising a hand to indicate that I should wait on the threshold, she turned to her right and I saw her expression soften slightly.

'Lyn?' she said, her voice softening too. 'Alex is here. Are you ready to speak to him?'

I heard no reply, which presumably meant that Lyn had nodded her compliance, for almost immediately Dr Bruce stepped aside, beckoning me forward. I entered the room, already knowing what I would see. If it wasn't for the trio of horizontal bars across the window and the red buzzer on the wall beside the bed, you might have thought this was a bright and summery room in a family-run hotel. The furniture, which consisted of the bed, a wardrobe, a bookcase, a chest of drawers, a dressing table and a couple of armchairs, was old but sturdy and well maintained. The carpet was a subdued coral-pink colour and the curtains and bedding were predominantly white and yellow, emblazoned with a pretty floral design. One of the two armchairs was positioned to the left of the window, where I know Lyn liked to sit and absorb the tranquil view of green lawns and well-tended gardens. The other chair, on the edge of which she was currently perched, was in front of the dressing table, which was positioned against the wall to the left of her bed. Usually the chair would be facing the dressing-table mirror (which I had once been told contained unbreakable glass), but today it had been turned to face the rest of the room.

I had half-expected her to be wearing the white nightshirt with the cherry design, but in fact she was dressed in a black jumper with a vertical pattern of multi-coloured lines and blue jeans. I had half-hoped too that she might have recaptured some of her former radiance, but she looked much as she had the last time I had seen her – her thin, lined face prematurely aged, her once-blonde hair now a dull mousey-brown.

As ever, too, her eyes were narrowed warily and her once-smiling mouth was set in a terse line. Her hands, bony as chicken feet, were locked together in her lap. Dr Bruce caught my eye and gave a brief nod.

The tacit suggestion that I required the doctor's blessing to speak annoyed me, but I tried to instil my voice with gentleness. 'Hi, Lyn, it's me, Alex. How are you doing?'

Although it made me feel both sad and condescending, I had been advised to confirm my identity at the outset of each visit, as Lyn sometimes became confused and forgetful. Much as I disliked doing it, I guess it was necessary, because there were times when Lyn simply stared at me as if she didn't understand what I was saying. I was pleased to see that today was not one of those times. In fact, as Lyn shifted in her seat, her dry hands rustling against one another, I was astonished to see the twitch of a smile on her lips.

'Yes, Alex,' she said in her quiet, deliberate voice. 'I know who you are. I've been dreaming about you.'

As if Lyn had passed some kind of test, Dr Bruce said, 'Right, well I'll leave you to it. Press the buzzer when you're ready to go, Mr Locke.'

I nodded vaguely, but kept my eyes on Lyn. Behind me I heard Dr Bruce cross the room, pulling the door closed behind her.

Something else I had been advised to do was check with Lyn before picking anything up or changing anything in her room, and so, indicating the chair by the window, I asked, 'Is it okay if I move that across here, Lyn, so that I can sit next to you?'

'Yes,' she said.

I carried the chair across the room and positioned it so that I could sit facing her, our knees only a foot or so apart. Now that I was here I suddenly found that I was uncertain of what to say, of how much she knew. I was aware from experience that I had to tread carefully, that she had to be eased through conversations for fear of becoming lost in them, and therefore stricken with panic.

'So, how have you been?' I asked.

She stared at me, as if she had no idea how to answer my question, and then she said, 'Every day is the same here.'

'And is that good or bad?'

'It's...' her eyes glazed a little as she searched for the right word. '... safe,' she said finally.

I paused a moment, considering how to proceed. 'Were you surprised to see me this morning?'

A slight frown wrinkled her forehead. 'I told you,' she said. 'I dreamed about you.'

'So you did. That's very interesting.' I made an effort to ensure that my voice was gentle, coaxing. 'What did you dream? Can you remember?'

'I dreamed that you could help me.'

'Help you in what way?'

'I dreamed that you could make the dark man go away.'

I licked my lips nervously. Mention of the dark man was often a sign that the situation was about to deteriorate. He, or more specifically his imagined presence, had been the catalyst for some of Lyn's more serious episodes over the years. I had been told by her doctors that the dark man was the embodiment of her psychosis, and that whenever Lyn mentioned him the best thing I could do was to be reassuring, to make her feel safe.

'Maybe I *can* make him go away,' I said. 'Where is the dark man now, Lyn?'

Her eyes flickered momentarily and I tensed. Her voice, however, remained calm, deadpan. 'He's here. He's always here.'

'And what is he doing?'

Her voice changed, became imbued with a note of almost childlike wonder, which I found both eerie and endearing. 'He's scared.'

'What is he scared of?'

'You, of course. He doesn't like you being here.'

'Well, good,' I said, resisting an urge to reach out and take her hands; sometimes she reacted badly to physical contact. 'In that case I'll stay a little longer, shall I?'

She nodded, and I looked into her eyes, trying to see something of the old Lyn, the Lyn that had appeared to me that morning. 'When was the last time you saw me, Lyn?' I asked. 'Can you remember?'

I knew this was a risky question; one thing that Lyn found hard to grasp was the concept of time. It wasn't unknown for her to freak out, suddenly and unpredictably, because of a question she couldn't answer or a concept she couldn't understand. When that happened it sometimes seemed to me that it was because she had had a sudden insight into exactly how mentally damaged she was, and that knowledge had terrified her.

This time, though, she merely pulled a face as if I was being dim. 'I already told you. In my dream.'

'But when was the dream, Lyn? Last night?'

She hesitated a moment, then nodded. 'Yes.'

I had a sudden weird notion that what I was looking at was not my wife at all but a chrysalis, dry and withered, inside which, waiting to burst into the light, was a dazzling butterfly. All I had to do was figure out how to break the chrysalis open without damaging the fragile creature inside.

'Did your dream tell you *how* I could help you?' I asked. 'Because I want to, Lyn. I really, really want to.'

She went very still, and instead of answering she slowly raised her hands and cupped them, dipping her head slightly as if she could see something tiny and delicate in there, something which she was protecting.

'The dark man carried darkness in his hands,' she said so quietly that I had to lean forward to hear her. 'He pushed it into me and I went away.'

She raised her head, looking at me as if her words explained everything. Not wishing to lose this moment, to lose *her*, I asked, 'Where did you go, Lyn?'

'Long ago and far away,' she said.

A spasm, a shock, went through my body, leaving both coldness and also a weird sort of exhilaration in its wake. But I tried not to react. I couldn't afford to alarm her, to snap the delicate thread between us. Keeping my voice steady, I said again, 'And how can *I* help you, Lyn? Did your dream tell you how?'

Again that quizzical look, as if I was being dim. 'You turn the darkness into light.'

I took a long breath, and that was when I felt the weight against my ribs. Seeing Lyn sitting before me, cupping her hands, I was suddenly struck by an inspiration.

'Can I show you something? It's in my pocket. Can I get it out?'

'Yes,' she whispered.

My heart was thumping, pounding. Not sure what I was doing, but feeling that it was right, I slipped my hand into the pocket of my jacket and folded it around the heart. Slowly, as though it was a delicate egg, or perhaps even the creature that had hatched from it, I withdrew it.

From the darkness into the light, I thought.

Raising my hand, I uncurled my fingers, showing Lyn the obsidian heart.

I held my breath, waiting for her reaction. For a long, excruciating moment there was no reaction at all; she merely stared at the heart, her eyes wide and fixed, her face expressionless. Then something changed in her. The tension went out of her body; the muscles in her face relaxed. I saw her eyes glitter, and then tears brimmed on the bottom row of her lashes and dripped on to her hands. It was so quiet in the room that I was convinced I could hear the little splashes they made.

'Are you all right?' I asked.

Her head tilted up, her eyes met mine, and I saw that there was something like rapture on her face.

'You took it,' she said. 'You took it from him.'

'Took what?'

'His darkness. You made it so that he couldn't hurt me any more.'

I felt a need to clarify what she was saying, to cut through the obfuscation. 'Is this his darkness?'

She nodded.

'You mean you've seen it before?'

'He put it in me. He put the darkness in me, and then I was in the darkness and I couldn't get out.'

'But is this what he used? The heart?'

'Yes. It is the darkness.'

I was stunned – but also confused. I didn't know what to make of this. Was Lyn speaking the truth? Had she really seen the heart before? Had it been used as a weapon against her, or was she deluded? Was she seeing the heart as a symbol of her own insanity, simply because it was black and because it represented the core of human life, the seat of human emotion?

I couldn't decide, but I knew that I couldn't risk pressing her on this without her becoming agitated. Besides which, I suspected that she had told me as much as she knew, or at least as much as she understood.

'Give it to me,' she said suddenly.

Her manner was neither aggressive nor insistent, and yet as before, when I had handed the heart to Benny at his request, my instinct was to say no. My instinct, in fact, was to tighten my grip on the heart, to put it back in my pocket and make some excuse as to why she couldn't have it.

Even as I struggled with my possessive thoughts I was disturbed by them. I could have reasoned that given the heart's track record I was merely anxious for Lyn's safety, but I knew that wasn't the case. Somehow I felt certain that Lyn *wouldn't* be harmed, that the heart would only become active if she seriously threatened me. And yet even though I felt as though some kind of breakthrough was being made here today, I still found it hard to accede to her request. In the end I fixed a smile on my face and said, 'The darkness is sleeping now. You must be very gentle with it. You mustn't do anything to wake it. And when I tell you, you must give it back to me. Do you understand?'

She looked at me, as awestruck as a child entrusted with the care of a vulnerable animal. 'Yes,' she whispered.

'All right then.' I hesitated a moment longer, and then I placed the heart carefully into her cupped hands.

She sighed in contentment and closed her eyes. I saw more of the tension seeping from her body. With the utmost care she bent her elbows and, still cupping the heart, pressed it to her bosom. She was weeping freely but silently now, tears forming glistening tracks down her cheeks. In that moment, haloed by the light from the window, her hands pressed together as though in prayer, she looked saintly.

The moment stretched, and for a split second I experienced a sensation of utter serenity. I felt blissful, complete; I had the oddest feeling that it was a projection of Lyn's thoughts momentarily and miraculously untangled by the ministrations of the heart. The feeling passed over me like a warm breeze, and I felt my fingers tingle, felt the now-familiar anxiety to possess the heart once again. Resisting the urge to snatch the object out of Lyn's hands, I said, 'You'd better give the darkness back now, Lyn. I need to keep it safe.'

Her eyes opened, and for a moment I felt certain she was about to protest. But then she sighed and gave the heart back to me. I took it eagerly, pushed it into my pocket, out of sight.

'Thank you,' she breathed. 'Thank you, Alex.'

TWENTY

MY DRUG

'You took your time.'

Benny sounded calmer than when I had last spoken to him, his voice only mildly reproachful.

'This is the first chance I've had to ring you back,' I said. 'I got your text at midday, but Clover and I have been together since then.'

He was silent for a moment, and then he said, 'And where's she now?'

'In the shower. We've checked into a hotel.'

'Which one?'

I hesitated, then replied, 'No offence, Benny, but I'd rather not say.'

I heard a dry chuckle from the other end of the line. When he next spoke his voice was a little warmer. 'None taken. To tell you the truth, Alex, I'm glad you're being careful, especially as Monroe's with you. How are you both?'

'Fine. How are you?'

'I'm all right. Lesley and I have spent the day clearing up. The conservatory's a fucking wreck.'

'I'm sorry about that.'

'I'll bill you when this is over, and we'll say no more about it.'

I grunted a laugh, though I wasn't entirely sure that Benny was joking. Clover and I had been on a train back to London when his text had come in earlier that day. I had been heading back from the buffet car with a bag of sandwiches and drinks when I had felt the phone vibrate in my pocket. The message from Benny had been short and sweet:

Call me. Don't tell Monroe.

I had considered ringing him back there and then, but the automatic door into our carriage had already hummed open and Clover had spotted me. When I got back to the seat she said, 'Have you had a message? I saw you checking your phone.'

Hoping my guilt wasn't written all over my face, I shook my head. 'It wasn't email man. Just work.'

Now, sitting on one of the twin beds in yet another London hotel, listening to the thrumming of water from behind the door of the en suite bathroom, I said, 'What did you want me for, Benny?'

'I might have some information for you. About your daughter.'

My heart quickened. 'Where is she? Is she safe?'

'Calm down,' he said. 'Don't get your hopes up. It might be nothing, but I've been given a lead.'

'What lead?' I said impatiently. 'Tell me.'

'I've been given the name of a bloke who might know something. It's tenuous, but I thought it was worth checking out. Can you meet me?'

'When? Where?'

'In an hour. A pub called The Cross Keys in Walthamstow. It's on Glenwood Road.'

'I'll be there,' I said.

'Can you come alone?'

Instantly I was suspicious. 'Why?'

'Because I don't know if this is a set-up. And if it is I don't want Monroe involved.'

Was he telling the truth? I had no way of knowing. I might be stepping into the lions' den, but was that any worse than sitting around here, waiting for something to happen? If I was going to find Kate, then I had to stick my neck out and snap up every crumb that was tossed my way.

'Fair enough,' I said. 'But why are you doing this, Benny? Why are you putting yourself at risk?'

It was only when I stopped talking that I realised he was no longer there. Had he been cut off? Or did he simply feel he had told me all I needed to know and there was no point in prolonging the conversation? I thought about ringing him back, but time was of the essence. The shower was still running in the bathroom, but Clover wouldn't be in there for ever. I swung my legs off the bed, crossed to the desk and scribbled her a note on hotel stationery. I felt bad for running out on her, but I hoped she'd realise it was for the right reasons. Crossing to the door, I opened it and then eased it shut behind me. I hurried to the stairs, expecting at any moment the door of our room to open and Clover to appear with wet hair and a towel wrapped around her, demanding to know where I was going.

The hotel was in Paddington, close to the station. It was a bit of a hike up to Walthamstow, and despite what I'd told Benny, I knew it would be a push to be there within the hour. Stepping out of the hotel into the chill of the early evening, I marched briskly along Praed Street, my hands stuffed in my jacket pockets, my shoulders hunched. I would have jogged if it wouldn't have drawn attention to myself, and if the pavements hadn't been so crowded. This was the first time I'd been out on my own since fleeing the scene of McCallum's murder, and despite the comfort of having the heart in my possession I felt paranoid and vulnerable, my head darting back and forth in an attempt to look in every direction at once, my eyes scrutinising the faces of everyone who came near me. So far the 'Wolves' that we had encountered (if that was what they were) had been bizarre beyond belief, but that didn't mean they were *all* just as grotesque. Wasn't it possible that some were human, or at least could pass themselves off as human, and so blend with the crowds? In which case the threat could come from anywhere, and my best option was to keep moving and be constantly on my guard. When I reached the station, I darted towards the escalators leading to the Underground, like a rabbit seeking the sanctuary of its burrow.

Not that there *was* any sanctuary to be found here. It was rush hour and the platform was packed, bodies crammed against one another. I squeezed my way to the far end, where the crowd was marginally thinner, and stood with my back against a metal stanchion, eyeing with suspicion anyone I felt was edging too close to me. When a Circle Line train sighed to a halt, I waited for my fellow passengers to board before darting towards the end door of the nearest carriage. I squeezed myself into the mass of humanity, dipping my head as the curved door closed behind me. The carriage smelled of sweat and stale perfume and damp cloth. The wall of bodies in front of me heaved and jostled as the train lurched into motion, an Asian man in a grey suit stumbling against me and inadvertently crushing the heart against my ribcage with bone-bruising impact. I grunted in pain, causing him to mutter an apology, but secretly I felt comforted by its unyielding presence.

As the train sped towards King's Cross, an illuminated snake slipping through subterranean darkness, I thought about the discussion that Clover and I had had that afternoon. She had been dubious about Lyn's claim that the heart, yielded by the dark man, had been responsible for taking her mind.

'Sorry, Alex, but she's deluded,' she had said. 'You said yourself that this "dark man" is the embodiment of her psychosis. So isn't it natural that after dreaming you can save her, she views the heart as the symbol of the dark man's power, which she's convinced herself you stole from him?'

In truth, I had been thinking along the same lines, but Clover's scepticism allowed me to voice a few of the doubts at the back of my mind, or more specifically to put forward the possibility that maybe Lyn's ramblings were not so far from the truth.

'I know what you're saying, but what if this whole thing *is* a lot deeper and more complex than we thought? Like I've said before, there must be a reason why *I* was chosen to steal the heart. Whoever's behind this went to a lot of trouble to get me involved.'

I could see she was readying herself to speak, so I held up a hand. 'Just hear me out. We know about the Sherwoods, and the fact that they'd been living across the hall from me for a year. So if our enemies can think *that* far in advance, why not further? Is it *so* inconceivable that breaking up me and Lyn was part of some great plan, and that they somehow used the heart to fuck up her mind?'

'It's not *inconceivable*,' Clover said, 'but it doesn't really make sense. If the Wolves or whoever had the heart five years ago, why didn't they hold on to it? Why was it in McCallum's possession and why did they need you to steal it?'

'Well... I don't know,' I said, exasperated. 'But you were there at the club and at Benny's house – you know what we're up against, and what the heart can do. Given what we've seen so far, *none* of this seems to make sense – but obviously it must do to somebody. The reason we can't see the big picture is because we're not privy to all the facts yet. But once we find out more, maybe it'll become clear.'

'Maybe,' Clover sighed. 'But I still can't understand why you were chosen, Alex. Don't take this the wrong way, but why are *you* so special?'

It was a question I'd been asking myself ad nauseam. Shrugging I said, 'Buggered if I know. I'm just a normal bloke from north London. My dad was a roofer and my mum worked at the Co-op. They bickered all the time and we were always short of money. My dad died of cancer in 2001 when he was fifty-two. Since then my mum's been trying to get compensation from the council, claiming it was due to asbestos poisoning. I had a normal upbringing, ran a bit wild when I was a kid just because all my mates did, and ended up in prison because I was greedy and wasn't strong enough to say no. Then I came to my senses and achieved the giddy heights you find me at today.' I smiled grimly. 'There's nothing I can think of that might have led to all this. There's nobody I've known, nothing I did or said, that might have marked me out for special treatment. I don't know, maybe I'm just unlucky. Maybe I was just in the wrong place at the wrong time.'

She looked at me long and thoughtfully. 'Do you honestly think you might have been targeted for this... this *whatever it is* years ago?'

'I don't know. And to be honest I don't care. If I can get Kate back, and a guarantee that we'll be left alone to get on with our lives, then I wouldn't care if I *never* got any answers.'

As I changed at King's Cross, jumping on a Victoria Line train bound for Walthamstow Central, I wondered if that was true. Perhaps it was simply the heart exerting some kind of mental juju over me, but I couldn't help thinking that its fate and my own were now inextricably linked. What really bothered me was the prospect of having to give the heart up. If it came to a straight swap, Kate for the heart, then I would do it, no question – but that didn't change the fact that somehow, over the past few days, the heart had become my drug, my heroin. My dependence on it terrified me, but it gave me succour too.

As the tube slowed at Blackhorse Road, the last stop before Walthamstow, I pulled out the London A–Z which Clover had given me the night McCallum had died, and plotted my route from the station to Glenwood Road, trying to commit it to memory. It was only a five-minute walk, but once I was off the train I wanted to keep moving. To have to stop for any length of time would make me feel like a target. It was just coming up to an hour since Benny had called, which meant I was going to be about ten minutes late for our meeting, but he would just have to lump it. I wondered what Clover was doing now, how furious she was with me, how betrayed she felt. She'd probably been trying to call me, had probably texted me or left a voicemail message, but I had switched my phone off. I was wound up enough as it was, and needed neither the hassle nor the guilt trip.

By the time I left the station, dusk had deepened into night and the shabby kebab shops, Indian restaurants and mini-marts lining Hoe Street were leaking light the colour of old teeth. I hurried along the pavement for a couple of hundred metres, keeping my head down, and then cut along a side road leading in the direction of Queens Road Cemetery, a sprawling, overgrown eleven-acre plot bordered by residential streets. Before reaching the cemetery I took a left down Glenwood Road, keeping my eyes peeled for the pub, The Cross Keys, which Benny had mentioned. After fifteen seconds or so I spotted it, a nut-brown, unobtrusive little building tucked between an Italian restaurant and a hair salon that specialised in 'Afro Stylings' and 'Real Human Hair Extensions'. The windows of the pub were tinted, the reddish glow which seeped from them reminding me of rheumy, bloodshot eyes. As I crossed the street I looked around for anything or anyone that might be construed as a threat, and then ducked into the pub's interior.

The bar was small and less than busy, and despite the dim lighting I spotted Benny immediately. He was sitting at a table beside a silent juke box, his face grim and his mobile pressed to his ear. He might have been calling me to find out where I was because the instant I entered the room he snapped the phone shut and put it in his pocket. As I approached I expected him to ask where I'd been, or tell me in no uncertain terms that he didn't like to be kept waiting. But instead he took a quick drink from a glass of what looked like fizzy water on the table in front of him and stood up.

'Let's go,' he said.

I was taken aback. 'Go where? I've only just got here.'

'There's someone we have to meet, and we're late already.'

'Why can't we meet him here?'

'He gets nervous in public places.'

I stood motionless as he strode past me and then I followed him outside. Walking back the way I had come I noticed that he had regained his old poise and confidence. Benny didn't exactly swagger

– he was neither crude enough nor obvious enough for that – but he still managed to give the impression that he owned the place and that you would cross him at your peril. Although I was taller than he was I had to hurry to keep up. At the end of Glenwood Road I asked, 'Where's the car?'

'We don't need the car where we're going.'

Reaching the junction I expected him to turn right, but instead he turned left, which gave me a sudden inkling of where we might be headed.

'Are we going to the cemetery?'

'Why? You scared of ghosts?'

'Course not,' I replied. 'It's just… well, if the Wolves of London are after me, isn't it better to stick to bright lights and lots of people?'

'If the Wolves of London are after you, they'll get you wherever you are. Do you want your daughter back or not?'

'Course I do.'

'You'll have to trust me then, won't you? You're not the only fucker running scared, you know.'

The streets were deserted, the multi-hued glow of lights from behind the curtained windows of the houses we passed giving the impression that the residents of Walthamstow had battened down the hatches, sealing themselves in for the night. Obscured by ribbons of cloud, the stars overhead were non-existent, the moon reduced to a silver smear. A chilly breeze caused litter to twitch fitfully in the gutters, and a nearby hedge rocked gently as though trying to dislodge the crumpled beer cans that had been pushed into it. In the distance a dog was barking, the sound flat and repetitive.

The grey stone pillars either side of the gated entrance to Queens Road Cemetery resembled sentry boxes petrified by time or ancient magic. The gates had been closed for the night, but Benny scaled them easily despite his age, dropping to the ground on the other side as soundless as a cat. Not to be outdone, I clambered up and over too, though my landing wasn't quite so elegant. Benny shot out a hand and grabbed my arm as I stumbled.

'Careful, son. You don't want to do yourself a mischief.'

Although flanked on all sides by residential streets, the cemetery was large enough for the majority of it to remain in darkness. Immediately beyond the gates the place looked neat and tidy, but closer inspection revealed that the graves, many of which had been here for well over a century, were in generally poor repair. Headstones were leaning or broken, monuments eroded and toppled, and many of the plots appeared to have succumbed to subsidence. Some of the long, flat stones which capped the graves were lying so aslant that it looked as if their occupants had pushed them up from below.

Barely making a sound on the gravel underfoot, Benny led the way towards a cluster of buildings. Silhouetted by darkness, the tall, slender belfry hemmed in by its pair of chapels looked as Gothic and forbidding as any haunted house. We passed through an arch beneath the long pointing finger of the belfry, and were plunged into instant icy darkness. Even when we emerged on the other side it was barely more enticing. Here, away from the public gaze, was where the cemetery was *really* falling to rack and ruin. The grass and weeds grew longer here, some of them so high that only the tips of gravestones could be seen, like the heads of drowning sailors slipping beneath an undulating sea. Undaunted, Benny pushed on and I followed, neither of us speaking. Struggling through the undergrowth, I jumped when I spied a figure lying in the long grass, only to realise that it was a stone angel as tall as a man, which had been pushed or fallen over and was now lying on its outstretched wings.

Eventually we came to a stone crypt, the entrance to which was enclosed by an iron fence whose railings had either rusted to almost nothing or were missing entirely. The crypt resembled a bomb shelter, albeit one fashioned with a Victorian penchant for over-elaboration. Into the lintel above the doorway was carved what I assumed was the name of the family whose mortal remains were incarcerated here, but it was too weathered, and my surroundings too dark, for me to make out the letters. The entrance to the crypt was a sturdy oak door behind a pair of fancy iron gates.

'This is the place,' Benny said.

'We're meeting your contact here?' I asked dubiously, peering at the surrounding foliage, which was rustling and shifting like a restless congregation.

'Not out here,' Benny said, and nodded towards the crypt entrance. 'Down there.'

I stared at him. 'You're kidding me.'

'Why would I be? It's as good a place as any.'

'But we'll be hemmed in. What if it's a trap?'

He reached into his pocket and pulled out the gun which I'd last seen pointing at my face. 'It won't be. But just in case...'

I shook my head. 'That won't do any good, Benny. You saw the thing that attacked your house. Bullets would be useless against something like that.'

Scowling, he said, 'Know what your problem is, Alex? You worry too much. Come on.' He stepped through the gap in the railings and walked up to the door of the crypt.

I expected him to rap on the gates with his gun or perhaps push his hand through the metalwork and knock on the door, but instead he reached out and, accompanied by the thin squeal of unoiled metal, tugged open first one gate and then the other. He grabbed the ornate brass doorknob, twisted it and pushed. The door grated inwards, revealing an expanding edge of darkness.

'How did you know it would be open?' I asked suspiciously.

'How do you think? I was informed.'

The door yawned wider. As Benny stepped forward I stood where I was, wary of committing myself. Behind me I heard a sound – a creak or a click. I twisted, peering into the shadows, but if there was something moving among the graves it was concealed within the restless stirring of the bushes and long grass.

'Are you coming or not?' Benny said. I turned back to see him standing in the open doorway. He was holding the gun loosely, its muzzle pointing at the ground. Behind him I could make out the top of a flight of wide stone steps descending into blackness. I patted my stomach, reassured by the solid weight of the heart in my inside pocket.

'Suppose so.'

Benny gave a curt nod and turned to face the darkness within the crypt. As he started down, I glanced behind me again and then followed. I wasn't sure about this – in fact, I couldn't shake off the feeling that this was a really bad idea. But what choice did I have? If there was a chance of finding out anything about Kate's whereabouts, then I had to take it. Passing beyond the threshold and into the crypt was like entering an icebox. Already Benny was descending into the gloom, his gun held out before him. The floor beneath my feet was gritty, each step I took echoing crisply back from the walls and ceiling. Benny, by contrast, was as silent as ever. Clenching my teeth, I picked my way down.

It was so dark I didn't know I'd reached the bottom of the steps until I stretched ahead with my foot to find I was back on level ground. Glancing behind me, I saw the crypt entrance was nothing but a tiny blotch of brownish dimness above. Wondering what would happen if someone were to slam the door and lock us in, I experienced a brief surge of muscle-tightening claustrophobia. Then I forced myself to calm down and think logically. Benny had his gun and I had the heart and both of us had mobile phones to provide light, should we need it, and a means of communicating with the outside world. So if we *were* locked in we'd have plenty of options for escape. Which meant we had nothing to worry about on that score.

Peering into the blackness and seeing nothing, I thought about using the light from my phone, but was reluctant to draw attention to myself. I hissed Benny's name, and when he didn't respond, I raised my voice to an urgent rasp. 'Benny, where are you?'

There was a click and mustard-coloured flame bloomed from the lighter in Benny's left hand. His face was a sickly yellow mask, his eyes twitching pools of shadow. The light glinted on the gun in Benny's other hand, and provided enough illumination for me to make out a low-ceilinged stone cavern with curved walls, which tapered to impenetrable blackness behind him.

'Boo,' he said mildly.

I forced a smile. 'So where's this contact of yours?'

Instead of answering, he said, 'Did you ever wonder why I took you under my wing in Pentonville, Alex? Why I looked out for you?'

Wondering whether it was a rhetorical question, I shrugged. 'I hoped it was because you liked me, or because you saw something in me. Something... worthwhile maybe.'

The shadows on his face shifted as his lips curved in a thin smile. 'Oh, I've got nothing against you, Alex. You're an okay guy. But the answer's simpler than that. I did it for money.'

I frowned. 'Money? You mean... someone *paid* you to look after me?'

'Yep.'

'Who?' I asked, baffled.

'Ah,' he said mildly, 'now that I *can't* answer. If I told you, I'd have to kill you.'

There was silence for a moment. My mind was whirling. 'I don't understand,' I said. 'Why would someone pay you? And how did they know we were in the same prison?'

'You clearly have influential friends,' Benny said heavily.

'If I do I wish they'd show themselves. I could do with some help at the moment.'

'You could probably do with more than you realise.'

'What do you mean?'

Benny sighed. 'You haven't asked me why I'm telling you this now, after all these years.'

Dread crawled in my stomach. 'Go on then – why *are* you telling me?'

'Because I've had a better offer. Sorry, Alex. Not that I give a shit one way or the other, but I just wanted you to know this is nothing personal.'

Casually he raised the gun and pointed it at my chest. For the second time in less than twenty-four hours I stared at the muzzle and tried to imagine what it would feel like if a piece of red-hot metal travelling at seven hundred miles an hour tore into the soft flesh of my body. Would there be much pain? Would I die instantly or would there be a split second when I'd comprehend the full terror and agony of what was happening? My hand itched to touch the weight of the heart in my pocket, but I didn't dare move.

I tried to speak and found that I couldn't. I was so scared my throat felt as though it had swelled, stifling my voice. Muscles jumped in my left leg and I pressed my foot harder to the ground in an attempt to quell them. I wanted to close my eyes, but at the same time I felt compelled to keep them open for what might be my last moments of consciousness.

As if reading my thoughts, Benny said, 'I'm not going to shoot you if that's what you're worried about. My job was just to bring you here.'

Whether it was this reassurance or my own willpower that enabled me to speak I don't know, but with an effort I croaked, 'For who?'

Benny shrugged. 'Your guess is as good as mine. All I know is that a lot of money was paid into my bank account this morning – more than enough to make this little trip worth the risk.'

I was surprised and also oddly grateful to feel anger surge through me, loosening my throat still further. Recklessly I said, 'I thought you were smart, Benny, but you're not. You're a fucking idiot.'

I thought he might get angry, but I didn't care. However, contrary as ever, Benny laughed. 'I'm not the one who blindly followed an armed criminal into a hole in the ground.'

'No, but that doesn't mean you won't be as dead as me when the Wolves of London show up. And then what good will your money do you?'

Again he shrugged, as though the prospect of his own death didn't bother him. 'At least Lesley'll be well provided for.' He flourished the gun. 'And if anyone *does* try to take me down, they'll find themselves with a fucking battle on their hands.'

I was about to make a disparaging remark when the scrape of stone echoed through the crypt, making me jump. Benny spun round, raising the lighter above his head. Insipid ochre light flowed into the blackness, giving our surroundings a murky definition. Behind Benny the low-ceilinged room opened out, and I saw a row of cobweb-festooned sarcophagi, their lids coated in a fine layer of dust and shrivelled leaves. The stone lid of one of the sarcophagi was lying askew, revealing a triangle of darkness, which was all we could see of the tomb beneath. A flurry of disturbed dust sparkled and spun in the light, which suggested that the sound had been caused by the lid being pushed aside from within.

'What the fuck?' Benny muttered, and then, as though reacting to his voice, the lid moved again. With a grinding of stone on stone it slid all the way across until its weight caused it to tilt and crash to the floor.

The echoes were still ringing through the dimly lit room when the occupant of the sarcophagus sat up.

At first, in the dim and wavering light, partly concealed by a rolling wave of pale dust, I thought I was watching the emergence of some vast, spindly-limbed spider. Then, as the dust cleared, I saw something long and white rising into the air and realised it was a face. I gasped and stepped back, recognising the tall man I had seen at Incognito. As he (or it) stretched out his long legs, which I had seen him use to leap from one rooftop to another across a gap of eight metres, and began to clamber from the tomb, I glanced nervously around, looking for any sign of his entourage of clockwork grotesques.

No sooner had the thought crossed my mind than I heard whirring and clicking sounds behind me. Turning, I saw that flooding in through the crypt entrance were dozens of waddling, lopsided, scuttling *things*. Benny was still directing the light towards the monstrosity unfolding itself from the stone coffin, which meant that the more nightmarish details of the descending freak show were temporarily hidden from view. Even so, I got the impression that leading the pack was some sort of armoured metallic crab spouting angry puffs of steam from apertures in its back as it lurched from step to step, and what appeared to be the frantically spinning workings of a grandfather clock atop a thrashing tangle of tentacles.

Then Benny spun round with the lighter, sending wavering blocks of light and shadow careening across the walls. As buttery illumination washed over the descending hordes I was assailed with a barrage of nightmarish images. I glimpsed a pair of bloodshot eyes glaring from a quivering mass of flesh inside a bell jar; an open mouth with serrated metal teeth in the shrunken, eyeless face of a child; a human hand, dragging what appeared to be a miniature cannon that had been fused to its wrist; a monstrous amalgamation of what appeared to be Siamese twins and some sort of wheelchair-like device, that moved not on wheels but on juddering, steam-driven pistons that tentatively probed the way ahead like the white sticks of the blind.

'What is this?' Benny's voice was a snarl, but I'm certain I detected a waver of fear in it. He spun back to face the tall man. 'Who the fuck *are* you people?'

Despite my own fear, I felt a savage satisfaction at seeing him so rattled.

'Out of your depth, are you, Benny?' I said. 'All this a bit outside your comfort zone?'

He turned smartly to face me, the light swooping again. 'Shut your fucking mouth or I'll shoot you where you stand,' he barked.

The tall man had unfolded himself fully from the sarcophagus now and was standing up. His movements were precise, unhurried. He made me think again of a spider, one which knew its victims were wrapped up tight in its web and couldn't escape. As he rose to his full height, he was forced to bend almost double, his upper body stretching along the ceiling like an elongated shadow. He towered over us, his thin slash of a mouth opening wetly in a red smile. The flat discs of his spectacle lenses reflected the yellow flame from Benny's lighter, which made it look as if glowing embers burned in his eye sockets.

Benny looked up at him and licked his lips. Though he still brandished his gun, he now looked no more dangerous than a small boy playing at cowboys.

'I don't know who you are, mate, and I don't care,' he said, fear roughening his voice, bringing his natural London accent to the fore, 'but I've done what you wanted, I've brought him here' – he jerked the gun in my direction – 'and now I'm going to leave.' He turned and took a couple of paces towards the stone steps, and then he hesitated, halted.

The menagerie, still wheezing and puffing and whirring and clanking, had come to a stop. They were ranged across the steps, some of them still halfway up, forming an impenetrable barrier. Somewhere in the darkness above our heads I heard things darting and buzzing, their tiny motors making me think of robotic flies. In the gloom I could hear the squelch of wet flesh too, as it expanded and contracted in tortuous respiration.

Benny waved his gun from side to side, a nervous and rather pathetic gesture. 'Out of my way.'

The menagerie didn't move. Benny levelled the gun at the centre of the mass of flesh and clockwork bodies.

'I *said* out of my way.'

Despite the threat the menagerie remained motionless. Suddenly there was a sharp clicking like ratchets aligning or tumblers falling into place, and to my surprise the tall man spoke.

'I would advise you against threatening us, little man.' His voice was plummy, the words pompous and a mite archaic. It was not entirely a human voice, however. It was underpinned by an insectile buzz, as though filtered through a vocoder.

Scowling, Benny looked up at the looming white face. 'We had a deal. I made the delivery you asked for. So if you don't mind, I'd like to leave.'

The tall man's face gave nothing away, but I had the impression he was considering the request. Finally he said, 'Very well. Go.'

Benny looked momentarily surprised, then gave a grim nod. 'Thank you.'

As he stepped forward, the clockwork army creaked and shuffled aside, making a gap for him. Benny turned briefly and looked at me, and I expected him to make some cutting remark. But he simply regarded me through narrowed eyes for a moment and then turned back to the steps.

That was when it happened. I had a split-second impression of what seemed like a colony of bats, disturbed by some commotion, suddenly exploding into life around me, and then I was plunged into darkness. My immediate assumption was that Benny's lighter had gone out, but then I realised that I was standing in silence too. I could no longer hear the clicks and whirrs and the fleshy, wet billows of breath from the clockwork creatures; nor could I hear the crunch of grit underfoot when I shifted my feet. The sensation was akin to the one I'd experienced in Benny's house almost twenty-four hours earlier, when the four of us had been engulfed by living darkness. The difference this time, though, was that I didn't feel as though my spirits were being crushed, stifled; on the contrary, I felt enclosed in a protective pocket, in a place where nothing could touch me. Even so, I had no idea how I would free myself. I didn't know which way was forward and which was back. I had lost all sense of direction.

I slipped my hand into the pocket of my jacket and squeezed the heart, but it was cold, unresponsive. *Okay*, I thought, *okay.*

'Hello?' I called, but the sound was flat, dead, devoid of echo. I took the heart from my pocket, squeezed it, stroked it.

'Come on,' I said. 'Come *on*.'

And then I saw a light.

I tensed – was this something to do with the heart? It didn't *feel* like it, but I couldn't be sure. The light glimmered brighter, as if something or someone was approaching. Nervously I slipped the heart back into my pocket, squinting to make out what appeared to be a dark shape, or at least some kind of nucleus, in the centre of the light. I couldn't run or hide; there was nowhere to go. The light drifted closer, a soft effulgence, and suddenly I saw that there *was* a shape within it.

It was the man I had seen at Benny's, the one in the demob suit. He was walking unhurriedly towards me, a slight pigeon-toed waddle in his step. If the situation hadn't been so bizarre it might have seemed comical. I watched him approach, until at last he was standing directly in front of me, so close that I could see a tiny shaving cut on his cheek, a rash of soreness where his shirt collar rubbed his neck.

He regarded me a moment, taking a final puff on his roll-up before dropping it and stamping on it.

'Hello, Alex,' he said, his voice slightly nasal, his accent pure south London. 'My name's Frank Martin. *Private* Frank Martin.'

He stuck out his hand and instinctively I shook it. His flesh was cold, his grip bony but firm.

'Right,' he said, 'now that's out the way, we'd better get down to particulars. If you want to stay alive you need to come with me.'

TWENTY-ONE

THE SOLDIER'S STORY

Ten minutes after he had introduced himself, Private Frank Martin and I were strolling side by side through the quiet, ill-lit streets of Walthamstow, heading in the direction of the tube station. As we walked I kept sliding sidelong glances at him, half-expecting him to disappear in a puff of smoke. But he seemed reassuringly solid and, despite his dated appearance, reassuringly normal.

My mind was boiling with questions, and the only reason I wasn't bombarding him with them was because Frank had assured me he would tell me what I wanted to know as soon as we had put some distance between ourselves and what he referred to as 'the Surgeon's mob'. Even so, I had managed to give voice to a few before he'd convinced me of the need for haste – the first of which, after he had instructed me to accompany him, had been, 'Why should I? How do I know I can trust you?'

Frank had sighed, his almost translucent eyelids drooping in weary exasperation. 'I was told you might be difficult.'

'Told by who?' I countered.

For a moment he looked as if he might be about to answer, and then he released an even longer sigh, perhaps realising what a can of worms he might be opening with his reply. Raising his hands he said, 'Look, Alex, this really ain't the time right now. What say we find a boozer and talk about this over a pint?'

Without the clamour of war that had swirled about his slight frame during our previous encounter, his threat seemed minimal, and yet still I was wary. 'You've attacked me once,' I said, recalling how he had dredged darkness from within himself. 'How do I know you won't do it again?'

He shook his head and offered a watery smile, which barely offset the haunted look in his deep-set eyes. 'That wasn't an attack, it was a rescue. I needed to get you out of there quickly, which was why I turned on the fireworks – to get you to respond. There were bad things coming.'

'Worse than you?' I asked.

He rolled his eyes. 'A lot worse. Believe me, mate, I'm one of the good guys.'

Suddenly he winced, as if pain had stabbed through his head, and despite myself I asked, 'Are you all right?'

His face cleared, though he looked more washed-out than ever. 'That Surgeon's a strong one. He'll break out sooner rather than later. We ought to scarper – and pronto.'

As far as I knew, I could have been heading out of the frying pan and into the fire, but deciding that even if I was I could barely make my predicament any worse, I nodded.

'Okay. But how *do* we get out?'

'You just stick close to me. Safest thing would be to hold hands, but I'm not that sort of bloke. So what say I go ahead and you follow with your hand on my shoulder?'

I agreed and he turned his back on me. Reaching out I did as he had suggested, aware of the delicate, almost bird-like jut of his bones beneath the cheap material of his suit jacket. I could smell his hair cream, combined with tobacco smoke and the faint whiff of mothballs.

'Ready?'

'Ready.'

'Right then. Best foot forward.'

I'm not sure what happened then. It was like being in a sensory-deprivation tank, or perhaps a trance, and then of having my senses restored one by one. There was no sensation that I could later recall of ascending the stone steps of the crypt, or of negotiating what I knew to be the uneven terrain of the cemetery. Nor was I aware at first of cold air moving against my skin, or of outdoor sounds like the almost ambient thrum of traffic and the susurration of branches and leaves and long grass, set in motion by the wind.

Yet gradually these things were returned to me, like small, unexpected gifts. I was walking with my hand on Frank's shoulder when suddenly I realised that I could feel grass brushing against my shins, or a breeze stirring in my hair. Or I could see the glow of a distant street lamp flickering through a jagged silhouette of leaf-stripped branches.

By the time we reached the entrance to the cemetery I had no further need of Frank's guidance. Letting go of his shoulder I cupped my hands to help boost his scrawny frame over the gate, and then I clambered after him.

We barely spoke again until we were sitting on a tube heading back into central London. The rush hour was well over by now and apart from us there were only four or five people in the carriage. I had deliberately led Frank to the seats at the far end, out of earshot of the other passengers, who had given him a few curious glances before turning their attention back to their iPhones and BlackBerries. London was full of weirdos, after all, and Frank in his retro gear was not all that strange compared to some.

As soon as the train began to clank its way out of the station, I leaned forward.

'Time for some answers,' I said.

Frank looked tired. From what he had said earlier, I guessed that manipulating the darkness was an energy-sapping experience. Sure enough he said, 'Have a heart, Alex. I'm all done in. Could do with a nice pint of stout to see me right.'

'I haven't got time for the pub,' I snapped. 'I need to get back to Clover.' Realising I was being a little harsh I raised my hand. 'Look, I'm grateful for what you did, Frank, but my daughter's missing, I have no idea what's going on, and I don't want to leave Clover alone for any longer than I have to. There's a bar at the hotel. I'll buy you a pint of stout there – I'll buy you *ten* pints – if you'll give me some answers.'

He slumped back in his seat and expelled a long breath.

'Right then,' he said. 'What do you want to know?'

'Well... for a start, who are "the Surgeon's mob"? And who are you? Where do you all come from?'

He smiled faintly. 'The Surgeon's mob I can't help you with – for the simple fact that I don't know all that much about 'em, except that they're a bad lot. As for me, I'm guessing you want a bit more than my name and place of birth?'

I raised my eyebrows and he nodded resignedly.

'Fair enough. Well, my name's Frank Martin, like I said. I was born in Lewisham in 1897 and died at Ypres in August 1917 during the battle of Passchendaele. I was twenty.'

My heart lurched. I raised a hand. 'Hang on,' I said. 'No. What did you say? You died? In the First World War? Are you... are you shitting me? Are you telling me you're a... what? Zombie? Ghost?'

Frank scratched his nose. 'Not entirely sure what I am, to be honest with you. All I know is that I'm here. I copped it from a bullet – then you brought me back.'

It wasn't just my heart that lurched this time. The whole world seemed to tilt. I felt dizzy, sick. I felt something akin to panic. As if I was clinging to a ledge above an abyss, and my fingers were slipping, and there wasn't a single damn thing I could do about it.

'No,' I said. 'Wait. Whoa a minute. What are you talking about? *I* brought you back?'

Frank nodded matter-of-factly. 'Well, you and that box of tricks of yours.' He leaned forward, winked, his voice dropping to a whisper. 'The heart.'

Perhaps it would be best just to let go, I thought, to drop into the abyss. At that moment oblivion seemed like a desirable option.

Frank looked at me, not unkindly. 'Knocked you for six, that one, didn't it? Thought it might,' he said.

Even so, I made an attempt to drag my reeling thoughts together. 'But... how?' I stammered. 'I mean... what...'

Frank's bony shoulders lifted in a shrug. 'I've no idea how your oojamaflip works, Alex. All I can tell you is what I know. We were both called up on the same day, learned the ropes together, got shipped out to the trenches. I wasn't long out of school, was training to be a draughtsman. I was shit-scared and as green as they come. You looked after me, took me under your wing. Like a regular big brother to me you was. We were sent to Ypres in Belgium – all the lads called it Wipers. It was like Hell – literally like Hell. Barbed wire, mud, rats, everything dead, the town bombed to shit, the stink of smoke and rotten flesh, slop to eat and not enough of it. We were too cold and wet and scared to sleep...' His voice faltered, and for a moment his eyes looked black, his face like a skull. 'But you got me through it. In my darkest moments you were there. And then I got shot. Stray bullet, ricochet, I don't know. Bull's-eye, right in the heart, snuffed out without so much as a by-your-leave. Then next thing I know I'm opening my eyes to find your ugly mug looming over me. And that thing of yours, that heart, is glowing or burning or some such. I can feel it inside my chest, fixing me up, working its magic. I am the resurrection and the life, all that palaver.' He grinned cadaverously. 'Only I came back changed, didn't I? I came back with something else inside me.'

'The darkness,' I murmured.

'That's right. It was like that bullet was an infection, like it was part of the war itself. Either that or it created a hole, and when I died everything that the war was – all the blood and pain and death and fear – came rushing into that hole and filled me up. Maybe it wanted to claim me, eat me, like a big fucking monster. But when you brought me back it... trapped it, tamed it somehow. And now it does what I tell it, it dances to my tune.'

This time his grin was savage enough to make me shudder. I reached out and touched his hand in an attempt to calm him, or bring him back, and was shocked by how icy his flesh was.

'But I don't understand,' I said, almost pleading with him. '*How* can I have saved you? I've never met you before. I wasn't around in—'

And then realisation hit me and the shock of it stopped the words in my throat.

Frank nodded slowly, a look of grim satisfaction on his face. 'Penny dropped, has it?'

My mind began to spin all over again. What I was thinking *couldn't* be true. And yet in the past few days I had been confronted by the impossible on too many occasions to entirely dismiss it. I goggled at him.

'You're talking about my future, aren't you? You're saying that somehow... I'm going to travel back in time?'

'Already have, as far as I'm concerned.' Frank jerked a glance at my pocket. 'All down to that box of tricks of yours, ain't it? The things it can do...'

I cupped my hand over the bulge of the heart. Could I feel it thrumming with energy or was that merely my own hot blood racing through my veins?

'Is this actually happening?' I said. 'Or am I hallucinating? Maybe

I'm away with the fairies. Maybe I'm strapped to a bed in a looney bin somewhere, dreaming all this.'

'You're saying I might be a figment of your imagination?' said Frank.

'It's possible.'

'How do you know that you're not a figment of mine?'

'Oh fuck,' I said. 'Oh fuck.' My head was throbbing, like a boiler under too much pressure. I wondered how much strain a human mind could take before it snapped or shattered.

'How can I believe this?' I said. 'I need proof. What else can the heart do? How does it work?'

Frank laughed. 'He asks *me*! That's rich, that is.' Stemming his mirth, he jabbed a finger at me. 'You're the organ-grinder, mate. I'm just the bloody monkey.'

I sat back, breathless, my head thumping, my heart racing. Could it really be true? Was I really going to travel back in time? To Ypres, to the trenches, to the First World War? The fact that I was even contemplating it as a possibility seemed ridiculous. And yet, and yet...

How far into my future would it happen, I wondered. And was it predetermined, unalterable? If Frank had already experienced it, and if he was here now, then surely it *had* to happen?

'What do I look like in the past, Frank?' I asked, amazed that I was even entertaining the notion. 'When you knew me, I mean. Did I look any different to how I do now?'

Frank shook his head without even scrutinising my face. 'Not that you'd notice. Different haircut, of course. Army short back and sides. But apart from that...' He shrugged.

'So you're saying this happens soon?' I said. The magnitude of it swept over me again, leaving me dizzy and breathless. 'Shit.'

Frank grinned, seemingly amused by my predicament. 'Least you've got an idea what to expect – from history books and that, I mean. How do you think *I* felt being sent in the opposite direction? Talk about a fish out of water.'

I stared at him, still trying to put together all that he was telling me. 'Are you saying it was *me* who sent you here?'

'To help you out. Gave me a right mission briefing, you did. Dates, times, all that.'

'So... you know what's going to happen to me?'

'Some of it,' Frank said, and tapped his nose. 'But that's classified information. No foreknowledge, you said. Too dangerous. Even I only know the bits I *need* to know.'

I rubbed my forehead. My hand was trembling and my heart was still beating hard. 'This is so fucked up.'

'You'd better get used to it,' said Frank. 'I've a feeling this is going to be your life from now on.'

I rubbed my hands briskly over my face, as if my confusion was a grey fug, a caul, I could shred and discard.

'What about Kate?' I asked, almost afraid of what his answer might be. 'What do you know about her?'

'I know she's your daughter and that you're looking for her.'

'But you don't know where she is?'

He shook his head and I felt something slump inside me. 'Sorry, guv'nor.'

When we reached Paddington, Frank got off the tube with me, telling me he would be sticking with me for a while. Walking back to the hotel I felt as if I were floating or dreaming, as if not only my surroundings, but my entire life was no longer real. It was hard to believe that only a few days ago everything had seemed set and immovable – time, the universe, life and death, whereas now it all seemed unstable, temporary, ephemeral.

Reaching the hotel, I drifted across the reception area, Frank at my side. It was only when we were ascending in the lift that I remembered the circumstances in which I had left Clover, and began to wonder what sort of mood she might be in and how she might react to my account of what had happened tonight, what I had discovered.

'Did I tell you about Clover?' I asked Frank, who was staring at the digital floor indicator on the panel beside the door as if suspicious of what it might do. 'Did the future me tell you, I mean?'

Still with his eyes on the panel, Frank said, 'Girlfriend of yours, ain't she?'

'No,' I said. 'At least...' I had been about to say 'not yet', wondering whether in my future – when Frank met me – my relationship with Clover might have changed. But I balked at even suggesting that it might become a possibility, for the simple reason that it seemed too weird and inappropriate to contemplate. 'No,' I said again. And then, after a pause, 'We're just friends.'

'Whatever you say,' Frank said, after which the lift reached the fifth floor and there was no time left for discussion. As soon as the doors opened, Frank stepped smartly out as if he didn't trust them not to slam shut on him. I exited behind him and looked across the landing at the door to our room. It was ajar.

Dread seized me.

There was no way, given the current situation, that Clover would have been so lax as to leave the door open. Which meant that something must have happened, almost certainly something bad. I shot across the landing, overtaking Frank, and leaped into the room, barging the door open with my shoulder and reaching for the heart in the same way that Benny might reach for his gun.

It needed no more than a cursory glance to see that the room was empty.

Not that the sight of it, nor even the fact that there was no evidence of a struggle, was any kind of relief. Remembering what had happened the last time I had found a hotel room unexpectedly empty, I crossed to the en-suite bathroom and (muttering a quick and silent prayer) pushed the door open.

The light was on, the harshness of the high-wattage bulb seeming to pulse at the backs of my eyes in time with my queasily pumping heart. Seeing that this room too was empty I allowed myself a small sigh of relief. There was still plenty of cause for concern, though; I couldn't believe Clover would simply pop out for a change of scene, or to do a bit of shopping, or even that she would have tried to follow me (I had given her no indication in my note of where I might be going). The alternatives, therefore, were that she had either been abducted or, like me, had been lured into a trap.

I scanned the bathroom again – toiletries around the sink, a damp towel on the heated rail, the plastic shower curtain still beaded with moisture – and then I went back into the main room. Frank was standing in the gap between the twin beds, hands in pockets, rocking gently back and forth on his heels.

'She's been taken,' I said.

He gave a brief nod. 'So it would seem.'

I narrowed my eyes suspiciously. 'Do you know something I don't?'

'I've *seen* something you haven't.' He looked pointedly across the room. 'There. Propped against that white jug.'

He meant the kettle. I followed his gaze and saw what appeared to be a business card. I crossed to it, snatched it up. The card was pristine, ivory-coloured, expensive-looking. Across the top, in gold, embossed script, was the heading: Commer House, followed by an address in the Isle of Dogs.

I handed the card to Frank. 'What do you think?'

Frank took it and read it. 'I think it's an invitation.'

'I think it's another trap,' I said, 'with Clover as the bait.'

Frank gave the card back to me and shrugged, seemingly unconcerned. 'Same difference.'

TWENTY-TWO

ISLE OF DOGS

Thanks to the still-expanding Canary Wharf development, the Isle of Dogs had become afflicted with something of a split personality over the past couple of decades. Enclosed within a noose-like loop of the River Thames, some of the most prosperous parts of the capital, if not the country, now stood shoulder to shoulder with some of the most deprived. Not that there was much evidence of the latter when Frank and I disembarked from the Docklands Light Railway at Mudchute, which cut between Millwall to the west and Cubitt Town to the east. After consulting my A–Z beneath a street lamp we began to walk up a road which would eventually bring us to the A1206, which looped all the way around the outer perimeter of the 'noose' like an artery serving a major organ, and thence to the dockside developments facing out across the wide stretch of the Thames. The address on the card that had been left for us in the hotel was Commer House, Britannia Wharf. Whether this was an apartment complex, an office block or an old still-to-be-developed warehouse was anyone's guess.

For an area with a once fearsome reputation, the long, meandering stretch of Spindrift Avenue, which Frank and I were following, was surprisingly quiet, even genteel. The houses and apartment blocks lining the road were neat, compact and modern, all sharp angles, red and black brick and port-holed windows. There was much greenery in evidence – regimented rows of identical trees and little patches of parkland squeezed into the urban sprawl. Yet, preferable though this was to the crumbling, rat-infested hovels and patches of litter-strewn waste ground that had once filled these streets, it was all a bit bland for my taste.

By the time we neared our destination it was creeping towards 11 p.m. We emerged from the tangle of streets on the outer edge of the A1206 to find that a low wall of shiny chocolate-coloured brick was all that stood between us and the rushing Thames. Across the river pinpoints of light combined to form a softly glowing halo above the buildings they illuminated. A cold breeze blew in off the water, freezing my hands and face and making me shiver.

'This way,' I said, pointing to the right. Frank and I hurried along a herringbone walkway which followed the course of the river, dwarfed on our right by the imposing, flat-fronted edifices of former warehouses converted into flats, their tiny, myriad windows bedecked with window boxes, their forecourts neatly paved and fenced and lined with shrubs.

Something flapped ahead of us, and I faltered for a moment, imagining the wing of a giant bird or bat. Then the sound came again, making more of a crack this time, and I realised it was only the loose edge of a piece of plastic or tarpaulin, animated by the wind.

Moving closer, I saw that beyond the apartment block on our right was a slightly smaller building, set back a little across a muddy patch of ground, as if timidly squatting in the shadow of its more illustrious neighbour. This building was encased in an exoskeleton of scaffolding, its upper floors wrapped in green netting. A chain-link fence formed a barrier in front of it, from which hung a pockmarked metal sign warning: DANGER! CONSTRUCTION SITE. Beneath, in smaller letters, was another sign: TRESPASSERS WILL BE PROSECUTED.

Even before I saw the Building Regulations notice stuck to the lamp post a few metres away, I knew that this would be Commer House. I looked at Frank and he looked at me.

'Here we go again,' he said.

The double gates, which allowed access to the construction crew and caged not only the building but the diggers and trucks that stood in front of it, were linked by a heavy chain wrapped in thick blue plastic and secured with a padlock. Frank dropped the roll-up he'd been smoking and stepped up beside me. He hunkered down and made a stirrup of his hands. 'My turn to give you a boost-up this time, mate.'

Before stepping into his linked palms, I reached out and gave the padlock an experimental tug, fully expecting it to be immovable.

However at my touch the looped bar at the top of the padlock slid free of the chain and the entire lock fell to the floor with a muddy clunk. I stared at it in surprise, but Frank only narrowed his eyes.

'Bloody eager for us to join the party, ain't they?'

'We'd better not disappoint them then,' I murmured, and unwound the chain, which was so cold it numbed my fingers. I tugged it free, then pushed the gate open just wide enough for the two of us to slip through.

As we entered the site I peered anxiously up at the building looming over us. If we had been observed squeezing through the gate there was no indication of it. The windows were black, and the only movement I could detect, aside from the billow and flap of the netting, was the restless prowling of a pigeon in a sagging gutter high up near the roof. Frank had moved ahead of me, and Commer House's shadow was already swallowing him as he picked his way delicately over the mud-churned ground. I followed, glancing nervously at the silent construction vehicles as if they were sleeping dinosaurs. By the time I reached Frank he had already wrapped his hand around the brass knob of the big front door and was pushing it open.

'Unlocked,' he whispered, glancing over his shoulder and raising his eyebrows.

I stayed him with a hand on the arm. 'They might as well have left a trail of breadcrumbs for us to follow.'

He paused. The blackness revealed by the wedge of open door looked every bit as profound as that which Frank could conjure out of himself. 'What do you reckon?'

'Let's not make it easy for them. Why don't we try round the back?'

'You're the guv'nor,' Frank said, and pulled the door closed again, as carefully and quietly as he could.

Picking our way through the ruts and puddles, we trudged round the side of the building. As soon as the side wall blotted out the waterfront lights we were plunged into darkness. I halted a moment, waiting for my eyes to adjust. Above me the green netting rustled like something big turning in its sleep.

'Don't suppose you can see in the dark, can you, Frank?' I whispered.

'Why would I be able to do that?'

'Well, you have a... unique relationship with darkness. And back at Benny's house you kind of... glowed. I just wondered.'

He chuckled drily. 'Sorry to disappoint you, but I ain't a bleedin' owl.'

Using the light from my phone, I was able to make out vague shapes ahead. Stepping around the icy metal scaffolding poles, I crept along the side of the building, the illuminated display screen angled towards the ground in order to avoid my stepping into holes or tripping over unseen obstacles. Even so, it wasn't easy; the phone-light wasn't great, and the side of the building was a higgledy-piggledy mass of abutments and recesses, which probably made perfect sense in the daytime, but in the dark was a confusing nightmare. And the ground was choked with debris: rocks, timber, clumps of weeds and nettles, chunks of metal and machinery.

At last we edged around the corner of the building, to find that the ground opened out at the back into a patch of wasteland, a tall fence marking the boundary at the rear of the property. All we had to do now was find a way in; I hoped that wouldn't prove too difficult.

As it turned out, it didn't prove difficult at all. Within a minute we came to a doorway across which a number of planks had been nailed. On the wall beside the doorway was another of those DANGER! CONSTRUCTION SITE signs. After tugging at the planks and finding they were nailed on too tightly for our fingers to dislodge, Frank wandered off in search of a makeshift tool and returned a minute or so later with a couple of sharp-edged rocks. For the next few minutes we battered and prised at the edges of the planks until, one by one, the nails came loose.

Beneath the planks was a rickety door, the wood warped, only a few jagged, grime-smeared fangs of glass jutting from the upper frame. By the light of the phone we saw nothing but a patch of blank floor, beyond which air so cold it seemed refrigerated drifted from the darkness. I grasped the sticky, dirt-encrusted handle and gave the door an experimental push. It juddered open a few inches with a horrible squealing, grating noise. I winced and gritted my teeth as though that might encourage it to fall silent.

'Maybe we should sing the national bleedin' anthem to drown out the racket,' Frank muttered.

'So much for the element of surprise,' I said, and gave the door a harder shove in the hope it would reduce the friction.

The warped wood still protested, but less vociferously this time. Frank and I slipped into the building, my hand again slipping instinctively into the inside pocket of my jacket, my fingers seeking the cool surface of the heart. In the phone's light I saw the pale ghost of my breath curling on the air as I exhaled.

'Freezing,' I said, thinking of how the presence of the supernatural was said to be accompanied by a drop in temperature. I was about to mention this to Frank when it struck me that he might be offended.

We peered ahead, my phone-hand moving slowly from left to right. Though the light didn't penetrate far, I got the impression of a large open space with occasional pillars or stanchions supporting what must have been a vast expanse of ceiling. Whether this had once been the shop floor or a series of offices which had been knocked through I had no idea.

'Where now?' I whispered.

As if in answer I heard a faint sound so fleeting that I couldn't tell whether it was a sob, a groan or a cry for help, and froze.

'Did you hear that?'

'I did,' Frank confirmed. 'I reckon it came from down below.'

'A cellar?'

'Could be.'

'But how do we get down there?'

Frank sniffed. 'Whoever that was, I reckon it weren't far away. There must be some stairs somewhere. But we'd better be careful. We don't want to fall through no hole in the floor.'

'You realise that sound could have been made deliberately as a lure?' I said.

'Course I do. But that don't mean we can ignore it, does it?'

We crept forward, spreading out a little, though not so far that we couldn't see one another in the darkness. As before I shone the phone-light ahead of me, my toes also probing the floor like a blind man's stick in case the boards were rotten. Sure enough, the wood creaked beneath my weight a couple of times, but otherwise seemed solid. After a minute or two, Frank said, 'Psst.'

I peered across at him, holding up the phone. Back at Benny's house he had been visible in the darkness, as if generating his own light source, but now – I guess in order not to give us away – he was nothing but a vague dark shape.

'What is it?'

I saw his arm moving and realised he was pointing at the ground. 'Stairs.'

I made my way over to him. As I got closer I saw metal stair rails emerging from the gloom, either side of a flight of steps descending into darkness. The first half-dozen steps were visible, but beyond that the light was swallowed by an impenetrable black pool that looked like liquid tar.

More freezing air drifted up, like the breath of something vast and ancient.

'Fuck,' I whispered. 'Doesn't look too inviting, does it?'

'We have the means to fight if needs be,' Frank said.

Feeling only minimally reassured by this, I gripped the metal stair rail with my free hand and picked my way down. A couple of the stairs creaked as I descended, and I paused, clenching my teeth, certain that the sound would encourage something to come howling out of the darkness. But the void beneath me remained silent, and the only movement was the occasional swirl of icy air.

Eventually, instead of illuminating the next few steps, the meagre light from my phone spilled out across a stone floor below, the coldness of which seemed to seep up through the soles of my boots as I stepped down on to it. A moment later Frank was standing beside me, his face wan, his cheekbones jutting and angular in the phone-light. The scent of his hair cream and roll-ups in the darkness was comforting, reassuring.

'Where now?' I wondered, angling the phone around and seeing only gloom beyond its range.

'Your guess is as good as mine.'

The words were barely out of his mouth when we heard a scuffle of movement from somewhere ahead of us and what sounded like a low groan of pain.

'That way,' Frank said unnecessarily, raising his right arm to point, and shoulder to shoulder we ventured into the gloom. My right hand was in my jacket pocket, clutching the heart, my left holding the phone out in front of me. Eventually we came to a stone wall, which loomed out of the darkness. Frank gestured to his left and hissed, 'Shine the light that way.'

I did so, and was able to make out the black arch of an opening.

We moved towards it, treading cautiously. We were no more than a couple of metres from the arch when Frank whispered, 'Turn off the light a sec.'

I did so without question, plunging us into darkness.

No, not quite darkness. From the depths of the arch came the faintest of glows.

'The light at the end of the tunnel,' Frank murmured drily.

'Maybe I should keep my phone off from now on,' I suggested. 'We don't want to give ourselves away.'

Frank nodded in agreement, and we entered the arch and crept down the tunnel or corridor beyond it. I felt my way along the wall in the dimness, which was damp, sometimes slimy, to the touch. Gradually the tiny square of light at the end began to get bigger and brighter. It was orangey-yellow and a little unsteady; not electric light, but a gas lamp or candle flame. We were about three-quarters of the way along the tunnel when again I heard the scrape-scuffle of movement. This time it was accompanied by a brief metallic tinkling sound. *Coins*, I thought. *Or chains.*

The sound made me pause. I glanced over my shoulder to check that Frank was still close. He was, his thin face sickly in the flickering glow.

'What's the plan, chief?' he whispered. 'Over the top, all guns blazing?'

I forced a smile, though I was so nervous I could barely get my facial muscles to respond. 'I think discretion may be the better part of valour.'

He nodded, and together we tiptoed to the end of the tunnel. All I could see through the opening was part of what seemed to be a large stone chamber, dimly lit, with further arched openings inset into the far wall, maybe fifteen or twenty metres away. I smelled damp earth and burning wax. The subterranean air was so cold it made my bones ache. Flattening my body against the wall, I peered around the corner.

The room stretched away from me. It was long, relatively narrow and high-ceilinged. At the far end was a cage, like the kind you might have seen rattling on carts in days gone by, designed to transport circus animals from one location to another. It was surrounded by fat white candles, their wavering tulip-flames exuding grey smoke like long, curling threads of spider-silk. Slumped in the cage, dark hair hanging over its face, legs tucked under its body, was a human figure. The figure's wrists were shackled in heavy manacles attached to chains set into the floor. Because of the glow of light and haze of heat from the flames the figure seemed to shimmer and blur.

I leaned further forward, and as though sensing my presence the figure raised its head. As its hair fell away from its face I saw that it was Clover. I was shocked, but not surprised. She looked exhausted, defeated, her eyes half-closed, her mouth half-open. I looked around the room again – at the expanse of floor between me and the cage; at the arched openings, evenly spaced, containing nothing but shadows; up at the high ceiling. If this wasn't a trap I'd be amazed, but it made no difference; I couldn't *not* attempt to rescue Clover.

Turning back to Frank I quickly explained what I had seen and what I was planning to do. He nodded his compliance and promised he'd watch my back. I took a deep breath, and then stepped out of the cover of the dark corridor and into the room. Clover saw me and her eyes widened. I put a finger to my lips, warning her not to call out, then began to run towards the cage.

It wasn't much of a tactic, but I figured that if there were potential assailants waiting in ambush in the dark arches, they would be expecting me to be cautious rather than reckless. It might only wrong-foot them temporarily, but any advantage was better than none. I gripped the heart in my pocket as I ran, hoping it would burst into life, perform its magic and spirit Clover and me out of there. However, it remained stubbornly inactive, a lump of hard, cold stone in my hand.

I reached the cage without being intercepted and threw myself against it. Letting go of the heart, I gripped the bars with both hands and tugged at them, more out of desperation than any real belief that I might prise them apart. The chains attached to the manacles around Clover's wrists jangled as she struggled to her feet. She looked tired and scared, but unharmed.

'Are you all right?' I asked.

She nodded rapidly. 'I'm fine. But you've got to get out of here, Alex. This is a trap. They want the heart.'

'Yeah,' I said. 'I guessed as much. They left us an address card.'

'But you still came?'

'Course I did. I couldn't just leave you here, could I?'

She looked tearfully grateful and at the same time full of despair.

Her eyes sparkled and her chin dimpled as her bottom lip began to tremble. Then she stiffened and her gaze shifted.

'Behind you,' she whispered.

I turned to see Frank standing in the middle of the room, looking warily left and right. 'Don't worry, that's just Frank. He's a friend. He's here to help.'

She shook her head. Her maroon hair was ratty and tangled, as if she had washed it, but had been interrupted before being able to dry and style it. In a tiny, scared voice she said, 'No one can help us.'

'Don't be too sure. The heart won't surrender itself that easily and Frank's got a few tricks up his sleeve. Remember the darkness at Benny's house?'

She sniffed, nodded.

'That was him.'

She stared at me, utterly confused.

'It's a long story,' I said. I inspected the bars, shook them again. I had no idea how I was going to get Clover out of there. I took the heart out of my pocket and held it up. 'Come on, heart, do your stuff.' Nothing happened. I grimaced at Clover apologetically. She shook her head again, slumping back to the floor, her legs folding beneath her.

'It's no good, Alex. You've got to go, before he comes back.'

'Don't worry,' I said, with a confidence I didn't feel. 'Frank can handle the Surgeon – that's what he calls the guy who attacked us at Incognito. He's already rescued me from him once tonight.'

Clover frowned. 'That wasn't who took me.'

'Who was it then?'

'It was me!'

The voice rang out behind me, echoing off the stone walls. I spun round, and beyond Frank, who was also turning, I was astonished to see Barnaby McCallum step from the shadow of one of the arched openings about three-quarters of the way down the room. He looked just as I had seen him a few nights ago (minus the hole in his head, of course): small, shrivelled and crooked. Wisps of dusty white hair floated about his flaking, cheese-coloured pate and his root-like hand was curled around a walking stick with a silver wolf's-head handle. He was dressed in a black suit, like an undertaker, and his face was puckered and sharp, like that of some ancient bird of prey.

I gaped at him a moment, and then I said, 'But you're dead. I killed you.'

'Appearances can be deceptive.' He raised a gnarled hand and pointed at the heart I was holding. 'Now, I believe you have some property of mine. Perhaps you should give it back before someone gets seriously hurt.'

His voice was screechy and jagged, like a rusty hinge forced into use after years of inactivity. He took a lurching step forward, but then Frank stepped into his path, hand upraised.

McCallum halted, and though his wrinkled mouth curled into a sneer, he seemed more amused than annoyed.

'What are you?' he mocked. 'His little bodyguard?'

'His chum,' Frank said. 'And I can't let you pass.'

'What do you think I'll do? Beat him to death with my walking stick? I'm here to talk, you silly fool. To *negotiate*.' Raising his voice he said, 'You've got something that belongs to me, Mr Locke. And I have information that will lead to the recovery of someone *you* hold very dear.'

My stomach lurched. 'You know where Kate is?'

Before McCallum could answer, Clover said, 'Don't trust him, Alex.'

Frank took another step towards McCallum, the fingers of his upraised hand stretching out as though to touch the air in front of the old man. I saw darkness, like threads of ink in murky water, coiling around Frank's fingertips and heard the brief, distant crump of explosives and the screams of dying men from a century before.

Then the sound – which had been no more than a murmur – faded and Frank said, 'She's right, Alex. This one ain't what he seems.'

McCallum sighed. 'I simply want what's best for all of us. What's *right*.'

'You're lying,' Frank said.

'Oh, for goodness' sake,' McCallum said, and then he came apart.

One moment he was standing there, and the next he seemed to shred, to unravel, to erupt outwards in all directions. His black suit became a mass of writhing snakes and scuttling insects; his head burst upwards into a fluttering cloud of moths. The myriad creatures advanced in a dark, fragmented wave, swarming across the floor, up the walls, over the ceiling. I caught only a glimpse of them, and heard the sound they made – an angry crackling and rustling, combined with the beating of myriad tiny wings – before Frank threw back his head and opened his mouth and the dark poured out of him.

I turned back to the cage, to Clover, and, like someone trying to unlock a magic door in a fairy tale, tapped the heart several times against the bars. 'Come on,' I muttered frantically when nothing happened, 'come on, *come on.*'

Clover watched me, her face taut with tension, her lips pulled back over clenched teeth.

'Hurry, Alex,' she said.

Anxiety made me snap, 'I'm trying. Can't you *see* I'm trying?' Then I felt ashamed. She was the one who was caged and shackled. 'Sorry,' I muttered. 'It's okay. Frank will hold them off.'

The words were barely past my lips when something stung me on the back of my neck. I jumped and turned. A fat grey moth, as big as a hummingbird, was hovering in front of my face. I flapped at it, but instead of retreating the entire front section of its dusty grey body transformed into a glistening, twitching mass of vicious, piranha-like teeth, which darted for my fingers. I jerked back, my shoulders and head impacting painfully with the bars of the cage. Clover screamed as the thing swooped for my face – whereupon the heart that I was still holding in my right hand abruptly turned red hot.

A sizzling white flash tore through my body and erupted out of me almost in the same instant. Before I knew what was happening I saw the moth-thing turn to ash and break apart before my eyes. As the charred fragments drifted to the floor I became aware that the wall of darkness that Frank had exuded was swelling and rippling like the surface of a black sea, trying to contain the wave of creatures, a number of which were even now forcing their way through. It was like watching seabirds floundering in tar, some of them shaking the stuff from their bodies and breaking away, others unable to escape the sticky, black, web-like strands that clung to them. As they struggled and fought, many of the creatures changed shape, losing their form and becoming glutinous, or simply sprouting extra limbs, or cilia, or antennae. In many instances the forms they adopted were monstrous, unrecognisable, a hideous conglomeration of flesh and muscle and bone. Occasionally, glimpsed within the flux, were suggestions of the mammalian or the avian, the aquatic or the insectile. Some of the creatures, having broken through

Frank's barrier, seemed little more than pulsing lumps of gristle with wings or legs, which buzzed and flittered erratically, as though physically damaged or driven mad by their passage through the darkness. Others adapted quickly, forming into vicious, darting projectiles, which came at me and were instantly vaporised by the heart-energy now gushing through and out of me. I saw, spilling out of the black, undulating wall, a litter of what looked like hairless, deformed kittens, slick with amniotic fluid, which crawled and mewled about the floor; they were followed by a baby with a ridged spine and huge eyes that tottered to its feet before being sucked back into the darkness like a thread of smoke into an open mouth.

Turning back to Clover, I was not surprised to see that the heart had changed shape and fused itself to my flesh. Once again it was as though I was wearing a black, pulsating glove, from which spiny antennae rippled as though tasting the air. I reached out and touched one of the bars of the cage, and instantly the metal turned brittle and crumbled away. I touched the next bar and that crumbled too. Within moments I had created a gap large enough to allow me to step into the cage. Clover was on her knees, gaping up at me, open-mouthed. Leaning down, I touched the heart to one of her manacles and it dissolved, falling in rusty flakes to the floor. I did the same to the other manacle and she stood up shakily, staring at me, fear and uncertainty on her face.

'Come on,' I said and turned away.

Although I didn't wait for her response I knew that she was following me. Thanks to the heart I was hyper-aware of my surroundings, was able to sense movement in every direction and react to it accordingly. None of the shape-changing creatures – which, the heart enabled me to perceive, were mere shreds, off-shoots, of a single entity – could get near to me. The instant they displayed any threatening intent, they were extinguished. In conjunction with the heart I felt inviolable, invincible; I was giddy with exultation. In my heightened state I felt certain that if ever my life was threatened the heart would protect me, rescue me, and as such my fears and anxieties were pointless, redundant. My enemies were nothing; the Wolves of London were nothing. Try as they might they would be able neither to kill me nor separate me from the heart.

I strolled towards Frank's wall of darkness. The candlelight spilled from the cage towards it, and was obliterated as effectively as a spill of black ink will obliterate the whiteness of a sheet of paper. The darkness was muscular, sinewy, a coiling, thrashing turmoil of despair and rage and terror. I sensed Clover shrinking from it, and extended the heart's protection around her as an adult will curl a reassuring arm around a small child. I raised my hand and the darkness shrivelled back at my approach, forming an opening, a tunnel, through which I could pass. I kept on walking, Clover behind me, the heart not only lighting the way, but guiding my feet so that I felt almost as though I were gliding. In that exalted, rapturous moment I was certain that if only I could work out a way to control the heart, to gain mastery over it, then I could use it to seek out Kate, to go to her and take her back, crushing all opposition. In this mood I swept back along the tunnel, up the stairs, across the expanse of wooden floor and out of the building.

The instant I set foot beyond the rickety door through which Frank and I had entered the warehouse my rapture and self-confidence didn't just dwindle, but nosedived. The cold and the darkness hit me like a train as the night sky swirled overhead, and my body was seized by a fit of feverish shivering and the most appalling stomach cramps I had ever experienced. I staggered forward, doubling over, nausea rushing through me. I heard Clover calling my name, her voice like a distant echo at the end of a long tunnel. I stumbled a couple more steps and then my legs collapsed under me and I fell. I vomited, convulsed, and everything went black.

TWENTY-THREE

SMOG

But only for a moment. Spurred by some instinct of self-preservation – or perhaps it was the heart giving me an extra nudge, warning me that I wasn't out of the woods yet – I jerked from unconsciousness with a wild gasp, breaking the surface like a swimmer who's gone deeper than he intended, and who's left it just that bit too long before kicking towards the light.

For a split second I was disorientated, confused. I opened my eyes to see something hideous, perhaps even demonic, leaning over me. I felt sure the claw reaching towards me was about to rob me of both my hearts – the now-dormant one of black stone clenched in my fist and the still-beating one in my chest.

'*No!*' I yelled, flailing like a child, causing the demon to lurch back with a cry of shock. My senses wavered, settled, and suddenly I realised I was staring not at a demon, but at Clover's shocked, round-eyed face. As for the claw which had been about to tear out my heart, I saw it was nothing but her pale, shaking hand hovering solicitously above my body.

'Whoa,' she said in a shaky voice. 'Are you okay?'

I jerked my head in a nod, though in truth I felt terrible. I was shaking uncontrollably and pouring with sweat, my limbs full of broken glass, nausea sluicing through me in waves.

'I'll live,' I muttered, and pedalled my legs in an attempt to climb to my feet. 'We need to get out of here.'

Seeing me scrabbling like an upended turtle, Clover knelt down and slipped an arm around my back. 'Let me help,' she said, clenching her teeth as she hauled me upright.

'Thanks,' I muttered, though being vertical only made my head swim all the more. Clutching her free hand for support, and with her other arm around my sweat-drenched back, I bent double and abruptly threw up again, shuffling my feet apart just in time to avoid puking on my boots. Wretchedly I spat out a string of bilious, phlegm-thick drool. 'Sorry,' I muttered.

'You're my knight in shining armour,' she said. 'You don't have to apologise.'

'That's me,' I murmured. 'Sir Pukealot.' I took several deep breaths and slowly straightened up. 'I think it's true what you said.'

'About what?'

'About using the heart. That it takes its toll on me, makes me ill.'

She frowned. 'As long as the effects aren't cumulative.'

I thought about the way I had felt – invincible, even omnipotent – when under the heart's influence. Nothing comes without a price, I thought. Maybe, if I used the heart *too* often, it *would* destroy me. Maybe even now the heart-energy was having an adverse and irreversible effect on my body. Maybe cells were mutating inside me, which would eventually lead to oedemas or tumours or God knows what else.

I pushed the thought from my head and concentrated on putting as much distance as possible between us and the thing in the basement. As Clover and I staggered along the riverside path and through the Isle of Dogs' quiet residential streets, like passers-by fleeing the aftermath of a terrorist attack, I thought about Frank and hoped he'd be all right. I felt bad about leaving him behind, but back in the warehouse I had been guided by the heart, and had not given my companion's welfare a second thought. Presumably the heart had its own agenda, and when it was active that effectively became my agenda too. I thought now about going back for him, but ashamed though it made me feel, I knew what a foolhardy venture that would be. The fact that walking willingly into a trap to rescue Clover had been equally foolhardy was neither here nor there. I tried to ease my conscience with the thought that Clover had been a helpless victim, whereas Frank had known what to expect and was able to look after himself. According to him, I had already brought him back from the dead, but that didn't make me feel any better. It didn't mean that his life was now mine to do with as I wished, and that I could therefore abandon him without a pang of conscience.

Even so, I didn't go back. If I had done, maybe the heart would have helped me – though the way I was feeling, another blast of heart-energy so soon after the last one might well have finished me off. I stopped once more on the way to the station and puked in some bushes, and was concerned to see that there were streaks of blood in it. By the time we got on the train, though, my stomach had settled and I was feeling more like myself again. Exhausted, but less feverish, less nauseous.

Clover and I barely spoke as we took the DLR back into central London. She hadn't yet mentioned my running out on her earlier. Maybe she would later, or maybe she thought I'd redeemed myself by rescuing her from McCallum.

No, not McCallum, I reminded myself. McCallum was dead. The thing that had used Clover as bait and tried to take the heart from us had been something new, something different, something that had the ability to *look* like McCallum – or, based on what I'd seen, anything else for that matter. A shape-shifter. An entity that could divide its body up and create an entire army of creatures out of its own... what? Flesh? Was such a thing composed of flesh? Or was it made of some other substance altogether?

I wondered how badly – if at all – I had wounded the thing by destroying some of its... *creations* with heart-energy. And again I wondered how Frank was coping, whether he was still alive.

I put my head back and closed my eyes. It had been a long night. Betrayed by Benny (was *he* still alive?), trapped by the Surgeon and his minions, rescued by Frank, lured into another trap by the shape-shifting thing... Was this really going to be my life from now on? I wondered whether the Surgeon and the shape-shifter were on the same side, whether they were both Wolves of London. The shape-shifter in the guise of McCallum had used a cane topped with a silver wolf's-head. A joke? Or an indication of his status? The fact that the cane hadn't been a cane at all, but part of the stuff of the shape-shifter suggested that here was a monster with a wicked sense of humour. But what did I know? As usual the questions far outnumbered the answers.

We changed trains at Bank, descending on to the Central Line platform, from where we'd catch the tube to Oxford Circus, and then get the Bakerloo Line to Paddington. Although all I wanted was my bed, I knew that once Clover and I got back to the hotel our best option would be to pack up our few belongings and leave. Perhaps the next hotel would be no safer than this one, perhaps the Wolves had so many fingers in so many pies that they could track our movements every minute of every day, but at least I'd feel superficially safer in a different hotel. Trudging down the steps to the platform at Bank I once again scrutinised every face. I knew that any one of these people could be a potential threat, and that knowledge depressed me. Would I ever feel safe, or be able to trust anyone, ever again?

It was late, nearly midnight, and the platform was filled with late-night revellers. A bunch of girls in short skirts and deeley boppers were screeching like banshees; a tall, skinny man wearing a brown suit and glasses was spitting invective at a pretty black girl, who was stroking his chest and urging him to calm down. I took Clover's arm and steered her away from the main throng, towards the end of the platform, where it was quieter. From the black arch of the tunnel came the distant squeal of metal and a smell like scorched dust. I glanced at the digital information board and saw that a train to Ealing Broadway would be along in two minutes.

Despite my previous conviction that the heart would always protect me, and that as long as it was in my possession I was invincible, I felt nervous, wary. Whenever the heart was dormant was when the doubts started to creep back in. Maybe it *would* protect me, but what was it doing to my body in the meantime? And was it *really* protecting me or simply using me, drawing on my energy, my life essence, to protect itself? Perhaps, when it had used me up, reduced me to a husk, it would move on, seek another host? Perhaps it was nothing but a parasite, intent only on self-preservation?

Beside me Clover coughed. I glanced at her. I was about to ask her if she was all right when I realised that our surroundings had gone a little hazy. I wondered whether the lights in the station were dimming, and then realised that a yellowish fog had crept on to the platform. Where had it come from? The tunnel? But even as I became aware of the fog, it grew thicker.

Clover coughed again. And suddenly I was coughing too, as the acrid-smelling mist caught in my throat. I wafted at it, but it became even darker and denser, obliterating my view of the other passengers further along the platform. It stifled the sound of their chatter, isolating

Clover and me as it coiled around us. I bent double, spluttering, my eyes stinging. In my head I was thinking, *Another attack! Pull yourself together!* But it was easier said than done.

Within seconds we were completely enshrouded by swirling, pus-yellow fog. No, not fog, I suddenly thought. Smog. Back in London's industrial past the combination of smoke from coke-based fuels and factories belching out pollution had meant the city was often coated in blankets of smog so thick and pungent they became known as pea-soupers. They were a thing of the past now, so how come Clover and I were currently stuck in the middle of one? Unless this was something different – a chemical attack perhaps, like the one on the Tokyo subway back in the nineties.

I touched the heart in my pocket, willing it to throw a protective bubble around us or something, but it was cold, unresponsive. Holding my breath, I zipped up the hoodie under my jacket all the way to the top and pulled the front of the collar over my nose and mouth, holding it in place with one hand. It helped a bit, enough to allow me to breathe without choking my guts out. I blinked my streaming eyes, then reached for Clover's hand in the murk. Behind her hazy form was a dark shadow, a shape. I thought it was the wall, or... something jutting *from* the wall. But then the shadow loomed towards us, became more defined, and I realised it was a man.

My first thought, that it was a fellow passenger, was quickly dispelled as the man came into blurry focus. Dressed in a long grey coat, checked waistcoat, knotted neckerchief and a bowler hat that looked as if it had been trampled underfoot then punched back into shape, he was not just dirty or grubby, but *filthy*. His hair jabbed from beneath the rim of his hat like matted, mud-clogged straw, and dirt was ingrained into the many creases and scars of his lumpy, pustule-pocked face. One of his eyes was milky and bloodshot, and between his thick, chapped lips I saw a mouthful of teeth so black and rotten it looked as though shards of coal had been embedded in his gums.

I took in these details in a split second, and then my attention was diverted to the hand he was raising towards me. It was as filthy as his face, smeared with dirt, black grime clogging his fingernails. However it was not the hand itself that concerned me, but the tarnished, jagged-bladed knife jutting from it. The man grinned, revealing even more of his blackened teeth, and then before I could react, he stepped smartly up behind Clover and slashed the blade savagely across her throat.

Her eyes and mouth gaped in horrified disbelief as every molecule in my body clenched in a sick, freezing spasm of shock. I saw the flesh of her throat part in a ragged tear and blood *gushed* out of her, the arterial spray so violent that it hit my chest like a hot, fierce punch. Her eyes rolled up and her head lolled backwards, and suddenly she was *all* blood – her entire front, her hands, were red with it. I was covered in it too, and so was the floor. It splashed against my boots and spread out in all directions, creeping and growing like something alive.

As Clover's body went limp and her feet began to kick and jitter, the man laughed, wrapped an arm around her waist and dragged her into the smog. Her jerking heels scraped through the blood, briefly forming white runnels in it, which were quickly filled as the edges oozed back together like the lips of a healing wound.

It was only now – far too late – that shock loosened its grip on me. Desperately hoping there was still time to save Clover, whilst knowing in my heart that there wasn't, I croaked, 'Hey!' and sprang forward. Though the cut-throat and his victim were receding rapidly into the murk, I could still discern them as a dark, diminishing blur. As I plunged forward in pursuit, however, *another* shape loomed out of the smog to my left. I was so surprised that I skidded on Clover's blood and my right foot shot from under me. Caught off-balance, I snatched no more than a glimpse of yet another filthy man – this one taller and thinner, and dressed in a long, ragged blue coat that looked vaguely military – before he stepped forward, exuding a rancid, pig-like stench, and shoved me hard in the chest.

This time *both* feet shot from under me and I crashed on to my back with enough impact to knock the breath from my body. For a moment the pain was so excruciating I felt sure I'd broken my neck or spine, and could only lie there, my mouth open in soundless agony. My brain was raging at me to move, to shake off the pain and leap up in pursuit of Clover's attacker, but it was another five or ten seconds before I was finally able to rise, groaning, up on to an elbow and then, slowly and painfully, to my feet.

Yellow smog still hung heavily around me, like wet sheets on a washing line. Stifling a cough, I tried to swipe it aside in an effort to see more clearly, but it was no use; there was neither sight nor sound of the two men. I stumbled in the direction that Clover's attacker had disappeared, still stunned by what I had seen, my mind refusing to relinquish the belief that she was not yet beyond saving. After only a few steps, however, I encountered the tiled wall of the tube station, and at the same time the smog started to disperse. Within moments I could see the dark shapes of people standing further down the platform, their collective stance and rising chatter suggesting they were oblivious to what had occurred.

It wasn't only despair that surged through me this time, but also rage. 'No!' I screamed, scrabbling in my pocket and pulling out the heart. I glared at it, clenching it so tightly that my knuckles turned white. '*Fucking save her!*'

The heart simply sat there, stubborn and smug. '*Save her! Fucking save her!*' I yelled again, half-aware of heads turning in my direction, of a few nervous giggles, of a partly amused 'You all right there, mate?'

Drawing back my arm, I smashed the heart against the wall, half-hoping it would drill clean through into whatever dimension the cut-throat had dragged Clover. Aside from the jarring impact that shuddered along the bone all the way up to my elbow, however, all that happened was that I dented the tile. Grimly I drew back my aching arm and smashed the heart against the wall again. And then again. And again.

It was the fifth impact that did it. No sooner had the heart connected with the now chipped and cracked wall than the cold black stone in my hand seemed to detonate, engulfing me in a blaze of blinding white light. I had once seen a TV documentary in which a war photographer had described the experience of stepping on a land mine. It had sounded something like this: an almost out-of-body experience of light and heat and weightlessness. I was vaguely aware of my head snapping back, my spine bending like a bow, my limbs going rigid. I opened my eyes and mouth wide as heart-energy poured out of me.

And then I was floating. Spinning. Falling.

I was not aware of losing consciousness, but the sudden transition from tumbling through space to bone-jarring pain was like falling out of bed after a dream about flying. For the second time in minutes I found myself on my back, though this time I was staring up into a night sky pin-pricked with stars. The ground beneath me was hard and bumpy (cobblestones?) and wet; icy liquid was oozing through my clothes and spreading across the flinching skin of my back and buttocks. And there was an awful smell. A stench. Raw sewage and something else. Something rank, animalistic.

My gorge rose yet again and I sat up, swallowing, willing my stomach to settle. No such luck, and for so long that I began to think it might never stop, I retched helplessly, my empty stomach attempting to turn itself inside out as it tried to expel contents that had already been expelled earlier that evening.

By the time my stomach had stopped convulsing I felt utterly wretched – weak, dizzy, my flesh tingling and sensitive to the touch, my innards full of a rough, raw soreness, as if they had been scoured.

I wondered if I was bleeding internally; wondered if my pounding brain was about to haemorrhage. There was no doubt that using the heart was fucking me up, that it was taking a gruelling physical toll.

When the ability to focus returned to my hot, smarting eyes I looked down at my hands. Were they a little more twisted than before? Were the knuckles swollen? Certainly they ached around the joints. I thought of Barnaby McCallum, the heart's previous owner. True, he was an old man, but had the heart contributed to the near-deformity of his twisted bones, his emaciated state? When had he acquired the heart, I wondered. When had he started using it? If only latterly, then I might well be putting myself at serious risk of an early death. Perhaps by using it so frequently – albeit largely unwittingly – in the few days since it had been in my possession, I had already dangerously exceeded my tolerance level.

With these worrying thoughts circulating in my mind, I looked around, taking in my surroundings. I appeared to be in a yard of some kind, surrounded on three sides by blackened walls of crumbling brick inset with filthy, narrow windows. Many of the windows were broken or simply unglazed; only a few were framed by grubby strips of colourless cloth that served as curtains.

I might have thought the buildings were abandoned, even condemned, if it wasn't for the candlelight flickering in some of the windows. This, at least, provided me with a modicum of murky illumination.

As my senses returned fully, I realised not only that I *was* lying on wet cobblestones, but also that the cobblestones were covered in filth. Scattered about were clumps of muddy straw, gnawed bones and other bits of unrecognisable organic matter – some of it rank with decomposition.

There was shit too, both animal – horse, dog – and what looked suspiciously like human. And among all this shit and rubbish was rustling, twitching movement. I peered at a particularly active mass of shadow and saw a fat-bellied rat, and then a second, dart from one patch of darkness to another. The thought of one of the creatures scuttling across to check *me* out was all the encouragement I needed to scramble to my feet. It was only as I winced at the sick, bone-deep pain in my back and put my right hand down to take some of the weight that I realised I still had the heart – cold and unresponsive again now – clutched in it. I dropped it back into the inside pocket of my blood and filth-smeared jacket, and then, groaning with effort, I stood up.

Where the fuck was I? And how had I got here? Crazy though it seemed, I could only assume that the heart had enabled me to teleport or something, like they do in *Star Trek*. As for where I was, I supposed I must be close to where the cut-throats had taken Clover. Unless I had damaged or angered the heart by bashing it against the tube station wall and it had deposited me somewhere completely random.

Once again I peered up at the slum-like dwellings that surrounded me. They appeared to be leaning towards me like a trio of giants perusing a tasty morsel. Were the cut-throats inside one of them? And if so, how would I find them? By bashing on doors like a lone copper doing house to house? And what if I *did* find them? Clover was surely beyond help by now.

I wondered why she had been killed and not me, why the cut-throats had made no attempt to grab the heart. Had they done it to isolate me? Break my spirit? Draw me here? Or had they killed her simply because they could?

More questions. Nothing *but* questions. Confusion and despair washed over me as I thought about the awful abruptness of Clover's death and how lost (in every sense of the word) I was. I shook my head, knowing that I couldn't give in to it, knowing that I had to think practically, constructively. My first priority was to find out where I was. Feeling stiff and achy and sick with guilt and grief, I trudged towards the only side of the yard that wasn't lined with buildings.

Stepping out of the shadow, I found myself in a narrow, cobbled street lined with yet more grotty-looking buildings. There were no street lamps to be seen, and even out here, where it wasn't quite so enclosed, the stink of rotting sewage was so thick it felt as though it was forming a slimy layer in the back of my throat. Somewhere to my right I could faintly hear a swell of chatter interspersed with an occasional burst of raucous laughter. There was the suggestion of light coming from that direction too, enough to cast a slithering orange reflection on to the surface of the filthy pools of water collected between the cobblestones.

I trudged towards the signs of life, my stomach fluttering with nerves. Wherever I was, I had seen enough to realise this wasn't a salubrious neighbourhood. In fact, the place was a slum, far worse than the run-down estate where I had grown up. At least there the housing, grim, grey and box-like though it was, had been modern and relatively sturdy. But these buildings were not only old but horribly dilapidated, some of them seeming to lean against their neighbours or even out over the street, as if about to collapse. They reminded me of Victorian rookeries, like the ones you see in Charles Dickens adaptations on the TV.

And then I stopped dead, struck by a terrifying thought.

Frank had said I'd saved his life during the First World War, which, impossible though it seemed, suggested that the heart had the ability to transport me through time. Although I hadn't disbelieved his story outright (I'd seen enough in the past few days to half-accept anything was possible) I suppose I'd still only been able to process it as an abstract concept – because being *told* something was true, however much you might be prepared to accept it, was a hell of a lot different to experiencing that truth for yourself.

But looking around now, and thinking about the two men who had emerged from the smog in the tube station, caused unease, even dread, to lodge in the pit of my stomach. Was it beyond the realms of sanity to suppose that I *might*, *actually*, be now standing in a Victorian street and breathing Victorian air? I barked a brief, shrill, hysterical laugh, which I immediately smothered with my hand. My thoughts began to race, my emotions to hurtle dizzyingly from disbelief, to wonder, to sheer, unadulterated terror. I felt a ridiculous urge to burst into tears, and even to find somewhere quiet and dark to hide, where I could squeeze myself smaller and smaller until I disappeared.

I must have stood in the same spot for at least a minute as the stew of thoughts and emotions swirled inside me. Still shuddering, I slipped my hand into the pocket of my jacket and gripped the heart. Although it didn't respond, its presence soothed me, and after a few moments I felt myself becoming calmer, my panic subsiding.

Finally, like a dog shaking water from its coat, I gave a final shudder and started walking again. I felt hollow and slightly spaced out, but generally okay; ready, at least, to face whatever I might come across.

It turned out the noise and light was spilling from a corner pub, The Princess Alice, a squat, red-brick building with soot-grimed windows. I stood about fifteen metres from the entrance, half-concealed in the shadow cast by a wooden hand-cart stacked with hessian sacks. Dressed as I was, and spattered with Clover's blood, I was loath to go in. I imagined stepping through the door and the place falling silent as the pub's patrons turned to gawp at me. I decided my best bet was to wait to see who came out, and then, if they looked approachable, to sidle up and speak to them.

I was so intent on the front of the pub that I failed to notice who or what was behind me. I almost jumped out of my skin when a gruff voice said, 'What kind of man are you?'

I spun round. Standing in the gloom was a portly man in a baggy, coarsely woven black suit, a shapeless cap perched on his head. He had ruddy, bulbous features and a thick white moustache that gave him the appearance of an elderly, bad-tempered walrus. At his feet was a white dog so stocky it resembled a barrel with legs. It had a square, blunt-snouted head, its muzzle criss-crossed with scars.

'Hi,' I blurted, and only realised my mistake when the puzzled frown on the man's lumpy face turned to startlement. 'Er... hello, I mean.'

Instead of returning my greeting the man eyed my filthy jacket, hoodie and jeans. Then he asked suspiciously, 'What's your business, mister?'

'Nothing,' I floundered. 'I mean... I'm lost. I was looking for someone.'

'Is that so?' he said. 'And who might that be?'

I hesitated before replying, and then decided to take the plunge. 'Two men. One of them's got a white eye and a scarred face. The other's taller and thinner. He wears a blue coat. Like a soldier's coat.'

The man said nothing. He continued to stare at me, his expression wary, hostile.

'I don't suppose you know them, do you?'

'What's your interest in 'em?'

'Last time I saw them they were... with a friend of mine,' I said, reluctant to say more.

'What friend?'

'A girl.'

His eyes narrowed. 'A girl, is it?'

'Her name's Clover,' I said. 'Clover Monroe.'

The man was silent a moment longer, then he seemed to come to a decision. Clicking his fingers, he said, 'Snap, watch him.'

The dog sprang to attention. Its sharp little ears pricked up and it scurried towards me, barking furiously. I stumbled back, half-turning to run, but the man growled, 'I wouldn't do that, mister. Stay still and Snap'll leave you be. But try to run and she'll sink her teeth to the bone.'

Although every instinct screamed at me to flee, I forced myself to stand still, raising my hands placatingly. Sure enough the dog came to a halt in front of me, its hackles up and its mean little eyes staring unblinkingly into my own. It growled menacingly, its muzzle quivering over sharp yellow teeth.

'Look,' I said, trying to keep my voice steady, 'I don't want any trouble.'

'You just stay still, mister,' the man said again, then he pushed past me and plodded towards the pub.

I looked over my shoulder and watched him go inside. Deprived of its master's control, I thought the dog might lose its discipline and fly at me, but it remained where it was, the blood-curdling growl continuing to rumble in its throat.

'Good dog,' I said, but that only made the creature stiffen in anger, the volume of its growl rising a further notch. I wondered whether the heart would defend me if the creature attacked, and whether I would want it to.

After a few minutes I heard movement and gruff voices behind me and looked over my shoulder. The white-moustached man was clumping back towards me, accompanied by four others. One was a skinny, slope-shouldered youth of about seventeen with a rat-like face and a black club in his right hand. Another was a man in a battered top hat and stained red waistcoat, whose bushy grey beard was matted with clumps of filth. The other two were the men I had seen earlier – the one who had killed Clover and his taller, skinnier companion in the blue military-style coat.

'I heard you was lookin' for us, mister,' barked Clover's killer, striding up to me. 'Well, here we are, so what's yer beef?'

He circled behind the dog to stand in front of me, glaring with his one good eye. His companions stood behind me, shuffling and sniffing; I heard one hoick up a mouthful of phlegm and spit it on to the ground.

My throat was dry, but I forced myself to speak. 'You know why I'm here.'

Clover's killer took another step forward, tilting his chin pugnaciously. A rank, unwashed odour came off him. 'Is that so? Well then, I confess it must have slipped my mind.'

Behind me his cronies cackled; the spitter spat again.

Glancing at the dog and knowing I had little to lose, I asked, 'Why did you murder my friend?'

Clover's killer raised his eyebrows. 'Murder, is it? That's an 'orrible accusation you is makin' there, mister.'

'There's no point pretending you don't know what I'm talking about. You did it right in front of me less than half an hour ago.'

'Half an hour,' he repeated, aping and mocking my speech, emphasising the 'h' of 'hour'. He glanced over my shoulder at the men behind me. 'Where was we half an hour ago, Mr Jackery?'

A weaselly voice replied, 'We was in the alehouse, Mr Hulse. We been there all day. In full view of our good friends and neighbours.'

Clover's killer – Hulse – nodded reflectively. 'That we have, Mr Jackery, that we have. Thank you ever so for reminding me.' He fixed his gaze on me again, his scarred face creasing into a leering smile. 'So there you has it, mister. I'm afraid your eyes has deceived you.'

I shook my head. 'I saw you. I know what you did. There's no point denying it.' But then I fell silent. What was I achieving by throwing the accusation back in his face? Trying to sound reasonable, I said, 'Just tell me why you did it. And... and at least give her back to me, so that I can give her a decent burial.'

Hulse's menacingly jovial manner slipped and he scowled. 'Is your brain addled, mister? I's already told you the facts of the matter. Now hold your tongue unless you wants to lose it.'

So saying, he reached into his jacket and pulled out the knife he had killed Clover with. It glinted rustily in the meagre light spilling from the pub.

From behind me one of the men said, 'Why not take his tongue anyway, Mr Hulse? Make a nice little titbit for Snap, that would.'

'Aye, and his eyes too so's he can't finger us as the coves what took his purse,' piped up a thin, reedy voice which I guessed belonged to the rat-faced youth. The other men laughed.

'What an agile mind you has, Mr Swann!' declared Hulse delightedly. 'Agile and inventive! Don't you think so, my lily-white friend?'

This last remark was directed at me. Instead of replying, I lashed out without warning, kicking the dog as hard as I could in the face. I had seen where the situation was heading, had known from the moment they confronted me that these men had no intention of allowing me to walk away. And so as soon as Hulse had drawn the knife I had decided that it was better to give them a run for their money rather than stand by and see events through to their inevitable conclusion.

Although the dog's head was as hard as a brick, it let out a loud yelp and lost its footing, rolling on to its side. Before it could recover, and before Hulse could raise the knife, I leaped forward and punched the cut-throat as hard as I could between the eyes. Dropping the knife, he stumbled sideways, and then tripped over the dog, which even now, though still on its back, was twisting its body like a fat white maggot to leap to its feet. As the two became tangled in a snarling, roaring heap I skipped past them and started running.

I had no idea where I was going, and no time to examine street signs or ask directions as I fled through the filthy, ill-lit streets. My only plan was to duck around as many corners as I could, and to aim for the narrowest openings and passageways in the hope of shaking off my pursuers.

I was so focused on staying ahead of the pack, and of keeping my feet on the slick cobbles, that I had no idea how close behind me Hulse and his men were, or even if they were following me at all. Certainly I could hear nothing but the thumping of my own footsteps, the pounding of my heart and the rush of my adrenaline-fuelled blood.

I had been running for several minutes, and making as many twists and turns as I could, when I finally rounded a corner and saw, on my right, a particularly narrow alleyway. I veered into it, my sudden change of direction causing me to catch the wall a glancing blow with my left shoulder. Though my body still felt tender and sore, I faltered only slightly, fat black rats scuttling in panic before my headlong rush. I burst from the other end of the alleyway on to a surprisingly wide street – wide enough, in fact, to have been granted the luxury of a pavement. Unfortunately, a young couple, strolling arm in arm, happened to move directly across my path as I catapulted from the opening. I cannoned into the woman, causing her to fall against her companion, and all three of us went down like skittles.

The ground rushed up to meet me, slamming into my left knee and elbow. The impact was so jolting that I felt a wrenching pain in my neck that instantly zigzagged into my head, momentarily blotting out my senses. When I came to, no more than a couple of seconds later, I was horrified to discover that my right hand was empty. Though it hurt to move my head, I looked up and saw the heart nestled in the gutter a few metres away. Gritting my teeth against the throbbing pain in my arm, leg and head, I propelled myself across the pavement and lunged for it. The relief I felt when my fingers closed around it was short-lived, because almost immediately I felt a searing pain in my ankle. I looked round to see that the white dog, its muzzle lathered with blood-smeared saliva, had clamped its teeth around my leg.

I kicked out with my other leg, my foot thudding into the side of its barrel-like body. However the dog simply snarled and tightened its grip, making me howl with agony. Out of the corner of my eye I saw the couple I had barged into clambering gingerly to their feet, the man aiding his companion, fussing over her as she whimpered.

'Help!' I shouted. 'Get it off me! Call the police!'

The man glanced in my direction, but I saw no sympathy or willingness to help on his face.

And then, behind him, I saw a flood of dark shapes spill from the mouth of the alleyway. Leading them was Hulse, his teeth bared in fury, his hand brandishing his knife. He saw me sprawled on the ground and howled in triumph.

Then, like a pack of wolves, he and his cronies were upon me.

TWENTY-FOUR

GHOSTS

Birds singing. The soothing orange glow of daylight on the inside of my eyelids. The smell of freshly laundered sheets and... something else. The warm, woody tang of tobacco smoke.

Frank, I thought, and opened my eyes.

And there he was, sitting quietly on a chair beside the bed in which I was lying, smoking one of his roll-ups. His skin was ethereally pale, so bloodless that it was not hard to imagine that he was a ghost, a vision from the past, and that if I blinked he would be gone in the split second it took me to close my eyes and open them again.

I blinked and looked. He was still there. One of his bony legs was crossed over the other, and he was casually brushing a spill of ash off his knee. He glanced at me with his mournful eyes, his face betraying no emotion.

'Back with us, are you?' he said, as if I had done nothing more than pop down to the shops for a pint of milk.

'What happened?' I asked, or tried to; my throat felt rusty through lack of use.

'Heart brought you home,' he said. 'You've been in the wars, old boy.' He smiled faintly at his own feeble joke.

My mind felt sluggish, as rusty as my voice. Memories blundered into view like slow, heavy animals emerging from a murky autumn dusk. Hulse and Jackery. The dog.

Clover.

I jerked up from the pillow as the memory of what had happened to

267

her passed through me like an electric shock. The sudden movement awoke points of pain all over my body – ankle, knee, elbow, wrist, back, neck, head – which in turn yanked a cry of pain from my throat.

'Calm yourself, chief,' Frank said, placing an almost weightless hand on my shoulder. 'You've been through a heck of an ordeal. You need to rest.'

Slowly I allowed myself to sink back into the bed. I didn't feel as damaged as I had when I'd woken up in the hospital after being beaten up by Glenn and his mates all those years ago, but it *was* true to say that the parts of me that *didn't* hurt were few and far between. My body felt like one huge bruise, although, after carefully wriggling my fingers and toes and flexing my limbs, I could more or less safely conclude that nothing was broken.

The main pain was inside. Not just the sense of scouring, of rawness, as if the heart was stripping me away layer by layer each time I used it, but the pain of loss, of grief. What was the point of the heart protecting me if it couldn't protect the people I cared about? Kate was still missing, and I was no nearer to finding out what had happened to her than I had been on the day she was taken. And now Clover, my partner and friend throughout this ordeal, had been taken too, her life savagely ended by a man who had been long dead before she was even born.

If this was what the heart did – protected me, but allowed those around me to suffer – then I wanted no part of it. Despite my reliance on it, like the reliance of an addict on his drug, maybe it was time to seek a way to contact Kate's kidnapper and arrange an exchange before I lost my daughter for ever. But how? By putting ads in all the London newspapers and magazines? By daubing cryptic messages on walls that only the kidnapper would understand? Or maybe I should just walk around London in plain view, offering myself as bait?

I wasn't aware I was crying until my eyes blurred and I felt the tickle of tears on my cheeks. Again there came the light pressure of Frank's hand on my shoulder. 'Don't upset yourself, guv'nor. You know what they say. Things are always blackest before dawn.'

The words were so trite I almost smiled. Given Frank's extraordinary nature it was easy to be in awe of him, to imagine that he possessed wisdom and understanding beyond the capacity of ordinary mortals.

But now and again I was reminded he was actually not much more than a callow youth from the early twentieth century. All right, so his experiences had aged him beyond his years, and he had returned from death as a vessel for the horror of the war that had killed him and thousands like him. But he was still just a boy underneath it all, one as naïve as he was haunted, as uncertain as he was powerful.

Reaching up slowly with an arm that was stiff and bruised, I placed my hand over his. His cold, waxy skin didn't bother me any more; I was comforted by his touch.

'Clover's dead,' I said simply. It was the first time I had spoken the words, and I was strangely shocked, hearing them out loud, how blunt they sounded, how final.

'That so?' said Frank with his characteristic lack of emotion. 'Want to tell me about it?'

Haltingly, croakingly, I recounted everything that had happened after Clover and I had fled the warehouse basement in the Isle of Dogs. I told him how Hulse and his feral companions had descended on me like a pack of wolves, and then I shuddered and looked at him, my neck creaking with pain. 'But what about you? How did you get away?'

'First things first,' he said. 'Nice cup of tea.'

It was only when he spoke the words that I realised how parched I was. I swallowed drily as he stubbed out his roll-up in a glass ashtray by his feet and stood up. 'Back in a tick.'

Left alone, I inched my body into a sitting position, wincing at the pain. I was in a double bed in the large bedroom of either a very nice house or a luxury hotel. The carpet was the colour of oatmeal, and the wallpaper, patterned with a subtly embossed Art Deco design, possessed a gold-brown sheen that made it look classy and expensive. The furniture was elegantly but sturdily Victorian, the main light fitting in the centre of the high ceiling just this side of ostentatious. The room was bathed in autumn sunlight which poured through a row of long bay windows to my right, beyond which I could see trees and railings and some sort of pagoda-like structure on a hill in the distance – parkland or the grounds of a private house?

Listening, I realised I could hear not only the chirping of birds but the low-level rumble of traffic. So I was back in my own time then, and from the sounds of it reasonably close to a main road. Was I still in

London? If so, that was probably Hyde Park I could see out there, or maybe Kensington Gardens.

Frank had said the heart had brought me home. But where exactly was 'home'? And, for that matter, where was the heart? With a sudden stab of alarm I looked around the room as quickly as my aching neck would allow, searching for my blood and filth-smeared jacket. I couldn't see it, but then I remembered that the last time I had seen the heart it had been not in my pocket, but in my hand. I had snatched it from the gutter after my collision with the couple in the street.

Shit. Had I dropped it? Left it behind? Had Hulse taken it? But if so, how had it brought me home? Then I saw it, sitting on top of a small cabinet beside the bed, and the breath of relief I expelled made me slump like a punctured balloon.

I reached for it – my drug, my lifeline to Kate – and clutched it gratefully to my chest, and a second later heard the creak of what sounded like stairs beneath the weight of an approaching presence. I looked up, expecting it to be Frank, even though the young soldier's previous movements had been all but soundless. The door opened and a woman entered carrying a tray.

It was Clover.

My heart leaped, and I let out a weird (and slightly embarrassing) high-pitched yelp. As she approached the bed with an almost triumphant smile on her face, I could only gape, too overcome to speak.

'Well?' she said, putting the tray on the chair by the bed. 'Aren't you going to say anything?'

My mouth moved, I licked my lips. 'It's... *you!*' I blurted.

She smiled happily. She was clearly enjoying this. 'Oh, *very* eloquent. I expected a bit more than that, if I'm honest.'

Something gave way inside me, some minor emotional dam, and I started to laugh. It made my ribs and neck hurt, but I didn't care. 'I thought you were dead,' I said. 'I *saw* you die.'

Lifting a teapot from the tray and pouring two cups, she shook her head. 'You didn't, you know.'

I frowned. 'What do you mean?'

I'd been so focused on the wonderful impossibility of Clover's being alive that I didn't realise Frank had slipped silently back into the room and was now standing at the end of the bed.

'The Clover you saw killed wasn't her, chief.'

I looked at him in bewilderment. 'Who was it then?'

'That thing from the Isle of Dogs.'

'The... shape-shifter?' I murmured.

Frank nodded. 'That whole thing with McCallum and what he turned into, and Clover in the cage, was a trick, a double bluff. He... if that thing *is* a he... *wanted* you to save Clover.'

'Why?' I asked, and then I realised. 'So that I'd drop my guard and make it easier for them to take the heart?'

Clover nodded, handing me tea in a proper china cup with a saucer. I put the heart back on the bedside cabinet before taking it. 'That's right,' she said. 'When he appeared at the hotel he looked like you, Alex. That's why he caught *me* off-guard. I think he must have injected me with something. Next thing I remember is waking up to find myself in a dark little room that stank like a toilet.'

'So the Clover that came with me,' I said, 'obviously meant to take the heart, but didn't get the chance.' I frowned, thinking hard for a moment. 'Which begs the question: did Hulse kill the thing that looked like you because he thought it *was* you, or because he knew it *wasn't*?'

Clover shrugged. 'Search me. I'd never even heard of this guy until Frank told me about him a few minutes ago.'

'That doesn't mean he hadn't heard of you, though. Or at least, it doesn't mean he wasn't given orders to kill you.'

'But why would he kill me and not you? You're the one with the heart.'

'Maybe because you were closer to him than I was? Or to make me follow him into his own time, where he'd feel more comfortable dealing with me? Or maybe he just killed you to break my spirit? I don't know...'

I broke off, frustrated. Frank remained silent, watching me intently, as if willing me to work things out for myself. I took the look on his face as my cue to try.

'If Hulse *did* know the woman he killed wasn't you,' I said slowly, 'then wouldn't that mean there's not just one group after the heart? I mean, if they're all Wolves of London, why kill each other? Maybe there are lots of different, weird, murderous factions, all after one thing?'

'Comforting thought,' said Clover.

Again I fell silent, my mind still working furiously. Then I said, 'There's another thing that bothers me.'

'Just one?' said Clover.

I looked at her, a worm of suspicion wriggling at the back of my mind. 'Instead of going to the trouble of locking you up, why didn't the shape-shifter just kill you when it caught you?'

She shrugged. 'No idea. Maybe it needs the real person close by in order to change into them?'

'But it changed into McCallum easily enough,' I said, 'and *he's* dead.'

'In that case, I don't know.' Then she saw the expression on my face. 'Oh, come on, Alex. Don't spoil the big reunion by saying you don't trust me.'

Sheepishly I said, 'I *want* to trust you. And I can't express how happy I am that you're alive. But given what's happened, how do I *know* you're who you say you are? How do I know *anyone* is?'

'You don't,' said Frank simply. 'But if we were your enemies, don't you think that instead of looking after you for the last three days, we'd have just killed you and taken the heart?'

It was a fair point – and then I realised what Frank had said.

'*Three days?* Is that how long I've been unconscious? What about Kate? Has there been—'

'Nothing on the news,' said Clover shortly. 'I'm sorry.'

I slumped back, but my mind was whirring. I felt frantic. *Three days.* Shit. In the present circumstances it was an eternity. Even though I knew it was barely my fault, I couldn't help thinking I'd let Kate down, failed her.

'We thought we were going to lose you at one point,' Clover was saying. 'You were delirious, running a fever. You looked like death.' She nodded at the heart. 'I thought maybe you'd overdone it with that thing.'

'Maybe I had,' I said distractedly, still thinking about Kate. 'Maybe the human body isn't equipped for time travel.'

'Time travel?'

'I'll tell you later.' I gulped my tea. 'How did you get away from the shape-shifter, Frank? What happened?'

The young soldier shrugged. 'War of attrition, chief. I wore the bugger down. It helped that you'd already singed its whiskers with the heart, and that it was in pieces. Soon as the bit that had disguised itself as Clover left with you, it lost a lot of its strength. Crawled away between the cracks in the walls to lick its wounds.'

'So you didn't kill it?'

'Don't think so. Not sure if something like that *can* be killed.'

I was about to respond, and then a wave of nausea hit me. It was as if the tea I'd drunk had suddenly rebelled on its way down and decided to turn back. 'Oh God, I think I'm going—'

And then it all gushed out of me. I puked on the bedclothes between my knees, filling the room with an acrid stench. Afterwards I felt shaky and feverish, my stomach hurting all over again, my head pounding, my skin sensitive to the touch. My hands felt stiff, and when I looked at them I was certain this time that my fingers were a little more crooked than usual, the knuckles swollen, as if the bones had become slightly distorted. Again I thought of how shrunken and twisted Barnaby McCallum had been.

Feeling wretched, I started to say how sorry I was, but Clover waved away my apologies. Briskly she pulled the covers back, bundled them up and carried them away. I shivered from reaction and because the sudden exposure to the air made me cold. I was wearing old-fashioned blue and white striped pyjamas, and I had a bandage around my ankle where the dog had bitten me. My feet were bare and looked long, white and veiny. Although they were probably no different to usual, I suddenly couldn't help thinking they looked like the feet of a sick old man. I had never thought of myself as old, or even middle-aged, before.

'Is there a hand mirror in here?' I asked.

Frank showed no surprise at the question. He gestured towards the back wall, where a Victorian dressing table sat beside a small sink. 'There's one on there.'

'Would you mind fetching it for me?'

He did so without comment and handed it over. I held it up in front of my face, afraid of what I might see. But it was the same old face as ever: long, bony, grizzled with three-day stubble, and wearing a pissed-off expression despite my best intentions. I was maybe a bit paler than usual, a bit darker around the eyes, but that was only to be expected. I'd had a horrible suspicion that I would suddenly look old, wrinkled, grey-haired, but there was no evidence of that. I let my arm with the mirror in it drop and sank back into the bed, groaning.

Clover returned with a fresh duvet, which she threw over me, then she moved the tea tray from the chair beside the bed and sat down.

'You need to rest,' she said, 'recuperate.'

'I've been resting for the last three days.'

'You've been fighting, not resting. This isn't the first time you've thrown up. You need proper rest now, and once you think you can keep something down, you need some food and liquid. You've had nothing solid for days and you've brought up most of the liquid that we've been able to get you to swallow.'

'But what about Kate?' I said. 'I've wasted enough time.'

'You're in no fit state to go running around London looking for Kate,' she said. 'You won't be doing her any favours by driving yourself into the ground. Besides, where would you go? What would you do? You've got nothing to go on. Everything that *can* be done to find her *is* being done.'

I knew she was right, but it didn't make me feel any better. I sighed, and winced. Even taking a deep breath was painful.

'Thanks for looking after me. Both of you,' I said.

Frank shrugged and nodded, clearly embarrassed.

'So where are we?' I asked, gesturing towards the window.

'Kensington,' said Clover, confirming my theory. 'It's a safe house. It belongs to a friend of mine.'

'Another friend?'

'You make a lot of useful contacts in my business.'

I decided not to push it – for now. Instead, looking out at the trees shedding yellow and brown leaves as their branches shivered in the wind, I asked, 'Can anywhere really be safe for us?'

Clover shrugged. 'We've been here for three days and nothing's happened so far.'

'Can I have my phone?'

She raised her eyebrows at the sudden change of topic. 'What for?'

'I want to see if I've got any messages.'

She looked thoughtful for a moment – perhaps she was deciding whether I was mentally strong enough to be reconnected to the real world – and then she crossed to the same dressing table from which Frank had taken the hand mirror. Opening the left-hand drawer she said, 'All your stuff is in here – wallet, keys, phone, that kind of thing.'

'What about my clothes?' I asked.

'Washed and dried.'

'But not ironed?' I muttered, teasing her.

She waggled my phone at me. 'You might not be well, Alex, but that doesn't mean I won't slap you if you don't behave.'

I smiled, though the humour was perfunctory, a vain attempt to relieve the tension I was feeling. Clover handed my phone to me, and I switched it on, pleased to discover that it didn't seem to have suffered any detrimental effects from its journey into the past. I had sixteen voicemail messages – a couple from Candice, four from DI Jensen, several from friends and colleagues, and a couple from Dr Bruce at Darby Hall – together with a bunch of texts, many from the same people, who were presumably following up the messages I hadn't responded to.

'Anything significant?' Clover asked, looking anxious on my behalf.

'Maybe,' I said, showing her the list, my heart thumping at the prospect of what Jensen could be ringing about. Bad news or good? I was almost too afraid to find out.

'We'll leave you to it,' she said tactfully, picking up the tea things. 'Do you feel like eating anything yet?'

After throwing up, my stomach had settled, and was now grumbling emptily, though it still felt tight with tension. I shrugged.

'I'll bring you some homemade chicken soup anyway,' she said.

I nodded. 'Sounds great.'

She left the room, Frank following silently. I took a deep breath, then dialled up my voicemail and listened to my messages.

The first from Candice was to ask whether I'd had any news about Kate. The second was more subdued, more concerned: 'Dad, where are you? I'm worried about you. No one knows where you are. The police have been in touch to say they're anxious to trace you. Please call me. I'm really, really worried. I love you.'

The batch of messages from friends, students and work colleagues were along similar lines, but more wary and restrained. From the tone of some it was clear they were not above thinking I might have had something to do with Kate's disappearance, and that I was now not so much lying low as on the run.

The two messages from Dr Bruce were short and to the point, the second containing a note of admonishment as if she believed I was deliberately ignoring her. In the first she requested that I call her at my earliest convenience, and in the second she said almost exactly the same thing, but replaced 'at your earliest convenience' with 'as a matter of urgency'.

Intriguing – and slightly alarming – though her messages were, however, it was the quartet of messages from Jensen that I was *really* concerned about. They were carefully worded, the detective inspector expressing thinly veiled concern for my welfare and asking me to contact him as soon as I could.

The moment the last of his messages, which were all virtually identical, had ended, I began to shake. What news did Jensen have for me? Or did he even *have* any news? Could it be that he was simply suspicious of the fact that I appeared to have fallen off the face of the earth and wanted to know where I was? I knew the only way to find out was to call him back, but I was scared; terrified, in fact. I told myself the news wouldn't be bad, that there was no way Kate's kidnappers would harm her, not while I still held the heart. But could I be sure about that? The answer was no, I couldn't be sure about anything. I took a deep breath and pressed 'Reply'.

It was a woman who answered the phone. I heard the bustle of an office behind her. Her voice was clipped, business-like. The only word she said that penetrated my racing mind was 'police'.

'Is DI Jensen there?' I asked, surprised at the phlegmy rasp that had replaced my voice.

'Who's calling please?'

'This is Alex Locke.'

I wondered whether I ought to elaborate, but my anxiety blanked my mind and froze my tongue.

'Hold on, please,' she said, but barely two seconds later there was a click, and the wordless clamour of the office environment was replaced by a split second of silence, and then a voice:

'Mr Locke. Where have you been?'

The voice was sharp, demanding, for which I was obscurely glad; it was not the voice of someone about to convey distressing news.

'Away,' I said, trying to remember what I'd told him the last time we'd spoken. 'Staying with friends.'

'Didn't you receive my messages?'

'I just have.' I tried to calm my racing mind, to not be intimidated by his admonishing tone and rapid questions. I took a breath, during which – even though it was only a second or two's reprieve – I wondered whether I should tell him I'd been ill.

In the end I said, 'The phone signal's dodgy here. I'm out in the sticks, I'm afraid.'

If he thought it odd or suspicious that I would knowingly remain out of contact when my daughter was missing he didn't immediately say so. 'Where are you?' he wanted to know.

'Do you have news about Kate?' I asked, ignoring the question, deciding to go on the attack.

There was a pause, as if he was contemplating whether to answer my question, or counter with another of his own.

Then he said, 'Not as such, I'm afraid.'

'Not as such? What does that mean?'

I heard a huff of resignation or exasperation at the other end of the line. 'We're pursuing several lines of enquiry, but I'm afraid at present I have nothing concrete to tell you.'

I considered cutting the connection, but knew that would only rouse his suspicions and his ire still further. Elaborating on what I'd already told him I said, 'Sorry, this is a very bad line. I can hardly hear what you're saying.'

I don't know whether he believed me or not, but he raised his voice and repeated what he'd just said. Then he repeated his earlier question. 'Where are you, Mr Locke?'

I counted to three, then said, 'Hello? Hello? Inspector, are you still there?'

He began to reply, but I cut in: 'I don't know whether you can still hear me, Inspector, but I've lost the connection at this end. I'll call you as soon as I can. Goodbye.'

I ended the call, cutting him off in mid-flow, and then sat, breathing heavily for a few moments, as if we'd just been engaged not in a verbal joust but a physical one.

Within a minute of ending the call, Jensen sent me a text, demanding that I provide him with the contact address and landline number of where I was staying. I didn't reply, thinking that I could always blame the lack of signal at a later date.

Much as I loved Candice, after speaking to Jensen I didn't think I could cope with my eldest daughter's emoting at that moment. I felt bad, but sent her a message saying that I was sorry I hadn't been in touch, but that I was staying with friends outside London and hadn't been able to get a decent signal. I said I was okay, but that there was still no news of Kate. I received a text back almost immediately, in which Candice said she was *so* glad I was okay and that I should call her as soon as I got the chance.

That just left Dr Bruce – aside from the messages from my friends and colleagues, of course, which I fully intended to ignore. I stared at the second of her texts for a few seconds, and then I sighed and pressed 'Reply'. The phone rang four times and I almost rang off, but then a female voice all but sang out the words, 'Darby Hall Psychiatric Hospital.'

I asked for Dr Bruce, and explained who I was and why I was ringing. As with my call to the police station I was put through within seconds.

'Mr Locke,' Dr Bruce said in her dry, reserved voice.

'Hi,' I said. 'Sorry I couldn't ring you earlier. I've been away. No reception.'

'Mr Locke,' Dr Bruce said again, ignoring my explanation, 'I wanted to speak to you about Lyn.'

No surprise there, I thought, but I didn't say so. 'Is she all right?' I asked. 'Nothing's happened, has it?'

'Something *has* happened, yes, but the development is very much a positive one.' She paused as though choosing her words carefully. 'Since your visit Lyn has shown a remarkable upturn in terms of her emotional state and cognitive abilities. I won't go so far as to say that her improvement is miraculous, but it's certainly encouraging.'

'You mean she's getting better?' I asked.

'Again, I wouldn't wish to make assumptions. It may be that her improvement is temporary – a flash in the pan. In fact, the breakthrough she appears to have made has been *so* sudden and dramatic that I'm inclined to feel...'

'Uneasy?'

'I was about to say *more* cautious than I might if her improvement had been gradual.'

I stayed silent. I could tell by her tone that she wanted to say more. Sure enough, after a moment, she said, 'Lyn claims that during your visit you banished the "dark man", which as you know is the phrase that she uses for her particular psychological condition. In fact, she claims that you... captured his darkness, took it away. Would you happen to know what she means by that?'

Reluctant to tell her about the heart, I said, 'Well, Lyn and I talked for quite a while. She was more lucid than usual. Maybe I just managed to get through to her.'

I half-expected Dr Bruce to pull me up on that, to waspishly inform me that getting through to Lyn was precisely what she and her team of trained psychologists had been trying to do for the past five years. But instead, speaking more animatedly than I had ever heard her before, she said, 'It seemed more than that. Lyn referred to the darkness as though it was a physical thing. She claims that you gave it to her, that you allowed her to hold it, and then you took it back.'

'She must have been speaking metaphorically,' I said.

There was a brief silence, and then, almost coldly this time, Dr Bruce said, 'Yes, I suppose she must have.'

'It's good to hear she's doing so well, though,' I said, beginning to wonder whether there was more to Dr Bruce than met the eye, whether *she* had been playing a long game too – or was I simply being paranoid?

'Yes,' she said again. 'When were you next planning to visit Lyn, Mr Locke?'

'Soon,' I said vaguely.

'The sooner the better would be my recommendation. I believe your visit would be of great benefit to her.'

'Yes, well,' I said, 'I'll see what I can do. Goodbye.'

I cut the connection, feeling oddly unnerved.

A minute later I heard the creak of ascending footsteps outside the door.

'You decent in there, chief?'

'Yes, Frank,' I called. 'Come in.'

He opened the door, allowing Clover, who again was carrying the tea tray, to precede him. On the tray this time was a steaming bowl of soup, a side plate of French bread, a glass of water and a couple of pink pills, which I assumed were painkillers.

I was about to say how delicious the soup smelled when my phone chimed to let me know I'd got a text. I looked at it, thinking it would be from Candice or DI Jensen or Dr Bruce – and then the blood seemed to drain out of my head, making me feel faint.

Clover set the tray down hurriedly. 'What's the matter, Alex? You're as white as a sheet.'

I swallowed but couldn't speak. With shaking hands I handed her the phone.

I watched her face change, her eyes widen, as she read the text. I knew what it said. The words were already burned into my memory:

Your daughter is with me. It's time to meet. Noon tomorrow at the house of the man you killed. Don't worry about the police, they've done with the place. Come alone.

TWENTY-FIVE

SCENE OF THE CRIME

As I cautiously approached McCallum's house I was hoping that I wouldn't have to run. If I did, then maybe the adrenaline would kick in and over-ride the fact that my body felt like one big bruise, but I really didn't relish the prospect of putting it to the test.

In addition to the pain, I was knackered. The text I'd received yesterday had whipped me into such a state that I had barely slept last night. I'd spent the long hours between then and now mostly pacing through the house, trying to build up my strength and get some mobility back into my battered limbs. My ankle, where it felt as though the dog had gnawed through to the bone, hurt like buggery, though Clover had assured me that the wound was healing and was not infected. Apparently, while I had been sleeping, I'd been given tetanus shots and antibiotics and God knows what else to keep me healthy and alive.

The building where I'd been recuperating was beautiful. A big old town house in an exclusive little enclave overlooking Kensington Gardens. Clover had told me our neighbours were mostly A-list movie stars, politicians and industry tycoons. When I asked her who owned the house she simply said, 'You do, for now. The real owner wants to remain anonymous.' When I said that secrets made me uncomfortable, she just shrugged. 'Sorry, Alex, but there's nothing sinister about this. Believe me, if I could tell you everything, I would, but I'm under strict instructions. The owner doesn't want to get involved. If that changes, I'll let you know. But in the meantime, just enjoy this place while you can. Why look a gift horse in the mouth?'

Once the nausea after waking up had passed, I ate ravenously, despite the apprehension gnawing away in my stomach. The fridge and cupboards in the kitchen were full of food and drink. The kitchen itself was modern, tasteful, expensive-looking and full of top-of-the-range gadgets and equipment. The rest of the house, I discovered, was an impeccably blended mix of the old and the new. Original fireplaces and priceless antiques rubbed shoulders with up-to-the-minute entertainment systems and computer technology. There was a vast library of books, a spotless home office that looked like something out of a science-fiction film, even a long attic room that had been converted into a home cinema. Yet although the place was beautiful, it was oddly anonymous – the show home to end all show homes. I was not restricted in my movements – I could go wherever I wished, delve into whatever nooks and crannies I could find – and none of the rooms I came across were locked. Even so, I found no indication, nor even the slightest clue, as to who owned the place, or (if the two things were not mutually exclusive) who might live here. There were no photos, no documents, no personal knick-knacks, nothing. The place wasn't bland – it was too luxurious and well-appointed for that – but, all the same, the personality of the owner or owners was peculiarly absent.

Although I had taken a long bath, changed into fresh clothes, and fed myself not only with food and drink but plenty of painkillers, I hardly felt fighting fit. I was grateful in a way that McCallum's house was not much more than a stone's throw from where I was staying, though at the same time I felt uncomfortable being so close to the scene of my terrible crime. It was like tempting fate. Or, in spite of the fact that the choice had not been mine, it felt arrogant, even disrespectful, to set up camp virtually on my victim's doorstep. Was it coincidence that the kidnapper had contacted me now and suggested McCallum's house as the venue for our meeting, or was it his way of indicating that he knew where I was staying and that there was nowhere I could hide that he wouldn't find me? I knew that over-analysing the question would only make me more paranoid, but I couldn't help it. As I limped slowly up Bellwater Drive, I was unable to shake off the notion that everything about this situation smelled bad – and yet at the same time there was no way I was going to turn down the possibility of meeting and speaking with my daughter's abductor.

Although it was daylight, the neighbourhood was no busier than it had been the last time I'd been here. It was a cold day, but the autumn sun in the bleached-bone sky was as harsh as light reflected off tin and gave everything a crisp, sharp brightness that hurt my eyes.

I was dressed in jeans and boots, a dark grey sweater and my black zip-up jacket. The jeans and boots were mine, but the sweater was from a chest of drawers in the house. I'd been loath to wear someone else's clothes at first, but Clover had told me she'd been unable to get the bloodstains out of my grey hoodie and so had burned it. The fact that the stains had come from the shape-shifter had also given her and Frank cause for concern. I saw her point: what if Hulse, Jackery and the shape-shifter had been working together and the death of the false Clover had been part of the plan? The false Clover might have been discovered after a short time in my company, but we'd be more likely to overlook the stains, to forget that they were part of the same living organism. Clover's argument was that at some point – while we were asleep, for example – they might have oozed from the fabric, formed into an entirely new entity and murdered us in our beds before making off with the heart.

Far-fetched? Paranoid? Maybe, but it was an example of the way we were thinking. Impossible as it seemed, we were trying to cover every angle, consider every eventuality. We knew that to find some kind of resolution to this matter we had to take risks, but at the same time we were trying to eliminate unnecessary ones.

Of course the necessary risks were often the biggest of all. We might try to keep our heads down, to cover our tracks, but if an open invitation came to meet with our enemies there was no way we could ignore it.

No way *I* could ignore it, anyway. I had too much to lose. After the text had come through yesterday, Frank and Clover had spelled out the dangers, had felt compelled to point out (as if I didn't know) that this was almost certainly another trap. And yet they hadn't tried all that hard to dissuade me from accepting the summons. They knew as well as I did that if there was even the remotest chance of seeing Kate again, of getting her back, then I had to take it.

'I'll be fine,' I reassured them. 'The heart will keep me safe. And *they* must know that by now, whoever *they* are.'

Clover nodded, but she didn't look convinced. We both knew that all manner of things could go wrong. What if Kate's kidnappers threatened her life in front of me and the heart did nothing? Or what if the heart *did* react and my weakened body couldn't cope with another symbiotic link so soon after the last one?

'I'll be close by,' Frank said, 'in case you need me.'

'No.' I shook my head. 'I won't have Kate's safety jeopardised. The text said I should come alone. If something goes wrong and they find out you're with me, hiding in the shadows... Sorry, Frank, but I just can't risk it.'

Alone aside from the heart, which as always was tucked into the inside pocket of the leather jacket, I came to a halt outside 56 Bellwater Drive. In the daylight the house, which I could see through the iron gate, looked shabbier than it had in the darkness – the stonework in need of re-pointing, the wooden window frames rotting at the edges – but it was still an impressive and imposing structure. A strip of yellow and black police tape hung limply from the gate itself, another from the frame beside the catch. Clearly it had once been a single piece, tied across the gate as a flimsy barrier, presumably after McCallum's body had been removed and the police had concluded their forensic examination. Now the barrier had been breached – pulled apart or simply snapped. Not that this was a sign that Kate's kidnappers were already waiting for me up at the house, of course. The tape might have been broken by a member of McCallum's household staff, or even by the police themselves returning to the house for a follow-up examination.

I stood for maybe ten seconds, staring up at the windows, trying to detect signs of life. Eventually, when it occurred to me that if I stood there any longer I might draw attention to myself, I reached through to undo the latch, pushed the gate open and went in. It was a still day and there was hardly any movement, only the very tops of the trees lining the high wooden fence that bordered the sides and back of the property nodding sagely as I passed. Unlike the last time I had been here I walked up the gravel path that encircled the house. My footsteps crunched slightly, but the sound seemed less pervasive in the daytime – besides which, I had no particular reason to conceal my presence this time.

I still had the key for the French windows that Clover had given me a week ago. As I was reaching into my pocket for it, I saw that I wouldn't need it. The French windows were ajar, an obvious invitation. I thought briefly of a spring-loaded mousetrap ready to snap shut when the bait was taken. And then I stepped inside.

My heart started drumming the instant I crossed the threshold. I knew it was crazy, but I couldn't shake the feeling that the house recognised me and was raising its hackles in memory of what I had done. I looked down at the now-faded pink bloodstain on the carpet and wondered who had cleaned it up. McCallum's housekeeper? Or did the police have a special team that dealt with such things?

The familiar smell, of old carpets and furniture polish, made me gag, not because it was unpleasant but because of its associations. Although the police must have swarmed all over this room since the murder, it looked no different to the last time I had been here. The body was gone, of course, and the broken glass from the smashed dome had been removed. But the rest of the room was just as it had been on the night the old man had died. There wasn't even evidence of fingerprint dust on the surfaces or the muddy boot prints of all the coppers who must have come traipsing through here.

My attention was snagged by something which I had been too preoccupied to notice the last time I'd been here. It was a large framed poster above the fireplace advertising a performance by 'The Great Barnaby' at the London Hippodrome on Friday, 10 December 1948. I remembered Clover telling me about the poster the first time we'd met. The main painting depicted a moustached and bearded man in a red eye mask, a top hat perched at a jaunty angle on his head. His hands, in white kid gloves, were upraised, fingers widely spread. An array of objects – playing cards, candles, pocket watches, juggling balls – arced in a glittering rainbow above him. Dressed in a black jacket, a red cravat and a cream-coloured waistcoat emblazoned with stars and ringed planets, the magician was grinning widely, almost crazily. I stared at the poster – and my heart gave a jolt. One of the objects he was 'juggling' was the obsidian heart.

Suddenly I tensed. As before, from elsewhere in the house, I could hear the slow, sonorous ticking of a clock. But now that sound was accompanied by another – a faint, rhythmic *squeak-squeak... squeak-squeak...* As this new sound grew louder, approaching the room, I took an instinctive step back towards the French windows. Though my body was stiff and aching I felt my muscles bunching, readying themselves to flee.

The squeaking sound halted right outside the room and then the door in the far corner started to open. Next moment a wheelchair entered, pushed by a burly man with a square jaw and dark, close-cropped hair, his pumped body straining to burst from a sombre pin-striped suit and tie. However I barely gave him a second glance. My attention was focused on the frail old man in the wheelchair.

It was Barnaby McCallum.

I stared at him, thinking of the warehouse in the Isle of Dogs. As his minder or carer pushed him further into the room I raised a hand and took another step back towards the French windows.

'Don't come any closer,' I said. 'I know you're not him.'

The old man in the wheelchair peered at me with an expression of... interest? Perhaps even sympathy? As if mirroring me, he raised one of the gnarled hands that were resting on a thick blanket across his knees, his face crinkling like a walnut as he spoke.

'I am, you know,' he said, 'though, of course, you're right to be suspicious.'

I licked my lips, aware that I was up on the balls of my feet, prepared to run. 'How can you be? You're dead. *He's* dead.'

The old man tutted. 'How long have you had the heart in your possession, Mr Locke? A week? Have you learned nothing of its properties in that time?'

Despite myself I felt offended by the question. 'I've learned plenty.'

'Ah. Then you're no doubt aware that it displays a certain... ah, *temporal* flexibility?'

I looked at him warily. 'Go on.'

His face crinkled even more alarmingly, as if it was folding in on itself, and I realised that he was smiling. 'Haven't you guessed? I've used the heart to travel forward in time. Today is... what? Monday the eighth of October?'

I nodded.

Tapping the arm of the chair, he half-twisted towards the burly man behind him. 'What day was it when we left, Hartson? The last Friday in September, wasn't it?'

'Yes, sir.'

'Which means that in... three days – or is it four? – you're going to kill me, Alex.'

My heart gave a jolt, causing me to gasp as my various bruises throbbed with pain. I opened my mouth to speak, but no sound came out.

'It's quite all right,' the old man said in his rasping voice, 'I know what you're thinking. You're wondering why, if I know this, I don't take precautions to prevent it?'

Dumbly I nodded.

McCallum sighed. 'You may not understand this, Mr Locke, young and fit as you are, but the truth is... it's simply time. I'm old and so very, very tired. It's time to pass on my legacy, to deliver it into your hands.'

I cleared my throat, forced myself to speak. 'But you tried to *stop* me stealing the heart.' Then I realised that the past for me was the future for him, albeit a future he was aware of. 'What I mean is, you *will* try to stop me.'

The suggestion of a twinkle appeared in McCallum's rheumy eyes. 'Well, I had to make it *look* good, didn't I? Would you have bashed me on the head if I hadn't attacked you?'

'No,' I admitted.

'No. Of course you wouldn't. You're not a violent man.'

This encounter wasn't going the way I had envisaged it at all. Despite the fact that I couldn't decide whether I ought to feel relieved to know that McCallum had *wanted* me to kill him, thus lifting my burden of guilt, or angry that he had chosen me to be his murderer, thus dropping me in the shit, I decided it was time to get back on track. 'Where's Kate?' I demanded.

The old man shrugged, resembling a bat drawing up its wings. 'How should I know?'

I felt the hope I had been offered slipping away from me. 'But that's why I came here! You *did* send me the text?'

McCallum gestured at the man behind him. 'Hartson here did it. My fingers aren't as dextrous as they used to be.'

'But you said you were the man who had Kate!'

'I lied,' said McCallum casually. 'I had to say something to get you to come.'

Despair and anger washed through me, as I realised I was as far away from finding Kate as ever. 'You bastard.' I glared at him. 'So why *did* you bring me here?'

'To talk,' said McCallum reasonably. 'I thought it was time you were given a few answers, time you stopped floundering in the dark.'

I half-raised a hand, then slapped it dismissively on my thigh. 'So tell me,' I said, as if it was an inconvenience. 'Tell me everything.'

McCallum looked at me shrewdly. 'Oh, I can't tell you *everything*.'

'Why not?'

'Too dangerous, Mr Locke. That wouldn't do *anyone* any good.'

Exasperated I said, 'Oh, for fuck's sake. This is a waste of time.'

McCallum simply smiled. 'I understand your frustration. But please allow me to tell you this. You're about to embark on a long and difficult journey, one on which you must, at all costs, protect the heart.'

'Why?'

'Because if you don't, terrible things will happen. Not only to your daughter, not only to you and your friends, but to *everyone*.' He paused, and suddenly his eyes seemed to glitter as he fixed them on me. 'If the heart falls into the wrong hands, if the balance of power tilts, things will unravel at an alarming rate.'

Despite myself I felt chilled by his words. 'But why me? Why was I chosen for this?'

'You killed me. Therefore it's your responsibility.'

I shook my head. 'No, it's more complicated than that. I was dragged into this against my will. I was *manipulated*. But this isn't me. I don't *want* any of this. So tell me again – why me?'

McCallum spread his hands. He looked genuinely sympathetic. 'There's only so much I can tell.'

'Bollocks!' I shouted and took a step forward. I saw the man-mountain standing behind McCallum's wheelchair tense, and I halted.

For a moment there was an impasse. I stared at McCallum, breathing hard. On the way here I had toyed with the idea of stopping to buy cigarettes. But I had kept walking, too hyped up, too anxious to break my stride. Now I wished I *had* bought some. I could have murdered one at that moment.

I grimaced at the unfortunate choice of phrase, a memory flashing into my head of McCallum lying on the carpet, a hole in his skull, blood pooling beneath him. I unzipped my jacket, slipped my hand inside.

'What if I were to give you the heart back right now?' I said. 'What if I were to return it and never kill you?'

'But you *have* killed me, Mr Locke,' McCallum said. 'The dirty deed has already been done and now it can't be *un-*done. Don't you see?'

'But if I were to give you the heart,' I said, drawing it from my pocket and holding it out to him, 'wouldn't that undo everything? Set everything back to normal?'

McCallum sighed. 'Time is a complicated thing, Mr Locke. But you'll get to grips with its quirks and contradictions soon enough.' He slipped his hand under the blanket spread across his knees, then slowly drew it out and held it up, showing me the object he was holding.

An obsidian heart, identical to my own.

'There are two of them?' I said, confused.

He smiled indulgently. 'Of course not. I've come forward in time. As far as I'm concerned you haven't stolen the heart from me yet. This is the one you'll flee with after killing me. The one you're holding right now.'

I looked from the heart in my hand to the one in his. 'How can the same object be in two places at once?'

He giggled, a cracked, rather awful sound. 'I know. It's mind-boggling, isn't it?'

Before I could reply I heard the faint wail of police sirens. I tensed, hoping they would fade, but alarmingly they seemed to be coming closer.

'Ah,' said McCallum sadly, 'my cue to leave.'

I could barely contain my own urge to flee, but I said, 'But you've hardly told me anything.'

'Another time, Mr Locke. See you last week.'

And with that he tapped the heart once, lightly, on the arm of his wheelchair. I staggered back, buffeted by what I imagined a minor aftershock of an earthquake would be like, and when I looked again McCallum, the wheelchair and his bodyguard were gone.

The sirens grew louder still, and then, with a final blip, seemed to halt right outside the house. I wondered what to do, whether to go deeper into the house and hide or try to make good my escape. I hovered for a second or two, then decided on the latter – decided, in fact, to adopt a casual, confident air in the hope that I could bluff my way out of the situation. I exited the way I had come in and instead of running or hiding, simply strolled along the gravel path towards the garden gate. My heart was pounding in my chest, but I was hoping my nervousness didn't show. I was about ten metres from the gate when it opened and two uniformed police officers appeared.

'Hi,' I said.

The officers regarded me a moment, and then the chubbier and older of the two said, 'Can I ask what you're doing here, sir?'

'Yes,' I said. 'I'm responding to a text.'

'A text?'

'Yes. My name's Alex Locke. My daughter went missing last week. I received a text, supposedly from the kidnapper, telling me to meet him here at noon. I turned up, but the kidnapper didn't.'

The chubbier policeman frowned. 'I see. Could I see the text, sir?'

This was the tricky bit. I shrugged. 'I'm afraid I deleted it.'

The chubbier policeman looked at me in disbelief. 'You *deleted* it?'

'Yes.' I couldn't tell him it was because the text had named me as McCallum's murderer. 'I did it by accident. I was trying to get the sender's number.'

The officers glanced at one another. It was clear from their expressions that they didn't believe me.

The chubbier one said, 'Are you aware that this house is a crime scene, sir?'

I shook my head. 'No.'

'So you didn't see the tape on the gate?'

'Oh,' I said. 'Yes. But...'

'But?'

For a moment my mind went blank, and then I said, 'I thought whoever sent the text might have put it there as a sort of... marker.'

The younger officer snorted softly. Looking over my shoulder at the house, his chubbier colleague said, 'May I ask how you gained access to the property, sir?'

'Through the French windows. They'd been left open.'

There was silence as the older, chubbier officer seemed to come to a decision. He leaned towards his companion and murmured something. His companion nodded. The chubbier officer turned back to me. 'I'm going to check the house, sir, so if you wouldn't mind accompanying my colleague.'

'Accompanying him where?' I asked.

'Our car is parked on the road, outside the gate.'

'It's all right, I don't need a lift anywhere,' I said.

His eyes narrowed as if I'd made a facetious remark. 'But I'm sure you're eager to notify the officer in charge of the inquiry into your daughter's disappearance of this latest development, sir? In fact I'm surprised you haven't already done so.'

I stared at him a moment, and then I nodded. 'Yes, of course,' I said.

The older officer gave an abrupt nod and stomped past me, up towards the house. The younger, slimmer one offered me a tight smile and gestured rather unnecessarily at the gate.

'This way, sir.'

TWENTY-SIX
STOLEN PROPERTY

The constable who escorted me to the interview room assured me that DI Jensen would be along 'in just a few minutes'. An hour later he still hadn't turned up, by which time my mind was jittery with questions.

How much did the police know about me? Why were they keeping me waiting? Were they trying to unnerve me or had they simply forgotten I was here? Had Jensen been detained or called away? And if so, was it to do with Kate and why hadn't I been informed?

I'd tried the door after ten minutes, to find it locked. Did this mean I was a prisoner or was it simply procedure? Were the doors to *all* the interview rooms kept locked, regardless of who was in them, purely as a security precaution?

I didn't know, but it was disquieting enough to make me restless. After texting Clover to let her know what was happening, I paced the room for a while before it occurred to me that hidden cameras might be observing and recording my every movement. So I sat back down, rested my arms on the table and lowered my head, trying to look as though I was using the delay to take an afternoon nap. After a while, the bland, duck-egg blue of the walls began to irritate me, so I closed my eyes. I kept them closed until, sometime later, the door abruptly opened.

I raised my head to see DI Jensen sliding into the seat opposite me, and placing a silver MacBook on the edge of the table. He was wearing a hairy grey jacket that had seen better days and his throat looked scraped and raw, as though he had had to use a blunt razor to shave because he had forgotten to buy new ones. He looked grouchy, and waited until he had pointedly smoothed down his green tie with one flat palm, as if to prevent it from curling up like old bacon, before leaning forward, clasping his hands on the table and locking his eyes on to mine.

'Sorry to keep you so long, Mr Locke,' he said, not sounding sorry at all.

'I expect you're busy,' I replied.

'We are,' he said, as if that was partly my fault. 'Very.'

Sensing a presence behind me, I glanced over my shoulder to see that a uniformed constable had followed Jensen into the room and was now standing like a guard beside the door.

'You seem nervous, Mr Locke,' Jensen said.

I turned back, trying to make it look casual. 'No,' I said, 'I'm fine.'

He indicated the MacBook. 'Mind if I record our interview?'

'Sure.'

He opened the MacBook and busied himself with it, his fingers dancing over the keyboard. Finally he nodded with satisfaction. 'There we go. Isn't technology wonderful?'

'Mm,' I said.

'Now.' He laced his fingers together again. 'Would you mind explaining to me why you were in the grounds of number 56 Bellwater Drive, Kensington, at approximately 12.15 p.m.?'

'I explained all this to the officer at the time,' I said.

Jensen's facial muscles twitched into something approximating a smile. 'I appreciate that, Mr Locke, but please indulge me. I would prefer to hear your explanation first hand. And also for the record, of course.' He nodded at the MacBook.

Trying not to sigh, I told him again about the text.

'May I see?' he asked.

'I deleted it.'

Although I suspected he had already been informed of this, he looked at me as if he was astounded. 'You *deleted* it?'

I told him what I had told the officer earlier. He stared at me as if to encourage or intimidate me into saying more, but I remained silent.

Finally he sighed and said, 'Was that the *only* reason you were at 56 Bellwater Drive today, Mr Locke?'

I felt my heart quicken. 'Yes.'

He was silent for another long moment, and then he said, 'Did it occur to you to wonder why my officers apprehended you at the Bellwater Drive house?'

Apprehended. It was only a small step from there to 'arrested'.

'I expect someone told you I was there.'

'You expect correctly,' he said, and fell silent again.

I wanted to ask him *who* had told him, but I waited patiently for him to continue. I had learned long ago that in situations like this it was best to say no more than you had to. After a moment he said, 'Were you aware, Mr Locke, that the house on Bellwater Drive was a crime scene?'

'Not until your officers told me, no.'

'And were you, or are you, aware who the house on Bellwater Drive belonged to?'

'No.'

'Were you similarly unaware that the owner of the house on Bellwater Drive was murdered during what is believed to have been a robbery last week?'

'No.' I felt a trickle of sweat run down the back of my neck. 'I mean... yes, I was unaware.'

'Have you any idea what was taken from the house on Bellwater Drive during the course of the robbery, Mr Locke?'

'No,' I said, and this time I couldn't prevent myself from blurting, 'How *would* I know?'

Jensen paused, looking at me a moment longer, and then he shifted his gaze slowly and deliberately to fix on his interlocked hands. He looked as though he wanted to give the impression he was thinking hard, mulling over my responses, though I suspected that he knew exactly what he was going to say next and was only prolonging the moment to exacerbate my unease. My lips were so dry they were sticking together, but I felt loath to part them with my tongue. I felt another trickle of sweat run down my neck and soak into the already damp collar of my jacket.

'What was taken was a small artefact about so big.' He held up his hand, indicating the size by spreading his thumb and index finger. 'It was a carving of a human heart, made of obsidian. Do you know what obsidian is, Mr Locke?'

This time I had to lick my lips in order to answer. 'It's a black rock,' I said.

'Correct. More to the point it's a *volcanic* rock. It resembles black glass. I'm told obsidian is formed when lava solidifies very quickly. An artefact like that would be very distinctive, don't you think?'

Aware that the trap had been sprung, I said, 'Yes.'

Jensen gave me a thin smile. 'Would you mind turning out your pockets, Mr Locke? Purely as a courtesy, of course.'

I felt suddenly enervated. My limbs were aching, my ankle hurting so much that it felt as though the dog was still gnawing on it. Delaying the moment, hoping that the heart would transform or even disappear, I half-rose from my seat and placed the contents of my jeans pockets on the table. Cash, receipts, keys (including the key to McCallum's French windows, which I hadn't needed on this occasion), my wallet, other bits and pieces. Then I patted my back pockets and the side pockets of my leather jacket, all of which were empty, before finally, reluctantly, slipping my hand into the jacket's inside pocket.

I knew, even before I touched it, that the heart had let me down. I could feel its weight, its solidity, resting against my ribcage. I closed my fingers around it, willing it to change. When it didn't I felt a spike of anger, a sense of *well, fuck you then* – and then I withdrew it from my pocket.

Even now I expected the heart to respond, to save me somehow. I wondered how this dour policeman would react if I were to disappear in a flash of light before his eyes. I put the heart on the table, but rested my fingers on it for a moment, giving it one final chance. Then with a sigh I let it go.

The air in the room felt heavy. Jensen looked at the heart, then at me. Pointedly he said, 'Mr Locke has produced a human heart carved out of obsidian from the inside breast pocket of his jacket and placed it on the table.' He took a long, slow breath, in and out, and then he said, 'Could you explain how this object came to be in your possession, Mr Locke?'

Before I could even think about it, I said, 'It was sent to me.'

'Sent to you?'

'Yes.'

'I see.' Another pause, his eyes burning into mine. 'And *how* was it sent?'

'Through the post. In a padded envelope.'

'Through the post?'

'Yes.'

Though Jensen's voice was low and, like his face, bereft of emotion, he managed to convey the impression that he didn't believe a word of what I was saying. 'And was there a return address with this package?'

'No.'

'Was there a message of any kind?'

Though I paused for no more than a split second before answering, I felt certain that my hesitation would not have gone unnoticed. 'Yes.'

'And what form did this message take?'

'It was a note.'

'Hand-written or printed?'

'Er... printed. In block capitals.'

'On?'

'Pardon?'

'What was the message written *on*?'

'A word processor, I suppose.'

He gave a brief, exasperated hiss. 'What kind of paper?'

'I don't know... normal. Typing paper. White.'

'Lined or unlined?'

'Er... unlined.'

'And what did the message say?'

'It said...' I paused, pretending to rack my brains, though in truth I was simply trying to avoid saying something that would trip me up. 'I can't remember the exact words, but it said that if I wanted to see Kate alive again, I had to look after what was in the envelope and keep it safe.'

'Is that all?'

'Yes. I think so.'

'And it didn't occur to you to inform us that you had received this package?'

'I was told not to.'

'By whom?'

'By the man who sent me the heart.'

'Oh, I see. He called you, did he?'

'No, he... in the note he said not to tell the police. That he'd kill Kate if I did.'

'But I thought you said that the note simply instructed you to keep the heart safe?'

'Yes. I mean, I forgot about the other bit.'

Jensen looked incredulous. 'You *forgot* that the sender threatened to kill your daughter if you told the police? Are you in the habit of *forgetting* when the lives of your loved ones are threatened, Mr Locke?'

'No, it's just...' I paused, took several deep breaths. His eyes were still drilling into me. I rubbed at my forehead to block out his gaze and said, 'I'm stressed, that's all. My head's all over the place. Wouldn't yours be if your daughter had been kidnapped?'

He didn't answer my question. Instead he asked, 'Where is this note now?'

'I threw it away.'

'*You threw it away?*'

'Yes. I didn't want it falling into the wrong hands.'

'You do realise that that note could have provided us with important forensic information? That it might have led us to your daughter's kidnapper?'

'Sorry, I didn't think.'

'Where have you been staying these past few days, Mr Locke?'

'What?'

He spoke slowly and deliberately, as if I was hard of hearing. 'Where have you been staying?'

'I told you. With a friend.'

'And does this friend have a name? An address?'

'Yes, but... I'd rather not say what it is.'

'Really? And why's that?'

'Because he wants to remain anonymous.'

'My last question applies. Why's that?'

'He's got a certain... reputation. A criminal record. He doesn't want his name bandied about. He doesn't want the police to jump to the wrong conclusions.'

'And what conclusions might they be, Mr Locke?'

I wafted a hand, as if to brush away his question like a troublesome fly. And then almost immediately I felt a welcome surge of anger, of irritation. Glaring at him, I said, 'Why are you treating me like a criminal? My daughter's been missing for bloody days. Why are you wasting time with me instead of trying to track down the real perpetrator?'

Jensen's eyes were like flint. 'Do you really want me to answer that question, Mr Locke?'

'Yes I do, actually.'

'Very well.' His voice remained calm, even. 'As I'm sure you will agree, it would be remiss of me not to thoroughly explore every avenue of enquiry in this investigation. And frankly, Mr Locke, your behaviour has become suspicious enough to more than warrant this interview. The fact that you have deliberately put yourself out of contact over the past few days, and that you now refuse to reveal your recent whereabouts, is suspicious enough in itself—'

I raised a hand to interrupt him. 'All right, point taken. But hasn't it occurred to you that someone might have set me up to make me *look* suspicious?'

'Of course it has. Which is precisely why I feel it would be in your best interests to be entirely honest with us.'

Touché, I thought, and slumped back in my seat. My collar and underarms were wet with sweat. I knew I'd have to give Jensen *something*, that he wouldn't let me alone until I did. But I couldn't tell him I'd been in London the past few days, not after letting him think I'd been somewhere more remote, where I couldn't get any signal – besides which, Clover had advised me not to reveal the address of the 'safe house' to anyone.

'All right,' I said, 'I'll tell you. But I'm going to be in so much trouble with my friend for dragging his name into this.'

'Given the circumstances, I'm sure he'll forgive you,' Jensen said evenly.

I hesitated a moment longer, then gave him Benny's name and address. It was a huge risk – I didn't even know if Benny had survived the confrontation at the cemetery – but I couldn't think of anything else to do.

'There,' Jensen said, 'that wasn't so difficult, was it?'

I shrugged. 'Whether he'll confirm I was there or not, I don't know.'

'Let us worry about that,' Jensen said. For the first time he reached across the table for the heart. I tensed. He picked it up carefully, as if it was so delicate it might crack at the slightest pressure of his fingers – or as if he knew what it was capable of.

'Do you mind if we photograph this?'

It was a request I could hardly refuse. 'Will I get it back?'

He pursed his lips. 'That depends.'

'On what?'

'On what we decide to do with it. The heart is evidence and needs to be examined. It may also be stolen property.'

I felt like a parent arguing with a social worker who was threatening to take their child into care. 'But I was told to look after it. Whoever's got Kate will kill her if I don't.'

'Do you really believe that, Mr Locke?'

'I daren't *not* believe it.'

Jensen raised his eyebrows slightly. 'If what you're telling me is true, then the way it looks is that the only reason you were ordered to keep the heart safe is so that you'd be found with it on your person leaving Bellwater Drive. Though why your daughter's abductor should want to set you up I have no idea. Maybe in an effort to discredit you? Or just to inflict even more hell on you than you're no doubt already going through – there are some sick and sadistic people about. But the good news is that if this *is* the case, then the threat from Kate's abductor is more than likely an empty one. You were told your daughter would be killed simply in order to ensure you were found with the heart in your possession. *Ipso facto*, Kate's abductor *wanted* that to happen.'

I stared at him. His logic was irrefutable. All the same, trying not to sound desperate, I said, 'What if you're wrong?'

He shrugged. 'Then who would know, besides the people in this room?'

I didn't know what to say to that. Partly because I was itching to snatch the heart from his hand and stuff it back into my pocket, I folded my arms and leaned back. I watched helplessly as Jensen stood, walked across the room and handed the heart to the PC by the door, murmuring instructions.

The PC nodded and slipped out of the room. I felt fresh sweat spring out on my scalp and run down my face. I palmed it away with a shaking hand as Jensen strolled back to his seat. Now I felt not like a parent losing a child, but like a junkie denied a fix.

'Are you all right, Mr Locke?' asked Jensen, sitting down again. 'You don't look well.'

'I've had a bug this week,' I muttered, hardly aware of what I was saying. 'Flu or something. Just run down, I suppose.'

Jensen arranged his features into an expression of concern. 'I expect it's the stress. Would you like me to get you anything? A glass of water? Cup of tea?'

'Yes, water would be—' Then I felt a sudden itch in my throat and barked a cough so violent it jerked my head forward. Pressing a clenched fist to my mouth, I was horrified to see that behind Jensen the air was shimmering, boiling, turning hazy. Jensen, unaware of the phenomenon, was frowning, his nose twitching at the acrid stench now creeping into the room. Abruptly the patch of hazy air thickened, erupting outwards like an underwater explosion, filling the room with yellow smog. Coughing now, also pressing a fist to his mouth, he began to rise from his chair, a look of bafflement on his face. I croaked a warning as a dark shape loomed from the yellow smog behind him, but I was too late. Jensen had barely begun to turn before Hulse stepped up behind him and, in one swift motion, slashed his throat.

The cut was so deep, so savage, that Jensen was almost beheaded by it. The wound gaped like a second mouth as his head tilted back, and instinctively I threw myself sideways as blood jetted across the table towards me. My chair toppled and I crashed to the floor, the jet of blood, followed by several others, shooting over my head and zigzagging across the wall. I felt pinpricks of it speckle my face as I slithered across the floor on my backside, kicking the chair away from me and propelling myself with my feet. I wanted to put as much distance as I could between Hulse and myself, but when I finally scrambled upright and looked across the table there was no sign of the cut-throat, and the yellow smog was already dispersing, rushing towards a central point as though being sucked into a hole. Within seconds I was alone with Jensen's body, which was now spreadeagled, face down, across the table. There was so much blood – on the table beneath him, drooling on to the floor and spattered across the far wall – that it looked as though someone had gone crazy with a tin of red paint.

Although deeply shocked by what had happened, my immediate concern, I'm ashamed to say, was for my own welfare. If someone had walked into the room at that moment they would have had no option but to assume I had murdered the DI. Later it would occur to me that there was very little blood on my hands and clothes and no sign of a murder weapon, but at that moment I was panicking. I glanced up at the walls, this time *hoping* to see a surveillance camera, but there was nothing to suggest that what had taken place had been either recorded or witnessed. I walked around the edge of the room, keeping away from the body, and taking care not to step in the blood which was already creeping across the floor. I reached the door and tried the handle and whispered a silent prayer of thanks when it opened. Clearly it hadn't been deemed necessary to lock it when Jensen was in the room.

I stepped into a corridor lined with doors. On the opposite wall a pair of fire doors led to a staircase, which I knew would take me down to the reception area, across from which was the main entrance that led to the outside world and freedom. From behind a closed door further down on my left came bustling office sounds – the buzz of chatter, the creak of chairs, the clatter of fingers on keyboards, the whine of a printer or photocopier. My over-riding instinct was to flee the building, but I couldn't leave without the heart. But where *was* it? How could I find it? I didn't have the first clue where to look.

I froze as the door to the large office opened, the sounds of activity swelling momentarily like a swarm of bees released from a box. A woman stepped into the corridor and pushed the door closed behind her. She turned to me and smiled. My mouth dropped open.

It was Lyn.

As on the previous occasions I had seen her beyond the confines of Darby Hall, this was the Lyn of yesteryear, before the 'dark man' had entered her life. And as before, she was pregnant and radiant, dressed in the white nightshirt with the cherry design, her feet bare, her fingernails and toenails painted a bright cheerful pink, her slim wrists bedecked with bangles.

Those bangles jangled now as she beckoned me. 'Come on, Alex,' she said. 'Hurry.'

She turned and began to stride away, heading deeper into the building. With a twinge of regret I glanced at the fire door and then hurried after her.

She was maybe ten metres ahead of me, moving quickly despite her bulging belly. As she reached the end of the corridor, I was striding past the long, busy office on my left, inside which I could see dark shapes moving through a row of frosted windows. Whoever might happen to look up at the windows from the other side would no doubt see the blur of my head passing from one to the next, but thankfully nobody emerged to check who I was or what I was doing. As Lyn turned right into the next corridor, I put on a spurt of speed, knowing that her presence was so ephemeral that to lose sight of her momentarily might mean losing her completely. My heart was thumping with anxiety as I rounded the corner – but there she still was, half a dozen metres ahead of me. Her blond hair swished as she shifted her weight from one side to the other, and her bare feet even made slight indentations in the carpet.

She stopped at a door two-thirds of the way down the corridor on her right. Although she glanced back as if to check I was still with her, she didn't say anything and she didn't wait for me; she pushed open the door and entered.

Or at least, I *thought* she had pushed open the door, but when I reached it I discovered it was still closed. Screwed to the door was a brushed-steel nameplate, the name itself indented in black: Detective Inspector F. Jensen.

I didn't knock and I didn't hesitate. I turned the handle and pushed the door open. Beyond was a small office, no more than half a dozen metres square. Directly in front of me was a neatly arranged desk, behind which a large window offered a view which was two-thirds sky and one-third birdshit-smeared rooftops. There was no sign of Lyn, but standing behind the desk, pulling open one of the desk drawers, was DI Jensen – the same DI Jensen whose throat I had seen slashed from ear to ear. Glancing at me with something like irritation, he reached into the drawer and withdrew the obsidian heart, which he brandished like a rock he intended to whack me across the head with. Immediately the air shimmered around him and his outline started to blur.

Without thinking what I was doing, and in defiance of my stiff and aching body, I leaped up on to the desk and hurled myself at him. I hit him like a rugby player making a tackle, my full weight causing him to hurtle backwards. With me still clinging to him, he hit the window at such a speed that the glass simply gave way, shattering outwards. I had the fleeting impression that we were surrounded by jagged chunks of glittering sky.

Then we were falling.

TWENTY-SEVEN

GASLIGHT

There was a smell.

Something chemical.

Chloroform?

Was I in hospital?

My eyes seemed to be glued closed and I couldn't summon up the energy to open them. I felt as if I was somehow *below* the surface of my body, as if my consciousness was wallowing in thick, black darkness, unable to influence my physical self, which was somewhere above me, out of reach. For the time being I could only think, remember. I recalled the uncontrollable, stomach-lurching sensation of falling from a great height. I remembered tumbling over and over, broken glass like shards of lethal-edged light cascading around me, the wind screaming, my hands gripping the lapels of Jensen's jacket and refusing to let go. And then...

Nothing. A blank. An absence. No sense of time passing, no dreams, not even darkness. I was gone and then I was... here. Aware but detached. Able to think, to smell...

To hear?

Yes. All it took was a slight shift in perception, and I became aware of sounds. Echoing clangs and clanks. A slight, persistent hiss. A wordless shout of pain or fear that seemed to come from far away.

And touch? Could I feel anything? I tried to connect with my muscles and bones, to imagine my fingers and toes twitching, even to tap into the memory of pain from my bruised and battered body. But

I couldn't. There was nothing. Was I dead? Was my consciousness, my soul, somehow trapped inside my mortally injured corpse? Panic surged, but it was slow and inexorable, like a vast, black wave of something more cloying, more terrible than water. I felt it rising above me, closing over my head. My thoughts broke apart and I let it fill me.

I slept.

When I next woke things were different. I knew immediately that I was closer to the surface. My eyes behind their closed lids felt hot and itchy and swollen. The pain that I could feel throbbing in my limbs was almost welcoming. The smells and sounds were sharper, more varied. The chemical odour was mingled with that of wood or pipe smoke, of hot oil or candle wax, of something dank and slightly musty. I heard footsteps, voices, the rattle of wheels, the clatter of hooves on stone, the general bustle of activity, all of which were muffled, distant, almost soothing. I was aware of something supporting my head, of my body from the chest down smothered by a covering that was prickly, and that smelled a little stale.

I tried to move my fingers, but again I couldn't manage it. Was I paralysed? Had I broken my spine in the fall from the police station window? Had I been in a coma, and if so for how long?

I struggled to communicate – to speak, to open my eyes. I felt the blood rushing to my brain. I felt trapped inside myself. I pushed and pushed, my eyes beneath the closed lids smarting, bulging, filling with heat as if about to burst. I wanted to scream, to thrash, but I couldn't move. I had an explosion building inside me, an uprush of energy with nowhere to go.

And then... light! Suddenly, unexpectedly. It was only a sliver, a chink, a tear, but it was searing, liberating, wonderful.

Once the breakthrough had been made it was easier. It was like cracking a carapace that had been encasing my body, like breaking out of an egg. I felt – imagined – the thin shell falling away. I struggled into the light, floundering, gasping, clawing at the air. I forced my eyelids apart, the tiny muscles around my eyes straining, aching, working like pulleys to prise open grit-encrusted window shutters. As the light seeped in, it flooded my brain, acting like a balm, soothing and reviving.

The first thing I saw was a row of windows to my left. Beyond them

I glimpsed movement – birds? Pigeons, maybe? It was hard to tell, not only because daylight was filtering through and making my smarting eyes water, but because the windows were small and high up and coated with a thick layer of grime. I blinked, tried to lift my hand to wipe my eyes, but it was unresponsive. Perhaps I *was* paralysed, though at that moment the thought didn't distress me as much as it ought to have done. I was just glad to have broken out of the darkness, to feel the daylight on my face. One thing at a time. Softly, softly, catchee monkey, as my dad used to say.

I blinked the tears away. Blinked and blinked until my vision was clear. I moved my head, looked around. I was in a small room, lying on my back on an iron-framed bed. The room had mustard-yellow walls, a bare wooden floor, wooden fixtures and fittings. To my left, below the row of windows, was a workbench stretching the length of the room, which was cluttered with equipment, all of it archaic. There were glass phials; test tubes in wooden stands; a bell jar containing a contraption that was all brass handles and curly wires and hand-blown light bulbs. There was a chunky box-like affair studded with brass dials beneath a half-moon display of hand-written numbers and a metal indicator needle, from the back of which rubber tubing trailed like an array of severed tentacles.

The right-hand wall was composed of a wooden frame divided into a grid of smaller frames, each no larger than a metre or so square. Each of these frames contained a mosaic of darkly coloured stained glass – no elaborate designs, simply rectangles of orange, brown and green glass fused together in haphazard patterns. The glass was thick, almost opaque, the effect of the design – though crude – autumnal, forest-like. It made me think of a screen of foliage through which seeped murky, dappled light.

The centrepiece of the wall of glass was a sturdy wooden door with a brass handle. There was no electric light in the room. Instead four gas lamps at head height provided what would presumably be the only illumination once the daylight faded.

Where was I? And more to the point, *when* was I? I could only surmise that the heart had done its thing, and that as Jensen (or the thing that *looked* like Jensen) and I had fallen, it had zapped us somewhere else.

So what year was this? Unless this place was some kind of museum, the evidence seemed to suggest I'd travelled back a century, maybe more. From my surroundings, and from the chemical smell, I would guess I was in a hospital, maybe a laboratory. The room reminded me of a set from a Hammer horror movie – not a pleasant thought. As I shook off the last muzzy threads of unconsciousness, I realised that the movement I could see beyond the grime-furred windows was people – or at least their legs and feet – moving to and fro.

So this must be a basement then, or at least a room slightly below ground level. From the echoing and often distant quality of the sounds beyond the door to my right, I'd guess that there was a corridor out there, or a series of corridors. I might have been wrong, but I had the impression of size, of a large building filled with many rooms.

I looked down at myself. I was wearing what appeared to be a white gown or nightshirt and was mostly covered by a coarsely woven grey blanket that made me think of the army. I tried to sit up, but realised that although I could now move my fingers and toes freely, I couldn't lift my arms or legs. I wondered again whether I was paralysed – and then suddenly it struck me. There was nothing physically wrong with me. I'd been restrained, strapped to the bed.

A wriggle of fear went through me and I looked again at the workbench on my left. I was only partly relieved to see there were no surgical implements on there, nothing that might be construed as a torture device. Presumably I was a prisoner here, but who were my captors? The Wolves of London? Hulse and his cronies? I was desperate to know, but at the same time reluctant to find out.

Clenching my fists, I flexed my muscles and pulled. The restraints held firm. Whoever my captor or captors were, he, she or they would be able to do whatever they liked to me. What did they want? The heart? Information? I guessed the latter, because otherwise why was I still alive? Which I supposed must mean that when I had arrived here, I hadn't had the heart with me.

Before I could think about it further, I heard footsteps in the corridor outside. They weren't the first footsteps I'd heard since waking up, but they were the first ones that were close, and getting closer. They were measured, casual, and – to my ears – ominous. I tensed, tugged again at the restraints, but they were immovable. I twisted my head to look at the door, a pulse jumping wildly in my throat. The knob turned and the door opened.

A man in a sombre tweed suit, albeit with black velvet lapels, stepped into the room. He was tall and bald with a pale, narrow face, his eyes encircled by small round spectacles. His lips were thin, but so red you might have thought he'd been eating strawberries. He was spindly, and he smelled strongly of the chloroform odour that I had detected when I'd woken up. Although he was just a man, and nothing like the monstrous creature I had encountered previously, I recognised him at once.

It was the Surgeon.

'Ah, the sleeper wakes,' he said, and smiled, displaying large yellow teeth, many of which were threaded darkly with decay. As he approached I began to squirm and thrash, to struggle frantically against my bonds.

'Get away from me!' I yelled. 'Don't fucking touch me!'

The smile slipped and he looked momentarily taken aback, but then his lips curled upwards and he unsheathed his teeth once more.

'Don't take on so, my friend,' he said soothingly. 'No one here means you harm.'

'Keep back!' I warned, and then as he took a step closer I began to shout as loudly as I could. 'Help me! Someone! Help!'

The Surgeon raised his right hand. In it was an old-fashioned hypodermic syringe with brass finger loops either side of the plunger.

'There really is no need to concern yourself,' he purred. 'You are entirely safe, I assure you. I have a suppressant here which will ease your agitation and enable you to relax.'

I continued to struggle, to scream for help, but no one came. The Surgeon placed his left hand on my shoulder and held me down with surprising strength. Then, yellow teeth gritted, he plunged the needle into my arm.

TWENTY-EIGHT

THE MAN FROM THE FUTURE

I was sitting in Benny's conservatory, sunlight streaming through the window. Basking in warmth, I felt relaxed, content. Suddenly aware that someone had entered the room, I looked round and smiled.

'Hello, Daddy,' said Kate. Her eyes, magnified by the lenses of her pink-framed spectacles, were the blue of the sky that was visible through the glass around us. When she smiled back at me her nose crinkled, reminding me of her mother.

'Hello, sweetheart,' I said, and noticed she was holding something in her hand. 'What have you got there?'

Kate raised her arm. Squatting on her palm, like a gnarled black bullfrog, was the obsidian heart. It was pulsating, throbbing.

'Where did you get that?' I asked.

'From here,' she said, using her free hand to pull open the white doctor's coat, which I only now realised she was wearing. She showed me the dark, ragged hole in her chest.

I lurched with shock – and awoke.

For a moment the mustard-yellow walls throbbed like the heart in my dream. I heard an animal-like panting, which it took me a few seconds to realise I was making myself. My eyes flickered about the room, snagging details – the gas lamps, the row of windows, the equipment on the workbench, the stained-glass wall.

As my thoughts settled, I remembered the Surgeon looming over me, the sudden cold pain of the needle penetrating my skin. Then numbness, my anger and fear dissipating, my consciousness crumbling.

My breathing slowed, quietened; the pulsing in my eyes began to recede. I felt relieved that the dream had been nothing more than that, and also surprised to be waking up at all. As the needle had gone in I had wondered whether my life was about to end, whether I would ever again see Kate or discover the secret of the heart.

Logically I should have realised that if the Surgeon had wanted me dead, he could have killed me any time I was unconscious. But why had he injected me, put me under again? I'd already guessed I was here because he wanted information, so why didn't he just torture me and interrogate me, get me to tell him where the heart was?

I wondered whether he would believe me when I told him that I didn't know. And if he *did* believe me, would that mean my usefulness to him would be over? Not for the first time I felt despair wash over me. How the hell was I going to get out of this? Even if I could break free of these restraints, which seemed unlikely, what would I do? Where could I even begin to look for the heart? And how could I get home without it?

I gave an experimental tug on my bonds, then slumped back, defeated. It was no use. Maybe it would have been better if I *had* died. At least then I'd have nothing more to worry about.

My stomach started to churn as I heard footsteps approaching, and I suddenly had a desperate urge to pee. I hadn't felt like this since my first few days and weeks in prison. I wondered now – as I had then – what was going to happen to me, how much pain I would be able to endure. To my shame I felt my bladder loosen, felt urine squirt hotly down my leg.

The door opened and a figure entered.

I had expected the Surgeon, and so gasped with relief when the newcomer turned out to be a nurse wearing a long, black, ankle-length dress beneath a white pinafore. She was somewhere in her twenties and rather stout, her lumpy, freckled face devoid of make-up. The most striking thing about her was her copper-coloured hair, which she wore pinned up beneath a white lace-edged cap. She was carrying a wooden tray on which stood a bowl of water and a neatly folded cloth. She looked so startled when she saw I was awake that she jumped, water slopping over the rim of the bowl and on to the tray.

I forced a smile, trying to put her at ease. 'Hello,' I said.

Clearly flustered, she took a step back. 'If you'll pardon me, sir, I'll inform Dr Tallarian that you're awake.'

'Please,' I said as she turned towards the door, 'wait a minute.'

She paused, her hand on the door knob.

'What's your name?' I asked.

She hesitated, then said, 'It's Charlotte, sir. Charlotte Moynihan.'

'And this Dr Tallarian,' I said. 'Is he a tall, bald man with glasses?'

Still facing away from me she muttered, 'He is, sir.'

'Then please don't tell him I'm awake,' I said. 'I think he means to hurt me.'

Slowly she turned, astonishment on her face. 'Oh no, sir. Dr Tallarian is a proper gentleman, and kind with it. There's many a soul in Wapping who considers him a saint on account of his good works.'

'Is that where we are?' I said. 'Wapping?'

'You don't know, sir?'

I shook my head. 'I'm afraid not. I have no idea how I got here.'

She regarded me a little fearfully, as if she was unsure whether I was telling the truth. After a moment, however, she took a couple of hesitant steps back into the room.

'What *do* you remember, sir?'

'Not much, I'm afraid. What happened to me?'

'You were found not two streets from here, sir, lying unconscious on the pavement outside the premises of Mr Jalcombe, the chandler. It was Mrs Jalcombe and her son, Henry, who discovered you when they opened up their shop yesterday morning. At first they thought you...' she blushed '...well, that you were a vagabond, or sleeping off the excesses of a night's drinking. Then Mrs Jalcombe noticed what queer clothes you were wearing – begging your pardon, sir – and considered you might have been a foreign gentleman who had been led astray and attacked. The Jalcombes found themselves unable to revive you, so they brought you here.'

'And where is here?' I asked.

'The Voluntary Hospital on Sovereign Street, sir. Dr Tallarian has been attending you since you arrived.'

'And that was yesterday morning, you say?'

'Yes, sir.'

'I see. And what did Dr Tallarian think might be wrong with me?'

'He was afraid you might be suffering from brain fever, sir, perhaps due to a blow on the head causing bleeding within the skull.'

'Did he now? And do I *have* a head injury, Charlotte?'

'Well... no, sir. But Dr Tallarian did say that an external injury is not always apparent in such cases.'

'And is Dr Tallarian in the habit of strapping his patients down?' I asked, tugging at my restraints to emphasise my point.

The nurse blushed again. 'You've been terrible feverish, sir, tossing and turning and throwing yourself this way and that. It was feared that you might hurl yourself to the floor and injure yourself.'

I gave her a smile that I hoped would convince her of my sanity. 'Well, as you can see, I'm fine now. So there's no reason why you can't release me, is there?'

Her eyes widened fearfully.

'I'm not going to hurt you,' I told her. 'I'm perfectly harmless.'

'Oh, I don't doubt it, sir,' she said unconvincingly, 'but it's not my place to make such a decision. I had better fetch Dr Tallarian.'

I could see there was no easy way out of this, no possibility of slipping my shackles and making my escape without encountering Tallarian again. However I consoled myself with the hope that Charlotte was telling the truth, that the doctor *was* a good man, and that whatever had happened to him, or *would* happen to him, was not yet part of his psychological make-up. Perhaps his transformation into the creature I would encounter in my own time was even my fault. Perhaps it would be as a result of taking pity on me that Tallarian would bring the wrath of the Wolves of London down upon himself and – maybe as a punishment – would be re-made into one of their monstrous foot soldiers.

The possibility that I might be indirectly responsible for the future downfall of a good and innocent man weighed heavily on my conscience, but I forced a smile.

'All right, Charlotte,' I said. 'I don't want to get you into trouble. But promise me one thing.'

Nervously she said, 'I'll try, sir.'

'Promise me that when I speak to Tallarian you'll be close by, and that if you hear me shout for help, or scream out in pain, you'll come running.'

She looked alarmed and unhappy, but she said, 'I promise, sir.'

'Thank you. Oh, and Charlotte?'

She had begun to turn away, but now she halted and looked back at me.

'You don't have to bother with all that "sir" stuff. My name's Alex.'

She looked bewildered, but gave a quick nod and left the room. Grimacing at the piss that was now cold on my leg, I lay back. I tried to breathe slowly and deeply to ease the cramping discomfort in my stomach, part of which was due to hunger and part caused by tension at the prospect of a further encounter with Tallarian.

After a few minutes I heard measured footsteps approaching along the corridor. I adopted what I hoped was a composed expression – neither welcoming nor hostile – as the man who I had come to know as the Surgeon entered the room.

'Dr Tallarian, I presume?' I said.

The doctor regarded me thoughtfully, his eyes unblinking behind his spectacles. 'You presume correctly. I trust you are feeling better now, Mr Locke? You certainly appear calmer than you did the last time we met.'

'You know my name?'

He confirmed this with a tilt of his head. 'After our last encounter, when you seemed unaccountably afraid of me, I took the liberty of examining your clothing in an effort to discover your identity. I confess that upon doing so I came across certain...' he hesitated, as if at a loss for words, and then with a wave of his hand he said, '...*items* on your person which intrigued me.'

From the hip pocket of his jacket he lifted a square of cloth that had been made into a bag by tying the four corners together. He carried it across to the workbench, put it down, and then carefully – as though afraid something might leap up and bite him – untied it and folded back the four corners. Frowning, he picked up my mobile phone (inactive, of course) between his thumb and forefinger and held it up.

'What is this?' he asked in a voice so thin and uncertain that in that moment I almost felt sorry for him.

I took a deep breath. This was going to be awkward. 'What do you *think* it is?'

He opened his mouth, then closed it again. His eyes seemed to cloud over. Looking at the utter bafflement on his face I realised that he had no frame of reference for the object in his hand. My phone might not be the latest model – only a couple of weeks ago Candice had sniggered at how archaic it was in comparison to hers – but it was still so far advanced from the technology of the age that Tallarian couldn't even *begin* to hazard a guess as to its function.

Not at first anyway. His mouth moved, but no sound came out. Then eventually, hesitantly, he said, 'Is it a... perhaps it's... these numbers? A calculating device of some kind?'

He put the phone back down with a grimace of distaste, as if it had squirmed in his grasp.

'If you undo these straps I'll tell you,' I said.

He looked at me, his eyes narrowing shrewdly. 'I'm not sure that that would be entirely wise.'

Pressing home my advantage, I said, 'Oh, come on, Dr Tallarian, I can see that curiosity is gnawing at you. So why don't we show each other a bit of mutual trust? You release me and I'll tell you about those items of mine. I mean, you can hardly keep me a prisoner for ever, can you?'

Tallarian was silent, though I could almost hear the cogs in his head whirring as he decided on the best course of action. At last he said carefully, 'It isn't that I *wish* to keep you a prisoner—'

'So don't,' I urged.

'...but the fact is, Mr Locke, I'm intrigued by you... so much so that I cannot afford to risk losing you. And, if truth be known, I am also a little afraid of what you might be capable of.'

I laughed as lightly as I could. 'Afraid? You don't have to be afraid of me. I'm not out to harm anyone.'

'That's as may be,' Tallarian said, and turned once more to the square of cloth. His hand hovered above it for a moment, and then, as if plucking up the courage, he lifted the mobile again. 'How do I know that this isn't a weapon of some kind? How do I know that you won't use this device to incapacitate me the instant I release you?'

'Who do you think I am?' I asked. 'Where do you think I'm from?'

His eyes clouded again. 'I'm certain I don't know.'

Was it my imagination or had a certain shiftiness crept into his manner? 'Oh, I'm not so sure about that. I think you at least have a theory.'

Instead of rising to the bait he put the phone down and picked up my wallet. Opening it he took out one of my credit cards. Holding it up, he said, 'What is this image? Why does it appear to have depth when it clearly does not?'

'It's a hologram,' I said.

'Hologram.' He scowled in bewilderment. 'What does that *mean*?'

I smiled. 'Undo these straps and I'll tell you.'

He dropped the credit card back on to the pile and wiped his fingers on his coat, as if afraid it might have contaminated him in some way. 'What are these items even *made* of? The material, the design, the manufacturing techniques, it's...'

'Impossible?' I said.

'Yes, impossible!' High spots of colour had appeared on his pale cheeks.

'Undo these straps,' I repeated.

He glared at me, and then plucked one of the coins from the pile. It was a ten pence piece. He snapped, 'Explain this to me. Who is this woman? Why does the date read 2008? Is this a ruse of some kind?'

Calmly, pleasantly, I said, 'The straps, Dr Tallarian.'

In an abrupt explosion of rage he hurled the coin at the wall above my head and brought his clenched fist down hard on the workbench, causing the items on it to rattle. 'You *will* tell me!' he hissed. 'I will *make* you tell me.'

My guts churned at the sudden threat, but I was determined to remain composed. 'By torturing me, you mean? Would you *really* do that, Dr Tallarian? Because I don't believe that's the kind of man you are.'

Tallarian leaned in close. His breath smelled bad, like rotting cabbage; I wondered briefly whether toothpaste had been invented yet. 'You have no idea what kind of man I am,' he murmured.

'That's true,' I said reasonably. 'But even so, I won't tell you a thing unless you release me.' I forced a smile and bluffed, 'Nothing you can do will make me tell you.'

His face was so red now that even the whites of his eyes had been stained pink with anger. He leaned in closer yet, and I wondered for a moment if he was going to bite me.

'We'll see about that, won't we?' he muttered.

TWENTY-NINE

THE MENAGERIE

After making his threat, Tallarian had gathered up my belongings, stuffed them into his pocket and marched out of the room, since when I had been attended to at various times by one or other of three nurses. As well as Charlotte, there was a thin, painfully shy girl called Agnes, from whom I discovered that the year was 1895, and a bustling, plump, red-faced woman with curly hair called Ruby. They had cleaned me up, fed me a thin, salty stew of vegetables and chewy bits of what I think was mutton, and had given me – surprisingly – a nutty, dark brown beer to drink. Charlotte had offered me milk too, but I had declined; it looked greasy, had yellow globules of fat floating in it, and smelled weird. At one point, the mutton stew having made me thirsty, I had asked Agnes for some water, but what she returned with was a glass of liquid the colour of weak tea swimming with black flecks.

'What's this?' I asked her.

Her voice was little more than a nervous whisper. 'It's the water you asked for, sir.'

'But it's filthy,' I said.

Her eyes widened in surprise. 'It is pure rain water, sir. We collect it in barrels on the roof. It has been strained twice over.'

Oddly, despite what I had already been through, it was this exchange which caused the full, stark reality of my situation to hit home for the first time. I suddenly realised that I had been hurled back into a society in which so many of the things I took for granted – clean water, pasteurised milk, refrigeration, antibiotics, telecommunications – simply did not exist. It wasn't that I hadn't been aware of this before, of course, but until this moment I had thought about it only in abstract terms – as though I was outside it all, as though it didn't really affect me because I didn't belong. It had taken the sight of a bewildered young girl holding what looked like a glass of dirty ditchwater for the terrible implications of my predicament to suddenly overwhelm me in a choking wave.

'I don't want it,' I said in a cracked, suddenly breathless voice. 'Please take it away.'

Unhappily, clearly wondering what she had done wrong, she scurried from the room.

When she had gone I clenched my eyes tight shut and tried to fight down what I can only describe as a kind of temporal equivalent of culture shock – time shock maybe? I wondered how I could ever hope to survive here – assuming, that was, that I managed to escape from Tallarian's clutches. I had nowhere to live, no job, no money, no identity. The food and water – if I could get any – was crawling with bacteria, to which I would most likely have no resistance. If I became ill or had an accident my prospects would become almost too horrendous to contemplate. I had fallen into a world with inadequate medical resources; a world that was only just stepping on to the springboard of technological advancement, but which, as yet, was still basically primitive, even savage.

Lying there I felt more alone than I had ever felt in my life. I felt like I'd crashed in the middle of a jungle, with no weapons, no means of communication, and predators closing in on all sides. My chest tightened and I started to hyperventilate, but with my eyes still closed I told myself to calm down, pull myself together. Whether that worked, I'm not sure; all I know is that I rode the waves for a while, until eventually, thankfully, I found myself drifting into calmer waters.

So okay, I thought, I had nothing in terms of material wealth or security here, but what I did have was intelligence, knowledge and foresight – all of which, surely, would enable me to get by? As for Tallarian, maybe I could drip-feed him tantalising bits of information, keep him dangling long enough to persuade him that I was too valuable to mistreat, perhaps even convince him I was his friend? Course, it would help if I knew what his motivation was for keeping me here. Was it simple curiosity or something more sinister?

I tried to get the nurses on my side, but it quickly became clear that they were all too fearful of Tallarian's austere manner and too respectful of his social standing to go against his wishes. He had told them I had been restrained for my own good, and although none of them said so, from the way they acted around me – cautiously, nervously – I suspect he might also have told them that, despite my friendly manner, I was unpredictable, even dangerous. Even Ruby, the oldest, shrewdest and least deferential of the nurses, couldn't be persuaded that I was being held prisoner for anything other than the right reasons. Neither could she be persuaded to undo the straps around my wrists and ankles, not even when I told her that my limbs were cramping up from inactivity – which they were a bit – and that I needed to stretch and bend them.

'You must think me born yesterday, sir,' she said cheerfully, tipping me a wink.

'I didn't mean all at the same time,' I said. 'You could release one arm, let me bend it a bit, just to get the blood flowing, and then strap it back down before you release the other arm.'

My half-baked idea was that with one arm free I could undo the rest of the straps and make my escape before Ruby could alert Tallarian, but she shook her head almost pityingly.

'I *could* do that, sir, but not without Dr Tallarian in attendance.'

I sighed. 'What has Tallarian told you about me, Ruby?'

'Why, nothing sir.'

'Has he told you I'm violent? That I'm a criminal of some kind? If so, he's lying. I mean, if those things *were* true, why hasn't he called the police?'

She looked at me with narrowed eyes, and for a moment I thought I was getting through, but then she wagged a chubby finger at me. 'You're a wily one, sir, and no mistake. A charmer, to be sure, but wily all the same.'

I sighed. 'You do realise that Dr Tallarian intends to torture me, don't you?'

This time she burst out laughing. 'Torture, sir? Well now, that *is* a story!'

'It's true,' I said. 'He isn't the kindly philanthropist you think he is. He threatened me earlier. He says he'll do anything to make me tell him who I am and where I'm from.'

She shook her head, still amused. 'If that's the case, sir, then why not tell him what he wants and have done with it? Why keep it a secret at all?'

'I can't tell him,' I said. 'The information might be... dangerous.'

'Dangerous!' she scoffed. 'Oh, I've never heard the like!'

Realising that this was getting me nowhere, I decided to change tack. 'How big is this hospital, Ruby?'

She regarded me suspiciously, and then, obviously deciding that I was doing no more than making idle conversation, she said, 'It's not as big as some, sir. This building was used to store tea before it become what it is now. There's room for forty beds here, though it's never enough.'

'So you're always full?'

'More than that, sir. We have the sick queuing outside the door most days. Soon as one patient takes his leave, be that feet foremost or under their own steam, there's another to take his place. One minute the bed's empty, the next it's occupied again, oft-times before the sheets have barely had chance to get cold.'

I thought of the sheets I was currently lying on and tried not to shudder. 'And how many staff work here, Ruby? Just Dr Tallarian and the three of you?'

She nodded. 'It's not enough, sir, truth be told, but there ain't the funds for more.' With a fierce frown, she added, 'Works his fingers to the bone, Dr Tallarian does. Hardly ever sleeps. We girls all thinks the world of him – and so do his patients.'

'Why does he do it?' I asked.

Her frown became a scowl. 'How do you mean, sir?'

'Well, he looks wealthy enough. Surely, if he wanted to, he could set himself up in private practice, earn better money in a more salubrious area? So why stay here? Flogging himself for a pittance?'

'He does it out of the goodness of his heart,' she said in a voice that dared me to contradict her. 'He's a veritable saint, Dr Tallarian is, and nothing you say about him will change my opinion one bit.'

After she had gone, huffing and scowling, I thought about what she had said. If Tallarian *was* going to carry out his threat to make me talk, presumably he would do it away from the eyes and ears of the staff and the other patients. Later that day I asked Agnes how many hours she and the other girls worked, and she told me that they each did a twelve-hour daily shift, albeit staggered. Currently Charlotte worked from 4 a.m. to 4 p.m., Ruby worked from 8 a.m. to 8 p.m., and she herself worked from noon until midnight. Which meant that for four hours out of every twenty-four – between midnight and 4 a.m. – Tallarian was here alone, apart from his assistant, a man called Thomas Huckerby, who, from what I could gather, acted as porter, general handyman and, if required, surgical assistant.

My guess, therefore, was that Tallarian would come for me sometime after midnight. And if he *did* decide to interrogate me somewhere out of earshot of the other patients, then I guessed there was always the possibility that he might first unstrap me from the table, in which case I ought to be ready to take my chance and flee. Of course, the likelihood is that he would drug me first, or even that he and Huckerby would hold weapons on me to keep me compliant. But even so, I resolved that if I saw even the smallest opportunity to escape, I would take it.

With this in mind, I dozed on and off throughout the day in order to be as energetic as possible when midnight rolled around. Which was why I couldn't believe it when, sometime after 10 p.m. (or 'ten bells' as Agnes had called it), with the windows showing nothing but blackness and the gas lamps providing the only illumination, I felt my eyelids growing heavy.

Angrily I blinked myself awake. What was I doing? I couldn't afford to fall asleep now, not with midnight creeping closer. I was surprised that adrenaline wasn't keeping me alert – and then it occurred to me that my tiredness might not be entirely natural. I had been so hungry when Agnes had turned up earlier with a bowl of beef broth that I had accepted it gratefully, thinking it would give me strength for whatever lay ahead. But now I realised that the food must have been drugged. But with what? What did doctors use in Victorian times to induce sleep? Laudanum? Alcohol? Not that it mattered, because knowing what it was wouldn't change the fact that I couldn't do a damn thing about the effect it was having on me. I felt woozy, detached from my body. I tried to fight it, but it was no use. Nothing could stop me from going under.

How long I slept for I don't know. When I woke, my head woolly and my stomach rolling with a faint nausea, I knew immediately and instinctively that I was no longer in the room with the stained-glass wall. *How* I knew I wasn't sure – I was still so out of it that I couldn't work out what my senses were telling me. When I tried to open my eyes I realised I couldn't even do that. Whatever had been slipped into my food had numbed me to such an extent that my body was completely unresponsive to the commands my brain was trying to give it. Wondering whether I had been paralysed, I imagined myself lifting my hand and rubbing gently at my eyelids, trying to prise them apart. And then I realised that I wasn't imagining the action at all, I was doing it! My fingers *were* rubbing at my eyes!

The knowledge was like an injection of adrenaline into my recumbent system. My body jerked, my head rising from the surface on which it was resting, and my eyes tore open. For a moment I was dazzled, but the glare quickly receded into a dullish orange glow. Something bird-like hovered in front of my face; I blinked at it, trying to make out what it was. Then it came into focus, and I barked out a laugh – it was my own hand! But what was my hand doing rubbing at my eyes and hovering in front of my face? Why wasn't it strapped down?

Looking quickly around, I saw that I was in a small room, dank and dark. Around me were stone walls with no windows, above me a low ceiling. The only light came from a candle in a tall brass holder that had been placed on the floor at the foot of the bed. Not that it *was* much of a bed. It was more a raised wooden board covered by a thin mattress. There was white fungus growing on the walls, water stains, still glistening with damp, on the ceiling. It was freezing cold and my shivering body was covered in nothing but the coarsely woven hospital gown I'd been wearing since I got here. My bare feet, sticking out of the end of the gown, were bone-white, though my toenails were purple with cold.

It wasn't the cold or the damp that had alerted me to the fact I was no longer in the room with the stained-glass wall, though; it was the sounds coming from beyond the arched opening to my left. They weren't the busy, purposeful sounds I had been used to – the clop of footsteps on wooden floors, the rattle of metal trolleys, people calling out to one another – but more the restless movements you might expect to hear in a hospital dormitory late at night: rustles and shuffles, snorts and groans. They were the sounds made by living things in close proximity to one another, mammals shifting uncomfortably and uneasily in sleep.

What was going on? Had I been moved closer to the other patients rather than away from them? But why was it so cold here, and why were my surroundings so grim? And, more to the point, why had I been freed from my restraints?

Still groggy, I tried to sit up, and felt a tugging on my right wrist. Looking down, I realised that there *were* restraints, after all, that my right arm was still secured to the bed (or was it a table?) by a leather strap. A quick check confirmed that there were restraints around both of my ankles too, that only my left hand was free. Strange. How could Tallarian have been responsible for such an oversight? Unless the restraint securing my left wrist had been deliberately unbuckled. But who would do that, and why?

With numb fingers I undid the buckles on the straps securing my right wrist and sat up, groaning at the creaking pain in my spine. I lifted and bent and stretched my right arm a couple of times, and then rotated my shoulders, wincing at the sharp crunching sounds they made. Gritting my teeth against the bolts of pain shooting through my upper body, I leaned forward and unbuckled the straps around my ankles. Despite my eagerness to find out where I was and to get away from here, I stretched my legs slowly and carefully, mindful of the knotting cramps that might seize my muscles at any moment, kneading the backs of my calves and thighs in an attempt to get some warmth into them.

At last, tentatively, I swung my legs from the bed and planted my feet on the floor. Although they were already numb, the wet stone was so cold that it cut through the numbness and made my bones ache. Clenching my teeth to stop them from chattering, I slid my backside from the edge of the bed and stood up. It had never occurred to me before quite how small feet were, how much we relied on them for strength and balance. I swayed a moment, my head swimming, and then moved cautiously away from the bed. I felt like Frankenstein's monster as I took one step towards the arch, and then another. Although I was gaining in strength and confidence with each step, it didn't escape my notice that my previous plan – to fight off my captors and run like hell – had been so ambitious that it now seemed risible.

It was only when I reached the arch that I realised it wasn't simply a doorway, but a short passage, which cut through a stone wall that must have been at least two metres thick. At the far end was a glow of brownish light, illuminating an expanse of floor, beyond which was what looked like a wooden surface heaped with clutter.

I plunged through the passage, my head still swimming, my breath rattling and phlegmy at the back of my throat. My limbs felt stiff and awkward through lack of use. After half a dozen shuffling steps, I was standing at the threshold of the next room, my left hand clutching the stone wall to stop me from swaying. I looked around, taking in the details, my mouth open in astonishment and horror.

The room was at least four times bigger than the one I had come from. It was a laboratory of sorts, or maybe more accurately it seemed to be part laboratory, part workshop and part operating theatre. The stone floor was dominated by a large central table, the wooden surface of which, although scrubbed clean, was covered in ominous dark stains. In an alcove in the corner furthest away from me, to the left of a closed wooden door, was a glass-fronted cabinet whose shelves were stacked not only with phials, bottles and items of medical equipment, but also a line of specimen jars, each of which was filled to the brim with a cloudy, yellowish preserving solution. In some of the jars floated small creatures (monkeys, cats, snakes), whereas others contained bleached bodily organs. From half a dozen jars at the end of the row peered a number of deformed human foetuses in various stages of development.

Stretching along the next wall, at a right angle to the cabinet, was what I had seen through the arch – a long workbench, on which stood the room's only illumination, a glowing oil lamp. The workbench was heaped with scientific equipment and what looked like the metallic paraphernalia from a number of dismantled engines. Many of these bits and pieces had been screwed and bolted together to create new and bizarre forms, the purposes of which I could only imagine.

My eyes barely skimmed across these details, however, intriguing and grotesque though they were. It was the wall to my left which snagged and held my attention. It was stacked from floor to ceiling with dozens of cramped wooden cages, and in each cage was a living creature. I could see rats, cats, dogs and, on the bottom row, most horrifying of all, children.

Because the room was dimly lit, my mind was reluctant to accept what I was seeing at first. The children, filthy and dressed in rags, had been forced into spaces so small they could do little more than lie with their knees drawn up to their chests. As I slumped against the wall, unable at first to do little more than stare, one of them raised its head and looked at me. When I saw what had been done to it, my gorge rose and I clapped a hand to my mouth.

The child, a scrawny boy of maybe six or seven, had had his teeth and lower jaw removed and replaced with a hinged, grotesquely oversized shovel-like contraption, inset with a double row of triangular metal 'teeth'. Though the light was dim, I could see that where the boy's flesh had been forcibly fused with the metal it was horribly infected. His face above the artificial 'jaw' was black and swollen, and around the heads of the screws that had been affixed to the bone just beneath his ears, the skin was split and suppurating with pus.

The boy was not the only prisoner to have been mutilated so horribly. As my gaze skittered from cage to cage, I couldn't see a single child or animal who hadn't been subjected to some kind of monstrous modification. A tiny girl of no more than six or seven had had her right arm removed and a metal limb, comprising a number of linked pistons operated by an intricate system of levers and pulleys, inserted in its place; an older boy had had the upper left quadrant of his skull – including his eye – replaced by a transparent dome, in which a seemingly haphazard assortment of tiny interlocked cogs whirred and spun within a tangled nest of multi-coloured wires. In the upper cages I could see a rat whose legs had been replaced with wheels; a cat with an exposed metallic spine and a raised scorpion-like tail; a dog whose working internal organs, including its heart, pulsed and twitched in an external glass container that was attached to its butchered body via a mass of rubber tubes.

As I peered into one cage after another I shook uncontrollably, not only with cold now, but with fear, pity, revulsion and disbelief. These were clearly Tallarian's early experiments; prototypes for his army of flesh and clockwork monstrosities that I had encountered in my own time. Horrific and pitiful though the creatures were, at least their presence here provided evidence that Tallarian had not become corrupted purely because of my proximity to him. On the contrary, I had stumbled into a world of madness, even of evil, so palpable that it seemed to poison the air. My instinct was to run, for fear that I'd become somehow contaminated by that poison, but I resisted the urge, and instead pushed myself away from the stone doorway and approached the stack of cages. As I got closer to them the boy with the metal jaw hissed like an angry cat. I opened my mouth to speak to him, and with an effort forced a few croaking words out of my dry throat.

'I'm not going to hurt you. I'm here to help.'

But how *could* I help? By opening the cages and letting the poor souls free? By putting them out of their misery? The boy stared at me as I spoke to him, though I saw nothing approaching comprehension in his eyes. He hissed again, his hideously oversized jaw creaking open and shut.

Some of the occupants of the other cages were stirring now too, turning bodies or heads to regard me. I heard scraping and clanking and (horribly) squelching. A cat began to yowl; a dog in an upper cage started to growl and then to make high-pitched yelping and whimpering noises. Afraid that the din would alert Tallarian, I raised my hands and made what I hoped were reassuring shushing sounds, but that only made things worse. The clamour increased, the yowls and barks accompanied by clicks and whirrs and creaks. It was like some hellish orchestra, a symphony of working machine parts and the tortured screams of living creatures.

Abandoning my attempt to placate the menagerie, I crossed to the workbench on the opposite wall and snatched up the oil lamp. I raised it to head height and swung round, looking for a weapon I might use to defend myself against Tallarian and his henchman, should I encounter them. The light fell across a wooden chair in the shadows to the right of the door, on the seat of which I was delighted to see my leather jacket. I hurried across and picked it up, and saw that my sweater, jeans, underwear, socks and boots were tangled together in a crumpled heap underneath. The clothes were a bit grubby, and a V of material had been snipped from the pocket of my jeans, presumably so that Tallarian could examine the denim in more detail, but they were generally okay. With no sense of self-consciousness whatsoever, I peeled off the smock-like gown I was wearing and dressed quickly in my own clothes. The jeans pockets were empty, and there was no sign of the items that Tallarian had taken from them, but I could live with that. It would be a pain to be without them if I ever got back to my own time, but as things stood, just *getting* back to my own time would be cause for celebration.

Psychological it may have been, but being dressed in my own clothes had an energising effect on me. It was as if I'd put on my battle armour; all at once I felt not only physically stronger, but more determined and confident than I'd been since arriving here. Skirting the stained table in the middle of the room, I crossed to Tallarian's workbench and rooted among the paraphernalia. I came across a half-metre length of copper pipe, which I hefted in my hand, swishing it through the air. It wasn't the greatest weapon in the world, but it was better than nothing. With the pipe in one hand and the lamp in the other I crossed to the door.

Tucking the pipe into my belt, I glanced back once more at the stack of cages on the opposite wall. The glow of lamplight reflected eerily from dozens of pairs of eyes, all of which seemed fixed on me. There was still some caterwauling from the occupants of the cages, but most had quietened down again now. Logic dictated that those watching eyes contained nothing but a primitive wariness of the intruder in their midst, but I liked to think there was expectation, even hope, in some of them too.

'I'll fetch help,' I whispered, and then, bracing myself, I opened the door. As it swung inwards, my hand moved quickly from the brass knob to the copper pipe, ready to pluck it from my belt and bring it down on the head of whoever might be lurking on the other side.

But there was no one. The door opened on to a flight of uneven stone steps leading upwards. Stepping forward, I noticed there was a key dangling from the keyhole on the outside of the door and guessed that this room was probably kept locked when Ruby and the other nurses were about. I assumed that Tallarian was more lax with his security when he was here alone, but as I began to ascend the steps another possibility struck me. Maybe Tallarian wasn't lax at all; maybe whoever had unbuckled the strap around my wrist had also unlocked the door for me. But who might that be? Huckerby? Could Tallarian's right-hand man be less tolerant of his employer's activities than the doctor realised?

No, that didn't ring true. If Huckerby was concerned about Tallarian's experiments, why had he left it until now before doing anything? Why, for that matter, was he relying on me to escape and alert the authorities instead of telling them himself? Wouldn't it be a long shot on his part to assume that a) I would wake up in time, b) that I would manage to get away once I *had* woken up, and c) that even if I *did* get away I would have enough of a conscience to go to the police?

I pushed my thoughts aside, deciding that the only important thing right now was not to look this gift horse in the mouth. The steps I was ascending were steep, and so narrow that I could have touched the walls on either side if I had wanted to. I was about halfway up them when I heard a noise – or *thought* I heard a noise. There was still enough of a racket coming from the cages below that I couldn't be entirely sure. I hovered in an agony of indecision, wondering whether I should carry on or wait until I was sure the coast was clear. Then my decision was made for me. The door at the top of the stairs started to open.

For an instant I was a rabbit in the headlights. Then I moved. Adrenaline flooding my system, I turned and raced back down the stairs. I didn't look over my shoulder, so had no way of knowing whether I, or the light from the lamp, had been spotted. Slipping through the door back into the laboratory, I hesitated for barely a second, knowing I had only moments to decide what to do. I realised that whoever walked in here would know immediately that I had escaped. Not only were my clothes no longer on the wooden chair beside the door, but my hospital gown was crumpled on the floor and the oil lamp which had been sitting on the workbench across the room was now dangling from my left hand. There was no way I'd be able to sort out all of these things *and* find somewhere to hide before whoever was descending the stairs entered the room. Which left me with only one option.

I scooted across and put the lamp on the operating table, then ran back and pressed myself against the wall beside the hinge side of the door. I was only just in time. Even as I was sliding the copper pipe from my belt the door began to open. I was half-tempted to throw myself against it, to slam it into whoever was entering the room, but I forced myself to wait. The best-case scenario would be to avoid violence altogether. If the newcomer didn't twig I was hiding behind the door, they might move far enough inside for me to slip out behind them and lock them in.

Nothing in life is ever that simple, though. What happened was that the door came three-quarters of the way open and then stopped. There was a pause, during which I pictured Tallarian standing with his hand gripping the door knob, his gaze sweeping across the room and taking in the discarded gown, the misplaced lantern.

Sure enough, it was Tallarian's voice which snapped, 'He's escaped.'

My heart sank as I heard another growling voice beyond Tallarian's. ''Ow's 'e done that then?'

Tallarian's response was cutting. 'Well, I don't know, do I? But the main door is locked, so he must still be in the hospital. Quickly, we must search the premises!'

The door began to close. For a second I considered allowing Tallarian and his companion to precede me up the stairs, and then it occurred to me that the doctor might lock the door and pocket the key, trapping me here. Acting on impulse, I leaped forward, grabbed the edge of the door and wrenched it open. Caught by surprise, Tallarian, who was still holding on to the handle, stumbled forward. As I stepped in front of him, his eyes widened in shock and rage.

Raising the copper pipe I whacked him as hard as I could on the side of the head. There was a sickening crack and he staggered sideways, blood instantly gouting from a wound above his left eye. As his legs crumpled, I thought about hitting him a few more times – but then with a roar the other man came at me.

He was huge! Grey-haired and grey-bearded, he was well over six feet tall. His shoulders were so wide you could easily have stood a couple of pint glasses on them. As he rushed at me, raising hairy, shovel-like hands, I backpedalled frantically. After three or four stumbling steps the base of my spine connected with something hard – the edge of Tallarian's operating table. I barely had chance to register the pain before the man-mountain was upon me. As he lunged for my throat I swung the copper pipe towards his head. He threw up his left arm, swatting the weapon aside as if it was a troublesome fly. Wrenched from my hand, the pipe spun through the air and hit the wall beside the arch with a metallic clatter. Desperately, fending my attacker off as best I could, I groped to my left, grabbed the oil lamp off the table and swung it with all my strength.

Glass smashed against the man's shoulder, dousing his hair, face and clothes in hot, burning oil. As he screamed, I jumped back to avoid getting splashed myself. Exposed to the air, the fire took hold instantly and within seconds the giant's hair and clothes were ablaze. His screams rose in pitch until they sounded barely human as he careened about, slapping desperately at his head and body, trying to douse the flames which even now were roaring and spreading, transforming him into a human fireball.

The heat coming off him was tremendous; I felt sweat rolling greasily down my face and chest. I jumped aside as he staggered towards me, and he crashed into the operating table and fell across it, still beating weakly at his clothes with hands that were already blackened and charred. As the fire continued to devour him the room started to fill with thick black smoke that stung my eyes and made me cough. The occupants of the cages were going frantic, screeching and flinging themselves against their bars in an effort to escape. I knew it was madness to try to save them, knew that most fire victims died of smoke inhalation and that I ought to get out of the room as fast as I could, but I couldn't just leave them to burn – I had made a promise. Bending double and pulling the collar of my sweater up over my face, I stumbled towards the cages.

Through the haze I saw that although they were made mostly of wood, they were secured by iron padlocks. Spotting the copper pipe lying on the floor, I snatched it up and used it as a jemmy, applying it to the hasp of the lock on the cage containing the boy with the metal jaw and trying to prise it free. It took several straining seconds before the padlock tore away from the wood, by which time my head was spinning and I was coughing so hard I could taste blood at the back of my throat. As the door swung open, the boy scrambled out, took one look at me as if weighing up whether I was his enemy, and then scuttled like a hunch-backed monkey across to the open door and up the stone steps. As I watched him go, I was aware of the blackened shape of the man lying across the operating table, still burning (as was the table itself), while, beyond him, Tallarian, blood pouring down his face, was floundering about on the floor in a semi-daze as if he couldn't work out what was happening.

I turned back to the cages, knowing that I could afford to have a go at releasing only one more captive before getting out of there. With no time to decide I simply moved to the next cage in line, that containing the girl with the metal arm, and rammed the ragged end of the copper pipe into the gap between the hasp and the wood.

Sweat poured into my eyes and my lungs laboured for oxygen. The airlessness caused my head to pound with the threat of unconsciousness, reducing the roar of the fire to a muffled throb. With my strength ebbing, I wrenched frantically on the end of the copper pipe, and after a moment of resistance felt rather than heard the gristly tearing of wood. The door to the cage swung open, but through the smoke-shrouded air I saw that the girl was unconscious, her tiny body heaving as it fought for breath. With what felt like the last of my strength I reached in, dragged her out and heaved her on to my shoulder.

Despite her grotesque metal appendage she seemed to weigh almost nothing. I turned, my chest convulsing with pain as coughs like barbed wire tore out of me, my lungs feeling as though they were on the verge of exploding. Through black smoke and raging heat I staggered towards the door. Just as I reached it a white hand lunged from the greyness and grabbed my foot.

It was Tallarian. I looked down to see him gaping up at me, his mouth wide in what appeared to be a silent scream of rage, but was probably nothing more than a desperate need for oxygen. The left side of his face was a mask of blood and his jacket was red with it. I snatched my foot back and his hand flopped to the floor like a dead fish. Leaving him to his own devices, I staggered out of the room.

Ascending the stone steps was like climbing a mountain. With the girl still unconscious over my shoulder, I literally crawled up them inch by inch, my fingers clutching for each jutting ridge, my body a dead weight that felt constantly on the verge of being torn apart by coughing. The heat and smoke felt *heavy* inside me, like wet sand which clogged my lungs and brain and weighed down my limbs.

At some point I passed out. I wasn't even aware it had happened until I felt strong hands beneath my armpits, attempting to haul me to my feet. I tried to protest, but all that emerged was a fit of coughing so violent I thought I was being turned inside out. I heard a voice, soothing and cultured. 'Try to relax, sir. We'll have you out of this dreadful place and back home before you know it.'

Home? I thought. *What do you mean, 'home'?*

But the airless, choking blackness swamped my thoughts once again and I knew no more.

THIRTY
HOME

My ribs and lungs felt as though they had been kicked and stamped on until they were pulped flesh and bruised bone. I woke up coughing, the ratcheting pain that ripped through me causing me to press a hand to my chest, for fear I might shake apart. Eyes watering, I struggled into a sitting position, trying to stifle the desire to keep coughing until all the smoke was out of me. I could still taste it at the back of my throat with each rasping breath; it was as if I'd been barbecued from the inside.

It was only when the initial bout of coughing subsided that I realised where I was. Through my swimming vision I recognised the room in the Kensington house where I'd recuperated after my encounter with Hulse and his men. To my right was the row of bay windows with its view of parkland and the pagoda-like structure on the hill. But the room had been redecorated since the last time I'd been here – the wallpaper was maroon and richly textured, the curtains and carpet thicker and darker. Plus it was more cluttered, knick-knacks and items of furniture taking up most of the floor space, and framed pictures cramming the walls.

Then I realised. Of course the house hadn't been redecorated; I was evidently still in the past and this is how it must have been before I had known it.

Although I was grateful to be free of Tallarian's clutches, my spirits were low, thoughts of Kate filling my head. The two of us were further apart than ever, and without the heart I could see no way of getting

335

back to her. But how could I even *begin* to search for it here? I was stranded, with no identity, no influence, nothing. I may have been in the middle of a city, but I felt as if I'd been cast adrift on a desert island.

Having said that, I clearly had allies here. The fact that I was recuperating in a familiar bed was evidence of that. Perhaps, then, I wasn't *completely* isolated. Perhaps there was *some* hope to cling to.

Moving slowly, I inched upright in the bed, fighting the urge to cough, and wondered if I could summon enough strength to call out. But then there was a creak on the landing and a tap on the door.

'Come in,' I wheezed, the effort bringing on a fresh bout of coughing so violent that it doubled me over.

When it subsided, and I was able to raise my head, I saw a tall, lean, immaculately dressed man standing at the foot of the bed. He was around sixty, the silver hair at his temples matching the silver waistcoat he wore beneath a dark, long-tailed jacket. His swan-like neck, rising from a wing-collared shirt, supported a head that was tilted in a way that, combined with his hooked nose, gave him the air of a Roman emperor. The austerity of his expression, however, was offset by the concern in his sky-blue eyes.

As I opened my mouth he raised a hand.

'If you'll pardon me, sir, I would advise you to rest your throat and conserve your breath. I shall endeavour to provide you with sufficient information to answer many of the questions you are doubtless clamouring to ask.'

I recognised his voice immediately. This was the man who had rescued me from the fire in Tallarian's laboratory. What was it he had said? Something about bringing me home? I watched in bemused silence as he crossed to the bedside table, lifted a beaded lace doily from the top of a jug and poured me a glass of water. As he handed it to me, I noted with relief that the water was clear and seemed free of impurities. I sipped, grateful for the soothing coolness of it against my throat.

'May I?' he asked, indicating a wooden chair beside the bed. I nodded and he sat down, though he remained straight-backed, his hands resting on his knees, as if relaxing didn't suit him. Without preamble he said, 'My name is Hawkins. I have been butler in this house for a little over two years. That is when I first met you, sir. You employed me shortly after you purchased the property from the estate of its previous owner.'

Reaching into the pocket of his jacket, he withdrew a small, ivory-coloured envelope, which he handed to me.

'If you'll permit me, sir, before I resume any further explanations I have been advised to give you this.'

Puzzled, I took the envelope from him. On the front 'Alex' had been written in block capitals. Opening the envelope, I took out the folded sheet of notepaper inside. The letter, covering both sides of the paper, was handwritten in black ink. With a jolt I recognised the handwriting as my own. I began to read:

Hi Alex,

First of all, I know how weird this is. But it's even weirder for me in a way, because I'm trying to remember exactly what this letter said when I read it in my past (your present).

I know exactly how disorientated you're feeling right now, because I've been there, but things are not quite as black as they seem. The house is yours, so you don't have to worry about finding somewhere to live, which I'm hoping means you'll be able to work out a few things.

But basically all I wanted to say was just listen to what Hawkins tells you and don't interrupt – not till the end, anyway. I know your chest and lungs are hurting and you're finding it hard to breathe, but you'll recover, trust me. Just take your time, be patient and <u>think</u>. I can't tell you too much, I'm afraid, not because I don't want to, but just because this is what I remember the letter saying when I read it and I don't want to risk messing things up by telling you more than I knew back then. I don't know if it <u>will</u> mess things up, but I daren't risk it. I don't have anything like all the answers, in case you're wondering (which I know you are), I don't even know whether time is set in stone and that by reading this letter it means that you're guaranteed to get to where I am now. Maybe things change all the time, maybe time is mutable, maybe the past me (i.e. you) will never even write this letter. Frankly, all this time-travel stuff does my head in. It's best not to think about it too much if you can help it.

In short, I'm winging it just as much as you are. But, as I say, do yourself a favour and listen to Hawkins. I know <u>exactly</u> how you're feeling just now – scared and confused and stranded – but although he's a bit uptight (don't tell him I said that – I <u>know</u> you won't) he's a man you can absolutely rely on. You'll learn a lot from him and he'll help you get by.

Okay, that's it. I'm dying to say more, but writing this is like taking dictation from my own memory, so I'd better not.

Good luck and take care, and I hope you get at least to where I am now. If not, God knows what will happen to me. Maybe I'll just blink out of existence or something.

All the best,
Alex (from the future)

I read the letter twice, and then again. By the time I put it aside I was as dizzy and sick as if I'd stepped off a roller coaster. I looked at Hawkins, and it comforted me to see the expression of polite sympathy on his thin, beak-nosed face.

'You don't have to say anything, sir,' he said. 'Although I haven't read the letter, I have been apprised as to its general content, and you yourself have explained the current situation to me and have described in detail precisely how perplexed you were when you first read it. Let me assure you, therefore, that it is my duty, and indeed my intention, to provide you with whatever aid you may – and will – require during this period of convalescence and readjustment. Although I'm aware that you don't know me at this stage, rest assured that I know *you*, and that I have your very best interests at heart.'

He paused, steepling his fingers.

'The date is the third of September 1895. As I'm sure you are aware, our current monarch is Queen Victoria and our prime minister, following his victory in the recent general election, is Lord Salisbury. However, in order for you to gain a more detailed knowledge of current affairs I have taken the liberty of arranging for *The Times* of London to be delivered to the house each morning, for your perusal.

'The address here is number 23 Ranskill Gardens, all the necessary documentation for which – together with your personal documentation – is held at the offices of your solicitor, the firm of Holman, Timperley and Bryce on Whitefriars Street in the Temple district. You are a gentleman of independent means, and have a bank account, containing a substantial sum of money, at Fulton and Co. on Lombard Street. Your current household staff numbers five – as well as myself, there is Mrs Peake the house-keeper and three maid-servants, Polly, Florence and Hattie. Mrs Peake and myself are fully aware of your circumstances, though as far as the girls are concerned you have just returned from a voyage to the West Indies with a malady which has resulted in a certain amount of temporary senility and memory loss.'

I felt I was taking in only a fraction of what Hawkins was telling me, but he paused for no more than a second or two before giving a regal-like waft of his hand. 'In the wardrobe to your left,' he said, 'you will find a selection of attire more suited to the current age than your own more, ah... avant-garde accoutrements. Undergarments and such-like can be found in the drawers of the dresser to the right of the window.

'It is currently a quarter to eleven and luncheon is served at noon. If you wish it, sir, I will gladly provide you with assistance in dressing should you prefer to take your midday meal in the dining room. That is not to say that your convalescence should be a rushed affair. On the contrary, aware though I am of how eager you are to begin your quest to re-acquire the obsidian heart, I must inform you that your, ah... future self did advise me to ensure that you don't bring more harm upon yourself by leaping back into the fray too swiftly. Indeed his – or rather, your – exact words to me were' – he paused, reddening slightly – '"Don't take any shit from me, Hawkins."'

Despite myself, I laughed – which instantly resulted in a renewed bout of coughing. Hawkins poured me a fresh glass of water, looking somewhat rueful. 'I'll have Mrs Peake prepare you a jug of honeyed herbal tea for your throat, sir,' he said heavily.

When my breathing had settled into the tight-chested rasp that I guessed I was going to have to get used to for a while, Hawkins said briskly, 'But enough of your domestic arrangements for now, sir. No doubt you are wondering about the events of last night and their consequences. Perhaps you have already guessed that it was I who unlocked the door to Tallarian's laboratory and loosened the restraint around your left wrist. I confess I did struggle to resist the urge to simply release you and carry you from the hospital and have done with it. The reason I did not was because I was acting on specific instructions – that is to say, *your* instructions – besides which, you were unconscious beyond my ability to rouse you, and it was unlikely that we would have made good our escape without encountering Tallarian and his brutish assistant.

'I had gained access to the hospital two days previously by posing as a patient. In this way I was able to observe Tallarian's methods and become familiar with his and his staff's routines. It quickly became clear to me that he was exploiting his exalted position to procure subjects for his vile experiments. You had already warned me of the horrors that I would encounter in his basement, sir, for which I am grateful. If it had not been for your warning, I fear I may have been quite unable to fulfil my duties in so clinical and efficient a manner. As it was, I don't mind admitting that I was shaken by what I saw in that dreadful place.'

It wasn't until he paused that I realised how much the experience had affected him. Throughout his recollection, Hawkins' voice had remained soft and steady, his spine ramrod-straight against the back of his chair. Yet, looking at him now, I saw that his facial muscles had tightened and his nostrils had flared slightly. Catching my eye, he swallowed and gave the briefest twitch of a smile, as if apologising for his weakness. When he resumed, his voice was as steady as before.

'The girl whom you rescued is alive,' he said, 'and recovering well. Indeed, she is proving quite a handful for Mrs Peake and her beleaguered staff. Aside from the horrific damage inflicted upon her arm, there is ample evidence that both her mind and body have been subjected to more general and prolonged maltreatment. In short, she is not so far removed from a wild animal. She appears entirely unable to speak, and is given to snarling and lashing out at whoever comes close to her. The girl Polly, and to some extent Mrs Peake, have managed, through persistent patience and kindness, to establish what can best be described as an uneasy rapport with the child. However that did not prevent Polly from suffering lacerations to her arm from the girl's metal claw when the two of them tried to bathe her. Filthy and stinking though the child is, the attempt to acquaint her with soap and water has been therefore abandoned for the time being. Instead

Mrs Peake is currently concentrating on persuading her to remain in her bed at night rather than building a nest from her shredded sheets in the corner of the room, and to... ah, use the chamber pot rather than the carpet for her evacuations.'

He smiled grimly. 'But Mrs Peake is a determined sort and I am certain that eventually the child will respond. In the meantime, upon your instructions, we have named her Hope.'

I nodded. It was good to hear that the girl had survived, but I wondered what had become of the boy I had managed to release, not to mention Tallarian's other victims, and even Tallarian himself. As if reading my thoughts, Hawkins' expression became sombre.

'I'm sorry to say that the other poor creatures kept captive by that fiendish man fared less well. I was unable to save them, as a consequence of which they perished in the fire which eventually caused the entire building to be evacuated. As for Tallarian himself, not a trace of him has been found. Forgive me if I sound callous, sir, but my hope is that he died along with his victims, his body burned beyond recognition. Although under the circumstances even that would be a kindly fate for him, I for one would be able to sleep more soundly in my bed, knowing that his black and craven heart had been for ever extinguished.'

I shook my head. Dredging breath from my smoke-damaged lungs, I wheezed, 'Sorry to disappoint you, Hawkins...'

His face fell. 'You have evidence to suggest that he survived, sir?'

I nodded. 'I've seen him...' The effort proved too much and I started to cough.

Hawkins held up a hand. 'Don't over-exert yourself, sir. In your own time, you mean?'

I nodded again, and Hawkins' face hardened. 'Then perhaps he is out of our reach for now. Or it may be that we can somehow stop him in his tracks, curtail his timeline and put an end to his wickedness.' He saw me looking at him in surprise and gave an abashed smile that instantly put an end to any doubts I might have had about his integrity and trustworthiness. 'Oh, I am not quite the stuffy retainer I appear, sir. I have something of a history – though I think we will save that for another time. For now, what do you say to getting out of that nightshirt and into attire more suited to a gentleman of the city? I can introduce you to the staff, and after a little lunch you could sit in the garden, take good, fresh air into those lungs of yours and peruse the newspaper. It may be a modest ambition for the day, but it is a realistic one, I feel.'

I almost gave him the thumbs-up, but then realised he may not understand the gesture, and so simply nodded again. I supposed that for the foreseeable future, nods and shakes of the head would be my primary means of communication.

With Hawkins' help, and with a lot of coughing, I got up and dressed. I could have done with a shower or a bath – which led me to wonder whether I had hot and cold running water in this house of mine – but I didn't have the energy; maybe tomorrow. It was odd having another man dress me like a child, but I was grateful for Hawkins' help. Besides which, he was a model of decorum, efficiency and patience, and I felt comfortable in his presence. It was a long, laborious process, but eventually I was ready. At Hawkins' suggestion I stood in front of the full-length mirror and admired myself. Admittedly I was unshaven, hunched over with pain, and my mouth was hanging open as I laboured for breath, but when Hawkins asked, 'Are the garments satisfactory, sir?' I nodded.

It was more than that, though. Seeing myself in my grey tailored jacket and trousers, my green and black embroidered waistcoat, and my wing-collared shirt and cravat, I had a sudden and overwhelming sense that time was shifting, that gears were grinding into motion to shunt me into a new and significant phase of my life. I felt the massive weight of expectation, of destiny even. Although the heart was no longer in my possession I felt it calling to me, felt as though it was still my mission, my duty, to find it and keep it safe. And I knew that if I could find the heart then I could find Kate too, for with the heart in my hand links would be made, timelines established and strengthened. And all at once I realised what I had meant in the letter when I had said that finding out the house was mine would help me to 'work out a few things'.

If I had bought the house and met and employed Hawkins two years ago, then I must have travelled back from my future to do so. And the only way I could have done that was with the heart. Which meant that I *must* find it, and that, if I didn't, who knew what would unravel, what terrible forces would come into play and what catastrophes would occur? I was trapped in a situation where my actions in the future were already having a massive impact on my present, and where so much and so many were relying on me. For that reason I *had* to succeed, simply to prevent everything from collapsing inwards like a house of cards.

The ripples of time. In that moment I fancied I could almost *feel* them. Slowly I raised my hand and touched my reflection in the mirror. Is that how close I was to my future self? Our fingertips almost touching? Is that how close I was to disaster? If I failed, would causality be like a series of mirrors, one shattering after another?

Behind me I heard the door open. I glanced in the mirror to see who had entered, but my raised hand was obscuring the doorway, smudging it out. I lowered the hand and stared at the figure that stood there. Astonished, I turned.

She was beautiful. Radiant. She wore a flowing silk gown, diamonds at her throat, and her hair had been teased into curls and waves. She swished gracefully into the room and smiled at me.

'Hello, Alex,' said Clover.

ACKNOWLEDGMENTS

Many thanks to my agent John Jarrold, and to my lovely editors at Titan, Cath Trechman and Natalie Laverick, for their enthusiastic belief not only in this book but in the entire trilogy, and for backing my cover ideas with grace and fortitude. I'm grateful to my ever-supportive wife Nel and to my children David and Polly, for listening to my occasional readings and making suitably encouraging noises. I'm indebted to my many wonderful friends (you know who you are), without whom this writing lark would be far lonelier and nowhere near as much fun, and particularly to those who provided me with a writing refuge during my travels, as a consequence of which bits of this book were written in Nicholas Royle's flat in Manchester, Sarah Pinborough and Lee Thompson's flat in London, Stephen and Patricia Volk's house in Bradford-on-Avon, and Johnny Mains's book-lined study in Plymouth.

ABOUT THE AUTHOR

Mark Morris has written over twenty-five novels, among which are *Toady*, *Stitch*, *The Immaculate*, *The Secret of Anatomy*, *Fiddleback*, *The Deluge* and four books in the popular *Doctor Who* range. He is also the author of two short story collections, *Close to the Bone* and *Long Shadows, Nightmare Light*, and several novellas. His short fiction, articles and reviews have appeared in a wide variety of anthologies and magazines, and he is editor of *Cinema Macabre*, a book of horror movie essays by genre luminaries for which he won the 2007 British Fantasy Award, its follow-up *Cinema Futura*, and *The Spectral Book of Horror Stories*, the inaugural volume of what is hoped will become an annual series. His script work includes audio dramas for Big Finish Productions' *Doctor Who* and *Jago & Litefoot* ranges, and also for Bafflegab's *Hammer Chillers* series, and his recently published work includes an updated novelisation of the 1971 Hammer movie *Vampire Circus*, the official movie tie-in novelisation of Darren Aronofsky's *Noah*, and the Shirley Jackson Award nominated novella *It Sustains* for Earthling Publications. Upcoming is a new short story collection from ChiZine Publications, two more novellas (for Spectral Press and Salt/Remains Publishing), and books two and three of the Obsidian Heart trilogy, which will be published by Titan Books in 2015 and 2016.

www.markmorriswriter.com